Ghost Dance II

A Novel

The Amulet

Gale A. Palmanteer

iUniverse, Inc.
Bloomington

Copyright © 2010 by Gale A. Palmanteer

All rights reserved. No part of this book may be used or reproduced by any means, graphic, electronic, or mechanical, including photocopying, recording, taping or by any information storage retrieval system without the written permission of the publisher except in the case of brief quotations embodied in critical articles and reviews.

Certain characters in this work are historical figures, and certain events portrayed did take place. However, this is a work of fiction. All of the other characters, names, and events as well as all places, incidents, organizations, and dialogue in this novel are either the products of the author's imagination or are used fictitiously.

iUniverse books may be ordered through booksellers or by contacting:

iUniverse
1663 Liberty Drive
Bloomington, IN 47403
www.iuniverse.com
1-800-Authors (1-800-288-4677)

Because of the dynamic nature of the Internet, any Web addresses or links contained in this book may have changed since publication and may no longer be valid. The views expressed in this work are solely those of the author and do not necessarily reflect the views of the publisher, and the publisher hereby disclaims any responsibility for them.

Any people depicted in stock imagery provided by Thinkstock are models, and such images are being used for illustrative purposes only.

Certain stock imagery © Thinkstock.

ISBN: 978-1-4502-8341-0 (sc)
ISBN: 978-1-4502-8342-7 (hc)
ISBN: 978-1-4502-8343-4 (ebook)

Library of Congress Control Number: 2011900106

Printed in the United States of America

iUniverse rev. date: 02/14/2011

Yea though I walk through
>the valley of the shadow of death
>I will fear no evil….
>>Psalm 23: 4

Prologue

Bastard's eyes glazed with fear, his nostrils flared…blowing blood and snot into the face of his terrified rider. Roy had a death grip on the loose reins and saddle horn as the big bay burst into the narrow opening to the spirit trail of the sacred black wolf.

The ghostly-white horse and rider he was chasing had vanished. He was alone and though Bastard continued to run for his life, he seemed to be stuck in place, as if on some unearthly treadmill. The bedrock bottom of the passage in front of them began to undulate like heat waves on a desert floor.

They were sinking!

As the powerful legs of the frightened bay fought to propel his rider forward, the hard rock trail softened and they slowly sank into what was previously solid granite.

Roy scanned the passage walls, glazed smooth by a thousand years of wind and rain. There was nothing to grab onto, no escape.

"So this is how it ends." His words were hollow and vacant, a reminder of lost chances and bad choices.

While the narrow passage closed in around him and his gallant steed, Roy reached a painful conclusion. Bastard deserved better! An agonizing pain ripped through his chest, and he fought for one last breath before Mother Earth consumed them, then there was nothing, total darkness, yet he was aware. Roy knew he was dead yet he could feel the powerful horse moving under him.

"Sheeit!" escaped his lips before a brilliant-yellow light emerged from a crevice in the total darkness.

"Sombitch!" His eyes adjusted to the scene unfolding around him. "So this is what happens when ya die!"

Chapter One

Janis Crossing

Standing Wolf left the valley through the sacred spirit cave. His mother, Bent Grass, was at his side when he exited the mysterious cavern. She gripped his hand, releasing it only when he stepped through the opening. He clutched the amulet close to his chest as if to release it would cause him to burst into flame.

Before leaving the valley of the Sematuse, Standing Wolf discarded his white man treasures; his fine western saddle and silver inlaid bridle in favor of a red fox riding pad and a rawhide hackamore.

Dressed in elk hide pants and a deerskin shirt, fringed moccasins that rose above this calf, his long black braids dangling midway down his back, his dark eyes darting from rock to bush, one would never have guessed he had once lived with the white-clay humans. The steel-bladed Bowie knife in its leather sheath tied to his leg just above the knee and the magnificent Arabian horse he rode were the only hints that he might be anything other than just another Indian.

The trail of the lone survivor of the apocalyptic uprising was easy to follow…his were the only horse tracks leading away from the valley. The soldier had made no attempt to cover his trail, so intent was he on simply escaping the ungodly carnage. Besides, where could he go except back to the fort?

Standing Wolf's thoughts drifted to his mother, the seer. "She is the real Messiah," he whispered to an attentive Whiskey. "The Great Spirit, *Ogle Wa Nagi,* is using me because I share her *tlchachie,* her spirit, her blood." Pride swelled in his chest and a lump formed in his throat as he pictured her in his mind.

He reached what he thought of as Roy's River, having left the outside entrance to the spirit cave. He felt a wave of sadness. He had liked Roy, scoundrel that he was. Without Roy, he would not have found his mother. Without his mother they would all be dead; Star Flower, Spotted Fawn, Little Beaver, Warm Hands even Ta-keen Eagle and Laughing Doe.

"I cannot let her down. I must find the amulet and return it to the valley," he said with conviction. "He will go back to the fort…safety in numbers." Whiskey nodded his delicate head in agreement. "But how do I find the one with the amulet? How can I sneak into the fort?" Whiskey snorted, blowing snot into the wind, clearly irritated at being asked the hard questions.

They don't know yet.

The runaway soldier had not had time to reach the fort. Unsuspecting soldiers at the fort would have no way of knowing Colonel Wolard, Bishop Donneli and a thousand men of the 5th cavalry, nearly a third of the fort population were dead, gone, killed and whisked away by a force more powerful than any they could have imagined.

"Do you think we can catch him before he reaches the fort, big boy?"

Standing Wolf rubbed the stallion between his black ears. A descendent of Arabarb, the big horse was bred for speed and endurance but a day or two was a lot of time to make up, especially when chasing a man who was running for his life.

He nudged the powerful horse and it broke into a smooth, ground-eating gallop. A thin smile creased StandingWolf's lips as he felt the animal under him. Never did he imagine he would ever own such an animal.

I can thank Roy for you, too.

To feel a good horse under you was a true pleasure and Standing Wolf was surprised to find the feeling exaggerated without the heavy western saddle. He really did feel like one with this great horse. Satisfied with the capabilities of Whiskey, Standing Wolf turned his thoughts to the task at hand…catching the soldier with the amulet before he reached the safety of the fort.

As the big black Arab ate ground, Standing Wolf's sharp eyes scanned the trail ahead. He had no expectation of spotting the fleeing soldier or even his dust until they were farther down river. His hope was to catch the man once they reached the broad expanse of the sand flats. "Unless he runs his horse to death first," he muttered to the wind.

With each pounding stride, the importance of catching the soldier before he was lost among the many soldiers at the fort became more and more apparent.

If the survivor reached the fort with news of Colonel Wolard's defeat at the valley of the Sematuse they would be on high alert. He could not just walk in and say, "Hello, I am your long lost scout and I am back." Besides, someone at the fort would surely recognize him…probably the guy with the amulet and that would, for sure, strangle his chicken.

Stopping only occasionally for water, a bite of grouse and a handful of grain for Whiskey, Standing Wolf was on pace to make a five day ride in three. His spirits soared. He should overtake the soldier on the sand flats as long as he did not run into a patrol or hunting party. Not that he feared either but it could cost him time…something he was short on right now. Time, he thought, sometimes it is everything and sometimes it is nothing.

All he wanted right now was to catch the guy, get the amulet and get back to Star Flower, the valley and his mother, the sooner the better.

Following the same fateful route he and Roy had taken when they discovered the spirit cave and the valley of rainbows, Standing Wolf was elated when he reached the place the Indians called Janis.

"How about a short rest?" he asked Whiskey, not expecting a reply.

As the big Arab drank from the river, Standing Wolf dug a pemmican paddy from a pouch and began to reflect on the enormity of the events in the last few days.

*

Standing Wolf was a believer ever since the day on the way to Buffalo Story when *Wakan Tanka*, Great Spirit of the Sioux, spoke to him, told him to return to the circle, and bring hope to the True People even though he was a half-breed and not Sioux but Sematuse. Spirit-walker, the ghostly white shaman with the glowing yellow hair had told the Sematuse they were the chosen ones, the True People. But, Standing Wolf wondered, What about the Sioux or the Cheyenne, the Paiutes or Minneconjous? What about the Indians of the Great Lakes like the Chippewa or the Apache and Comanche of the plains?

Ogle Wa Nagi, Great Spirit of the Sematuse, did not speak directly to him as had *Wakan Tanka*, but rather to his mother, Bent Grass. But it was he, following her command that summoned the spirits of so many warriors to rise up against the soldiers and drive them from the valley of the Sematuse into a world without souls.

"Why me? Why not Ta-keen Eagle or Little Beaver or my mother?" Standing Wolf spoke to the slow moving, shallow river as if seeking wisdom from its dark waters.

"I am the Messiah. *Ogle Wa Nagi* has made it so, and my people are safe for now because of me and the Ghost Dance, but why me?"

What about Spirit-walker?

He was the one who warned the soldiers and Roy more than once, then led the armada of ghostly warriors the dance resurrected. It was he, who then destroyed them and mounted on that amazing white stallion, whisked away all the whites, except Roy and the soldier with the amulet, off to an unknown place…maybe hell.

If there is a hell.

"There was something eerily familiar about that shaman," Standing Wolf mused. The whole experience defied any attempt at a logical explanation.

Standing Wolf was yanked from his reverie by an ear-splitting whinny emitting from somewhere deep in Whiskey's gullet. The blaze-faced Arab held his head high, pointy ears aimed directly across the river.

Scanning the strange rock formations to the east, his gaze was drawn to what appeared to be moving bushes. The green shrubs seemed to scurry about only to stop occasionally as if halted by an unknown order.

Whiskey again sent a chrill signal echoing off the shear bluffs and up the deep-ragged canyon across the river. "What is it, boy? Are there horses over there?" Standing Wolf asked quietly. He watched in bewilderment as the top of the layered-lava bluffs came alive with moving green trees and shrubs.

Grasping Whiskey's mane, he sprung easily aboard the big Arab. "There is something very odd over there." His curiosity was peaked but he had a mission. "I do not have time to chase after a trick my eyes must be playing on me." Whiskey bolted, nearly unseating his agile rider.

"Ieeeyah! Ieeeyah, Ieeeyah!" The unmistakable cries of warriors on attack were interrupted by the rapid bursts of gunfire.

Standing Wolf pressed his right knee against Whiskey's side, turning him toward the river. Curiosity turned to urgency. As the big horse hit the river, shallow in the August heat, Standing Wolf's mind raced to assess the situation. It sounded like a fight but who would be fighting? His people, the Sematuse, were all in their valley…of that he was sure. Whatever was happening amidst the odd rock formations across the river had the distinct sound of war. Clearly there was a battle going on between whites and Indians and it was close and fierce.

Whiskey lunged out of the river on the far side and up through the dense foliage that protected its bank while Standing Wolf scanned the mouths of numerous canyons, seeking to match site with sound. The war cries continued, incessant, but the gunfire was now randomly infrequent.

Standing Wolf guided Whiskey toward the nearest and largest of the canyon openings. If there were a fight between Indian people and whites, maybe he could help. He had no idea who or how but with his newly bestowed status and the amulet, he had to try.

As Whiskey carried him farther up the canyon, the sounds he sought became muffled and distant. "Are we in the wrong canyon?" he questioned Whiskey. Slowing the Arab to a smooth walk, he focused, trying to locate the origin of the fading yelps. Discouraged and frustrated he pulled the horse to a halt.

"If I am Standing Wolf, Messiah, the Chosen One sent to save all Indian people, then why can I not tell which canyon the sounds are coming from?" His words were lost in the labyrinth of crevices and canyons known as Janis.

Turning back, he headed for the river. Upon exiting the canyon, the yelps became infrequent and the gunfire ceased. Riding down river at an easy lope, his eyes scanned the rocks and crevices for any movement.

Whiskey saw it first…his steady gallop interrupted by a sideways leap, his alert ears riveted on the rider-less horse headed their way.

The frightened animal shied away from Standing Wolf and Whiskey as it turned up river. Standing Wolf recognized the smooth pommel and skirt-less stirrups as a McClellan enlisted man's saddle, the kind used by the 5th Cavalry, the kind used by Colonel Wolard's troops.

His anxiety level elevated and he wondered… Are troops from Fort Okanogan looking for the colonel and if so, what happened in this rocky canyon? Without hesitation he urged Whiskey forward, back-tracking the wide-eyed mount that just passed him without a rider.

The trail was easy for an experienced tracker like Standing Wolf to follow and had it not been made by a rider-less horse, he might have worried about being led into a trap.

Less than a mile in, the canyon narrowed and large boulders were strewn about the canyon floor so he slowed Whiskey to a cautious walk. His eyes wandered anxiously up and down the smooth, weather-polished walls of the deep ravine and a chill crawled up the back of his neck. His eyes returned to the boulders…some as large as a horse, scattered about the dusty canyon bottom. The chill persisted, now accompanied by an empty feeling in his gut.

Just beyond the boulders, Standing Wold saw horses…dead horses. Strewn amidst the equine slaughter were men…naked, dead men. Dismounting, he examined the carnage. The men were white, clean-shaven with short hair.

Soldiers!

Some were scalped, which was not a common practice among the Indians of the *Okinakane,* but then neither was it common to attack a military patrol.

Leading Whiskey through the trail of dead horses and soldiers, the canyon made a turn to the right. Rounding the bend, Standing Wolf stopped in his tracks. There were more dead men, white men, but these men wore beards and long hair. He saw half-a-dozen wagons and dead horses with double trees still hooked to leather harnesses.

Most of the dead men had arrows protruding rudely from their still bleeding bodies, some with their throats cut, others missing genitals cut from their naked bodies with dull flint knives. Wandering through the grotesque scene looking for any sign of life, he came to more large boulders blocking his way.

"This was a trap," he stated, as if he needed convincing.

Rocks had been rolled off the bluffs into the narrow ravine blocking the advancing wagon train, then behind them closing off any chance for escape.

"This was a wagon train with a military escort," he told the black Arab.

No women or children. If there were, they must have been taken captive. As a scout for Colonel Wolard, Standing Wolf spoke with most of the bands of the upper *Okinakane*. They were not a hostile people but they were possessive of the land they believed was a gift from the Great Spirit for them to hunt and fish.

It struck him as odd that there were no bodies of braves killed in this battle. Could this have been an ambush so well planned and effective that no Indians were killed? He had heard the gunfire. Did all of the gunshots miss their mark or did the warriors take their dead with them?

Standing Wolf remembered telling the colonel, "If there was going to be trouble moving any Indians onto the Sand Flats it will come from those up north, farther from the Columbia."

Of course none of that mattered now, not after that fateful day in the valley of the Sematuse.

*

Where are the Indians? He wondered…Were there any survivors? Why the brutality?

The Indians of the *Okinakane* might fight to protect their way of life but he could not imagine them mutilating their victims. They would be more likely to honor them for having died bravely.

"Something is very wrong here," he told his equine companion who shook his noble head in apparent agreement. "If any of the northern bands did this they have gone crazy," he whispered to himself thoughtfully. He wondered if news of what happened in the valley could have somehow reached the *Okinakane,* inciting such violent action.

Standing Wolf realized he had a decision to make. He could easily track the perpetrators of this attack and find out who they were and why they acted so violently, or he could return to the pursuit of the soldier with the amulet…his only reason for leaving the valley of the Sematuse.

When put in perspective the decision was easy. The one with the amulet held the secret to the valley and possibly the future of his people. He had an obligation to his mother, to Star Flower and all of the Sematuse.

The attack on this wagon train and the mutilation of the dead bodies was very curious to him but someone else would have to solve this mystery.

With a light touch of his heels to Whiskey's ribs, Standing Wolf urged the animal into a swift gait. Precious time was already lost if he was to catch the amulet thief before he reached the fort.

They crossed the river just above what would be rapids in higher flows but were now barely white water rivulets. Heading south his thoughts returned to his mission. So transfixed had he been by the canyon scene that he lost track of time.

He easily picked up the trail where he last left it and tried to focus on making up ground that was lost. His thoughts were divided. He had to get the amulet and return it to the valley but he could not shake the vision lingering in his head.

The brutality and mutilation was so unlike any of the bands he met as a scout. It was a small wagon train of only a few wagons and it looked as though each wagon was occupied by just one driver. "Why would such a small train merit a military escort? Who were the soldiers? Had they come from the fort?" He asked the questions aloud as if hoping for answers from a shaman or spirit.

Choo-pin-it-pa-loo. Could the train have been ambushed by the feared, People of the Mountains, believed by some to live in the vast upper reach of the *Okinakane*?

Standing Wolf remembered his encounter with Little Moses. Were not the People of the Mountains his people, the Sematuse…or were they imaginary? Were they a figment in the minds of the superstitious tribes along the Columbia and Okanogan?

Using knowledge gained from numerous trips up and down the Okanogan, Standing Wolf guided Whiskey away from the river, past a small lake and along the base of a sheer rock wall. He maintained a steady course until the bend of the river drifted back in to meet him. He was losing light and he was tired…really tired. Patting the horse on his sleek black neck, Standing Wolf pulled the powerful animal to a comfortable walk.

A cottonwood thicket near the river beckoned him like a feather bed. "Let's take a rest," he told Whiskey. "We'll both feel better in the morning."

He awoke with new resolve. "We will catch the soldier today," he declared to a wide-eyed stallion, "and return the amulet to my mother and the Sematuse."

Refreshed, man and mount moved south along the river the Indians called *Okinakane* at a ground-eating pace, eyes fixed on the sandy trail ahead. The sun rose high overhead, then faded slowly into the western sky. Still he and his gallant mount moved downriver.

Then he saw a plume of dust rising above the distant horizon. Nudging Whiskey lightly with his heels, he picked up the pace. Still a day, day-and-a-half from the fort, he guessed. I have to think this through, he cautioned himself. With a change of heart he pulled Whiskey into a comfortable walk. If the soldier stopped for the night Standing Wolf would catch him tomorrow. If not, he would catch him tomorrow night. Either way, Standing Wolf was sure he would catch his prey before he reached the fort. His heart soared at the thought of returning the amulet to his mother, and his masculine needs to Star Flower.

Standing Wolf rode all night, not pushing but determined not to lose ground now that he was closing in. As the first rays of the sun peaked over the eastern skyline, he found the dust plume, no closer but no farther away then when darkness settled in last night.

Who the hell is this guy?

Standing Wolf was astonished that he had gained little or no ground on the soldier over night. "Here I am riding a bonafide descendent of Arabarb. What the hell is he riding?" he whispered, shaking his head, unwilling to believe his eyes.

"We will get him today," he asserted and felt the big Arab respond to his nudging with a long smooth stride. Not only do I have a better horse, Standing Wolf thought, but I still know a trick or two. With that, he aimed Whiskey for the riverbank, plunged over the edge and dropped into the shallow water.

"Instead of fighting, sage, sand, dust and heat, we will follow the river. It will be easier going and cooler since the water is so low. And," he added, "he will never see us coming."

As they reached the area known as the Sand Flats, it was clear he was gaining ground on the elusive cloud of dust but not as rapidly as he expected. "I am not going to push you any harder," he assured Whiskey.

He expected the dust plume to disappear at any moment, proof that the fleeing soldier had run his horse to death. The cloud remained but the distance was steadily diminishing. Standing Wolf estimated he was now within a mile and closing fast.

"Finally," he muttering in reluctant satisfaction, and began to plan his overtaking of the man and the retrieval of the amulet.

He could wait until he caught up to the dust of what he now believed to be a very desperate man, exit the river bottom and over take his prey, or he could surpass the dust plume and wait in ambush for the fleeing soldier. "I have to catch him first," he reminded himself. "And do not forget, although I have been chosen by the Great Spirit to free the True People, I am still a man, not a shaman, so do not get careless."

Standing Wolf believed his power came from the Great Spirit, his mother and the amulet…his trilogy. As if he needed more reminding, he thought of the man he was pursuing.

"Desperate people do desperate things," he whispered. "So stay vigilant."

As the Arab's hooves pounded across the damp sand between water and bank, his delicate head held high and alert, he pulled even with the elusive plume of dust they had been chasing for days. Standing Wolf watched for a suitable place to ascend the river bank and found a spot broken down by frequent game use. He decided to ride in behind the fleeing man and run him down. He was sure by now that the man was terrified, running for his life.

"The sight of us bearing down on him should add to his fear," he told Whiskey. "Fear can be an ally when confronting the enemy and I will give him plenty to be afraid of, scared people sometimes do stupid things." Standing Wolf's conclusion was based on past experience.

Breaking out of the riverbed and through dense alder and dogwood, he avoided the scattered hawthorn and broke into the tall black stalks of greasewood. Then Standing Wolf saw him. A quarter mile ahead was a lone rider on a horse the color of the dust plume it created. Can I take the amulet without killing him, he pondered, or does he have to die? He is the only survivor of an unearthly attack that clearly did not intend for any of the invaders to leave the valley of the Sematuse alive.

Urging Whiskey to pick up the pace, Standing Wolf felt the big horse's stride lengthen and saw the gap between him and the fleeing rider begin to shrink. He was sure the running man did not know anyone was behind him, especially not right on his ass. It would not be long until he would be painfully aware of the unusual half-breed Indian in pursuit.

"By then it will be too late," he whispered into Whiskey's flowing mane.

As he anticipated overtaking the soldier and retrieving the treasured amulet, Standing Wolf's heart pounded and his spirit rose. The joy of anticipation suddenly melted into the despair of disappointment. Beyond the soldier on the gray horse loomed the unwelcome site of Fort Okanogan. His sharp eyes assessed the fort and his hope of catching the man evaporated when he saw the stockade gate swing open. It was too late.

Pulling Whiskey in and guiding him into a cluster of cottonwood near the river, Standing Wolf dismounted.

"If only I had not been distracted at Janis," he said quietly.

Chapter Two

Reflection

Sam had to admit he did not know much about Indians. What he did know was that he had seen enough of them to last him a lifetime, however long that happened to be. Corporal Samuel DeSoto left Fort Okanogan under the cover of thick black clouds. He was in a panic and had no clue what direction he and the little sorrel mare were headed, except that it was away from the fort, Major Denton and what was left of the 5th Cavalry Brigade assigned there.

He pushed the little mare into the bleakness of night, unseeing and depending on the sorrel's night vision to carry him away from the memory of the ungodly carnage still gripping his mind like the unforgiving jaws of a wolverine.

It was enough to cause him to question his sanity, his memory. He'd seen Indians in full war regalia burst from aspen leaves and funnel clouds in an otherwise clear sky. He'd seen thousands of painted warriors on thousands of ghostly ponies ride on a river of no return. He had heard the anguished cries of dying soldiers, screaming as if their souls were being ripped from their bodies, screams he knew he could never forget. It was like a bad dream but he need only reach into his pocket to know it was very real. He fingered the leather necklace as he rode farther into the darkness. He had no idea how long he had been riding or how far he and the sorrel had traveled. Not far enough, was his only thought.

Advancing precariously, the sure-footed mare carried Sam on into the night. His legs ached, his head hurt, one rein slipped from his tired fingers and he barely caught it before it dropped to the ground. Alarmed, he tied the reins into a simple knot and draped them over the pommel of his military issue saddle. He didn't need them, he couldn't see where he was going anyhow.

"Can't stop," he muttered to himself, startled by the sound of his own voice. He was suddenly filled with a desperate anxiety. "They won't come after me until mañana," he assured himself. "They don't even know I am gone yet. Unless that damn stable guard talked to the duty officer," he said, not allowing himself even a brief solace.

A faint glow emerged in the distance. He rubbed his eyes, trying to focus. "Daybreak!" he exclaimed, surprised by his own exuberance. His excitement was quickly dampened by the realization that Major Denton would be ordering a patrol to find him.

"The major might want me back alive," he surmised, "but I would rather die here than go back to that god-forsaken valley."

As light slowly filled the sky, Sam looked around. He was surrounded by sage and sand with scattered large pine trees providing the only hope of shade or cover. Now he began talking to himself in earnest.

"How far from the fort am I? Where am I?" He was full of questions and he had only one answer. "We need to rest," he stated, patting the sorrel on the neck.

Need a place to hide and get my strength back.

The thoughts bounced around Sam's head like loose shells in a buckboard. He had been on the run day and night for nearly a week since leaving the valley of carnage. He was getting careless and he was lucky the little mare had not fallen in the darkness.

Through dry, burning eyes, he squinted, looking around the landscape for anything that could afford him and the sorrel a hiding place. When the first rays of sun peeked over the horizon, he rode into a dry wash.

"At least I won't stand out like a pimple on a princess," he told himself as he dropped below the rim of the gorge.

There was no water but there was a small channel where water flowed in the spring and perhaps during substantial rains. Riding on, the wash became narrower and the vegetation denser by the time he neared the head of the wash.

"I would rather be lucky than good," he whispered. The ravine began to pinch off and its bottom filled with dogwood, ocean-spray, serviceberry and hawthorn.

Dismounting, Sam would have fallen but for his grip on the pommel. His knees buckled and pain shot from his feet up his legs and into his back. Steadying himself against his horse, he took a deep labored breath. The pain in his feet slowly transformed into a cool, wet sensation. With a twinge of panic, he looked down and found his feet immersed in shallow water. He was so tired he did not realize the sorrel mare already discovered the stream and was noisily slurping the cool liquid.

"Need to get some sleep," he muttered, then tied one rein to a sturdy bush and lay down on the cool stream bank.

He awoke drenched in sweat. The hot August sun was directly overhead heating up the narrow chasm like a Dutch oven. "Goddamn it!" he shouted, startling the little mare and causing her to rear back, breaking the bridle rein at the bit. "Goddamn it!" he repeated as if his first expletive hadn't done enough damage.

Getting to his feet slowly, he began talking softly to the frightened mare like she was a lover. "Easy girl," he mouthed quietly and held his hand out. The mare's pupils were rimmed with the whites of wide-eyed fright. "Please don't run," he pleaded. A wave of panic washed over him like cold water on a cat, leaving his gut feeling empty, realizing his life might depend on catching this horse.

"Patience," he told himself as he extended his hand toward the mare, hoping to dupe her into believing it contained grain or some other goody. Holding his breath, fearing the mere act of breathing might spook the high-strung animal, Sam inched steadily closer, ten feet, five, two. Slowly his free hand reached for the remaining rein as he continued to rub his thumb and fingers of his extended hand, hoping to simulate the sound of grain in a bucket.

"Gracias," he whispered to some omni-present deity when his hand gripped the dangling rein. Slowly it was joined by his other hand, no longer needed for deception but used to insure a secure hold. Retrieving the broken rein, he inserted it through the empty ring of the bridle bit and tried tying it. The leather was too stiff.

"Well shit," he mumbled, "I guess one rein will have to do."

His transportation now secure, Sam began assessing his situation. Speaking softly to calm his nerves and the little mare, he pondered aloud. "How far we are from the fort? Denton surely has a patrol out after us."

Remembering where he'd seen the bright light of dawn, Sam felt sure he knew where east was but had no idea which way he'd ridden in last night's darkness.

"I know that valley was northwest of the fort so east sounds pretty damn good right now," he declared with confidence…a confidence quickly doused by reality. "I don't know where in the hell I am, half of the 5th Cavalry is probably chasing me, I've got a bridle with one damn rein and some ghostly Indian is probably looking for this. Shit!" he repeated as he reached into his pocket, reaffirming the presence of the strange piece of leather.

After a brief one-sided discussion with his horse about whether to hide or ride, Sam decided to keep moving. "Our trail can't be hard to follow," he surmised. His desire to put distance between him, Major Denton and that god-awful valley was powerful. "I hope you enjoyed the rest, chica," he said, "because it may be the last you will get for a while."

Riding along in the hot August sun he was both relieved and concerned as dark clouds began to boil up in the distance. The cooler air felt good but Sam was worried about finding his way through another dark, moonless night. As the light began to fade, he and the mare approached a small pond surrounded by short flat-bladed grasses.

He was hungry and thirsty. Holding tightly to his rein as he drank, he allowed the mare to drink and nibble away at the sedge-like grasses. Sam hadn't eaten for at least a full night and day and his stomach was aching. Patting the rifle, taken from the stable guard, he muttered, "Sure would be nice to find some game before dark."

As the mare struggled to maneuver the short grass around the bridle's bit and her tongue, Sam watched the pond, turbid from their disturbance, slowly clear. As the ripples subsided and the murky water cleared, he was transfixed by his own reflection.

His blue uniform was now a dusty gray, only the bright-yellow corporal stripes appeared clean and shiny. His lanky six-foot frame looked gaunt, he wore no hat but his hair was neatly trimmed in contrast to his week-old black beard and tired dark eyes.

"What happened to my hat?" he whispered, not able to remember if he lost it or forgot it at the fort.

Again, the strong fingers of fear gripped his gut as grim reality sunk in. If the army caught him he would be shot for desertion! Then an even more terrifying thought struck him. What if the Indians from that valley were after him? He felt the talisman in his pocket and a pang of fear shot into his abdomen nearly causing him to loose control of his bladder.

"How could this have happened?" It was more of a plea than a question before his mind flashed back over his short life.

As a boy, Sam lived on the family ranch called Destino, ironically meaning 'fate', in the shadow of the Sierra Nevada Mountains where they raised fine Brahmas and fast horses. His father's family had moved from Spain to Mexico around the time of the Conquistadors. His father, born with an adventurous spirit, had wandered north into California during the gold rush. Good fortune went with him and he was one of the few who actually found gold. After successfully staking his claim and working it for a relatively short time, he sold the mine and purchased a ranch. It was then he met Sam's mother…a brilliant lady doctor who, after training in France, traveled to America with her parents. They, too, came west in search of gold. She was a French and Irish beauty with long, straight, coal-black hair and turquoise eyes.

Life for Sam had been good…privileged even. They lived in a fine house and he developed a love and talent for training horses. He also found time to pursue the art of quick draw and trick shooting. His father liked to take him to local celebrations where Sam could show off his abilities. By the time he was sixteen Sam had become a local legend; so much so that his father feared for his son's safety. Real gunfighters, men with cold hearts and fast hands, wanted prove they were better than this upstart kid.

Three days before Sam's eighteenth birthday everything changed. His mother fell ill with a fever and despite her training and the best medical attention money could buy, she died on his birthday. Sam really lost both parents that day. His father slipped into a deep depression and six months later killed himself by shoving the barrel of a Colt .45 in his ear and pulling the trigger. Sam heard the shot from the stable and found the gruesome remains of his father's head in the kitchen sink.

He'd grabbed a horse from the barn and ridden in blind despair to the neighboring ranch for help, knowing that nothing could help his father. The neighbor and his wife had taken Sam in and when it became apparent that he could not, or would not go back to the ranch, they arranged for him to join up with the US Army, 5th Cavalry, assuring him they would look after his ranch interests.

Dropping to his knees from the pain of the memories, Sam splashed water over his face to escape the sadness and clear his head. "I must think," he told himself. "Maybe I should head for Destino."

He quickly discarded the idea. California was too civilized, too much law, too much military. Besides, the ranch would be the first place the army would look for him…if there was still a ranch there.

The treaty of Guadalupe Hildago marked the end of the Mexican War and with the discovery of gold at Sutter's Mill, California was placed on a fast track to statehood by President James Knox Polk. With statehood it was only a matter of time before all Mexicans would be run off their land or killed.

"I am sure my father feared that," Sam lamented. "The fact that my padre's heritage was Spanish rather than Mexican meant little to anyone but him."

Ready to ride, Sam grasped the pommel with one hand and for the first time noticed the brass molding over it, along with the cantle and pigskin-covered padded seat depicting an officer's saddle. Gripping the cantle with his other hand but before he put his foot in the stirrup, his eyes froze on the saddlebag hanging just below his right hand. US

ARMY 5th Cavalry was branded into the leather and underneath were the initials, B.D.

"Benjamin Denton!" he exclaimed. "Madre de Dios! I didn't just steal a horse…I stole the goddamn major's horse!"

"BD could pass for Been Discharged. I hope it doesn't stand for Bad Decision," he mumbled, finding little humor in his weak joke.

The little mare began nervously prancing in anticipation of his mounting. His mind back on track, he stuck a foot in the stirrup and swung into the military saddle; one more reminder of the predicament he was in.

"You need a name," Sam suddenly announced to the sorrel horse. Reality now firmly in place, he knew that if he escaped what ever demons might be on his trail, he would owe it to this tough little mare. "Major," he said as if stating the obvious. "You will be my constant reminder to stay vigilant," he added, patting Major on the neck, "and the army's first femenino major." Sam smiled at the thought.

Canada.

His normally quick mind was now functioning again. "If we can make it to Canada we should be safe. The Queen doesn't much like America anyway, so she should not be thrilled by the idea of the US Army crossing the border after a deserter. Hell, we might be heroes in Canada," he said. Major shook her head up and down in apparent affirmation.

Pulling on the single rein, Sam guided Major toward what he hoped was north. With darkness settling in he could only guess based on where he thought he'd seen the sun rise.

"Have to keep moving." He kept up a one-sided conversation with Major, who while seeming genuinely interested, had nothing to say.

Sam had read all he could find on the American/Indian Wars, finding an incongruous similarity with the Mexican/American Wars. In both cases, the natives were fighting for their land…the land of their ancestors.

Joseph.

"I can not make the same mistake Chief Joseph made," he confirmed.

According to written accounts of Joseph's run for Canada from General's Miles and Howard, he had camped in the Bear Paw Mountains either thinking he was already in Canada or that he was so far ahead of One-Armed Howard that he could not be caught. That mistake cost Joseph his freedom and the lives of many of his people, including Chiefs White Bird and Lookingglass and Joseph's brother, Alokut.

Ka-boom!

A sudden flash of lightning accompanied by a deafening crack of thunder sent Major into a series of crow hops. A stunned Samuel DeSoto tried desperately to get control of the startled horse, using the one rein to pull Major's head around against her shoulder.

Suddenly and furiously, rain began pummeling the exposed horse and rider. The brief flashes of light did little to help Sam get a bearing on his location or the direction in which he was traveling while moving though the darkness at a brisk walk.

"At least our trail will be washed away," he said confidently. That was all he was confident of as he rode on into the night and the storm.

Give a horse its head and it will take you home.

The words of his father sent a pang of emptiness through him. In the darkness and left with only one rein, he allowed the little mare to have her head.

"You are NOT headed back to the fort for a helping of grain are you?" he asked with a new sense of dispair sticking in his throat.

Riding on through the thunder, lightning and rain Sam realized he would need a little more than luck if he were to escape a firing squad or a ghostly band of painted warriors. Reaching in his pocket Sam ran his fingers over the leather circulate.

Chapter Three

The Pack

Ross Riley stomped on the iron foot-pedal and the long, curved tines of the buck-rake lifted, releasing the sweet, green meadow hay into what was becoming a series of straight windrows. A large-brimmed straw hat shaded his wind-tanned face from the hot August sun. A billowing tan pioneer shirt concealed broad shoulders and muscular arms. He was a powerful man with hands some described as 'meat hooks' because if Ross Riley grabbed you with one of those big hands, you were not likely to get loose.

He maintained a steady banter of gees, haws, whoas and giddy-ups as the fine Belgian team of Jake and Jim pulled the rough-riding rake around the freshly cut meadow. Plenty of warm sun along with timely rains had produced a fine crop and he was anxious to get it out of the meadow and stacked into strategically placed hay pens.

Once in windrows it would need a couple of days to dry, then he would have the kids, Larry and Lilly, shock it; placing it in small stacks of thirty- to forty-pounds each. It would then be loaded onto a wagon and hauled to the pens. The pens were eight- to ten-feet high and built out of rough-sawed fir planks. These pens were necessary to keep not only the free ranging cattle out of the stacks but also the plentiful deer and elk herds that, if allowed, would tear down the stacks and ruin the hay.

Ross liked ranching but he learned the hard way that he could not depend on what seemed like ample pasture to hold livestock over a severe winter. After loosing nearly a quarter of his herd, including two prize bulls during just such a winter, he discovered that by harvesting the meadows in August he could avoid losing his equipment or draft horses in the hard-to-see bogs. The grass would then grow back sufficiently in the fall to provide enough grazing, should the winter prove to be a mild one.

Ross always worked hard and smart since moving along with his wife Ruth to what the Indians called 'Flathead' almost twenty years earlier. Of course, there were many hardships along the way but he put the past behind him. Things were good now. Their son, Larry, at seventeen was old enough to take on many of the responsibilities of the ranch and Lilly at sixteen was a big help to her mother, although she was also a huge help to him…especially at roundup time. At sixteen, Lilly was also becoming a woman and wanted to be called Lillian. She could out-ride and out-rope her brother; a fact she smugly held over him and one to which Larry begrudgingly conceded. Then there was Ruth, Ross' lovely wife and mother of his children; but for her he would not be here.

The thought of Ruth made him hungry. "Better not tell her that," he whispered under his breath and grinned. It must be about lunchtime and he was looking forward to a bowl of her beef stew. Chunks of shoulder roast, beef broth, carrots, onions, tomatoes, spuds and some secret seasonings only Ruth and Lilly were privy to.

Unhooking Jake and Jim from the double trees and dropping the chains, Ross drove them, shy the buck-rake, first to a small pond for water, then to the barn for grain and a bite or two of grass hay.

With the animals cared for it was now time for lunch. Nearing their fenced in garden he saw Ruth, barefoot, legs spread, bent at the waist, putting freshly picked ears of corn into a white cloth bag. She was wearing a light cotton dress that in her current position allowed its hem to pull up well above the back of her knees. Ross felt a tightening in his groin.

"The kids around?" he asked, walking up behind her, gently taking her hips and pulling her to him.

She shrieked, dropped the bag of corn and turning, pounded him playfully on the chest. "Lilly is in the kitchen warming up some stew and Larry is repairing a stack pen over by the north meadow, AND you have too much work to do to start with me. DO NOT start something you don't have time to finish." Her green eyes were gentle but teasing, full of the impishness and promise you might expect from a much younger woman.

Making sure she was facing him as Ruth bent to pick up the corn. The effect was no less arousing as her partially unbuttoned dress hung open revealing a generous portion of her alluring cleavage. Catching him stealing a glimpse, she handed him the bag of corn and scolded, "Behave yourself. Lilly could come out here any time and catch you with something you can't hide."

"I hope *Lillian*," he stated, emphasizing what she liked to be called and knowing he was usually the one guilty of calling her Lilly, "has the stew ready because that may be the only thing that will take my mind off your butt." He knew that came out wrong the minute the words left his mouth.

"Fine, see how you like sleeping with a pot of stew tonight," Ruth said coyly.

Not sure if being surrounded by beautiful women was a curse or a blessing, Ross admired his daughter when she set a steaming kettle of stew on the large wooden table. Lilly was a little shorter than her mother, maybe five-foot-three, but she already showed signs of developing into a young woman with all the feminine charms of her mother. Her hair was an orange-red and flowed softly to the small of her back, her eyes as blue as a mountain lake and her teeth as white as fresh snow; still free of tarnish from coffee or tobacco. Freckles dotted her otherwise flawless creamy-white skin. She wore blue jeans with boots, as usual, and light cotton top. He could not help but notice her cute little butt and perky breasts. Somewhere out there, he thought, is a young man who has no idea how lucky he will be. His gaze shifted back to his wife and he finished the thought…maybe even as lucky as me.

Ross was just finishing the last spoonful of stew and preparing to wipe the bowl clean with a slice of bread fresh from the oven when Larry burst excitedly through the door. "The wolves are back!" he exclaimed. "I saw about a dozen over on Wild Horse Creek and heard more off toward the Cabinets." Larry was tall, a little over six feet with a lanky frame and curly brown hair.

Wild Horse Creek ran through the north meadow and was grazed heavily by cows with three- to four-hundred pound calves this time of year. Those calves, if discovered, would become a favorite meal for a hungry wolf pack. Deer and elk, the normal diet for wolves in the Montana wilds, was giving way to beef; especially six- to eight-month old calves. They were a bigger meal and a helluva lot easier to catch.

"I need to finish wind-rowing," Ross told Larry. "Better take Lilly with you and move any cows and calves you find down to the Big Arm."

"It is *Lillian*, Daddy, *Lillian*, and yes, I will go and move the cattle to the Big Arm and Larry can help **me**." Tossing her hair proudly, she headed for the barn to get her Palomino mare, Buttercup.

The Big Arm was their pet name for a long, shallow ridge running just north of the house and barns. It was usually saved for fall pasture but it would be better to lose a little pasture temporarily than to lose any calves permanently.

"Be sure and take a rifle along," Ross told Larry as the boy headed for the door.

"And don't shoot any wolves unless they are attacking the cattle or you," Ruth added. She liked the wolves…liked hearing them at night and was always excited to see one. For nearly twenty years, they had lived with wolves and lost only a few calves and never a full-grown animal. The way she saw it, they knew there were wolves here when they settled this land. There were also bear and cougar, wolverine and badger, mink and weasel; all were a threat to farm animals. There were only a few critters Ruth would prefer not to be here; skunks, grizzlies and moose were at the top of that list.

"No problem Mom. If they make a lunch out of Lilly I'll leave them be so long as they don't come after the cows or me," Larry replied as he closed the door behind him.

"Now the kids **are** gone," Ross said with a mixture of love and lust.

"I thought you had raking you needed to finish," she teased.

"I do but I have something more important to finish first." He grasped her shoulders and pulled her gently to him. Then with one hand moving over her hair to the back of her head and the other sliding to the small of her back, he kissed her; gently at first, then with more urgency, his tongue parting her lips. His hand moved lower to the swell of her bottom and he felt her press against him. She moaned softly when he slid his hand slowly down over her firm butt to the back of her thighs then moved his free hand to her back and lifted her into his arms, his lips never leaving hers.

Carrying her up the short flight of stairs, he released her lips and took a deep breath. She raised her hand to the back of his head and pulled his mouth back onto hers. Reaching their bed, he lay her down and moved his fingers to the buttons of her summer dress. With the release of each button, more of her soft, white breasts were revealed. When the last button was free, his hand slid under the material and over one breast, her nipples now hard and erect. She was breathing heavily as he moved the fabric aside and lowered his mouth onto her nipple. Again, she pulled his head to her, forcing more of her yearning breast into his mouth.

Pulling her skirt up around her waist, Ross slid his fingers into the waistband of her panties and pulled them down over her thighs, past her knees and then off. He pulled his shirt off, barely taking time to undo the buttons then struggled to free himself of his pants and underwear, hampered by the size of his engorged manhood. Spreading her legs, he lowered himself onto her, feeling his hardness throbbing against the soft, moist entrance to her core. Ruth took him in her hand and guided him…the hot, wet essence of her womanhood enveloped him.

Their lovemaking ended in a climax of thrusting, quivering, gasping and moaning that finally settled into gentle stroking and whispered endearments.

After a brief nap, Ross sat up and stated, "Ruth, I have raking to do. Have you no shame, distracting me in the middle of the day?"

"Seems like you've been doing more plowing than raking but what do I know about farming?" his wife crooned.

Rolling off the bed, Ross looked at his wife's still exposed body. Only the threat of August thunder storms forced him to put his clothes back on and return to the meadow and the task at hand.

Larry and Lilly were nearing the place on Wild Horse Creek where he saw the pack of wolves earlier in the day. "You know, Lilly, it's an interesting thing about wolves," he stated, deciding it was time for big brother to start educating little sister.

"They mate for life. The parents take care of the kids just like people…they even do the grandparent thing. Their home range for hunting is really big and they mark it as they move around in a circle so they don't over kill their prey. Kinda' like how we move our cattle from pasture to pasture so they don't over graze. They probably won't be around here for more than a couple of weeks, so we just need to move the cows and watch them closer for a little while. It will probably be a year or two before this pack comes back by here. And unless something happens to the alpha male, no other pack will be allowed to hunt this pack's loop."

"Sounds like you like wolves," Lilly said quizzically. "I doubt Dad shares your enthusiasm."

"That's because he listens to the old farts who think the only thing that belongs on this land is cattle…their cattle. The Indians lived here for hundreds, maybe even thousands of years and shared their food with wolves and neither one went hungry."

"Don't you think our cattle belong here?" Lilly pressed.

"Sure, but that doesn't mean we need to shoot every wolf we see. You kill a wolf and you've killed a mother or father, brother or sister. Besides, if we kill all the wolves, there will be more elk and we will have to kill them because they will be eating the grass we need for the cows."

Their conversation was cut short when they began finding cows and calves along the brushy banks of Wild Horse Creek. Each busied themselves with the task of moving cattle to a small meadow where they would be held until enough were gathered to make a drive back to the Big Arm.

It was a hot dirty job trying to move cows from the shade of the creek into the August heat. Lilly saw it as a challenge, determined to move more cattle to the holding area than her brother. So intent was she on pushing cattle out of the brush she failed to see the large black bear working the stream for early fall-run Chinook. A loud splash and a muffled "woof" got Lilly's attention just as the big bear reared up on its hind-legs, looking squarely at her.

Black bear, she thought, instantly relieved that she was not face-to-face with a dreaded grizzly. Then she heard a strange noise behind her, almost like a baby crying. Turning in the saddle a sharp pang of fear shot though her body settling in her belly. Not twenty yards behind her were two bear cubs! She was caught between mama and her babies and mama was not happy about it.

All hell broke loose in a heartbeat. The sow bear let out a deafening roar and charged intent on destroying what stood between her and her young. Lilly sunk her spur-laden heels into Buttercup causing the Palomino to leap forward, barely avoiding the claws of the angry beast.

Hawthorn barbs ripped her shirt, her hat flew off, bouncing off Buttercup's butt. Lilly gripped the saddle horn as her mare lunged through the dense brush, nearly unseating her. When Buttercup broke free of the dense foliage lining the creek Lilly looked back only to see brush falling before the charging bruin.

Buttercup was stretched out into a flat-out run by the time the bear broke free of the brush-laden bank, its hind-feet reaching beyond its nose as it bore down on the fleeing horse and rider. Lilly watched as the beast closed the gap between them, then begin to fall back and the distance between them widened. Thankful that bears tire quickly, Lilly pulled Buttercup to a halt when she saw the cubs catch up with their mother. Then the three bears wandered off as though nothing had ever disturbed them.

Lilly dismounted and began assessing the damage to her face, hands and shirt. The scratches, while painful were not serious…her shirt on the other hand was pretty much a mess. A large three-cornered tear exposed one cup of her brassiere, three of the five buttons were gone and one sleeve was little more than ribbons. "Good thing I'm out here with my brother and not one of his jerk friends," she whispered to Buttercup, and stuffed the torn corner of her shirt into the top of her bra-cup, hoping to avoid the teasing she knew Larry would not be able to resist bestowing upon her.

"What the hell happened to you? You fall off your horse?"

At first, Lilly was greeted with little regard for her welfare when she and Larry rendezvoused with a respectable number of cattle to move to the Big Arm. Looking closer, he became suddenly serious. "No joke, Lilly, what happened? Are you alright?"

Lilly told him her tale of the encounter with the bear and cubs as they pushed the beeves toward the Big Arm.

"Never really thought much about black bear," Larry mused then added, "It's a good thing you can ride. You could have been in damn bad spot."

"Not 'could have been'." Lilly corrected. "Was!" she stated, patting the Palomino on the neck.

Ruth busied herself making lemonade and mashing potatoes; the aroma of pork roast permeated the kitchen. Ross was washing up, feeling good about having finished the windrowing in the meadow. Both were reminiscing about the afternoon delight they had shared, tempered only by a nagging worry about Larry and Lilly. It was getting dark and they should be back from Wild Horse Creek by now.

When the door opened, Ruth heaved a sigh of relief that stuck half way out of her throat when she saw the tattered and torn Lilly. "Lilly!" she shouted, bringing Ross out of the bathroom, face lathered and a straight razor in his hand. He stood with his mouth open as his eyes moved from her torn shirt to her bloody face.

"It's alright," Larry said quickly as if somehow responsible for Lilly's plight. "She just had a little run in with a bear."

"Oh, my God!" gasped Ruth. Rushing to her daughter, she took Lilly's hand and led her into the bathroom, leaving Ross with a stunned look and shaving cream on his face.

Once Lilly and Larry were cleaned up and Lilly's bear story told and retold, they settled in around the wooden table for dinner and the conversation turned to wolves.

"So, did you see the wolves again?" Ross asked the question open-ended for either Lilly or Larry.

"Nope, didn't hear any either," Larry offered.

"You think they were just passing through?"

"Not likely. My guess is they'll be around for a couple of weeks then they will probably move on." Larry quickly added, "There might be two packs because I herd howling off toward the Cabinets at the same time I was watching the pack on the Wild Horse."

"Maybe they are Mormon wolves and have a really big family," Lilly said with a giggle. She was referring to the Johnston's who had a ranch and fourteen kids over toward the Thompson River.

"Don't make fun of the Johnston's," Ruth admonished her daughter, while grinning widely. "They believe God wants them to have a big family."

"Well, then either the Johnston's or God is stupid. No woman should have to have that many kids," Lilly stated.

"Let's forget about the Johnston's," Ross said firmly. "We are talking about wolves and wolves are no laughing matter."

"They are not the end of the world either, Dad," Lilly retorted. "They were here for hundreds of years before us and things were fine."

Larry and his mom could see this conversation was going downhill fast. He felt a little responsible for having told Lilly how he felt about wolves but he knew she had her own opinions without his help.

"Why don't we all take a ride up to Wild Horse Creek tomorrow?" Ruth interjected. "I know I would like to get out of the house and its good weather. It would be a nice ride and we can bring any stray cows and calves back to the Big Arm. Lillian and I will make a lunch and we can have a picnic." Ruth was not about to let a wolf pack or two lead to a family feud.

Chapter Four

Fight or Flight

As the night sky paled into daybreak, Sam found himself in the middle of a large flat covered with sage, bunchgrass and scattered pines. It was still overcast but the rain had reduced to a light drizzle. Evidence of the intensity of last night's downpour remained as water ran in small rivulets in the sandy soil.

"Whoa," he whispered. Not a hundred yards away stood a mule deer doe, her big ears pointing toward them in curious wonder.

Slowly Sam pulled the guard duty Spencer from its scabbard. Dismounting, he laid the gun across his saddle, flipped up the adjustable rear sight and took aim. With the lone rein firmly gripped in his left hand, he squeezed the trigger. **Crack!** The sudden report of the rifle startled both him and Major. She jumped and he dropped the rifle, grabbing the rein with both hands. Speaking softly, Sam coaxed the horse into believing that all was well, while he watched the doe kick one last time before lying still.

Not taking time to gut the doe, he skinned the deer, then relieved her of her back-strap and cut small strips of meat from the hindquarters and shoulders. Chancing a fire, Sam cooked all the meat, ate three slices of back-strap and stuffed the rest into a saddlebag. Now full, he stomped out the small fire and rode away with a new sense of confidence, pausing only for a moment to lament the amount of the doe he was leaving to waste.

"The Indians would be pissed but the coyotes and wolves will say muchas gracias," he resolved.

Without the consuming nagging of hunger, Sam began to take stock of himself and his situation. Removing his blue coat, he pulled the talisman with the broken leather cord from his pocket. Taking the two strands of leather, he looped them into a simple knot and slipped the cord over his head. With the amulet resting safely on his chest, he felt a sense of *alivio*, physical well-being.

"Probably, it is the venison," he concluded.

As he topped a rise, Sam found himself looking over a nearly dry, serpentine creek bottom framed by a desert-like sage flat. A tree-covered mountain range in the distance looped around him like a horseshoe.

Then he saw them. Six, maybe eight Indians on horseback, motionless like ornaments atop the tall sage, were looking directly at him. He pulled Major to a halt. His blood ran cold as fear surged through his body and his mind struggled to make a decision.

Fight or flight?

Sam remembered the last Indians he'd seen…thousands intent on killing every soldier in sight.

"They can't be from that valley," he assured himself. "They have to be locals. Maybe they are friendly." His words did little to calm his fear, a fear rooted in the memory of what he'd seen in that strange place a week or maybe a lifetime ago. It remained like yesterday in his mind.

Friendly Indians…Peace Treaty.

He managed a weak smile as he equated the oxymoron.

Memory overpowered reason. Quickly removing the broken rein from its secure location on the saddle's strap ring he folded it double. Aiming for the near side of the horseshoe Sam smacked Major on the butt with the rein-turned-whip and broke into a flat-out run for the cover of the mountains.

Surprised by the speed of the little mare, Sam grasped the pommel with his free hand as they raced over sand and sage. After cutting the distance to the trees in half, he chanced a glance over his shoulder. He saw not six or eight but fifty or more Indians in blood-thirsty pursuit.

Leaning forward over the pommel, he smacked Major again as they sped toward cover. Major's foot caught in a sage and she stumbled, nearly unseating Sam. Clinging desperately to the smooth pommel he managed to regain his seat and the mare returned to her ground-eating gait. Looking back, he realized the stumble had cost them valuable ground and their pursuers were gaining.

"Go! Go! Go!" he shouted, urging the little mare to a newfound speed. "If these are friendly Indians, they've damn sure got me fooled," he muttered in the wind. The sound of the yipping Indians reached his ears like a chorus of hungry coyotes.

Rushing at breathtaking speed toward the timber Sam was struck with a stark realization. The trees, that looked to be so close across the vast flat, remained far in the distance, a deception common to desert travelers. Mind numbing fear crept into his being when he felt Major's swift pace begin to slow. Desperately he applied the whip but there was nothing left in her, her big heart and lungs were willing but her legs were worn out.

Panic infiltrated his mind and body like blood in water. "Run goddamn you, run!" he yelled at the top of his lungs. Then a calm acceptance set in. "It's alright chica," he said to the gutsy little horse. Feeling contrite, he patted her on the neck and pulled her to a stop. "It is not your fault I'm in this mess."

Yipping Indians rode along side shaking fists that held spears and bows. Surrounded, Sam closed his eyes awaiting the searing pain of an arrow in the gut or a spear through his heart. Neither came.

After a twenty-four-hour minute, Sam slowly opened one eye, then the other. He'd never seen so many Indians so close. Unlike the unforgettable encounter in the hidden valley, these Indians were not covered in war paint and except for their dress and long hair didn't look all that different from him. They seemed more curious than menacing.

A stocky brave on a fine looking Appaloosa rode to within arm's length. "What are you called? Why do you run like a *kamita*, a dog?"

Sam had no idea what the brave was saying. "Cuanto dinero for that Appaloosa?" he replied, knowing the brave would not understand a word he said and thinking no response might be taken as an insult.

The Indian's eyes moved to the butt of the carbine protruding from its scabbard. He motioned to a brave on a brown-and-white pinto who rode forward and reached toward the gun.

Sam raised his hand, palm facing the Indian, hoping he would recognize the sign to stop.

He did.

Sam quickly wrapped the bridle rein around his saddle horn then slowly reached for the Spencer. Grasping it by the butt, he cautiously removed it from the scabbard. Still gripping it by the butt he held the rifle out at arm's length as excited Indians clamored for a closer look. Vigilantly lowering his upraised hand, he grasped the stock and held the carbine out for their inspection.

A murmur ran through the group and several braves pulled their ponies back, opening a path to a fine-looking Indian with broad shoulders and muscular arms. He extended his arms toward Sam. In his hands, he held what appeared to be a Winchester or Henry lever action. He stared at Sam for what seemed like a full minute, mimicking him as he showed off the rifle then began to laugh, a joke that seemed to be much appreciated by his comrades.

"Well hell," Sam mumbled. "I guess they are not all that impressed by me having a rifle."

The stocky brave closest to Sam reached out and grasped the guard duty carbine. Sam saw little point in resisting and released his grip. "Just try to stay calm and don't show them fear," he resolutely told himself.

With him disarmed, the small Indian armada quickly closed in around him. A leather bag, apparently meant for carrying roots or mushrooms or maybe harvested animal parts like hearts, livers or testicles, was slipped over Sam's head and tied around his neck with a leather drawstring.

Suddenly recognizing the gravity of his situation, he whispered to a God he wished he could believe in, "This ain't good."

"There is no in way in hell these Indians could know about Colonel Wolard, that valley or this totem," he assured himself unconvincingly.

Encased in total darkness, Sam felt Major begin to move, slowly at first then at a brisk walk. He began to sweat while the smell of rancid meat and blood invaded his nose…he could even taste it. Feeling dizzy, Sam gripped the saddle pommel in an effort to steady himself and regain his equilibrium. Vomit boiled up in his throat and he fought the growing nausea.

If I puke I could drown in my own vomit, he thought. I have to think of something else, bueno…something good.

Mind control.

Sam thought of his mother.

After an unknown period of time a claustrophobic panic gripped him. He couldn't breath! Disoriented and desperate he grabbed at his throat and the drawstring. It slipped, and a rush of cool sweet air invaded the bag along with a glimmer of light. "Damn," he muttered. "That was close."

The rocking of Major's gait and thoughts of his mother became Sam's world until he realized the faint light within the bag had again turned to darkness. He was puzzled and perplexed. Where were they taking him? Were they going to ride all night?

The answer to his last question came abruptly when his mount came to a halt and he was roughly pulled to the ground. Strong hands gripped Sam's arms and his hands were lashed around what he guessed was a small tree.

"Sweet Madre de Jesus," he whispered, hoping he was tied to a tree and not some post used for ceremonial torture.

The excited chatter of his captives faded into the distance and Sam was left in an awkward position with aching arms, burning hands and a growing fear that threatened to consume him. He had always been proud of his ability to stay cool under pressure, to re-act instinctively to any situation. It was what had made him a good soldier. It was what had saved him that day in the valley.

Now Sam had a new problem. There was no element of surprise, no chaos in which to re-act, no chance to observe his surroundings and find an opportunity for escape. He was bound and blind, helpless and hopeless.

If only I can get this hood off.

Leaning his head back against the obstacle he was bound to, Sam began sliding down. The hood moved but stopped at his chin. He'd loosened it enough to breath but not enough to slide off over his head.

Caught in a squatting position, his legs began to ache then to cramp. Painfully he managed to slide into a sitting position. Straightening his legs he breathed a sigh of relief…the comfort was brief but welcome.

Panic was now a constant companion, an empty feeling in his gut, a growing lump in his throat threatening to invade his brain and push him beyond the edge of sanity.

He awoke to the clamor of voices and the thumping of hooves. "Oh God," he groaned then, "Dios mio."

The pain in his neck, shoulders, arms and legs ripped through him like a flint-tipped arrow. He didn't feel the binding removed from his completely numb wrists and hands. Only when pulled to his feet did Sam realized his hands were no longer bound.

Instinctively his hands went to the heart-sack-turned hood, trying to pull it over his head. Strong fingers grasped his wrist and jerked his hand away, the drawstring was pulled tight. His breathing was again labored but he tried to stay calm. Do not fight it, take small breaths, he mentally coaxed himself. Sam was feeling lightheaded and again, slowly this time, reached for the hood. He managed to loosen the tie a little before being led to his horse and his foot placed in the dangling stirrup. Grasping the pommel he swung aboard his mount. The lone rein was missing. Sam no longer had control of his horse…he was being led by his captors.

After unfathomable time, encased in the dank dark bag, interrupted only by infrequent stops in which he was freed to relieve himself but never free of the hood, Sam began to develop an acute awareness. Sound became more distinct and he was able to identify individual sounds and their locations. He could feel each muscular movement of his horse and began to visualize the ever-changing terrain by the adjustments in balance needed to stay in the saddle. He knew he was still aboard Major, having become one with the little horse and able to sense and anticipate her every move.

What he lost track of was the grueling days and painful nights. He had did not know how long they had traveled, how far they had gone or where they were going. He remembered gruesome stories old soldiers told of torture at the hands of savages.

The captive white man was shirtless, his hands tied behind his back. The Indian's face was painted red with streaks of white and yellow running straight down from his forehead to his jaw, the vertical line intersecting menacing cold eyes. In his hand he held a jagged flint-blade knife. Slowly the Indian drew the knife downward from the man's sternum, ripping the skin and allowing intestines to roll from the man's stomach.

The screaming man dropped to his knees, barely conscious, entrails spilling from his body, his screams turning to agonizing groans and sobs. The painted Indian joined the rest of the war party and waited. Soon magpies began to circle and land near the dying man. First one then another and another landed on the blood-stained ground and hopped like black-and-white demons toward the gut pile. The man slowly died while the scavenger birds poked holes in his innards, searching for any tasty morsel.

A nude woman was staked spread-eagle on the bare ground, the hot sun burning her white skin. Indians in full ceremonial attire danced in jubilant light-footed bounds around their captive. The horrified woman's eyes darted from side to side, wide with fear and trepidation.

A chanting warrior moved beside the prone woman and slowly poured a golden liquid over her breasts, stomach and thighs, letting the final drops leak out over her exposed womanhood.

Then, caught in a torture driven frenzy, dancing chanting Indians poked sticks in a nearby anthill then threw them on the honey-coated prisoner.

Her agonizing screams echoed off the mountains and through the valleys as the voracious ants bit and crawled over her, into her eyes, ears, nose, mouth and private parts.

Sam shook his head violently, ridding himself of the horrible images. *Get a hold of yourself.*

There was no reason to believe any of those damn stories. They were whisky-talk and old-timers trying to scare the hell out of privates.

His mind spun off in a different direction.

Venison…

He was starving and the damn Indians were probably eating his back-straps.

Now that is enough to piss off even a good soldier.

Sam had no idea where he was or how far he'd been taken. He'd felt Major travel up and down hills, across at least one river and several small streams. There were too many excruciating nights spent tied to trees to count. His stomach was cramping to the point of spasms and his mouth was so dry his tongue felt swollen.

A new fear emerged.

They will not torture me; they will let me die of hunger or thirst. Probably the thirst will come first, he concluded.

When Major stopped and he was pulled to the ground again, he was glad for the break but dreaded another night bound to some sapling. There was much talking in excited or angry tones. He wondered if his captors had reached their village.

Maybe now they will torture me.

He lamented, realizing that his parched lips and tongue could no longer emit a sound.

Sam felt the drawstring of the rancid bag jerked and suddenly the hood was yanked over his head. It was as if he was being born for the very first time. His knees buckled and he nearly collapsed as light invaded his retinas and sweet fresh air drenched his nose and mouth. Squinting in an attempt to adjust to the light he realized it was night. Sam could not look directly at the moon or stars. It was like the night sky was filled with a million suns so he covered his eyes with his now free hands. Slowly he spread his fingers letting light in then cupping his hands to hood his eyes until they adjusted to a world outside of the bag.

Finally able to see, Sam found himself encircled by Indians; no war paint, no tomahawks or war axes…just curious, cautious Indians. "You have much *orenda*, powerful medicine." The one who rode the good-looking Appaloosa said. "And some good venison," he quickly added, then burst into laughter.

A taller, thinner brave with long black braids stepped closer and handed Sam a rawhide pouch. Pointing at the pouch and then cupping his fingers to his mouth he said, "*Wasna*, pemmican, good, you eat."

Sam got the message.

You don't need to send me a smoke signal.

He was starving. Opening the pouch, he quickly pulled out the flat, dried piece of venison, saskatoon and bear fat. Taking half of the paddy in one bite he chewed voraciously, the sweet juices of the paddy resurrected taste buds he'd given up for dead. "You would think I have not eaten for a week," he chuckled. Swallowing small amounts of juice soothed his parched throat and prepared his empty stomach for the foreign substance…food.

An Indian handed him a gourd and made a motion for him to drink. Again, he did not need to be told, the pemmican had done much for his hunger but little for his thirst. Sam was now feeling better but very much aware of the pickle he was in. "Be just like you to feed me before you kill me," he said to the tall one, who grinned and nodded as though he understood.

"Damn Indian probably thinks I just thanked him." Sam's feeble attempt at humor did little to bolster his spirits but the pemmican and water helped considerably.

Wispy clouds drifted across an August moon while Sam's eyes adjusted to the night sky. He looked for anything in the stars that might hold a clue to his location. He found the big dipper but it was in the same relative location it had been when he was at the fort. In fact, it seemed to be in the same place it was when he looked at it from the veranda at Destino.

Two Indians with white feathers in their hair took Sam's arms and led him to a small pine. They pulled his arms behind his back and around the tree and tied him. He dreaded another night in such an uncomfortable position but was relieved when they left without putting the hood over his head. He never gave much thought to what it would be like to be blind, now he knew. He wondered, if he was forced to choose between being blind and living or dying, which would he choose? He was dog-tired but could not close his eyes to sleep; he just wanted to see, to take in the stars, the moon, the slow moving clouds and even the shadows.

Sam began to wonder about his captors. "Whoever they are they must be a long way from home," he was now talking to himself on a regular basis. "We have been traveling for days with no sign of a village. At least none my eyes could see," he sickly joked then quickly stammered, "Eso no tiene gracia. That was not funny...nothing about this is funny."

Without the hood Sam began to think about escape. He was pretty sure these Indians weren't taking him back to that dreadful valley but he had no desire to spend the rest of his life living with Indians anywhere. Still, he was feeling some kind of connection to these people.

Maybe it is empathy, he thought. They are losing their land and way of life the same as my people in California. De oro, gold...it was gold in California and it is gold here.

For the first time in what seemed like a lifetime, Sam began to think about something besides the terrifying spectacle of the un-dead Indians and his determination never to return to *that* place. His current situation was only slightly less concerning. He was a prisoner of fifty or more Indians with intentions completely unknown. Even if by some miracle he escaped, he was still a deserter. He had run in the face of the enemy, fled a battlefield leaving his comrades to die and then deserted his post in defiance of a direct order.

"Major Denton surely has a patrol looking for me," he assessed. "If they find me I will be shot or forced to lead Denton back to that valley. I would rather be shot," he confirmed. "But they will have to find me first."

"Maybe it is a good thing these Indians caught me," he mumbled, while further contemplating his predicament. The army would never find his tracks amidst half-a-hundred Indian ponies. That thought was only slightly comforting.

Sam awoke to an overcast sky and a threat of rain. Granite cliffs worn smooth by wind and rain towered high above him and a small river meandered through dense vegetation nearby. A brief surge of panic raced through him. The similarities to that dreadful valley were uncanny but he quickly realized this valley was only similar, not the same. He breathed a sigh of relief.

When he was untied, fed and watered, Sam wondered if this was how animals felt...completely dependent on their owners for their care.

A commotion drew his attention toward the river where several braves were speaking with loud voices and animated gestures. When the small group became more and more emphatic they were joined by others in the excited banter. With each forearm held securely by a strong brave, Sam watched the antics of the group with guarded curiosity.

From within the group was an occasional muffled, thumping sound that sounded like someone's head was being pounded into the ground.

Could they be fighting over what to do with me?

Sam felt his knees weaken and a cold wave swept through his belly causing him to feel like he needed to pee.

Suddenly the group broke apart and two large Indians came toward him. Looking past them, curiosity turned to panic. Evenly spaced were four wooden stakes; now he knew what was being pounded into the ground.

"Madre de Dios," he whispered. "They have tired of playing a game with me. They will stake me out and kill me or leave me here to die."

All the stories he had ever heard about Indian torture came rushing back like a flash flood. "Never let em take ya alive," Sergeant Podunski, after a couple shots of army whisky, used to expound to any wide-eyed private who would listen.

The braves closed in around Sam. Two grabbed each leg and two took his arms, lifted him off the ground and carried him toward the ominous looking stakes, then the hood was slipped back over his head. He was again in total darkness. Lowered to the ground, first one leg and then other were tied to stakes with rawhide cords. His arms were roughly pulled toward the stakes on either side of his head and it felt like his shoulders were being dislocated.

This is no way to die.

Sam closed his eyes and thought of his mother. "Por favor, please," he muttered to some omni-present being. "If I die here, let me see my madre... and my padre?" he added with doubt, wondering if you paid for suicide in hell.

When his left wrist was secured to a stake, Sam felt a sudden surge of adrenaline and with all the strength of a cornered animal, he jerked his right arm free.

I will not go to my death without a fight!

Swinging wildly with clenched fist, he wanted to hit something, to inflict a little pain before being left to die, or worse. He struck out hitting only air and ground.

"What the...!" The words stuck in his throat as he grabbed at the hood and pulled it over his head.

He'd seen things on that fateful day in the valley he would not have thought possible but still he was totally unprepared for what happened next.

The horses saw it first; their heads came up from the lush grass and their ears snapped forward in unison, pointing toward an aged cottonwood rising from the surrounding brush near the riverbank.

"Iieeeyah!" A frightened cry escaped the throat of a nearby Indian.

Choo-pin-it-pa-loo, People of the Mountains... The cries of running Indians filled the air.

Scrambling to untie himself, Sam searched for the source of the excitement.

Then he saw it!

"Griz," he stated flatly as the huge animal crawled out of the river and emerged from the thick brush. The next words that fell from Sam's mouth came without benefit of thought. "Wolf! Madre de Dios! It is a goddamn wolf!"

The animal walked toward Sam and his captors, water spraying from its jet-black coat as it shook violently.

Yipping and shouting rang in Sam's ears while his eyes danced between fleeing Indians and the wet wolf, its fur shining like greased coal. When its advance stopped some fifty yards short of where Sam stood, there was no one left in sight except Sam and the wolf. The Indians had disappeared leaving only a cloud of dust and their lingering screams.

"What the hell?" Sam said, desperately trying to reign in his runaway mind. The attempt was quickly aborted when the big wolf began to glitter and glow, its black coat fading to gray and then pulsating as if emitting some kind of electrical charge.

"Santo Madre de Dios!" Sam exclaimed, suddenly wishing he'd run off with the frightened Indians.

The wolf's yellow eyes glowed in the overcast morning light and Sam remembered the necklace. His hand reached for it, again in what was becoming a far too frequent occurrence. Samuel DeSoto was scared, really scared!

Indians would not run from a wolf.

But this was no ordinary wolf. Sam pulled the totem-like circulate from inside his shirt as if offering it to this shimmering lobo as a sacrifice. He stood pillar-still with the painted-leather amulet in his hand while the colossal canine drew nearer, its eyes like two glowing orbs.

"What is this thing?" Sam questioned, looking at the ornately painted leather in his hand. "What do you want with me?" he asked, fully expecting the animal, or the amulet, to answer.

The beast took a long, seemingly quizzical look at Sam, then shook its magnificent head and was suddenly enshrouded in a smoke-like fog. When the fog cleared the wolf was gone. Sam could hear the whoops and yelps of the fleeing Indians in the distance. Nearby, a blue jay bragged to all who would listen about what he had just seen. A squirrel excitedly scolded the jay and a raven mocked them both.

Sam was alone somewhere in the land of the *Okinakane*. He was alone again with his horse, his saddle, his knife, his clothes, the strange leather talisman and his life. The horse, saddle and clothes weren't his; they belonged to the army…an army he was no longer a part of. He was scared, bewildered with no idea where he was or where he was going, only where he had been and where he could not go back to.

At least they left my horse.

Sam was sure that had more to do with fright than favor.

Chapter Five

Risky

Standing Wolf set up a small camp with a distant view of the fort. He cooked on a small fire made from dry wood that burned hot and did not smoke. He maintained a constant surveillance of the fort, confident the soldier with the amulet was inside.

Days passed with no activity outside of the stockade walls and Standing Wolf was becoming restless.

"Something is not right," he told Whiskey. "They should have sent out a search party as soon as the survivor made it to the fort and told what happened…unless they do not believe his story. A month ago I would not have believed what happened to Colonel Wolard, Roy, Bishop Donneli or the soldiers but still they are gone, they have not returned to the fort. Were I in command that would require an explanation." He was talking to himself and it made him think of Frank and Spotted Fawn, then his mother and Star Flower.

As days turned to weeks, Standing Wolf became increasingly agitated. "I should be back on a bed of boughs with Star Flower by now."

He watched as a few small patrols of a dozen or more soldiers left the fort only to return before nightfall. "The guy with the amulet is probably with them if they are looking for the colonel," he said in frustration, realizing there was no way of knowing which soldier that was. He looked hard at every man on a gray horse but soon realized that was hopeless. For one with the power to call his native ancestors to battle, one who had been called the Messiah, Standing Wolf felt powerless.

"I have to try something else," he told the black stallion.

His mind returned to Janis and the dead soldiers and civilians.

Are they still there?

If the dead soldiers were from the fort, a patrol should have found them by now and brought them back. He watched every patrol come and go and none returned with bodies.

"If only my mother were here. If I could speak with her perhaps she could tell me how to find the man with the amulet." He spoke to the wind as his mind darted about like a frightened hare. "If I am Standing Wolf, the Chosen One, why am I not guided to the amulet by *Ogle Wa Nagi*, the Great Spirit, so I can return to the valley of the Sematuse?"

Standing Wolf was feeling helpless and frustrated. Somewhere inside the log walls of the fort was a soldier with the amulet, a sacred totem painted by his mother with the guiding hand of the Great Spirit. He considered his options; he could ride to the fort and announce himself as Breed…the scout hired by Colonel Wolard and lie about any knowledge of the colonels whereabouts and hope to find the one with the amulet, or he could go to the fort and claim to be a survivor of a great battle along with one soldier and that he and that soldier could lead the army to the colonel and his men.

He liked the second idea best…for about one beat of his heart, he realized both ideas were just frustration. Neither would work. The man with the amulet knew what happened in the valley and would have told his story to the entire fort. Even if no one believed his account of what happened it would not help Standing Wolf.

If I go to the fort they are sure to arrest me, he concluded.

Unless…

It was risky but it just might work. Standing Wold knew the fort and how it worked from his time as a scout. He wondered whether anyone was living in his cabin within the fort's walls. The fort stable was located some distance outside the walls of the fort and was watched over at night by a single armed guard. If he could take out the guard and if his uniform would fit, Standing Wolf might just be able to slip into the fort unnoticed. He could then listen and watch, maybe get lucky enough to at least find out who he was chasing.

"You are going to have to stay here and be quiet for a while," he said to the big black, not knowing how long a while might be.

Not very damn long, I hope.

With darkness settling in, Standing Wolf disrobed, leaving his clothes stashed in a hollow log. As he moved in the direction of the fort, he wore only a rawhide belt and a sheath holding his Bowie knife.

Nearing the stable, he looked for a guard. "I hope things have not changed too much since Colonel Wolard's demise," he said under his breath. He hoped they had not increased the number of stable guards and he hoped the no-dogs-rule still applied. The colonel had banned dogs at the fort because he hated stepping in dog poop.

"I can sneak up on anything but a damn dog," Standing Wolf lamented.

He hunkered down, careful to keep his privates out of the dirt. 'I sure am glad it is August and not December,' he mused.

The night was quite. Only a light breeze rustled the leaves of the nearby aspen and cottonwoods. The mournful cry of a screech owl was reassuring and for a moment he thought of the valley and Star Flower.

Focus.

He mouthed the word, bringing his thoughts and instincts back to the task at hand.

He heard voices. A horse snorted and stomped prompting a flurry of activity in the stable that quickly died down. The night grew quite again. Standing Wolf moved toward the murmur of voices. Two soldiers sat on the ground next to the stable door. A rifle leaned against the stable wall and another rested across the lap of the soldier nearest the door. It was too dark to see what rank they were but guard duty went to mostly privates and corporals.

I hope they are privates, he thought. They went mostly unnoticed around the fort.

Waiting and watching he hoped they were the changing of the guard and that one would take his rifle and return to the fort. He soon realized they were not a change in the guard…they *were* the guard.

They have doubled the guard on the stable, he surmised. This was not a good sign. They were clearly on high alert. What did he expect with the fort commander and a thousand soldiers missing?

His attention quickly returned to the guards. The one nearest the door stood up, leaned his rifle against the building and walked toward the far corner. As the guard rounded the corner, Standing Wolf moved silently toward him. The guard stopped, fussed with the front of his pants then with legs slightly spread he straightened, arched his back and with one hand apparently grasping something important, a sigh broke the silent night air.

Standing Wolf struck!

The man's piss was cutoff in mid-stream. The forearm hit him in the neck just below his chin. The blow knocked his head backwards causing a disconnection between his spinal cord and his brain. His world went blank.

Standing Wolf grasp the fallen soldier under his arms and dragged him deeper into the surrounding darkness. Coyotes yipped in the distant night as he removed the soldier's uniform and slipped it on his own naked body. At least he is a private, Standing Wolf thought, noticing the thin yellow stripe on the uniform arms.

Struggling to tuck his long braids into the tiny blue cap, he finally gave up and shoved them under the coat collar. "Lucky the coat is a little big," he muttered, squirming, attempting to feel comfortable in the unfamiliar clothing.

Returning to the barn, Standing Wolf approached the seated guard, a rifle leaning against the wall on either side, and caught a glimpse of the two-striped chevron on his sleeve. Should have known one would be a corporal, he thought.

Now it starts to get tricky.

I wonder if my survival skills have gotten rusty, he thought as he approached the corporal. It had been nearly fifteen years since that awful war that turned him into a finely tuned killing machine, and he wondered if he might have lost his edge.

"Took ya long enough," the seated guard quipped. "Have trouble findin' it?"

"Yeah, ya wanna help me look for it?" Standing Wolf responded, remembering the tone of military banter among the enlisted soldiers from his days with Custer.

"Not unless yer a woman pretendin' ta be a man," the guard said standing and stretching. "My turn shouldn't take me so long, mine's easy ta find." He laughed as he walked away into the darkness.

Standing Wolf was alone, dressed as a cavalry private with two guns and a decision to make. Should he see if the corporal knows anything about the guy with the amulet or just take him out and sneak into the fort and take his chances?

As the lone, remaining guard emerged from the darkness buttoning his blue trousers with their faint yellow stripe, Standing Wolf picked up the .50 caliber Spencer Carbine leaning against the stable wall and pointed it at the approaching soldier.

The guard stopped dead in his tracks, his mouth dropped open but no words came out.

"Stay calm, do as your told and you will live to see tomorrow, do something stupid and I will be the last thing you see on Mother Earth." Standing Wolf picked up the second rifle and moved away from the faint light emitting from the stable door. He motioned the bewildered guard to the site.

The corporal barely made it to the barn door before his trembling knees gave way to mounting fear and he slumped against the wall, sliding down to a sitting position.

"You ain't Joe," he finally managed to wheeze breathlessly. "What the hell's goin' on? Who are you?" The question was only slightly more forceful than the statement.

"You do not want to know who I am," Standing Wolf told the man with certainty. "Do you know of a soldier who came to the fort with a talisman like this? A sacred amulet?" he asked, grasping the ornament hanging around his neck.

"Who the hell are you and where is Joe?" the man insisted.

Standing Wolf took a step closer and pulled back the hammer on the rifle.

"OK, for Christ sake! I don't know nothin' about any sacred anything. I just know that Sam came back all crazy and sayin' that they was all dead…even the colonel…killed by some kinda ghost Injuns."

So his name is Sam, Standing Wolf thought. Now how can I get him out here?

"I need to see Sam and you are going to help me," he told the corporal. "Any tricks and you will find out where Joe is."

Fear can make an ally out of the enemy.

The words of General Custer came back to him.

"He ain't here!" the corporal blurted. "He left the same night he got back with that crazy story. He just went plum nuts…stole Major Denton's horse and lit out in the middle ah the night. The major's still pissed! Now who the hell are you and what did ya do with Joe?"

"Gone where?" The question escaped his lips before the obvious answer reached his brain.

"If I knew where, I'd be the new sergeant major!" the corporal retorted. "The major's been gonna send a patrol out lookin' for Sam. He ain't gonna be happy till he's got 'em in the brig. Only thing is, he don't wanna lose another patrol."

Standing Wolf's heart sank.

Gone!

This changes everything, he thought. "He could be anywhere and he has had a week to get there." The words seeped from his mouth as his mind wrestled with what to do now.

Pointing the cocked carbine at the frightened guard, Standing Wolf unbuttoned Joe's uniform shirt and slipped it off, one arm at a time, then the boots and pants.

Completely naked, long black braids now visible and holding the wide-eyed soldier at gun point, he spoke. "I am Standing Wolf. I was known at this fort as Breed, Colonel Wolard's guide and interpreter. Sam's story is true. The colonel, his brother, the priest…they are all dead and so will you be if you tell anyone of what you have seen."

Picking up the other rifle Standing Wolf continued, "Joe will come to in an hour or two. You must tell him to remain silent about this night. There are Indians with powers you can not understand. Just know that they will not bother you unless you alert the others in the fort. If you do, they will find you in the darkness as I have and remove your heart and soul from your body. They will use your brains for fish bait."

In an instant Standing Wolf disappeared into the night, hoping he had scared the corporal enough that by the time he explained to Joe what had happened neither would speak of this night…when guard duty took on a whole new meaning.

By the time Standing Wolf reached the hollow stump and his clothes, he was on the verge of despair. Never had he considered the panic-stricken soldier, Sam, might leave the security of the fort.

"We have ourselves a new problem," he said to Whiskey.

The big black rubbed his dished, blazed face against the chest of Standing Wolf as if he understood.

Chapter Six

Hot Water

FRANK was in a dither. Normally that would not have been unusual but since finding his daughter, Sarah...now called Spotted Fawn... and reuniting with Charlie, who was now Standing Wolf, he was feeling at peace with the world.

The euphoria of the appearance of ancestral warriors, and the annihilation of the intruders, was still highly present among the valley inhabitants.

While Ta-keen Eagle and Warm Hands were in seemingly endless discussions about how and why such a revelation could have occurred, Laughing Doe and Willow quickly returned to their free-spirited, flirtatious ways.

Little Beaver and Spotted Fawn were completely absorbed in each other, marveling at the mysterious way *Ogle Wa Nagi* had brought them together...soul mates for eternity.

The reason for Frank's fretting was that everything in the valley was returning to normal so quickly. The memory of that soldier yanking the revered amulet from around his neck haunted Frank. He wished he had seen it coming but so much was happening so quickly there was no time to react.

To his credit, the soldier reacted swiftly...not a fact that made Frank feel any better. Because the soldier escaped with the amulet, Standing Wolf left the safety of the valley, Star Flower and Bend Grass in pursuit of the talisman. The future of these people and this magnificent valley might depend on its safe return.

And then there's Willow.

Since Frank got sane and clean, he was a target of her playful but seductive nature, including her very obvious female charms. Women were something Frank hadn't thought about since that awful day so many years ago. Julie had been the love of his life, the only woman he'd ever known, in the Biblical sense, and it cost him his sanity and nearly his life...*it had killed her.*

Tormented as Frank was by the past, Willow's sensuous ways were beginning to have an unexpected effect on him. He found it difficult to look away when her large smoky-gray eyes grabbed his with a come-hither look.

She's just teasing, he told himself but it didn't matter. It was not that he had any expectations. It was that she caused him to feel things... like the tingling ache in his groin that he had long ago forgotten.

He was not at all sure he liked the feeling. With it came a cold shower of guilt, but he could not ignore it. During his time in the valley Frank came to understand these people. They had no concept of jealousy or guilt in matters of the heart or body. Physical pleasures were the Great Spirit's way of rewarding them for being His people, for living in the old ways.

Frank tried to stay clear of Willow although every time he saw her a faint smile tickled his lips. She was so special, such a seriously beautiful woman and yet so playful and unaware of her undeniable feminine attributes. She was like a child in a woman's body.

Again, he thought of Julie. If only he could shake the guilt.

"I can't wait till winter," Frank mumbled as he spotted Willow in her deerskin vest; low cut and held together in the front by leather loops and deer-antler buttons, revealing a generous portion of her firm breasts. Her skirt made of eel grass attached to a strip of leather clung to her hips, the grass just touching the tops of her knees. Her tiny waist accentuated the bare skin between the vest and skirt. With each step her hips swayed and a bare leg was exposed well above mid-thigh.

"She dresses like that this winter she'll be covered in goose bumps," Frank fussed and began walking briskly toward the teepee of Spotted Fawn and Little Beaver.

"It's a fine morning," he announced, approaching their abode and hoping for a response that would allow him entrance and avoid further beguilement.

Spotted Fawn pushed open the teepee flap and tied it back; her dark-brown hair in braids hung well past her shoulders. "Good Morning Father," she said in a soft caring voice. Her big brown eyes danced with happiness.

Frank entered the teepee and saw Little Beaver seated near a bed of boughs and furs. He had the contented look of an opossum.

Is everyone in this place in love?

The thought bounced off Frank's mind and fell harmlessly to an array of more meaningful thoughts.

"I am concerned about Standing Wolf," he stated. "Since I was the one who lost the amulet I should be with him, at least helping to get it back."

"Oh, Father," Spotted Fawn cajoled, "losing the amulet was not your fault and besides, I doubt Standing Wolf needs any help. I believe he could take a salmon from a grizzly bear if his life depended on it."

"I know, but I have a bad feeling…like something is wrong, something unexpected, and I feel helpless. All I do is run from Willow like a rabbit from a coyote," Frank fussed.

"So that is what this is about," Spotted Fawn said with a giggle, and Little Beaver gave her a knowing glance.

"Now this is serious, *mahkin*, my wife." Little Beaver said stern-faced. "I survived the attack of the white hump-back and even I am afraid of Willow." His stern look shifted to one of sheer amusement.

Spotted Fawn flashed the powerful young brave a look reserved for one with an intimate understanding then looked back at Frank. "Perhaps you should not run too fast, Father. I am sure most of the men in this village run after her, not from her." Again, she gave Little Beaver a coy smile.

"I do not know of anyone that Willow has left permanently injured," Little Beaver interjected, "although some have been known to wander aimlessly for days after falling prey to her spell."

"Enough!" Frank snorted. "I will find Warm Hands or Ta-keen Eagle…someone who understands the mystery surrounding this valley and why a woman like Willow should not be taken lightly."

He ducked as he exited the teepee and pulled the flap shut, pausing briefly to admire the lifelike beaver standing on hind legs against a partially chewed aspen tree. Near the aspen lay a spotted fawn, head tucked into its flank in a blissful sleep.

Bent Grass, Frank thought, no doubt the exquisite painting had been her gift to the new couple. Bent Grass is the one who understands the mysteries of this valley. I should talk to her, he mused. If only I didn't feel so guilty over losing the amulet she painted especially for me. She may not blame me, but that doesn't change things. Standing Wolf is gone and something is wrong.

Bent Grass was also troubled. Not because Standing Wolf was gone, though she did miss him and felt bad for Star Flower's loneliness, or because she feared for her son, or the return of the amulet. She had complete confidence in his finding and returning with the sacred talisman. The source of her concern came from deep within the cave of spirits.

Since the apocalyptic event that reduced a regiment of the 5th Cavalry to a thousand riderless horses, her visions changed from warnings of horse soldiers attacking their village to visions of strange lights in the night sky and a river of fire and ice. She saw little Indian children hand-in-hand with white men, their Indian parents sobbing and overcome with grief.

She saw great chiefs from unknown tribes in full-feathered headdresses weeping like children. She saw many Indians in shirts like those worn by the white-clay humans except the shirts bore beautiful paintings; some of aspen groves, some of buffalo, others of the long-eared deer…some even displayed the likeness of *Sunk Manitu Tanka*, the sacred black wolf.

Bent Grass was walking with a determined stride toward the teepee of Chief Ta-keen Eagle and Laughing Doe when she spotted the loco one. Only Frank was no longer loco. Something had happened to Standing Wolf and Frank in the spirit cave. Even she, the seer of the Sematuse, did not understand it. It was as if they had known each other…been friends in another life. What ever they saw in the spirit cave made the loco Frank sane. She was given many visions in the cave, some strange and unexplained, and had seen sane men go crazy but never a crazy man go sane. And what of her son and Frank's other life…the one they spoke of since returning from the cave? Sure, they had a life before they came to the valley, but did they return from the dead? She did not have much time to think about those things because the attack by the soldiers and the Ghost Dance happened so quickly.

Frank, also, headed for the chief's abode when he saw Bent Grass and quickly looked away then almost reluctantly walked toward her. She stopped, awaiting his approach.

"At least she isn't like Willow," Frank whispered under his breath as he drew nearer to Bent Grass. She was a small woman, around five feet tall. She was shapely but without the prominent breasts so proudly displayed by Willow, her tiny waist and flaring hips less apparent.

"It's a fine morning," Frank greeted her, wishing there was something more profound or important to say.

"It is," she said smiling; never one to overstate the obvious.

Her beauty momentarily held Frank hostage; the big dark eyes, the white teeth behind full lips and her crowning jewel…the long, straight black hair framing her delicate face and falling to her waist.

He thought about apologizing, again, for having lost the amulet but decided he'd already beat that dog to death. He wanted to talk to her but felt inadequate. Besides the language barrier, his feeling of inadequacy around this woman was compounded by the fact that she spoke to the gods…and was his friend, Standing Wolf's, long lost mother. Frank remained silent.

"Do you think Standing Wolf has found the soldier with the amulet yet?" Bent Grass asked, pausing to make sure he understood.

She is trying to make polite conversation, he thought. *She would be more likely to know what is happening with Standing Wolf than I, since the Great Spirit keeps her informed.*

Frank had even lost track of how long Standing Wolf had been gone from the valley but replied. "I'm sure he has and he will be back with you and Star Flower soon."

At least I hope so.

Frank felt the cold pang of guilt gnaw at his gut. *I should be with him,* he silently scolded himself.

"I must speak with our chief," Bent Grass said. "Good hunting," she added dismissively and regained her stride toward the teepee of Ta-keen Eagle. After greeting the chief and Laughing Doe, Bent Grass sat on a small carved-out log covered by the pelt of a river otter and began speaking of her disturbing visions.

"I believed when Standing Wolf danced the Dance of the Ghosts and the white soldiers were taken from our valley, all our troubles with the white-clay humans were over and I would no longer see them in my visions. I no longer see horse soldiers, but I see the people being very sad. It is as if their *tlchachie*, their spirit, has left them and they no longer believe in the *yandoo*, prayer." She shifted her weight on the log, crossing her legs and exposing a generous portion of her dark-skinned thigh.

Laughing Doe smiled. When Laughing Doe smiled it was not an in-significant matter. Her name was a reflection of her large, soft brown doe- eyes and her flashing smile that seemed to light the space and brighten the lives of those around her…especially her *mihakin*, her husband, and chief of the Sematuse, Ta-keen Eagle.

"Might your visions be because you are worried about your son and the amulet that was taken by the soldier?" Ta-keen Eagle inquired.

Bent Grass was much respected, even revered by the Sematuse, including Ta-keen Eagle and Warm Hands, their medicine man. If she was troubled, all the Sematuse were troubled. "I am anxious for Standing Wolf to return home but I do not fear for his safety. I do not believe we are in danger but I see a great river of sadness spreading across the land. Perhaps this sadness will not affect those in this valley…only those who live beyond our sacred borders."

Laughing Doe studied the woman seer. Sometimes it was hard to remember she was human, one of the True People, like herself, like Ta-keen Eagle, Warm Hands and Willow. The Great Spirit had chosen Bent Grass to speak through to the people. He had given her the talent to tell stories through paintings, made her the mother of Standing Wolf, the Messiah.

"You should talk with Fire-hair Frank," Laughing Doe said quietly. Her soft voice had a sexual sultriness even when the subject did not. "He has lived in the land beyond our boundaries and might be able to help you understand the meaning of your visions."

It was Ta-keen Eagle's turn to smile. He loved this woman and was constantly amazed at the wisdom hidden behind the dazzling smile and shapely body that was Laughing Doe.

"Laughing Doe is right," he said, feeling amused at how many times he said those words since becoming chief of the Sematuse.

Bent Grass left the teepee without further discussion. She would like to talk to the one called Fire-hair but he knew little of their language and she knew little of his. Standing Wolf had taught her some English words and could help her because he knew both Salish and the English. Of course if he were here she could just talk to him for he, too, had lived beyond the valley of rainbows.

Patience, she thought. I must wait until Standing Wolf returns or *Ogle Wa Nagi* gives me the meaning of these visions.

"She is such a pretty woman but so sad," Laughing Doe told Ta-keen Eagle after Bent Grass left. "It is as if *Ogle Wa Nagi* gives her only bad visions. Should the Great Spirit not have some good visions to give her?"

"Perhaps the sadness in her visions comes from her own sadness, not from *Ogle Wa Nagi*. Perhaps if she had more joy in her life there would be more happiness in her visions," Ta-keen Eagle offered, then somewhat perplexed, rejected his own theory. "The return of her son brought her great joy, so why is she still sad?"

"I would be sad without you, even if I had a child. Standing Wolf brought the news of the death of her *mihakin*. There are reasons why a woman needs a man even if she thinks otherwise. As a seer, Bent Grass has many gifts to satisfy her soul. As a woman, she needs to satisfy her body as well." Laughing Doe's look left Ta-keen Eagle with little doubt of her meaning or her wisdom.

"Are you feeling a little sad, my *mahakin*?" Ta-keen Eagle said, feeling the familiar tingle of arousal when his manhood began to move within his leather breechcloth.

"Not so sad that it cannot be fixed by the right man," she teased and slowly slid the leather straps of her dress over one shoulder, then the other, allowing the dress to rest briefly on her bulging breasts then slip down over her taunt nipples.

Ta-keen Eagle pulled her to him, pressing his hardness against her as he lowered her onto the bed of boughs. After removing each other's clothing in a passionate frenzy, he took her long and hard, lustfully not even aware that the flap to their tent remained wide open.

When Frank saw Bent Grass leave the teepee of Chief Ta-keen Eagle and Laughing Doe he waited until she was a safe distance away then moved slowly toward the chief's tent. He wanted to talk to Laughing Doe as much as he did with Ta-keen Eagle. Laughing Doe was Willow's best friend. Maybe she would tell Willow not to bother him, that he had more important things to think about and that he had no time for her playful games.

Guilt!

That was the real problem. Frank felt guilty about the amulet, guilty about Julie, guilty for Bent Grass and Star Flower being alone. At least he no longer felt guilty about Sarah.

He sighed, thinking, I have her back and as Spotted Fawn she is happy, loved and has the best kind of life I could ever have imagined for her. I do feel good about that.

Approaching Ta-keen Eagle's teepee, Frank walked quietly, careful not to talk out loud to himself, fearing that to do so might cause him relapse into insanity.

He heard the moans at the same time his eyes froze on the lustful scene inside the teepee. While fighting to tear his eyes away from the carnal sight Frank felt the steel blade of panic rip into his heart, sinking to his very core. On weak knees, he managed to veer away from the open, teepee flap and out of view of the couple inside. Shaken, he wandered for a ways, his mind unable to rationalize what saw. It was like he'd run head-on into his darkest past!

"Git a gol'darn grip on yerself." The sound of his voice jerked Frank back to reality. It also sent a bone-chilling scare through him.

"Son-of-a-dead-trapper's aunt," he muttered then very carefully whispered. "You're not crazy again, Frank, you've just had a shock. So calm down, take a deep breath and quit talking to your goddamn self!" he finished emphatically despite his efforts to remain calm.

Shaken, Frank left the village and found solace near a large cottonwood on the bank of the stream the Indians called Chewaken. He began to sort out what he'd seen. He knew these people were carefree, passionate about life and loving. They knew no guilt, shame or embarrassment. They were totally open and un-inhibited about matters of sex. He admired that about them.

"If only I was more like them back then." He let the words slip out in a sudden flash of remorse. "Or even now," he added as an after thought. As his head began to clear he became aware of a situation that was even more shocking than his unexpected voyeurism. He had an erection! "What in the hell is this?" he almost shouted. It was so long since he'd had any such feelings even the Indians thought that part of him was dead.

Frank fought to free the image of the lovers from his mind, ashamed and confused that the scene had somehow aroused him.

Willow!

It was because of her…the flirtatious, sensual woman had managed to resurrect feelings that died so many years ago…feelings he was not at all sure were welcomed.

Finally recovered from and relieved of his unfamiliar condition Frank tried to focus. Why should he care what happens outside of this valley? He had his daughter. She was safe there, she was happy. Still, something was wrong. He could feel it. Not here in this place but outside. Maybe it was Standing Wolf but why, how? He certainly could take care of himself and he apparently had all the Indian Nations awaiting his call.

I should try and speak with Bent Grass, he decided.

If anyone knew anything about Standing Wolf or what may be happening outside of the valley it would be her. But first, Frank was going to visit *no-wha hee*, the hot springs. The unexpected events of this fine morning left him tense and a little irritable. The soothing waters of the hot springs might improve his attitude.

Frank could have caught a horse and ridden to the hot springs. Most were broke, thanks to Crazy Crow, Talks-to-Horse and Little Beaver. There was even a little sorrel mare Frank was especially fond of but he decided the walk would do him good. Running his trap line had been physically demanding but since arriving in this valley he did little to stay fit.

All the more reason I'm gettin' cranky, he reasoned, feeling on edge.

Walking through the lush meadows and along the deep quiet waters of the river of rainbows, Frank began to relax. Seeing the low arch of the grotto in the distance he lengthened his stride, the muscles of his thighs and calves stretched and responded.

"Now this feels good," he sighed, drawing a deep breath. "Yer not dead, ya old dog, yer just gettin' fat and lazy."

Frank laughed, it felt good to laugh and it felt good to act crazy knowing he was perfectly sane. His gaze drifted from the arched entry of the hot springs on to the north and the big mountain the Sematuse called *Chopaka*. The mountain always did give him the chills but he was now convinced the Sematuse's Great Spirit, *Ogle Wa Nagi*, really did live there. From the mountain his eyes followed the valley's east rim to location of the spirit cave. He could not see the tiny opening in the rocks leading into the cave from this distance, but simply casting his eyes in that general direction was unnerving.

Passing through the archway of the springs, Frank felt the hot steam on his face. The cavern was shrouded in a hot mist that caused beads of sweat to form on his forehead and run down his cheeks into his fiery-red beard.

"These whiskers were a lot more fun when I was crazy," he muttered and began pulling the leather shawl-type shirt Spotted Fawn made for him over his head. Removing his prized, denim pants he stepped off the rocks into the hot soothing water.

"Aahhh!"

The cry that escaped Frank's throat was equaled only by the one emitted by the woman, also naked, and only a few feet away in the steamy grotto. His surprise elevated to panic when the woman spoke.

"Fire-hair, you frightened me!" she managed breathlessly.

"Bent Grass!" Frank barely squeezed out the words.

Of all the Sematuse women he could have found himself naked with, Bent Grass was by far the most embarrassing and unnerving.

She is to the Sematuse what the Virgin Mary is to Christians.

"Excuse me," Frank said, turning away and pushing his legs together to insure that his man-parts didn't decide to do anything to further his embarrassment.

"I should have called out," he said apologetically, hoping she could understand his mixture of Salish and English. "I was lost in thought and it never occurred to me that someone might be in here. I will leave and wait outside until you are finished."

"No, wait, it is good. You stay and we will talk." Bent Grass spoke in a calm voice, fully recovered from her start. "I have had visions of much sadness among Native People, people outside of our valley, people I do not know but whose sadness touches my heart." Remembering Laughing Doe's advice, she continued. "You have lived outside of the valley of the Sematuse. You know the ways of the outside world."

Looking at him through the foggy mist, Bent Grass smiled. Frank's red hair and beard hung straight, dripping like a wet cat, his face turned away, afraid to look at her. "Why would those Natives be sad? Are their ways so different from ours?" she asked.

"I wish I knew. I never spent much time among the Indians… whites either for that matter. I mostly stayed away from people. I met a few trappers and that was about all."

Frank remained partially turned way from her, afraid he would not be able to hold his gaze on her face if he looked her way.

"Standing Wolf is the one who knows all about the Indians. It is too bad he is not here to ask." Frank was pleased he was not having as much trouble with the language barrier as he expected.

I can actually talk to her, he thought, and relaxed a little.

"How far is the place you call the fort from here? How long will it take Standing Wolf to go there and return?" Bent Grass pulled her wet hair back from her eyes, curious why Fire-hair Frank did not seem to want to look at her.

"The fort is five, maybe six days, suns, from this valley. He could be to the fort by now *if* there were no problems and *if* he can find the amulet he could be back in a few days."

Turning his head, Frank risked looking at her, careful to focus on her eyes. Even through the mist, he sensed a warm softness about her. She speaks to the Gods, he thought, yet she seems caring and gentle. Not like the preachers I remember, shouting hell and damnation!

"Standing Wolf is brave and strong, he will have no trouble returning the amulet to the valley." Bent Grass' pride in her son was apparent in her tone.

Frank did not respond. He was captivated by her. In the dim-mystical light of the hot springs, her face and hair, wet from the mist, shone like an onyx in firelight.

She is beautiful.

The thought struck Frank without warning. So in awe of her spiritual powers had he been, he never before really dared to look at her closely.

His mind darted back to his academy days. This would have been the worst scenario possible to be seen in for the women who hung around West Point; at least the wet hair and no make-up part.

Finally breaking the spell, brought on by her natural beauty, Frank confirmed her opinion of Standing Wolf and added, "There should not be a problem unless the soldier gives the amulet to someone, or throws it away afraid of what it might mean. He did see what happened here and probably knows that he only survived because of it."

"A white man would do that?" Bent Grass asked, puzzled. "If an Indian possessed an omen he thought to be sacred he would die before giving it up." She moved closer, causing Frank to flinch. "Would a white man really throw such a thing away?" she asked again in dismay.

Frank anchored a stare on Bend Grass' forehead, afraid that to blink might cause his eyes to avert to some part of this seer's body that would give the Great Spirit cause to turn him to stone, or worst yet just one part of his body to harden.

"White men can do some strange things," he blurted. "Some have even been known to bury gold in caves just so they can die rich." He chuckled, amused by an obsession that no longer had any use or meaning to him.

Bent Grass looked at him as if maybe he had gone crazy again. "Gold," she said. "What is this thing, gold? Spirit-walker once told me there is gold in the cave of *tlchachies* and that it must be kept a secret from the whites. I am not worried; you are the only white man who has ever entered the cave of *tlchachies* and lived…you and French," she corrected, giving Frank a knowing smile. He flushed as if he'd been blessed by a deity.

"You should ask *Ogle Wa Nagi* about gold," Frank said, feeling some urgency. "Gold is an obsession of the white man. It is a greater danger to the Indian than the white man's guns or horse soldiers because for **it** the white man will stop at nothing. They will send soldiers with guns. They will kill women and children and break promises made by their chiefs."

He watched as her face became drawn and serious. "Spirit-walker was right. You must never let the white man know there is gold on your land."

"But it is not our land," Bent Grass said quietly. "It is the land of Mother Earth, of our ancestors, our children and our children's children."

"Believe me," Frank said emphatically. "If the white man finds gold, he will take the land from you and your children. It will be his land!"

"I must speak with my chief about this gold," Bent Grass said. She stood without warning to leave the warm waters of the hot springs and her conversation with Fire-hair.

Frank closed his eyes as quickly as he could but not quick enough to avoid catching a glimpse of her petite body. The image of her pert breasts with wet nipples protruding and her tiny waist flaring into firm, full hips burned into his brain.

"How will I ever sleep?" he muttered when he eventually opened his eyes to find her gone, but knowing the moment he closed them again that intriguing image would return.

Chapter Seven

Trails End

"Joe!" he called repeatedly, his voice quivering with anxiety, as he stumbled through the darkness in search of the private. Corporal Daniel Bone was desperate. He had Joe's clothes under one arm and his guard duty rifle in his grip; a second rifle in his free hand provided a false sense of security.

"Joe, where the hell are ya?"

In the darkness the only thing Daniel could see was the image of the naked Indian with the long black braids burned into his brain. 'If I didn't have Joe's clothes I'd swear I had a bad dream,' he thought, trying to make some sense of what he'd seen. The damned Indian had been like a ghost. He appeared out of nowhere in Private Joe Wright's uniform, made a few threats, shucked the private's clothes and disappeared into the night.

"The major would sure like ta know there's some Injun prowlin' around so close to the fort," he whispered then quickly added, "but I ain't gonna be the one ta tell him. No sir-eee, that Injun done got inta my head."

Moaning and slurred attempts at speech reached the corporal's ears from somewhere in the darkness. He stopped, held his breath and listened, intent upon locating the sound.

"Ohhhh," the groaning was faint but growing louder and more incessant. Daniel began walking, he hoped, toward the sound.

"Joe!" he called again, "Joe, are you alright?"

Stupid question, he thought, continuing to hone in on the moans and groans.

Then he saw Joe.

The private's white, naked body laid face down, his ass shining like a beacon in the faint moonlight. Rushing to the hapless looking form, Daniel grasped Joe's shoulders and shook him.

"Joe," he said trying to get the man's attention. Bone started to turn him over but thought better of it. Joe's white ass looked ridicules enough; he didn't need to see anymore.

"Oh God," Joe finally muttered, "Oh God, my head."

"Git yer damn clothes on," Daniel said quickly. "Then I'll take a look at ya, see if yer bleedin'." He dropped the bundle of clothes, including Joe's boots on the prone man…a boot landing on the fallen soldiers head.

"Ouch! Cheerist!" Joe exclaimed. "My goddamn head is killin' me."

He turned over slowly, sorting through his uniform pieces looking for his underwear. "OOuhh," he groaned again. "My head…my neck, what the hell happened and why am I naked?" he demanded, suddenly angry.

"Git yer ass dressed and I'll tell ya," Daniel asserted, relieved that Joe was only sore and humiliated, apparently not in danger of dying.

Once back in uniform, Joe listened dubiously while Daniel tried to explain the lone Indian and what had happened to them.

"We gotta tell the major," Joe stated, still hurting and still angry.

"You want ta tell him, go ahead," Daniel replied. "But I ain't sayin' nothin'. That Injun told me ta keep my mouth shut and that is just what I'm gonna do. Unless you want ta lose more'n yer uniform next time, I'd suggest you just forget about what happened tonight."

"But its just one Indian and he might know somethin' about the colonel. The major is for sure gonna want to know what ya saw." Joe argued.

"That's just it. It's what I saw. You didn't see nothin' because ya got yerself naked and fell asleep on guard duty. That's what I'm tellin' the major if ya say a word about tonight. If yer smart, private, you'll keep yer mouth shut, stay in the fort and try not ta go on guard duty…that's what I'm doin'."

The walk-through gate at the fort squeaked and their replacement sauntered out to the stable. Private Joe Wright and Corporal Daniel Bone handed over their rifles and headed for their bunks; neither said a word to their replacements or to each other.

Inside the fort, Major Denton was still uptight but seemed to be over his mad. He was busy putting together a search party to look for Colonel Wolard and his men. Private Wright went to sick bay, suffering from severe neck and head pain while Corporal Bone tried to decide if he should volunteer for the search party or risk being called for guard duty again. At least if he was with the search party he wouldn't be alone.

First Lieutenant William Radcliff, a lanky 'boy' in the view of some of the more experienced non-coms, was picked by Major Denton to lead the search party. Known as Will by the other officers, Lieutenant Radcliff had thick, curly blond hair, blue eyes and baby face. He exuded the quiet confidence of the West Point graduate that he was.

In his mid-twenties, the young lieutenant was considered neither an 'Indian lover' nor 'Indian hater' by Major Denton. Will always demonstrated a respect for the Indian's culture and a healthy regard for their gorilla warfare style fighting tactics. If this patrol got into a sticky situation, Will Radcliff was exactly who Denton wanted in charge.

Briefed on their mission, the patrol of a dozen soldiers set out with three scouts recruited from a band of Methows, now living on the reservation, but familiar with the upper *Okinakane*. It was early, the sun not yet above the eastern horizon, but it promised to be another hot August day.

The squeaking of saddle leather and the jangling of cavalry issue spurs was comforting to Corporal Daniel Bone. This was one detail he was glad he'd volunteered for. "This here sure is better'n sittin' around the fort waitin' ta be attack," he said to a buck-sergeant on a big bay horse.

"Might be," the sergeant replied, "long as this young lieutenant don't get us caught ass deep in Injuns."

As the patrol moved north along the river, a lone half-breed on a black Arabian watched from the cover of rim-rocks. The patrol continued steadily up river, stopping occasionally to talk with Indians already adjusted to reservation life. These conversations were brief with the Indians being very animated, waving arms, shaking fists and pointing fingers.

Leaving the Sand Flats, the small search party proceeded up river onto the deceptively steep sage-covered slopes that slid toward the river. Standing Wolf concluded they were looking for the colonel and his men, not the AWOL soldier.

Confident that Sam had not gone up river toward the hidden valley, and convinced he would not go west of the river, Standing Wolf decided to work a large arc east of the *Okinakane* and south to the Columbia in hopes of picking up the trail of a lone rider. Then the thought occurred to him that there could be two search parties; one patrol looking for the colonel and one after Sam.

"Just have to keep a lookout," he muttered and guided the Arab back down river, intent on finding a starting point for a reconnaissance of his own.

Overhearing the translation of what the reservation Indians said about the *Choo-pin-it-pa-loo*, a strange band of Indians believed to live in the sacred mountains of the Pasayten, gave Corporal Bone cause to question his choice of volunteering for this patrol.

"This whole thing about ghost Injuns is a little creepy, doncha think?" Daniel asked his newfound buddy, hoping to hear something encouraging.

"Might be," the sergeant replied. "Depends on if your superstitious or not. I'd feel a hell of a lot better if I knew where the colonel and all those men were. I'd like to think all this yappin' about sacred mountains and ghostly Injuns is bull crap but that don't explain what happened to the colonel."

"Sam said they're all dead…the colonel an' all them men…before he run off. Do you think they're dead?" Corporal Bone asked, still looking for something comforting.

"Might be," was the reply, two words Daniel had heard just about enough of.

Riding into a lush bowl of a meadow stretching out a mile or so from the river, Lieutenant Radcliff halted the group. "We'll camp here tonight," he stated, then ordered a couple of privates to unload the two pack mules. "You will each have to cook for yourselves. That way I don't have to listen to any bitching about the camp cook."

As the men set about pulling saddles, mostly 1859 model McClellan's, from their mounts and looking for a suitable place to tether them, Will began to assess the site for the placement of nighttime sentries.

More concerned about the vulnerability of the horses than the men, he decided to post two guards with the horses and have one patrolling the campsite.

Corporal Bone was relieved the patrol of twelve men consisted of six privates, more than enough to ensure he would not have to pull guard duty on this detail.

"Guess ya know I'll be sleepin' with Henry tonight," Daniel quipped to the sergeant as he secured his mount to the tether line.

'Henry' was his army issue 1860 model, lever action carbine patented by B. Tyler Henry and now manufactured by the New Haven Arms Company for the U.S. Army.

"How 'bout you sarg, ya gonna be keepin' yer rifle in yer bed with ya?"

"Might be," was the familiar response. "But I'd prefer Henrietta." Both laughed as they rummaged through the pack-boxes in search of an evening meal.

The night was uneventful and the group was cleaning up after a breakfast of venison, eggs and taters nearly deep-fried in a cast-iron pan half-full of lard, when two of the scouts rode back into camp and rushed excitedly to Lieutenant Radcliff.

"The valley narrows up ahead, Sir. We found the colonel's trail. It has to be him because the trail looks to be four to six horses wide and by the way the ground is chewed up there had to be a lot of horses."

This was the news Will was hoping for. He did not see how you could just lose an entire cavalry regiment without a trace. Of course, it is an awfully big country and the thin line made by a cavalry column could be hard to find.

With the night's camp picked up and the patrol mounted, Will gave the order and they headed up river, the two scouts leading the way. Once on the trail, following it was as easy as finding warts on a frog.

The whole patrol buzzed with excitement and a hint of trepidation. If this trail was going to lead them to the colonel, what were they going to find at the trail's end?

When they reached a bend in the river the scouts said the local Indians called Janis, they stopped for lunch then continued following the colonel's trail, which left the river, passed over a plateau then returned to the river. There were many mule deer on the plateau and the scouts killed and dressed two small bucks. The back-straps they would have for dinner, the rest cut and dried into venison jerky.

"Ya hear that?" Daniel asked as he and the buck-sergeant chewed on jerky mixed with dried apples, raisins and apricots. "There's a racket goin' on across the river, up in them blasted rocks."

He was looking at a foreboding rock formation that appeared to be made up of a series of crevices and canyons, their layered walls rising hundreds of feet above the river bottom.

"There's somethin' up there makin' a helluva fuss. Sounds like crows or buzzards. Ya suppose there's somethin' dead up there?"

There were no flocking crows or circling buzzards above the rocky horizon.

"Might be," was the predictable retort. "I don't think the lieutenant's gonna be lettin' ya wander over there ta find out."

"Don't think I even wanna go pokin' around in them rocks but it does make me a little curious, ain't you?" Daniel probed.

"Might be," said the sergeant.

Lunch finished, the patrol mounted up and headed north on the well-worn trail. Will Radcliff's mind was busy chasing down worst-case scenarios. He couldn't see how he could lose the trail, so the concern was what he would find when the trail ended. Could the colonel simply be lost? That didn't seem possible because Colonel Wolard had his brother Roy with him, and he knew this country better than anyone except for that missing half-breed scout.

"This can't be another Little Big Horn," he confided to Corporal Bone who happened to be riding alongside the lieutenant. Every man in the United States Army knew about Custer, especially those with the good fortune to have attended West Point.

"No, Sir," Daniel concurred, his stress level elevating another notch.

As the sun faded in the west, casting long shadows over the small contingent of horse soldiers, they encountered a small river merging with the *Okinakane* and cause for much excitement. Here, scattered over an area a quarter-mile squared, was an assortment of debris. Broken wagons, rotting meat and eggs, coffee, beans, salt, even bibles were strewn about the hardpan earth. A shallow mound of dirt with a crude wooden cross marked an apparent impromptu grave.

"We'll be camping here tonight," Lieutenant Radcliff ordered. Looking directly at Daniel, he continued, "Corporal Bone, take a couple of men and see if anything is salvageable. I'm going to try to figure out what happened here. If you find anything that indicates an Indian attack, arrows, spears, a war ax, I want to know about it immediately."

Enough good lard was salvaged from five containers to fill one, a couple of the wagons could be repaired, but that would mean sending a detail from the fort with the needed parts. Lieutenant Radcliff asked for the opinion of each of the twelve soldiers on the merits of exhuming the body from the shallow grave. Since there was no evidence of an Indian attack it was agreed that identifying the dead body and possibly determining a cause of death did not merit disturbing the grave. A man's grave was a sacred resting place and to disturb it meant disturbing his eternal life. Many of the soldiers were very superstitious where death was concerned; even some of the more educated were paranoid.

Over an unusually fine dinner of venison back-strap, beans and carrots, Daniel inquired, "Got any idea as ta what happened here, Lieutenant?"

"No I don't, Corporal. It doesn't appear they were attack but something certainly raised havoc within their ranks." Will paused. "Do you have any ideas?" he added in what appeared to be an afterthought.

"Ya don't suppose they coulda' seen them ghost Injuns, them *Choo-pin-it-pa-loo*, do ya, Sir?" Daniel asked sheepishly.

"No, Corporal, I don't think they saw any ghost Indians but that still doesn't explain what happened here," William said, a little condescendingly.

Daniel wasn't quite so sure. He had heard the warnings at several of the villages on the Sand Flats about the ghostly People of the

Mountains. If the natives were afraid of them, that was enough for him.

"Well, that could explain it, Sir," he answered with a touch of agitation for being so easily dismissed.

No one slept well that night, not even the horses. Daniel lay wide-eyed, stealing an occasional glance toward the shallow grave some fifty yards away.

"It's like tryin' ta sleep in a friggin' cemetery," he muttered, unable to get the idea of ghost Indians or the dead man out of his head.

When morning finally came, Daniel was both exhausted and relieved. The men around him had tossed and turned in their bedrolls and the horses had stomped and snorted all night, apparently agitated by some unseen presence.

No one was happier than Daniel Bone when the patrol mounted up and left the camp site, following the obvious trail of Colonel Wolard and his troops. His joy was short lived. The trail led the patrol upstream on this major tributary and headed directly toward the mountains the Indians called Pasayten; the mountains they had been warned about.

"Somethin' killed a guy back there," he said to a tense private aboard a good-looking gray mare. "I kinda wish we'd dug him up. Sure would like ta know what killed him. I got a feelin' he mighta just been scared ta death."

The private did not respond but Daniel was sure the man's knuckles turned a little whiter as he gripped the bridle reins with his left hand, his right hand reaching up to touch the stock of his lever action carbine. He took a little deeper seat in his McClellan.

Another day of tracking went well. The trail was easy to follow and the terrain along the river manageable. The sun set earlier as they neared the mountains to the west, the shadows seemed somehow darker and more ominous. Daniel began to dread the thought of another sleepless night. His thoughts burst into words surprising even him.

"At least I ain't gonna be lookin' at no poor devil's grave." He looked around quickly, hoping no one heard his sudden outburst. No one did, they were lost in thoughts of their own.

Riding into an aspen thicket, it was clear the colonel and his men had camped here. Another day on the trail drew to an end, another day closer to the colonel, another day closer to some answers. Will threw a leg over the cantle of the McClellan and stepped down onto solid ground. Stretching his arms over his head, arching his back and working the kinks out of his legs and knees, he wondered how much farther this trail could lead. He was already at least a couple of days out of his comfort zone. Janis was the end of the world for most of the men stationed at Fort Okanogan and few patrols, except for the colonel, ventured farther north than there.

For Daniel, the night was a little better than the previous one; probably more due to sheer exhaustion than to any improvement in his psyche.

For Lieutenant Radcliff, responsibility was weighing heavily. Colonel Wolard had led a thousand men on the trail he was now following; neither the colonel nor any of his men, except one, returned. William had a new understanding of why Major Denton was so upset by the disappearance of Corporal DeSoto. The man had the answers to all of the questions. *If he hadn't run away, I wouldn't be out here second-guessing myself*, Will concluded.

The following day did little to ease Lieutenant Radcliff's burden. The trail, while still easily followed, rose above and away from the river bottom, and into timbered mountainous terrain. An ominous rock bluff dominated their right flank, the trail became narrower and serpentine, reduced from six horses abreast to single file as it worked its way around brush-choked canyons and pockets of windfall.

Advancing slowly along the more difficult trail, Will halted the patrol to wait while two of the scouts dismounted knelt to study the trail, advanced a few yards, knelt again, then returned to Will and the patrol.

"One set of horse tracks going that way," said the scout, pointing down the trail from where they had come. "The horse is running, and on top of the trail we follow."

Those have to be the tracks of Corporal DeSoto, Will surmised. His anxiety level rose as he sensed the answers to the mystery of the missing colonel and one thousand horse soldiers may not be far ahead.

Following a miserable half-day, the terrain improved along with Will's attitude. Confident that his small patrol must be gaining ground on the colonel and his regiment, he was encouraged.

"We could overtake the colonel and his men anytime, Corporal," he commented to Daniel, who had ridden alongside when the group paused while the scouts examined the trail.

Daniel tried to imagine what the colonel and his men could be doing that would keep them from returning to the fort. He also wondered about DeSoto's wild story. They're not lost, that's for sure, he concluded. They would have to have been struck blind not to be able to follow their own trail home.

While Daniel's imagination ran unchecked through bizarre possibilities, Lieutenant Radcliff searched for logical solutions. He tried to envision what they would find when the finally overtook the colonel. Would they just find them riding along, single file through the woods, oblivious of the fact they had been considered MIA for nearly a month? Would they find them bivouacked in some mountain meadow enjoying the serenity and the time away from the fort?

The lieutenant found those scenarios comforting but unlikely. The most logical option was that the colonel and his men had been ambushed and were surrounded by hostile Indians, pinned down unable to move but holding their position in hopes help was on the way. If that turns out to be the case, I'd like to be part of the firing squad when they catch DeSoto, Will thought. If the corporal managed to escape the attack but ran away instead of getting help, he deserved to die.

"Whoa."

The word fell from Will's mouth. It was to rein in his runaway thoughts and a reaction to a sudden sharp turn in the trail they were following. The southbound trail had taken a turn to the west, leading directly toward the imposing rock wall towering nearly a quarter-mile high.

"Now where are they going?" William posed the question to one in particular.

"It's for damn sure they ain't goin' up that bluff," Daniel blurted before adding, "Sir."

As the trail led directly toward the sheer rock wall, Will was becoming uneasy and perplexed. This made about as much sense as confederate cannons in a coal mine.

Was it a trap?

Could there be a hidden opening? Did they see something? Thoughts bounced around Will's brain like BB's in a barrel.

Daniel's buddy, the buck-sergeant on the big bay, decided it was time to speak up. "Sir, if the colonel rode inta some kinda trap, we don't wanna make the same mistake. Sir, if there's enough Injuns out there ta trap a thousand soldiers, what good's a dozen more gonna do?"

"We're going to do the best we can, Sergeant. If it means sending someone for help while we monitor the situation then that's what we will do."

"Mind if I volunteer ta go fer help, Sir," the sergeant joked…sort of.

The first sign something was terribly wrong came when the three scouts who were riding in advance of the patrol, returned at full-gallop and without hesitation rode past the on-coming patrol and on back down the trail.

"Get those men and bring them back here!" Will shouted the order to no one in particular but was determined not to lose his scouts to panic or any other reason.

The buck-sergeant and the bay were the first to break rank in pursuit of the wayward scouts. Any excuse to head back toward the fort rather than where they were going worked for him. The thought caught up with him along with two privates, also quick to respond to the opportunity to retreat.

None of the remaining patrol needed an order to pull their rifles from their scabbards. On high alert, weapons in hand, they scanned the nearby timber and bluff for any cause of the unexpected exodus of the Indian scouts.

As William moved the group forward, Daniel's eyes scrutinized every bush, tree, rock and stump, fully expecting the surrounding forest to materialize into painted warriors, intent on the removal of his scalp.

Lieutenant William Radcliff, while less intimidated, he was still baffled by the behavior of what he perceived to be dependable Indian scouts. While anxious to know the cause for their sudden retreat, he had no intention of waiting until they were caught and returned to find the answer.

Riding at the front of the line, like any good First Lieutenant, Will was the first to find a clue to the mystery of the missing colonel and the panic-stricken scouts. Dismounting, he walked the five feet or so to the sheer rock wall, a large gnarly pine protruded from a narrow fissure that shot up the face of the bluff like a lightning bolt.

The trail disappeared at the base of the tree and led directly into the rock wall!

Will knelt in the trail and felt the rock bluff and the tree. They were solid, the tree having somehow grown out of the fissure for a hundred years or more. Joined by the rest of the patrol, the lieutenant sat alongside the obvious trail, removed his hat and placing it on his bent knee, scratched his head in disbelief.

"What happened here?" he asked, as soldiers examined the trail, the bluff and the tree. "It has to be some kind of practical joke," he stated almost hopefully. "But that is impossible."

"Not as impossible as ridin' through solid rock, Sir," Daniel contemplated.

"Check back up the trail and along the bluff; see if there is any way those scouts could have faked this trail," Will ordered.

He was grasping at straws. There was no way for three men to fake a trail left by a cavalry regiment.

"I need some ideas here. There has to be a solution and I'll see that the first man to find it gets a promotion."

It's like a training problem at West Point, Will thought; remembering the way cadets were often given complex military problems to solve. Often there was no right answer, only the best answer, but here there appeared to be no answer.

After two or three hours of combing the area along the base of the massive bluff, even attempting to find a way over or around the barrier, Lieutenant Radcliff was baffled and frustrated, his men were scared, bordering on panicky. Even he felt the hair on the back of his neck stand up as he rubbed the goose bumps from his arms, and looked up at the foreboding bluff and pondered the impossible.

High above the mounted patrol, hidden among the crevices and bushes along the rock wall, four-dozen Indians, bodies painted with streaks of brown and black, watched with hawk-like eyes.

They carried longbows made of ewe wood and spears carved from willow and dogwood. They could easily have destroyed the small group of soldiers with a rain of arrows and spears, but were more interested in their reaction to the lost trail.

"The white man believes he is so smart. He has many guns and forts made of wood. He has missions and schools where he teaches himself and even Indians about Indians. Let us see if he is smart enough to follow a trail through solid rock," a warrior stated.

Satified the soldiers were baffled and would return to their fort with another unbelievable story, the painted warriors watched the troops ride away. Silently and unseen, the ghostly alliance melted into the crags and crannies of the bluff and the dark shadows of the nearby forest.

"It is good. The white soldiers, like the rest of the white men, will become frightened and run from what they do not understand. The land will again be at peace."

The Indian spoke not to another Indian but to an unseen presence, a presence known only to a few…and to the *Choo-pin-it-pa-loo.*

On their return trip to the previous night's camp site, the patrol met the three soldiers escorting the reluctant scouts.

"They ain't makin' no sense, Sir," the sergeant greeted Will. "They keep yappin' 'bout some sacred place and them mountain people."

"It's alright, Sergeant," Will said, "nothing about this makes any sense."

The buck-sergeant and the two privates sat in total silence while the discussion of what they found that day went around a campfire, burning in spite of the warm August night.

"So now what?" the sergeant asked. "What are we gonna tell the major? He'll throw ya all in the brig if ya tell him that story. It ain't that I ain't believin' ya, but that's as crazy a story as what that AWOL corporal told him."

The discussion continued well into the night, no one seemed anxious to retire to a bedroll and the sounds of the night. Even Will was unsettled by the events of the day. He couldn't return to the fort after nearly two weeks and just tell the major he'd lost the colonel and his regiment into the side of a mountain. There was no plausible explanation for what they had seen. An entire cavalry regiment could not have ridden into a solid rock bluff…yet they apparently had.

One by one, the soldiers drifted away from the discussion, retiring to individual bedrolls. Will spent what was left of the night restlessly tossing and turning while he racked his brain for some rational explanation. Finally convinced there was none, he fussed over what to do in the morning. Should they go back to the bluff and look until they found a way over or around, or head back to the fort and think of something to tell the major?

By morning, he had made a decision. They had done all they could, following the colonel to the trail's end. That was their story and they would stick to it…every member of the patrol. There was no further explanation.

Major Denton was not going to like it but William had a feeling this was going to be one of many things the major was not going to like.

Chapter Eight

Backtrack

Sam's trail was easy to find. He was headed northeast from the fort and toward the hunting grounds of the Nespelems. The people of Little Moses, Standing Wolf thought, remembering a night he spent at Long Rapids a lifetime ago.

Encouraged by having picked up the trail of the lone, shod horse he was disturbed by the number of setbacks that had cost him another two or three days on the man's trail. "We don't have to make it up all at once this time. Sam no longer has a destination, no fort, no more safe-haven. Now he is just running and we have the advantage," he told Whiskey, choosing to dismiss the couple of lost days.

Following the lone horse tracks through sandy, sage country was like following a herd of stolen beef up the *Okinakane*. He and Whiskey traveled the trail at an easy lope, daylight until dusk. Part way into the third day Standing Wolf suffered another setback. Disappointment spread over him like an infected blanket. The soft, gray sand turned hard and brown, gullies and dry washes spread out like spiderwebs.

"Cloudburst," Standing Wolf muttered.

Sam had ridden into shrub-steppe country where sudden, isolated rain storms washed away surface sand, shrubs and any sign of tracks… animal or human.

"Sam is a pretty lucky fellow," Standing Wolf said, thoughtfully, to a disinterested Whiskey who was intent only on grasping a few tufts of bunchgrass up rooted by the storm.

Experienced tracker that he was, Standing Wolf knew his only choice was to ride until he found the end of the storm's path and work an arc again until he picked up Sam's trail. He was confident he would again find the trail but it would cost him more time.

Standing Wolf ran his thumb and forefinger down the leather strap around his neck to the amulet. His mind raced over the times when faced with adversity or life-threatening situations he had the good fortune, skill and/or luck to survive. The amulet was with him every time; his father's death, the Civil War, Custer, Roy and the Ghost Dance. Sam, too, has an amulet, he pondered.

Is it really just luck?

It took another day-and-a-half to pick up the trail of the lone horseman again. "This guy should have been a scout," Standing Wolf commented to a more attentive Whiskey.

Sam had managed to maintain an almost constant course to the northeast.

"He should be riding in circles," Standing Wolf cracked, "considering the state of mind he must be in."

The remainder of the day he spent traveling through a transitional zone between shrub-steppe and mountains. The climb was gradual but constant and the vegetation, while still dominated by sage, greasewood, prickly pear and pine, began to show signs of fescue, fir and saskatoon.

After a decent nights sleep, Standing Wolf resumed following Sam's trail with a renewed exuberance. "He is making no attempt to hide his trail," he confided to his mount. "I am guessing he thinks he is being followed and that his advantage is his head start and he is intent on maintaining that distance. He also probably thinks that little rainstorm washed away his tracks. Guess he does not know who is trailing him, huh big fella'."

The trail led to a large plateau rimmed by a low mountain range. They were now deep into the land of the Nespelems. If Little Moses and his small band were any indication, this was not a good place for a lone soldier to find himself.

"If he knew what he was getting into, he would just stop and wait for us to find him." The Arab snorted in agreement.

The first sign of trouble came when Standing Wolf found the *mowich*, or mule deer, carcass with the back-strap removed and strips of meat cut from the hindquarters.

"He is getting hungry, maybe thirsty too," he muttered to himself, taking note of the fact that Sam had a gun. "He did not choke that deer to death," he whispered to affirm the fact.

The next sign of trouble was far more disturbing. It started when the trail of the lone horse broke from a comfortable walk to a flat out run.

"Something has frightened our boy," Standing Wolf stated, running through a checklist of possibilities.

Cougar, Grizzly, Wolves…Nespelems?

The answer came quickly. Sam's tracks were overtaken by first ten, then many more unshod horses.

"Nespelems! Nothing is ever easy," he sighed in exasperation.

Standing Wolf was unable to find the shod tracks of Sam's mount among the many unshod Indian ponies but he did find Sam's boot tracks among many moccasin tracks.

"Well, they have him," he confirmed to Whiskey, while trying to access the ramifications of this development. "It is going to slow him down that is for sure. But what are they going to do with him… and the amulet?"

He could not be sure how far he was behind Sam and Sam's new companions. They had ridden through another rainstorm and the soil was sufficiently soaked to prevent hooves from disturbing dry dirt. There was no way of knowing how long it had been since the storm or how hard it had rained. The tracks looked fresh but they always looked fresher on wet ground.

"Could be a week, could be a couple of days," Standing Wolf said, patting Whiskey on his serpentine neck. "Not to worry big boy," he assured the proud horse. "We will catch them soon enough, it is what we find when we catch them that I am concerned about."

The trail led him over a shallow mountain range and into a deep and foreboding canyon. The trail into the canyon worked its way along a small stream and the descent was gradual. Once he reached the canyon floor, the small stream delivered into a small river. Standing Wolf was perplexed.

This was more than a hunting party.

There was a campsite at the confluence of stream and river with the remains of numerous small cooking fires. The area trampled and grazed indicated the group was substantial in size.

Standing Wolf let his gaze wander up and down the canyon. Except for the way he entered, sheer bluffs rising thousands of feet from the valley floor guarded it. The similarities to the valley of the Sematuse were uncanny. However, there were no rainbows and this valley was much narrower and covered with dense foliage. Large cottonwood lined the river and aspen whispered to him in a light summer breeze. Much of the ground cover was wild rose, raspberry and blackberry bushes. He concluded that whoever this band was that had Sam they were not just wandering, they knew this country. As he followed their trail upstream, the towering bluff pinched the valley tighter.

Box canyon!?

He was not sure where that thought came from, somewhere in his past he had heard about Indians leading soldiers into box canyons, sealing off any escape and waiting for them to starve or go crazy. Standing Wolf was reasonably sure there were no soldiers following this band and that this was not a trap or a box canyon. His thoughts ricochet back to Janis and the obvious trap set there but quickly discarded the idea of any connection between the two.

The thought persisted when the massive walls closed ever tighter into the valley floor and the small river winding through it. Dense vegetation forced the trail he was following into the river itself. With the water low in the August heat, the going was easy and the sandy bottom between the water and the banks looked as if it had fallen victim to a herd of wild horses.

Adrenaline rush through him as he peered through the dense cover surrounding the river trail. The sheer bluffs appeared to merge a quarter-mile or so up river. He reflected on the valley of rainbows.

"There can not be another such place on Mother Earth, much less within riding distance." Standing Wolf spoke as if to a deity.

He took a deep breath and smiled at his folly. The giant bluffs stopped a couple hundred yards short of merging, leaving a narrow passage with the river running through it. With the light fading, Standing Wolf spoke softly to Whiskey.

"We better bed down for the night, my friend."

He knew the high canyon walls could bring the onset of night quickly and he did not want to risk losing the trail of Sam and his apparent captors to darkness. Freeing Whiskey of his hackamore and riding pad, Standing Wolf surveyed the area for a suitable site for his bed. A swale between two cottonwood roots prevailed and using his riding pad for a pillow, he lie on the soft mulch of leaves and let his eyes focus on the slowly emerging stars in the night sky.

"Beats the feather bed I had at the fort," he commented with a sigh, knowing the only audience he might have would be frogs, lizards and hoot owls. He set his mind to more serious matters; the killing and mutilation at Janis where even horses were killed. None of it fit with what he knew of the bands along the *Okinakane*. Now, Sam as apparently captured and being held prisoner by a large band Standing Wolf guessed were Nespelems.

"But if they are Nespelems, where are they going?" he asked the night sky. He was confident they were no longer within the traditional hunting grounds of the Nespelems. What did they want with a white soldier?

Most Indians in the *Okinakane* would not see a single soldier as a threat and would either kill him to settle a score or ignore him as unimportant.

"Did something happen while I was inside the valley that so angered the Indians of the *Okinakane* they are now seeking revenge? Could the ancestral warriors that rid the valley of soldiers have been seen by Indians outside the valley?"

If logic had anything to do with anything, what happened in the valley that Standing Wolf was convinced was a world within a world, stayed there. However, he knew logic was not a factor in spiritual matters. He thought about the white buffalo and the black wolf, both seemed surreal, part of another life, another time.

When Standing Wolf first passed through the spirit cave into the valley, he felt a sense of euphoria, of physical well-being unlike anything he ever experienced before, even as a fearless teen. He realized now he felt more troubled, less euphoric…he felt mortal.

He touched the amulet hanging around his neck. Could its powers and his be limited to within' the foreboding rock walls of the sacred valley of the Sematuse?

Standing Wolf was unceremoniously awakened by the 'pluft' sound of Whiskey blowing in his ear. Looking up at the big black horse standing over him was unnerving. Must be how it feels to be an ant, he thought.

The trail continued upriver at what appeared to be a leisurely pace. Ground, while disturbed, was not torn up and grass was chewed down indicating the horses were allowed to spend considerable time grazing.

Refreshed and encouraged, Standing Wolf patted Whiskey on the neck.

"We just might catch up with Sam and his entourage on this fine day," he cracked flippantly.

He was sensing an end to this chase. As the day wore on, the imposing bluffs gave way to an expansive swamp, the river he had been following was now lost amidst the emergent vegetation of the boggy bottomland.

The tracks averted to higher ground, skirting the edge of the swamp for a considerable distance before passing over a low mountain range and encountering a large, emerald-green lake. Light was fading and the sun settled behind the western horizon.

"We better stay here for the night," he told a sweating Whiskey.

It had been a tough day, pushed by Standing Wolf in the hot August sun, the shallow mountain pass proved a grueling end to a long day. Besides, an inner voice that he came to trust was telling him he was closing in on his quarry.

"If we catch up with them tomorrow, what could I offer these Indians in trade for their white captive?" he asked Whiskey, half expecting the horse to have an answer. The obvious answer was Whiskey, but that offer was not on the table.

Standing Wolf found their campsite, not on the lake but on a new and larger river. They had camped on a sharp bend with a sandy beach. Small cooking fires, while no longer smoking, held burnt embers warm to his touch. Horse tracks led to and from the water but they had obviously been staked or tethered away from the campsite.

Leaving Whiskey on a ground tie, he walked around the site searching for Sam's boot prints or other sign to insure he had not somehow slipped away.

"Fat chance," Standing Wolf scoffed.

He had been careful to watch the perimeters of their trail for a lone rider leaving the band, though he was more concerned about the group splitting up, leaving him with a decision to make. He was also becoming increasingly concerned about finding Sam dead and the amulet gone.

In a grassy meadow not far from the sandy campsite, Standing Wolf found where the horses had been kept. He also found something very disturbing. Unlike the trail he was following for days, the band left this site in a hurry. Sod was torn up and chunks of turf up-rooted, the hoof imprints showed the deep gouges of horses running flat out.

"They left here in a damn big hurry," he accessed, wondering if he was the cause of their haste or if something or someone else suddenly spooked them.

Soldiers were his first thought, but was quickly rejected. If soldiers were pursuing them there would be some sign of them. If they were close enough to cause the Indians to run, they would have already over run the campsite. No such sign existed.

What else was there?

He pondered, as he returned to Whiskey, what would cause this many Indians to bolt as if they had seen a ghost. Did Sam run with them?

The sun was setting on the following day when Standing Wolf finally caught up with the band. He was watching for a dust plume, sensing that the trail was getting more and more fresh. Topping a rise, with eyes peeled vigilantly on the trail ahead, he was startled to see forty, maybe fifty Indians, all warriors and engaged in the process of making camp. Some were gathering limbs, sticks and bark for cook fires while others were leading horses to water or staking them out in lush grass.

The light was not good and he was a couple hundred yards away but he began to get an empty feeling in the pit of his stomach and it was not from hunger. He could not see a soldier anywhere. They could have stripped him of his uniform but he did not see a naked man either. He could be off relieving himself or they could have him hidden. None of the options were adding up.

"How in the hell could we have lost him?" he questioned, as if the horse was somehow responsible.

His anxiety level was elevating while he retraced the trail in his mind. He had been careful to watch for a lone horse leaving the group, unless Sam somehow slipped away while Standing Wolf was on the trail after dark. But that made no sense because this band captured Sam for a reason. They would either keep him or kill him.

Standing Wolf continued to watch the camp until he could see nothing but the scattered fires. Even then he peered into the light, hoping to catch a glimpse of a blue uniform. Only when the fires died and darkness prevailed did he lie down near an aspen, comforted by the belief that the tree leaves harbored the spirits of his ancestors.

He awoke at daybreak and watched silently as the small armada scurried about, spearing fish, rebuilding smoldering fires and rounding up mounts that were strayed from those tethered or staked. As the full light of day enveloped the camp, Standing Wolf's empty feeling crawled up to form a lump in his throat.

"Our soldier is not there," he whispered, disappointed and dismayed. "I lost him, damn me, I lost him," he muttered, relieving Whiskey of any complicity.

Where? How?

He tried to retrace a trail now grown hazy in his head.

"Just like at Janis," he told his patient and understanding equine friend. "I let myself be distracted."

By becoming enthralled with the strange band that held Sam, either as a prisoner or compatriot, Standing Wolf believed he had taken his eye off the target. He was too curious who these Indians were and where they were going, where they were taking Sam.

"I have to backtrack. It is going to be slow and tedious and may not produce any answers." Patting Whiskey affectionately on the neck, then rubbing him between his ears Standing Wolf conceded, "At least we will be moving slowly, you should enjoy that."

Backtracking proved to be every bit as tedious and frustrating as Standing Wolf anticipated. Less than a half day past on the return trail when he suffered another setback. It began with a distant rumbling then thunderheads billowing above the southern horizon. Soon he felt a cool breeze slide over his skin, warmed from the hot August sun. As the sky darkened and the thunder became incessant, large raindrops began falling, scattered at first then increasing until he was caught in a downpour.

The rain felt good but there was nothing good about a cloudburst to a tracker on the trail of a quarry. Standing Wolf guided Whiskey under a large pine as the pounding rain fell around him, and his thoughts drifted to the valley and Star Flower. Women held no interest for him until he saw her; not as a boy in the union army, not as an officer in Custer's command, and not as a drunk in search of his mother's people.

All that changed the first time he saw the back of her head… well, a little more than her head. Actually he was seated behind her at a council meeting and spent much of the time focused on her long shiny, black braids, the line from her narrow shoulders to her tiny waist merging with the flair of her promising hips and bottom. He smiled as he recalled watching Star Flower dance, it was then he had been awestruck by her beauty and grace.

Shaking his head to rid himself of images that could only be distracting to the task at hand, he threw a leg over Whiskey's neck and slid to a light-footed landing. Gathering a few of the plentiful cones scattered about under the tree, he started a small fire, ran a dogwood stick through a small forest grouse he manged to bag before the rain, and began cooking it. As he did so, Standing Wolf considered his current dilemma.

Did the Indians let Sam go and he had missed the trail? Did Sam give the amulet to the Indians in trade for his freedom? Had they killed Sam and dumped him and the amulet in the river or left him for animals to drag off, or killed him and kept the amulet?

It was becoming all too apparent that Standing Wolf did not know and had no way to know where the amulet was or who was currently in possession of it.

"I hate gambling," he muttered to the totally disinterested bird he was cooking.

The odds seemed even that the amulet was either with Sam or the curious Indian band, but if he bet wrong it could be lost forever.

"This is turning into a real head scratcher," he said.

While working the trail backward there was always one persistant thought. Something happened on the sandy beach at the river bend. Until then, the pace of the Indian band had been steady but unhurried, yet they left the beach in what appeared to be a panic.

Could it be?

Standing Wolf wondered. Sam escaped the valley by reacting to the panic around him; could he have taken advantage of that situation again?

"I am beginning to find this Sam to be a very interesting fellow," he stated to the omnipresent being he always sensed was watching and listening.

Chapter Nine

Pair o' Dice

The Riley family fell asleep listening to the mournful yet intriguing sound of wolves howling in the distance. Ross and Ruth slept a sound and satisfied sleep, the result of their afternoon lovemaking while Larry and Lilly spent a restless night filled with anticipation and anxiety.

Ruth was up before the morning sun and soon the smell of coffee, taters, eggs and pork sausage permeated the house. Ross rolled from his side to his back under the light cover and stretched. His first thought was of Ruth and the passionate way she responded to his lovemaking yesterday…the next was wolves; how many there were and how much of a threat to his livestock did they pose? He would know more after today.

Ross knew Lilly and Larry thought the ranchers should be able to live with the wolves, not eradicate them. He'd had that conversation before and it never seemed to end well. He understood Indians lived for many, many years in harmony with wolves, but the Indians weren't raising beef or sheep. This was something that was not going to change; as long as the white man was here, there would be ranchers.

When he reached the kitchen, Ruth was busy setting plates on the table. "Good morning sleepy head," she smiled as she chopped an onion in half, sliced, diced, and added it to the potatoes.

Ross slipped up behind her and sliding his arms under hers, he cupped her full breasts and teased her nipples through her light, cotton shirt. As he began to press his pelvis against her firm backside, she spun facing him, kitchen knife still in hand.

"What did I tell you about starting things you can't finish?" Ruth scolded, her eyes belying the fact that she really enjoyed his teasing.

Ross sat down at the table and was soon joined by Lilly, as Ruth was setting hot plates and platters of food on the table. Eventually, Larry moseyed in. "Smells really good, Mom," he said, sniffing the air in an exaggerated fashion.

"No offense, Mom," Lilly cracked. "But he thinks dirty socks smell good."

"Mom, Lilly thinks your breakfast smells like dirty socks."

"Lillian, jerk, it's Lillian."

"Don't start, you two," interjected Ross. "Save your energy for today. We have a long ride ahead of us and you will have all day to insult each other."

Quickly changing the subject he stated, "If we have time today, I'd like to swing over by the Thompson River and see if any Running R cattle are over there. We can check for any sign of wolves while we're at it."

The brand, a straight iron with a forward leaning R belonged to Ruth's Dad back in Missouri and when Ross and Ruth headed west in search of gold, they brought the branding irons with them. Ross wasn't sure why except that maybe it helped Ruth to feel like she had a part of her Dad with her.

While Lilly and Ruth cleaned up the breakfast dishes, Larry led their horses to water before starting the long day. Ross pulled his Spencer Repeater from over the fireplace mantel and moseyed to the barn; a big log building with ten horse-stalls and two mangers for milk cows, a tack room large enough for a half-dozen saddles and related gear and work harness for the Belgium team. There was even a small blacksmith shop for shaping shoes and repairing farm equipment and wagon wheels.

Entering the barn, Ross took a moment to reflect.

*

When they were first married, Ross was nineteen and Ruth was fifteen. Her parents wanted her to wait for a couple of years but there was talk of a Civil War in the south. Abraham Lincoln was the newly elected president of the United States and he seemed determined to free the slaves, something Ross knew the slave states would never agree to. In March 1861, Jefferson Davis was elected as President of the Confederate States and war, Ross figured, was inevitable.

Ross never saw himself as a coward but he, like a lot of his friends, saw no reason to fight and maybe die for slaves. Hell, he could end up fighting friends or maybe even relatives. Besides, Ross had heard stories about prospectors finding gold in California since he was a little boy. The decision was easy…marry Ruth and go west looking for gold or not marry Ruth, stay home and wait for either the Union or Confederate Army to force him to fight. Hell, he didn't even know which side Missouri would be on.

Ruth's parents were not happy at first. She was their only child left at home and they feared once she left they would never see any of their children again. Once they were finally convinced that Ross and Ruth really loved each other, they reluctantly blessed the couple…an act that meant a great deal to Ruth. Convinced their only chance for a life together was to go west…maybe if they were lucky they would even find gold…if not, the government was offering free land to settlers, they would just find a piece of ground and settle on it.

Ross and Ruth headed west along the Missouri River, filled with hope, energy and a lust for adventure. It was in October when the couple decided the Missouri River was headed north, not west, and choose to leave it and head upstream on a river called the Cheyenne. They soon learned Cheyenne were also a notorious Indian tribe credited with killing many white prospectors and settlers. However, they would have died on that beautiful but treacherous river had it not been for the 'notorious' Cheyenne.

A blizzard caught them by surprise, and with their wagon stuck and their supplies running out, they started tearing the wagon apart to keep a fire burning. When the storm finally ended, there were three boards and a wheel left to burn. All of their food was gone, they were freezing and they were terrified! A small group of Indians were riding toward them through the knee-deep snow.

They were Cheyenne braves.

Ross was especially afraid for Ruth having heard stories along the trail about what Indians did if they captured a white woman. He knew he would die before letting anyone, white or Indian touch Ruth. At least this was a fight he believed in and fight he would!

Ross wrapped his arms around Ruth, determined to protect her or die trying, when to their mutual amazement a young brave rode directly up to them and spoke in poor but understandable English. "Bring horses, come with us," the young brave said, pointing at the dapple-gray draft horses.

Afraid but with no real choice, Ross and Ruth were helped onto the draft horses, harnesses still in place, and rode bareback to a village in a valley along a small stream. There was no wind in the valley and many teepees had smoke rising through an opening at the top. On arrival, the young Indian motioned for them to dismount. "Come in teepee, get warm then eat," he simply stated.

They spent the winter with those Cheyenne and were treated like honored guests. The way Ross and Ruth would think about Indians and their own lives, were changed forever by that one young Indian. In the spring, that same brave, along with a small hunting party, led them to a place they called Flathead. The young brave had friends and relatives there. Because of his help, the Riley's were able to settle a homestead among the Indians, and by treating them with respect and giving them a few 'slow buffalo', as the Indians called cattle, they were able to prosper and grow into the successful ranch operation they called the Running R.

The young Cheyenne to whom he and Ruth owed everything was called Wolf Chief, a fact that Ross now found amusing and ironic.

"Dad, you want to ride Drifter or Roy?" Larry's question snapped Ross out of his reminiscent trance.

"Drifter will do fine, Son." Ross liked the stout Morgan bred horse, a dapple-gray with two black socks reaching all the way to his knees.

The sun was low in the western sky when the family, in good spirits, rode out of the ranch complex to the north past the Big Arm and on toward Wild Horse Creek. It was going to be another warm day and they were traveling light. Dressed in jeans or riding pants and light, cotton shirts, spurs jangling on cowboy boots; only Ross and Larry wore straw hats, brims turned up in a Texas curl.

The women's long hair fluttered in a gentle breeze as they engaged in conversation, and the sound of their voices was like chimes to Ross's ears. Life is good, he thought. Even if we lose a couple of animals to wolves, life will still be good. What would not be good, was if a pack of wolves got used to feeding on beef and abandon their normal prey for the taste of cattle.

"If we run into any wolves today, just blow some dust up at them. We don't need to kill them; we just need to make sure they are more comfortable back in the high country."

Ross was speaking to Larry but clearly for the benefit of Ruth and Lilly. Inwardly he was grinning, contemplating the rewards Ruth might bestow upon him for his compassion.

"I've got a feeling they have already moved back to the Cabinet Mountains. That's where it sounded like they were last night," Larry replied, knowing wolves would often move sixty miles or more in a day.

"So you think the pack you saw was just passing through?" Ross asked, knowing Larry took, what seemed like, an unusual interest in wolves. He knew Larry learned a lot about them by talking to local trappers and a few Indians on the nearby reservation.

"Don't know, Dad. But unless we find a kill, chances are they're long gone. If we do find a kill then they'll probably hang around for a few days."

Larry looked at his mom before adding, "Of course if they've killed any cattle, just sprinkle cayenne pepper on the carcass. That should convince them that elk taste a whole lot better than cows."

"Cayenne pepper!" Ross blurted. "Where did you get that crazy idea and where would we get cayenne pepper anyhow?"

"From Mom," Lilly interjected with an ear-to-ear grin. "Mom and I thought it was a good idea, even if it was Larry's. We each have a small bag full in our saddlebags."

Ross shook his head and shoved his straw hat back in dismay. "I can't believe you'all would go to this much trouble to save a few wolves."

Sixty miles northwest of Wild Horse Creek, a gabled gray, or timber wolf pack, were on the trail of a small herd of elk. Two bulls lifted their noses to sniff for the scent of nearby danger. With their heads lifted, their sharp-tipped antlers reached their rumps. Four cows and three calves made up the rest of the herd.

Lobo, a one hundred twenty-five pound alpha male, was the first to locate the herd…first by smell then by sight. He had a healthy respect for the big bulls, even the cows with their sharp cloven-hooves, but they were of little interest. It was the calf with a severe limp that attracted his attention, along with that of his mate, Lola, a ninety-pound alpha female.

The rest of the pack was this year's young, now about four months old, and last year's pups, still not old enough to breed. The pack totaled twelve in all.

The calf's right, hind foot was turned inward, the result of an apparent genetic deformity, making it difficult for the animal to walk and even more difficult to run.

The plan was basic; if they could spook the herd into running they would chase them off then backtrack and the calf will be theirs.

It was an age-old strategy, proven successful time after time. The pack burst from the timbered ravine not more than twenty-five yards from the grazing herd. Startled, the elk formed a defensive line, the cowering calves falling in behind the bulls and flanked by the four cows.

Lobo and Lola feinted attacks on the flanking cows while the rest of the pack circled the prey, each time drawing closer to the defenseless calves in the rear. As the circle grew tighter, a calf, unnerved by the close proximity of the snarling, growling predators, broke rank. Soon the defensive posture of the elk unraveled and the entire herd bolted in an attempt to outrun certain death. Instinctively, a couple hundred yards into the chase the herd scattered, leaving the crippled calf exhausted and alone.

Lobo, Lola and family would feast for two days on the carcass while a link in the chain of a genetic abnormality was broken. The herd would be healthier for it.

After a lunch of roast-beef sandwiches, dill pickles, hard-boiled eggs and apples, Ross and Ruth split up from the kids hoping to cover more ground in their search for stray cattle and/or wolf sign. Ross was also hoping to find a secluded place where they could find another use for the picnic blanket.

The plan was for Ross and Ruth to follow Wild Horse Creek west toward the Thompson a ways, then loop back around to the southeast. Larry and Lilly were to go east to the lake, then south and they would all meet back at Big Arm, hopefully before dark.

They were about twenty-five miles southwest of Blacktail Mountain and nearing the Thompson River when Ross dismounted to relieve himself. Walking a short distance from the trail he undid his button-up fly and while peeing his gaze wandered to a well-worn game trail not more than ten feet to his right. He focused on what looked like a large track in the dusty trail.

Cat.

From where he stood, it looked like a large mountain lion track, not uncommon to this part of the country. Once finished with the task at hand, so to speak, Ross walked over to the trail and knelt for a closer look. As he studied the track his heart began to beat faster and his pulse pounded his temples.

He called to Ruth, "Come over here and tell me what kind of track you think this is."

The track had a pad and four toes, it was not round enough to be a lion, to symmetrical to be a wolverine, not enough toes to be a bear. It looked like a wolf or a big dog but measuring the track with his hand, it was a good eight inches long and five inches wide.

Could it be a big dog, like a St. Bernard? Ruth wondered. She had never seen a St. Bernard or their track but that was the biggest dog she could think of.

Ross was baffled. He did not know what a St. Bernard track looked like but he did know what a wolf track looked like…like this, except only about half this big.

"I think a St. Bernard track would be rounder," he said. "This looks like a wolf to me…a wolf the size of a grizzly bear," he finished with a grin and a disbelieving shake of his head.

To make matters worse there was only one track. The animal did not walk down the game trail but crossed it, leaving a single foot print. "I sure wish Larry could see this," Ross lamented. "I would love to hear him try and explain how a wolf could have made this track. If a wolf made that track I'd sure like to see him through my rifle sight."

"You wouldn't shoot it just because it was a trophy, would you?" Ruth quizzed and scolded at the same time.

"No, I'd shoot it because it would be worth a fortune, probably a thousand dollars, maybe more…and because a wolf that big could eat a cow a day."

"I just wish Larry was here," Ruth sighed, knowing how difficult it was going to be to convince him of the size of this footprint.

Larry and Lilly were scarcely seperated from their folks for an hour before they made a troubling discovery. Lilly noticed it first; a scattering of leaves and needles that seemed to be a pattern. It was just off the game trail they were following and there was something that didn't look right. Larry stepped off the pinto he called Weasel for a closer look. Instinctively he picked up a stick and began stirring and poking around in the loose leaves.

SNAP!

He tripped the release on a trap, the jaws snapping the stick in half.

"Aghhh!" Larry gasped and jumped back, hurling the remainder of the stick over his head.

Buttercup snorted and leaped sideways, frighten by Larry's sudden movement and the flying stick. Lilly grabbed her saddle horn to catch her balance then laughingly teased her brother.

"What's the matter, did the stick bite you?"

"No but that trap sure could have. Why would anybody be trapping in the summer? The furs are no good, unless they are just trapping to kill."

"What kind of trap is it?" Lilly questioned.

"Well I'm not sure but I'd guess it must be for coyote or wolves. It's too small for bear and the wrong kind of set for cats and it's definitely not left over from last winter, this duff is fresh. Who would be out here trapping at this time of year? It's certainly not a good time to trap for furs. It could be a rancher if he just wants to kill wolves or coyotes."

"But who? Larry do you know any ranchers who would do that?"

"I know a lot of ranchers who hate wolves but most of them are too busy to spend time setting traps hoping to catch a wolf," he said thoughtfully, "unless there is a kill around here and this is not a random set."

"We'd better look around," Lilly said. "Dad is going to want to know if something is killing stock.

A thorough search of the area did not reveal a kill of any kind, wild animal or domestic, however they did discover another trap. Larry sprang it as well and gathered both traps for a closer examination. There was no bait in either of the traps, just a powerful odor. Being neither a trapper nor an animal scent expert, Larry had no clue what the scent was, just that it smelled awful…worse than skunk.

"Are we going to take the traps to show Dad, or are we going to leave them?" Lilly inquired.

"Let's take 'em. I don't see any marks on 'em but I'm sure Dad is going to want to know someone is trapping on the Wild Horse. You carry these in case we find more." Larry wrapped the long drag-chain around Lilly's saddle horn.

"Eeuuuh!" Lilly sputtered. "They smell awful! You carry them… you stink anyway," she said, laughing.

"I hope all girls aren't sissies like you. If they are then I'm never gettin' married," he scoffed, then un-wrapped the chains and hung the smelly traps over his saddle horn.

"We'll see who's a sissy. Race you to the lake!" Lilly touched her rowels to Buttercup and the Palomino bolted down the trail attaining full stride in about three jumps.

Larry sank his spurs into Weasel's ribs and the race was on. He liked the pinto though his dad thought the horse was too high strung. He considered, perhaps his dad was right when Weasel nearly jumped out of his skin at the sudden departure of his companion, and the sharp rowels in his ribs.

Larry caught his hat with his right hand and a trap with his left, just in time to avoid taking the trap squarely in the mouth. The traps were bouncing off Larry like bats in a barrel, dirt and rocks hitting him in the face as Buttercup tore up the trail in front of him.

"Never underestimate me or the Weasel!" he shouted ahead, hunkered down and screwed his hat on tight.

Lilly never heard him. She was grinning like a cat with a carp, thrilled by the flying feet of her speedy Palomino mare. She was unaware the swift pinto was gaining ground until Weasel's pounding hooves, rattling traps and Larry pulled alongside.

Stealing a quick look across at Larry, Lilly urged Buttercup forward, focusing her eyes on the lake and the finish line, determined not to let her brother return home with any kind of bragging rights. The two impetuous youngsters thundered across the flat leading to the lakeshore.

Willing mounts responded to their urging when, as Larry turned his head to look at his sister, a flying trap smacked him in the ear, transforming his vision of Lilly's face into red and green spots on a black background. Larry grabbed the horn for balance and pulled in on the reins, trying to slow the fired-up Weasel. Slowly, Larry's head cleared and he shoved his feet forward in the stirrups then grasped a rein in each hand and began working one rein then the other, finally getting control of the leap-frogging pinto.

Lilly, twenty yards ahead, looked back and sensed something was wrong. Buttercup was easy to pull in without the racing pinto alongside. She stopped and waited for Larry to catch up.

"What's the matter, give up cause you knew you were going to lose?" Lilly razzed then saw the blood covering Larry's face, his shirt, everywhere. "What happened?" she screamed, alarmed.

"Damn trap hit me. Probably cut my goddamn ear off!"

"Come here and let me look at it."

Lilly dismounted and met Larry as he stepped off Weasel. She pulled a napkin left over from lunch out of her saddlebag to clean the blood from the gash in Larry's ear.

"Eeouch!" he yelped as Lilly wiped the blood away for a closer look.

"You took a pretty good piece out of your ear. We better go to the lake and clean it up but you need to keep pressure on it until it stops bleeding." Her stern look of concern slowly morphed into a playful smile of relief. "Now that you have a notch in your right ear, all we need to do is get a brand on you and everyone will know you belong to the Running R."

"Very funny, Sis, You're the one who's going to get branded. Some young stud will take one look at your cute ass and decide to put his brand on it."

"Don't you be looking at my butt, and any guy who thinks he's going to put a brand on me better be bullet-proof!"

Riding south along the Thompson River, Ross and Ruth found a couple-dozen Running R cows and decided they would move them east to the Big Arm. Even though they found only the one track, wolf or not, there was definitely something roaming this part of the country that could be a threat to cattle.

Picking up the cows threw a wet blanket on Ross' plans for a second picnic, one where food was not part of the menu. Even his daydreaming was messed up. Just when he was focusing on Ruth's tight riding pants encasing her smooth firm bottom or her full breasts straining against the fabric of her cotton blouse, images of what made that huge track would horn in on his intimate visions.

Ross had spent the last twenty years in the western wilderness along the Missouri, to the Dakota Badlands, to the Flathead country of Montana. He'd never seen anything like that track. He ran a mental checklist of possibilities: black bear, grizzly bear, wolverine, fisher, cougar and lynx; all were discarded as quickly as they crossed his mind. Even the Indian legend 'Sasquatch' did not fit that track. Ross was convinced it had to be a wolf track but he was equally certain there was no wolf in existence big enough to have made it.

So where does that leave me?

He pondered if could be a wolf with a deformed foot that made the track.

That has to be it.

Maybe a wolf managed to escape from a trap somehow and was left with a badly swollen foot.

"I think I have the answer," Ross blurted and repeated his theory to Ruth. "That is the only possible explanation."

"Why would anyone be trapping wolves this time of year?" Ruth questioned.

"Could have been last winter, it was more likely a coyote set caught a wolf and he managed to pull his foot free leaving it mangled and it healed that way."

Satisfied with his deduction, Ross returned to the more pleasurable act of picturing his wife's naked body lying on their bed, her blond hair spread out like a halo around her angelic face.

When they reached Big Arm, Larry and Lilly were waiting. Larry's ear was no longer bleeding but his bloody clothes alarmed his mother and father. He and Lilly went into great detail about finding the traps and their diligent search for more. The details how his ear got notched like a prize steer were a little vague, neither wanted to confess the injury was the result of risky and childish horseplay.

Ruth, while relieved that her son's injuries were not serious, was very concerned that he would have a deformed ear.

"You need to see a doctor, young man," Ruth stated, her green eyes flashing like emeralds in sunlight. "Otherwise you are going to end up with an ear that looks like a hunk of califlower."

It was the perfect segue for Ross to tell his wolf-track story along with his 'deformed' theory… a theory he was somewhat pleased with until Larry said, "If he's deformed, he's probably been driven out of the pack and is gonna' find cattle a lot easier to catch than deer or elk."

"Oh, great," Lilly piped up. "Now everybody's going to think we have a monster wolf running around eating cows. Ranchers are going to want to kill every wolf they see so they can check and see if their feet are normal, not like it will matter once they're dead."

"Relax Lilly," Larry cajoled. "Any wolf with a foot like that would be limping so badly you could spot him a mile away."

"You should be more concerned about who is trapping in the summer than somebody killing a crippled wolf," Ross told his daughter, almost condescendingly.

"Okay fine," she replied with the sass only a budding sixteen-year-old beauty could muster.

"Let's head for home, Ross," Ruth cut in. "I want to take a better look at that ear. I think Larry and I will ride into Paradise tomorrow and see if Doc Jensen is there. If not we will have to go to Horse Plain."

"But, Mom," Larry pleaded. "It's only a little cut. It will be all right."

"You will do what your mother wants," Ross spoke up. "So you may as well see what the Doc says. If he can't fix it then I guess we'll call you One-eared Larry."

Ross and Lilly laughed but Ruth's green-eyed stare quickly sobered the mood. Ross knew Ruth could see nothing funny about one of her kids being hurt and Lilly was feeling more than a little guilt for having started the horse race, and for being wimpy about the smelly traps.

Pair o'Dice was located at the south end of the Cabinet Mountains, not far from where the Flathead River runs into the Clark Fork. Ruth found the name humorous, not because she found anything funny about gambling, but because it sounded like 'paradise', which in her opinion it was not…except for the hot springs. Ruth, not totally sure if she did it for fun or spite, insisted the place should be called Paradise…like it or not.

It was forty miles from the ranch house to Paradise and another ten or so if they went on to Horse Plain. There was not much in Paradise; a livery stable and blacksmith shop, a saloon, a general store, a boarding house and a church. Doc Jensen kept a room in the back of the saloon where he delivered babies, mended broken bones and patched up cuts. He sometimes even treated dysentery, gout, pneumonia, consumption and diphtheria. He tried to be in Paradise every other Wednesday.

Trouble was unless you lived in Paradise, and not many people did, it was hard to remember what day of the week it was…much less every other week. Of course if there was an emergency in Horse Plain on the day he was suppose to be in Paradise, well then shit, the whole rest of the year was messed up.

The thriving competition between the Hudson Bay Company and the North West Trading Company in Horse Plain…plus the town being at the hub of the wild horse business… had brought an influx of settlers like Ross and Ruth Riley. Soon Horse Plain turned into a growing community with an obvious need for a doctor. The Indian problems throughout the Walla Walla region, especially the uprising at the Whitman Mission, made moving an easy decision for the middle-aged Doc Jensen and his family.

When the railroad arrived, places like Pair o'Dice, Horse Plain and Thompson Falls…especially Thompson Falls…grew and though the trading companies left, the wild-horse business remained in Horse Plain…and so did Doc Jensen.

The doctor was five-feet ten inches tall with a slight build and weighed one-hundred fifty pounds, if he was holding a full-grown goose under each arm. His hair was white, long and shaggy but his face was always clean-shaven.

When Ruth arrived in Paradise with Larry, his ear now badly swollen and the color of a rotten apple, they went straight to the saloon.

"Please tell me Doc Jensen is here today," Ruth said hopefully to the small man with the doorknocker beard behind the bar.

"All right, Doc Jensen is here today," the bartender responded. "But he ain't. He will be tomorrow though, 'less he has an emergency over in Horse Plain."

"Isn't this Wednesday?" Ruth asked, puzzled.

"No Ma'am, this here is Tuesday, but I'd be glad ta tell ya its Wednesday if ya'd like."

Tiring of having a little fun with the lady, he asked, "Can I get you or the boy anything ta drink?" He quickly added, "Sarsaparilla, coffee, water? We got good water here from the well outback."

Larry felt a flush of anger at being called a *boy*. After all, he was seventeen, and a man by most any standard. The impulse quickly waned when a rush of blood resulting from the emotion reached his ear. The throbbing, burning ache caused him to respond weakly, "I'd have a sarsaparilla."

"That's one nasty lookin' ear," the barkeep stated. "Ya get into a fight with a mountain lion, or bitten by a girl?"

Ruth didn't know this mouthy bartender, and she thought she knew everyone in Paradise. He was obviously new in town.

No great addition.

"My **son** and I are going to need a room."

She hoped the emphasis on son would nip any more smart remarks in the bud. They could have stayed at the boarding house but Ruth wanted to be close when Doc Jensen arrived.

This was obviously a woman of means who was not used to being played with, and it did not go unnoticed by the bartender that the young man with her wore a pearl-handled Colt low on this right thigh.

Enough fun, he cautioned himself, and proceeded to show Ruth and Larry to a tidy room with two beds.

Returning to the bar, the man pondered the possibilities. What was a fine-looking woman like that doing in the middle of the Montana wilds? Women always laughed at him because he was short, maybe he would show this beauty just because he wasn't tall didn't mean he wasn't big. There was just one problem…the boy, and something about the way that Colt .45 hung on his leg. He got the feeling the kid used that gun for more than shooting snakes and squirrels.

The bartender had seen it before in the small desert towns of the southwest. Young boys, just kids really, but with the lightning reflexes of youth and immortal belief of those too young to know better. It nearly cost him his life in Tucson when he underestimated a kid and wound up with a bullet in his belly. The bartender felt the scar, about two inches above his bellybutton and dead center. It reminded him never to make that mistake again. He'd been fortunate there was a good doctor in Tucson and no one knew who he was, or believed what started the fight.

By time the town was convinced of what he had done to that young-gun's mother, he was well enough to ride, and had been riding and running ever since. He probably wouldn't stay here long either, but he sure would like to see more of this kid's mom before he moved on.

"You can bet yer life if that little gal found Clarence Hobbs between her legs it would be an experience she'd never forget," he mumbled on his way back to the bar.

The question was…would Clarence Hobbs bet his?

Morning brought Doc Jensen and bad news. Larry's ear was seriously infected. Once the Doc was able to get Ruth out of the examining room and discovered the source of the injury was a steel trap treated with some type of animal scent, he knew there could be more than concern over the cosmetics of an ear; it could lead to blood poison, tetanus and death.

After lancing Larry's ear and giving it a good soaking in alcohol, Doc Jensen left the room to speak with Ruth.

"Mrs. Riley," he began, "at this point I can't be sure what I can do for your son's ear cosmetically. A more urgent matter is to eliminate the infection. I have lanced the ear but need to watch it for a few days as it may need lanced again. I would like him to come to Horse Plain with me. I can clean the ear with alcohol and iodine and soak it in Epsom salt, see if I can get rid of the infection. Once that is done, I can evaluate the cosmetic possibilities. I don't mean to alarm you but you need to know your son has a potentially serious injury. If the infection gets into his blood stream and he gets blood poisoning, tetanus or lockjaw, I may not be able to save the ear… or him."

Ruth gasped, tears streamed down her cheeks uncontrollably. She had been worried about how the ear would look; it never occurred to her that her son's life was in danger. After all, it was only a cut on his ear.

"You mean he could die?" She was barely able to force out the words.

"Ma'am, please understand, I think I can get ahead of the infection but if for some reason I cannot then yes, he could die."

"But my husband is expecting us home tonight or tomorrow at the latest. He will be worried sick."

"Your son will be fine for the next few days, by then I will know if I have gotten a handle on the infection. I suggest you go home and that you and your husband come to Horse Plain in three or four days. By then Larry will be getting better and we can discuss possible cosmetic remedies, or I will have lost the battle and we will all have to pray for a miracle."

"My husband and I don't cotton much to prayer," Ruth mumbled.

She was in shock; she could barely feel her arms and legs. When she attempted to stand, she discovered she didn't have the strength to get to her feet.

Doc Jensen studied her carefully. "Mrs. Riley, perhaps it would be best if you stayed here another night and returned to your ranch tomorrow. I am sorry for having to upset you but I have always tried to be honest and up front with my patients. I believe we have a good chance of getting this under control. The injury is still fresh and that is on our side. Often by the time I see this kind of injury the infection has spread throughout the body…by that time it is too late."

"Can I see him?" Ruth managed to ask quietly.

"Of course, but try not to alarm him, right now he only has a sore ear and a bandage around his head. He is probably going to want to go home but I need you to make Larry understand that he needs to let me keep an eye on that ear for a few days. Remember, I can only treat him if he lets me. I can't force him."

"I understand."

Wiping stubborn tears from her eyes, Ruth took a deep breath, fighting to regain her composure. It took all the authority she could impose as Larry's mother and all the persuasion she could muster to convince her son that he needed to go to Horse Plain with Doc Jensen. In the end it was one word 'lockjaw' that convinced Larry to follow the doctor's orders.

The next task was to convince Larry that he didn't need his gun while under the doctor's care. It wasn't that he fancied himself a gunfighter; he rarely carried his .45 on the ranch but he did know how to use it. Ross had taught his son well and he did like to have it with him when going to town.

As the pain from the lancing and cleaning turned to an agonizing throbbing, Larry's concern about his pistol waned. Ruth watched as Doc Jensen made a place in his buckboard for the young man to lie down.

With tears in her eyes and burdened with bad news, Ruth headed for the Running R. She had Larry's horse in tow, his .45 slung over her saddle horn. She had plenty of time to make it home before dark, the days were long this time of year and she knew she had to tell Ross, the sooner the better.

From an upstairs room at the back of the bar, Clarence Hobbs watched with anxious anticipation as Ruth rode out of town, leading a gray horse with no rider.

"Clarence, you are one lucky bastard," he whispered and headed for the livery stable.

Chapter Ten

Contact

Finally confident the Indians were not coming back and using a small stream as a trail, Sam led Major to the river. Call it paranoia or instinct, he now felt an impulse to cover his tracks. He had no idea how far he was from the fort and couldn't imagine anyone would still be on his trail but with his life at stake, he couldn't be too cautious.

Once he reached the river Sam crawled on Major, briefly looked up and down stream and easily decided he would go downstream… the opposite way the Indians had gone. He rode for days through the shallow waters of the riverbed; no longer sure of what direction he was traveling except it was downhill. However, from brief glimpses of the sun, it seemed at times the river was flowing to the north, then the south, then east. He began to wonder how every direction could still be downhill.

Eventually, he saw the river was merging with a larger one and coursed through a deep rock gorge. There were no banks and it was obvious the water was too deep for him to ride through. He rode to a rock point that extended out into the larger river where a distant roaring sound reached his ears.

Pulling Major to a sudden halt, Sam froze. What he saw left him breathless. Across the river and downstream not more than a mile or two, he could see several buildings at the edge of the timber.

Trading post…or fort?

Sam had no money and nothing to trade and damn sure didn't want to risk running into any military outposts. He was curious about the roaring sound but not that curious.

"Better just keep your Spanish ass moving unless you want to face a firing squad from the business end." He reasoned.

Turning upstream and away from any sign of civilization, Sam rode for days until he reached what appeared to be the river's headwaters. The weather turned clear and hot and he was able to start each day moving toward the morning sun, away from the fort and that unholy valley. So paramount was his fear that he avoided any sign of possible towns, trading posts or farms.

Early on, he started the habit of making a mark on Major Denton's saddle each night; partly out of boredom and partly as a means of measuring the distance he traveled. It was a rough measurement at best but Sam figured he could travel forty to fifty miles a day when it was easy going.

Scratching one more mark into the military saddle, he took a deep breath and let it out slowly. Based on his marks, Sam guessed he'd been on the run a month, more or less, and four or five hundred miles from the fort. He was pretty sure he was somewhere in Canada and that was just fine with him. He decided it was time to stop worrying about being followed and start thinking about what he was going to do with the rest of his life.

Hunger was his constant companion, though the rivers and creeks supplied a steady diet of fish. He began to think about things like sitting down to a table for a home-cooked meal and a bath with actual soap; especially to wash his hair and a shave. Sam's whiskers had stopped itching but he couldn't get used to the hair all over his face, and clothes…he needed clothes. His were so dirty they could sit in the saddle without him, and if he was in Canada, a U.S. Cavalry uniform would be like rat shit in sugar.

Confident he had lost anyone who might be following him and no longer concerned about covering his trail, Sam figured it was time to change his appearance. He began looking for signs of civilization.

"I need new clothes and money and you need a new saddle, blanket and bridle," he told the little horse for which he'd developed a growing fondness. "Only way I know to get any money is to sell you."

Major snorted, blowing snot in the air, obviously seeing no humor in Sam's jesting.

"All right, I could rob a bank or a stagecoach. I know…I could start looking for de oro, gold, in some of these creeks!"

As was often the case with Sam, his sarcasm led to solutions; it had happened more than once, especially when mixed with some good old-fashioned luck.

Removing the amulet from around his neck he stared at the life-like painting and the golden-yellow eyes. The collision of two thoughts exploded in his brain. He was certain the amulet was a good luck charm and much, much more. Still, if those bright eyes were made from flecks of gold, he could probably sell it for enough to get new clothes, a saddle and a grubstake. He might even be able to get a gun so he could kill his own food.

Sam quickly rationalized that it made no sense to sell a good luck piece for a little money when with it he could, maybe, find a lot. The whole idea reminded him of something his dad used to say about teaching a man to fish. Besides, the amulet meant more than luck, it meant life; a life he was sure he would have lost without it.

He was yanked from his reverie when he topped the head end of a ravine and found himself on a well-traveled road. There were horse tracks, cattle tracks, even wagon tracks. Impulsively, he spun Major around toward the ravine and cover. When his mind caught up with his reflexes, he pulled Major in and contemplated his discovery.

Sam knew he could not avoid people forever; he was neither a mountain man nor a recluse. Hell, he liked people and missed the interaction. He was lonesome, but he couldn't just ride into town and have a beer. He looked like hell, smelled worse and the only clothes he owned could only belong to a deserter.

He heard horses and leaped off Major like he was shot at.

"I need to see people," he said breathlessly, "but not now."

Rubbing the little mare's forelock and talking quietly, he willed her not to whinny or otherwise give away their position as the sound of the horses drew near. In his current state of mind, Sam was totally unprepared for what he saw next.

A Woman!

He could barely process the thought. He hadn't seen a woman for, well, since before he was a corporal, and now his first contact with the civilized world was the sight of a woman. A damn pretty woman, he thought as he watched her pass by on a magnificent chestnut mare and leading a good-looking gray gelding.

Sam didn't risk even a breath until the woman was out of sight. She must be meeting someone, he thought, contemplating the gray horse with the empty saddle. Maybe she lives close by or I'm very near a town. His thoughts bounced around like babies in a buckboard. He struggled with his trepidation of meeting people and wishing he could do something about how he looked. He wondered whether he should follow the woman, take the road in the opposite direction or forget the road completely.

His thoughts were again interrupted by the sound of pounding hooves, this time a lone horse and rider moving at a comfortable lope and intent on the road ahead. Again, Sam thanked whom ever the omnipresent being might be that kept Major quiet.

"Town must be that way, chica," he advised his horse, his only friend.

He determined that based on the scant evidence that both passing riders were going the same direction; a conclusion that did nothing to help Sam with his next move.

Clarence Hobbs's kind of luck was holding. He almost missed the chestnut and the gray tied in a lodgepole thicket no more than thirty yards off the road. The gray turned its head to look at the passing rider and the movement caught Hobbs's eye. Reining in his tough little cayuse, Clarence dismounted and led the horse over an embankment into a ravine. Tying the gelding to a sapling, he removed a rag and several short strands of rope from a saddlebag and stuffed them inside his shirt. Cautiously, he climbed back onto the road and moved toward the thicket. Kneeling behind a large boulder, he watched the horses for any sign of the woman.

She's probably taking a pee.

The thought caused a lustful tingle in his groin. When Hobbs saw her, she was meandering toward the horses, cinching her belt around a tiny waist. He studied her for a moment. She was everything he remembered from the saloon; long blond hair hanging nearly to her waist, the swell of her breasts and the flare of her hips.

"Oh, this is gonna be good," he mouthed silently and trembled slightly, excitement gripping his body.

Clarence felt the oxymoron of pleasure and pain as his over-sized manhood strained against his tight-fitting Levis. Women called him a freak of nature but that didn't keep them from howling with pain… or pleasure…it was all the same to him. Once they felt 'the beast' they changed their tune.

When he stepped out from behind the rock, Ruth's mouth dropped open and she stared as if trying to process his sudden appearance before she screamed. The sound barely escaped her lips when with surprising quickness he charged, knocking her to the ground. They struggled and Hobbs was surprised by her strength when Ruth repeatedly jerked her arms from his grip.

He managed to turn her onto her stomach, and with the speed of a rodeo-style calf roper he slipped the loop of the piggin' string over her wrist and made two, quick half hitches. Before Ruth's face was forced into the dirt and duff she screamed again. Hobbs reached around her head and forced a dirty rag into her mouth. With her hands tied behind her and his weight in the middle of her back, she lay still.

Terror, panic, disgust and resolve swirled together like a deadly cocktail as Ruth struggled to comprehend her plight. It's that awful bartender, she thought. There was no doubt what he wanted; the way he looked at her yesterday had given her the creeps.

With his prey now secured, Clarence began to imagine the spoils he was about to claim.

"First, little lady, we need ta get away from the road."

The chestnut and the gray were gone, apparently spooked during the struggle. That was good. He would have cut them loose anyway.

Shoving his hands under her arms, Hobbs lifted Ruth but she let her legs go limp, not wanting to go anywhere with this monster but he gripped her arms and lifted. The pain of her own weight forced her to get her feet under her and walk. Reaching a grassy hollow, he released her. She tried to run but in her panic and without arms to balance, she fell hard after only a few steps.

"Ya better get used to this," he said in a condescending tone. "The more ya fight the more it's gonna hurt. Now it's my turn ta have some fun," he smirked and lashed her ankles together so the most she could do was rollover.

Looking squarely into her tear-filled eyes, his hands moved to the buttons on the front of her shirt and unbuttoned them one by one. The shirt gapped open revealing bulging breasts in a tight brasserie. Ruth shook her head violently, trying to rid her mouth of the stifling gag.

"God I love it when a woman cries," Hobbs muttered.

Grasping her brassiere with both hands, he pulled and the clasp in the back gave way. Her breasts burst into full view, nipples protruding, not in arousal but in fear. Sitting on her stomach, Clarence cupped each breast in his hands, the silky smooth softness causing a rush of lustful pleasure to permeate his body.

"You got some damn nice titties, girly," he growled in a voice ragged with lust.

Purposefully, he tweaked and rolled her nipples, then crazed by the sight and feel, leaned forward and took one of them in his mouth.

"Just like lickin' the business end of a bullet," he groaned, admiring the smooth pink surface.

Palming the side of each breast he pushed them together and moved his mouth and tongue back and forth from one nipple to the other. Ruth silently sobbed and twisted her body in an effort to move, to get her breasts away from the madman's persistent assault.

Hobbs' hands and mouth left her breasts and worked slowly down her body. He repositioned himself moving from her belly to her thighs until he reached the waistband of her jeans. He sat up and Ruth tried to sit up, too, but he put a hand to her throat and pushed her back down.

Squealing from the pain, a white-hot flash of anger flooded her mind along with a silent promise.

I will kill you!

Slipping his fingers under the waistband of her jeans, Hobbs lifted her briefly then let her back down. The buckle of her belt came apart easily and he undid the button on her pants and pulled down the zipper. The fly pulled apart and Ruth's white panties came into view like the pearl-handled grips of her son's pistol.

Clarence took a deep-ragged breath.

"Gotta slow it down, this is way too good to rush."

His whisper trembled with lustful desire. Placing his hands on her flat belly, he slid both thumbs under the waistband of her panties and pulled down. Ruth's pale-blond pubic hairs immerged from her panties as his thumbs moved further down her belly. Her body jerked with an involuntarily spasm when his thumbs neared her most intimate place.

He tried pulling her jeans farther down but he had no leverage and she wasn't helping. She tried to jerk her knees up but with him on her thighs, the attempt was futile.

"You're a real fighter, missy, but I got all night. I'll wear ya out more ways than one."

Slipping his hands underneath her backside, Hobbs grabbed her jean pockets and jerked. With Ruth's hands tied behind her back, her bottom was elevated just enough to allow him to pull her pants down over the swell of her bottom. Now, only his position on her thighs prevented him from further access.

Ruth was tiring; her arms ached from their awkward position behind her back, her own weight threatened to rip them from their shoulder sockets. Ross and Lilly wouldn't expect her home until late, she was helpless and this monster was going to play with her until she no longer had the strength to resist. The thought sickened her, but she knew if she vomited, she would choke on the gag.

Crawling off her legs, Clarence worked her jeans down to her bound ankles. He took a moment to admire his work while she lay helpless before him. Her proud breasts were red from his abuse, the nipples taunt from his teasing, her smooth flat tummy tapering to a tiny waist then flaring again over shapely hips and legs. He left her panties on to prolong the ultimate thrill of seeing her completely naked and helpless…of making her his.

Ruth clenched her legs together as tightly as she could with her waning strength. He forced his hand between her knees and slid it upward along the inside of her thighs, the nearer his hand came to the precious junction of her thighs the less pressure she could apply to stop it. When he came in contact with the dampness of her panties Ruth jerked as if she'd received an electric shock.

Anger consumed her and she tried to focus on her revenge. She knew who he was, where he worked. If he thought he could treat her like a common whore and live, he'd better think again.

Clarence also reacted to the contact. With his lust beyond containment he stood, undid his pants, pulled her knees apart and forced himself between them. Kneeling between her legs, his breath now labored and raspy, he slipped his fingers under the waistband and his thumbs under the leg bands of her panties and jerked.

Clarence Hobbs didn't hear the sound of the panties ripping from Ruth's trembling body. He never saw the final fruits of his savage, selfish, lustful attack. All he saw was blackness, all he felt was the sudden sharp pain when a powerful fist stuck him in the face; the blow sending him flying backwards. Landing flat on his back, he fought to clear his head and find the reason for his sudden pain. Rolling instinctively in a defensive maneuver, Hobbs saw the blurry bulk of a man just before the attacker landed on him.

Ruth had her eyes closed, desperately trying to block out the revolting reality of her situation when there was a loud 'crack'. The legs she was so valiantly trying to keep together suddenly slammed shut, banging her knees against each other with a resounding smack. Her eyes popped wide open and she watched helplessly while two men fought over her like she was a prize at some stock show.

Clarence continued rolling, trying to regain his senses and his feet. He wasn't a big man but he was strong and agile, he'd fought a lot of men and left most bleeding in the dirt, but now he was confused. What had hit him? Who had hit him? The 'who' grabbed his arm and jerked him to his feet, a blow to Hobbs' gut doubled him over and an upper-cut left him dazed, bleeding and suddenly scared.

"Don't kill me!" he yelled, running half-blind as blows continued to rain down on his back, head and shoulders.

He reached the road in full-flight and fell face down bleeding, covering his head with his arms, waiting to be struck again. Nothing happened. Recovered enough to figure out where he was, Hobbs struggled to his feet, located his horse and made a run for it, no longer thinking about the woman or his lustful plans. He knew he'd be lucky if he could escape with his life.

Ruth, bound and terrified, watched her attacker run from his assailant. She saw the victor, who was dirty with an un-kept black beard, turn to walk purposely toward where she lay, naked and helpless. When he reached her side he removed his shirt and she closed her eyes, wishing she could die before having to endure more humiliating abuse.

"Are you bien, alright, Señora?" Sam blurted, instantly regretting the stupid question.

Covering her exposed body as much as possible with his shirt Sam moved to Ruth's feet and untied her ankles. It was then he realized her hands were tied behind her back.

"Bueno, this is awkward," he whispered, then said aloud, "Señora, I must turn you on your side to untie your hands, please do not be afraid, I will not hurt you."

He realized he was speaking slowly and carefully as if talking to a child. So focused was he on getting her untied, while not looking at her exposed body, Sam failed to notice the gag in her mouth until he freed her hands. Though she quickly removed it, Ruth was unable to speak, her body convulsed with sobs, pain and revulsion. Sam tried to comfort her to no avail. Feeling helpless and at a loss, having no experience with any woman except his mother, he turned to leave.

Ruth's mind slowly began to function clearly. This man saved her and meant her no harm. Quickly standing, she pulled her pants up, fastened them and buttoned her torn shirt.

"Wait," she called to him, then noticed the stripe down his trouser leg.

He's a soldier!

Relief cascaded over her like a waterfall on a hot day.

"Don't go, don't leave me alone. If you leave me that horrible man will come back." Her voice was weak and pleading.

Sam turned and for the first time since finding this woman, and a scene that challenged his senses, he actually looked at her. Until now he'd been intent on saving her from the unthinkable abuse she was suffering and destroying her evil abuser. After driving her attacker away, he was humiliated and embarrassed for her vulnerable, exposed condition. Having never seen a naked woman, Sam was stunned and carefully averted his eyes to focus on her bindings. He was almost afraid that looking upon her would cause him to turn to stone or the biblical pillar of salt.

She is beautiful, he thought, like my mother. He unexpectedly felt an inexplicable compassion for this vulnerable stranger. He knew he would do anything he could to help this woman, even if it meant risking his own freedom, or his life.

"How may I help you?" he asked cautiously. "Do you live around here, do you need a doctor? Is there a town nearby?"

She answered him with questions of her own. "Who are you and how did you find me? Are you a soldier?"

She began to sway and her knees buckled slightly. Sam rushed to her side before she collapsed.

"Sentarse, sit down," he said, and taking her arm eased her to the grassy surface. "It is going to be alright," he said softly. "Esta bien. Try to relax, breath slowly and deeply. I will be glad to take you to a doctor if you know where we can find one."

Looking into her frightened green eyes, Sam realized her pupils were dilated and her face was ashen. He stepped away to give her space. She turned away and vomited…one body-wrenching dry heave after another.

Sam felt as if like his guts were being twisted while he watched and listened to the poor woman. He thought of his mother, how he watched her suffer during her sickness, helpless, praying that God would give him her sickness and make her well. Thankfully, this woman was not sick but in shock, her body not at the mercy of some unrelenting illness with no cure. She was suffering but for her there was hope, she just needed time, care and understanding.

Gradually, Sam noticed color returning to the woman's face. With her condition improved, he was struck with a mind-jerking realization. So concerned was he for this poor woman and her well-being, he'd forgotten about the son-of-a-bitch that attacked her. What if he had a horse and a gun nearby and came back to get even with him and the woman? Quickly assuring Ruth he wasn't leaving her, that he would be back for her, Sam headed in the direction where he last saw the man.

The search did not take long, he found where the man crossed the road, obviously still on the run, and had gone over the bank. There he found a single set of horse tracks leading back onto the road and headed in the opposite direction from which Sam first saw the riders pass. With little to do but hope the man didn't plan to ambush them later, he nervously returned to the woman, still sitting where he'd left her.

"Mi llamo is Samuel, Señora. Samuel DeSoto."

Sam was surprised he did not lie and use a fake name, he just didn't have time to think, so concerned was he about this poor lady.

"Ruth Riley," she said, embarrassed at her lack of social protocol. "You saved my life," she blurted. "If you hadn't come along when you did I would have died, whether that awful man killed me or not." Her voice cracked and again she fought back tears. "How can I ever repay you? Come home with me, we have horses, cattle, we have money, I want to pay you for saving my life."

It was Sam's turn to be embarrassed. He had given no thought to being rewarded. He simply found a woman in trouble and did what any man would do; at least he hoped it was what any man would do. In the back of his mind he heard the words; 'Do not be stupid, this is your chance to have your own horse and saddle, your own clothes and money!'

"I found your horses, ma'am, they are tied a ways from here along with mine. I will get them and come back for you and then I will go with you until you are safely home," he said.

"No!" she screamed, startled, Sam dove for the ground, searching for the source of her exclamation. She almost smiled at the sight of Sam flat on the ground, eyes darting from tree to bush.

"No," she repeated less emphatically. "Don't leave me alone. I can walk. I'll go get the horses with you."

Sam was acutely aware that this woman's physical injuries were going to heal much faster than the psychological damage. He felt a responsibility to get her home to her family where she could be taken care of.

When Ruth saw Cocoa she sobbed again and dropped to her knees while Sam watched, feeling helpless. Seeing her horse jolted Ruth's mind into thoughts of home, of Ross, Larry and Lilly, mixed with shame and relief. A wave of panic swept over her. Ross will want to kill the bastard when he hears what happened. She thought of Larry, depending on Doc Jensen to stave off an infection that could threaten his life, the shattering of Lilly's innocence when she heard what someone did, or tried to do, to her mother. It was all too much.

Sam was beside himself, for the time being he forgot about his problems, significant though they were. He was getting a crash course in women and the fragility of their emotions and was beginning to regret letting the asshole that did this get away. Not only might he be out there somewhere with a gun, stalking them, but it was becoming apparent to Sam the man deserved to die for what he did to this woman…this Ruth Riley.

He remained silent as Ruth slowly regained her composure. It was almost dark when they rode into the ranch complex that was the Running R. Ross rushed to meet them, stopping abruptly to assess the rider-less gray, the scruffy looking soldier accompanying his wife, and his wife.

"What's going on Ruth, where's Larry?" Ross asked, not sure he wanted to know.

With all the self-control she could muster, Ruth firmly said, "Ross let us take care of the horses then we'll go in the house."

Ross knew instantly, something was very wrong.

Despite Ruth's protests, Sam insisted that if shown where things were, he would be glad to take care of the horses. She and Ross should go in the house and leave the chores to him. Ruth finally agreed, saying she would send Lillian out to help him.

It was Ross' turn to protest, he didn't like the looks of this very un-military looking soldier.

"I don't think that's a good idea Ruth," he said, giving Sam a skeptical eye.

"It will be fine, Ross," she said, with a do-not-mess-with-me edge to her voice that could cut ice blocks from a frozen lake. "Come in the house and I will explain everything."

Ruth had found her inner strength; she was past shame and vulnerability…she was mad as hell.

Sam was leading the horses toward the barn when Lillian caught up with him. She opened her mouth to speak but no words came out.

Yuk, she thought.

He was awful; he was dirty, he stunk and the hair on his face looked like a home for rodents. Quickly taking her mom's chestnut, Cocoa, and Drifter from him, Lilly motioned toward an empty stall at the far end of the barn.

"You can put your horse in there, might want to stay there with her." Embarrassed by her own rudeness, she added, "I'll get your horse some grain and ask Mom where she wants you to stay tonight."

"Stay tonight." Were the only words Lillian spoke that registered with him, everything else was like a harpsichord he heard one once in California, and it was the most beautiful sound he'd ever heard…until now. Not only did this girl have the voice of an angel, she was beyond beautiful, she was devastating. He remembered his reflection from the river and was suddenly sad and humiliated.

"I look like death before breakfast," he whispered in disgust.

Lilly quickly went about the chores of feeding, watering, brushing and putting away tack. Sam felt useless along with ugly and dirty.

Finally finished, Lillian said, "Wait here, I'll go see where Mom wants you to sleep. I'm sure the loft would be fine but there's no smoking up there."

"That will be perfect, Señorita," he managed to reply adding, "I do not smoke anyway."

For Sam, the loft in the Riley's barn might just as well have been his own room in heaven. He didn't sleep well because his mind was too busy replaying the nearly overwhelming events of the day. Still, it was the best night he'd spent since the night before he and one thousand soldiers had followed Colonel Wolard into that unspeakable valley of death.

The next morning, Ruth bore only a few outward signs of her ordeal. Her wrists were red and a little swollen from being bound, her eyes were red from crying, there was a small cut on her lip from the gag being forced into her mouth, and a scratch on her cheek from when she tried to roll away from her attacker. Ruth withheld the sordid details from Ross for his own good, making light of the attack but praising Sam for arriving in time to run the man off.

Ross was livid, furious that his wife was attacked, furious that anyone in the Flathead would dare to mistreat her, furious that the man who did it was still on the loose. His anger was tempered only by gratefulness to the man in the barn for saving Ruth from even greater harm, and his concern for Larry.

Lillian was full of questions; questions no one seemed willing to answer.

"Who is the guy in the barn? When was the last time he had a bath? Why is he here anyway? and why are you wearing your gun? Where's Larry? And why are you wearing your gun?" she repeated.

She was addressing Ross and the bone-handled .45 holstered at mid-thigh. Her dad never wore his gun in the house.

"Larry is with Doc Jensen in Horse Plain, the doctor is very worried about infection in his ear," Ruth explained. "Your father and I are going there and with good luck we will bring him home soon."

Ruth's concern for Larry was the only thing holding off the awful memories of the humiliation and abuse she'd suffered.

"I'm going too," Lillian stated, fighting the guilt of **not** packing the traps and starting the race to begin with. "He's my brother, even if he is a jerk, and I want to see him."

"We could be gone for a few days, Lilly," Ross began. "We need you to stay and take care of the stock, and you know I like to take my gun to town."

"Hopefully, we can convince Sam to stay here with you," Ruth interrupted. "He can help with the chores and you will be completely safe with him. And Lilly, after Sam is cleaned up, have him make up a bed in the bunkhouse. I don't want him sleeping in the barn while we're gone."

"Are you completely out of your mind?" Lilly exploded. "I'm not staying anywhere near that filthy bum." The fiery redhead stomped her foot for emphasis then in a subdued tone said, "I can't believe you'd even think of leaving me here with that…that…man!" Tears welled up in her sparkling blue eyes.

"Lilly," Ruth said softly. "When we get back with Larry I will explain, but for now please believe we would never put you at risk. We know you can take care of yourself but trust me, Sam is a good man and will treat you like the young lady you are. Your dad and I will have enough to worry about with Larry so please; we need you to do this for us…and for Larry."

"You call him Sam. Sam what? I don't even know his name and you want to leave me here with him? And besides he stinks!" Lillian protested.

Ross and Ruth were united on one front. The guy in the barn was welcome no matter who he was, though he did need a bath and a shave.

"I'll talk to him," Ross said. "I'll tell him his first chore is to take a bath and we'll set out some of Larry's clothes. They should fit him pretty well."

Lillian knew this matter was settled whether she like it or not, and she did not.

Chapter Eleven

Exhumation

"Does it really matter so much?" Ta-keen Eagle asked Laughing Doe.

"The one called French took the amulet and left the valley. It was gone for many winters before Standing Wolf returned with it. I wish Standing Wolf would return to the valley and to Star Flower and forget about the amulet. The one who took it has no reason to return to this place."

The Sematuse chief was more concerned about the emotions of his sister, who was very sad and lonely without Standing Wolf, and about Bent Grass. She was so important to their tribe and since her son left the valley, she had become obsessed with the Spirit Cave. She spent nearly all her time, day and night, in the cave waiting for a sign, a vision of his whereabouts, his well-being.

Laughing Doe rolled onto her back and threw the light covering of rabbit fur aside, revealing her exquisite feminine charms and purred, "So now the first thing you think of, with the rising of Sister Sun, is the amulet. Am I no longer your first thought causing *you* to *rise* before Sister Sun?"

A quick smile broke Ta-keen Eagle's otherwise stone face. With everything that had happened, his wife did not change. She was still the most playful, sexually charged, sensuous woman he could imagine. "It is only because as chief, I have a great many things on my mind."

Sitting, Laughing Doe pulled the rabbit-throw up over her breasts and with a proud toss of her long black hair, she rose to start her day. It was elderberry-gathering time and she and Willow had a cluster of bushes already selected.

"Will you speak with Star Flower? She, too, does not understand why Standing Wolf feels that retrieving the amulet is so important," said Ta-keen Eagle. "She worries he may return to the *ska ha wicasan*, the white-clay people, as do I."

"Willow and I will ask Star Flower to gather elderberries with us. We can talk but it will not be easy to make her feel better as long as her man is gone."

Knowing Laughing Doe and Willow would do what could be done to ease his sister's anxiety, Ta-keen Eagle set out in search of Warm Hands. After that fateful day, the chief's worries about the white-clay humans driving his people from this valley were greatly diminished. He understood the True People were protected by a powerful Great Spirit, *Ogle Wa Nagi*, which could be called by many names but was the force that would keep his people free to live in the old ways.

Ta-keen Eagle's mind was at ease but he remained perplexed by the unexplained arrival of the three visitors. Lone Frank, Spotted Fawn and Standing Wolf, who did what occurred only once before in the memory of his people; they entered the sacred valley of the Sematuse. This would have been strange enough but it turned out they were connected to one another beyond the valley. In fact French, the first visitor to the valley was Standing Wolf's father, Lone Frank was Spotted Fawn's father and Standing Wolf, Frank and Spotted Fawn had known each other outside the valley.

"It all means something," he muttered as he wandered through the village toward the medicine man's cupola.

Warm Hands council was always helpful to Ta-keen Eagle. The medicine man had an understanding of things beyond *pezuat*, medicine. He found Warm Hands staring at a basket full of willow bark.

"What are you planning for that?" Ta-keen Eagle asked, motioning at the basket of bark.

"I am not sure," replied Warm Hands. "It is very good *pezuat*. I am thinking that adding a little to our teepee fires in winter might be good. The smoke would be like taking medicine every day. I thought

I would start with a small fire as the nights cool. If it works for me it should work for all, especially the little ones. It is Spotted Fawn's idea," he added proudly, always ready to give credit to others, especially his self-proclaimed daughter and protégé.

"I wish to speak with you of Spotted Fawn, my friend, and of Frank and Standing Wolf. All came to this sacred place from a world outside of this valley, yet all are connected." Ta-keen Eagle said and studied the medicine man for a reaction.

Warm Hands motioned for Ta-keen Eagle to sit. He realized this was going somewhere and knowing his chief, it could take a while.

"Are you saying their arrivals were not random events, my chief?" he inquired, encouraging Ta-keen Eagle to continue.

"It is clear the arrival of Standing Wolf was no accident. He was sent by *Ogle Wa Nagi* to protect us from the white soldiers. Yet he knew both Frank and Spotted Fawn outside our valley. Does that not seem strange to you?"

"Strange, yes, but not a fact that caused us harm…it actually brought us peace and happiness. They have taught us much. We now know Standing Wolf is the Chosen One and will protect us by calling upon our ancestors when needed. Does it not make your heart soar to know our ancestors are with us; that they live in the aspen leaves and the thunderclouds even when we can not see them? Frank and Spotted Fawn were a gift to me from *Ogle Wa Nagi*, they tested my medicine and taught me how to care." Warm Hands sober expression turned to a sly grin. "Like you, my chief, I know little of the world outside our home but because of Frank and Spotted Fawn, I know there is good among people…even *ska ha wicasan,* white-clay people."

"Do you not wonder why *Ogle Wa Nagi* told our people we can not leave this valley, yet Standing Wolf has come and gone with the talisman given to him by his mother? Even that white soldier who stole the amulet was able to leave. Perhaps, as her chief, I should instruct Bent Grass to make such an amulet for you and me so we can go out and look over that other world. Perhaps there are other *ska ha wicasan* we should invite into our valley."

"Do not forget, my Chief," Warm Hands calmly replied, "except for Standing Wolf, who possessed the amulet, all others who entered this valley have done so accompanied by *Tlchachie Manitu*, the Spirit of Death.

Perhaps the amulet allows you to leave but you can only return with *Tlchachie Manitu*."

"If that is true, then I must leave you behind, my friend so you can steal my *tlchachie* from the darkness and return it to the light," Ta-keen Eagle joked.

"Perhaps," Warm Hands turned serious. "You have enough light here in the valley of rainbows. This is our world and had I been asked for my advice by Standing Wolf, I would have told him to forget about the soldier and the amulet, to stay with his people as chosen by *Ogle Wa Nagi*, to be happy with what is, not what might be." He paused for a moment, then holding his hands out, palms up, added, "But he is the Chosen One, not I, perhaps he gets his advice from *Chopaka*."

"I would not be concerned for Standing Wolf. I believe he is guided by *Ogle Wa Nagi*. It is only because my sister weeps for him and I must wipe away her tears that I fret. I believe when he has done what he must do he will return to Star Flower and this valley, with or without the amulet."

Ta-keen Eagle let his eyes wander around the cupola, filled with assorted herbs, barks, feathers, claws and the various skins that adorned the abode.

"What is it he must do besides find and return the amulet?" Warm Hands queried.

"*Ogle Wa Nagi* called him *Waboka*. Bent Grass speaks of a time when *Waboka* will call on all the Native People to do the Dance of *Tlchachie*, Ghost Dance, a dance in which all of the Native People will join hands and dance in a circle like the sun circling Mother Earth. It is then that all *ska ha wicasan* who have mistreated the Native People will be swallowed by Mother Earth. It will be a time of *exhumation* when the Native People rise from the darkness and reclaim the land. At that time, the veil protecting our valley will be lifted and we will be free to roam the land as our ancestors did without fear of *ska ha wicasan*. There will no longer be reservations; the land will again belong to the people and the animals."

"Maybe that is why the visitors were sent to our valley, maybe they were chosen by Standing Wolf to be saved. That could be the connection, Standing Wolf knew they were good *ska ha wicasan* and sent them here to be saved. Now he is free to go start a Dance of *Tlchachie* that will lead to the end of reservations and the oppression of the True People." Warm Hands was beginning to warm up to this conversation.

"Why would *Ogle Wa Nagi* choose one who is half Sematuse and half *ska ha wicasan* to be *Waboka*, the Messiah?" Ta-keen Eagle pressed, sensing he was gaining the medicine man's interest.

"If you were given the power to save one animal, say the bear or the fox, would it not be better if you could live as a fox and a bear before choosing?" Warm Hands asked.

"Perhaps, but I do not believe Standing Wolf has the power to choose, the choice was made, he was given the power to act on it."

"If Frank and Spotted Fawn are here because of Standing Wolf, do you think the time of *exhumation* is near?" Warm Hands wanted to hear more of Bent Grass' proclamation.

"It is difficult to say but if what happened to the soldiers was a sign, then it could be soon. That is another matter I wish to speak with you about; what the *ska ha wicasan* call time. We count time from daylight until dark, from moon to moon, from fishing, to gathering, to hunting. Outside our valley I think time may be different." Ta-keen Eagle halted his speech abruptly, seemingly puzzled by his own words.

"Different how?" Warm Hands coaxed.

"I am not sure, but Lone Frank told me *ska ha wicasan* use something called 'clock'. It tells them when to start their day and when to finish. He said many great battles have begun when 'clock' said it was time, no matter what sign Sister Sun and Brother Moon gave them." Ta-keen Eagle studied his friend for a reaction, then added, "Even Spotted Fawn said they could only eat at the place she calls 'orphanage' when 'clock' said it was time; no matter if you were hungry or not. Of course she said she was always hungry."

"If Sister Sun or Brother Moon did speak to *ska ha wicasan* I doubt he would listen. No wonder Frank was loco when he came to the valley; he spent too much time listening to 'clock'." Warm Hands laughed and slapped his knee, amused by his own joke then added, "I really doubt Frank listened to 'clock', I think he listened only to wood rats." Warm hands then asked, being only slightly more serious, "Does 'clock' tell *ska ha wicasan* when to make love to his woman and when the berries are ready for wine?"

Ta-keen Eagle replied, "I believe the thing called time does not matter. When the dance is done and the *exhumation* occurs, it will **be**, no matter what 'clock' or Sister Sun or Brother Moon says. If there is a sign to tell us of the *exhumation,* Bent Grass will be the first to know." Ta-keen Eagle's awe of the seer was apparent.

He said, "*Ogle Wa Nagi* is known to us in many ways and by many names, *Chopaka, Sunk Manitu Tanka, Wakan Tanka* even *Waboka.* Perhaps we have missed the greatest *Tlchachie* of all living right in our midst…Bent Grass. She practically lives in the cave of *tlchachies* and sees things that have yet to happen. She even sees things that happen outside our valley."

Warm Hands was becoming impatient. "You seek many answers, my Chief, let us go speak with Bent Grass; perhaps she will share with us the knowledge of the ages."

Ta-keen Eagle understood Warm Hands well, and knew this conversation was finished. It would start again only if Bent Grass was in a mood to speak to them.

They were surprised to find the seer sitting in the shade of an aspen grove talking to Lone Frank. They seemed unlikely friends but actually had quite a lot in common. Both were loners, both experienced life-changing experiences in the spirit cave, Frank had known her son in another life outside the valley, and Bent Grass had made an amulet for Frank.

An amulet with the painting of the sacred black wolf with golden eyes was such a sacred symbol, not even Chief Ta-keen Eagle or his father Chief Chewaken possessed it. It allowed someone to leave and re-enter the valley without harm. The only other way for this to happen was for a person to be guided by *Sunk Manitu Tanka*, or the sacred black wolf.

"It is a fine day to be a Sematuse," Ta-keen Eagle greeted Bent Grass, then acknowledging Frank added, "or a dead trapper who was given back his life by an amazing medicine man." It was a rare attempt at humor by the proud chief.

"That would be a pretty good joke if it was not true Chief," Frank retorted, not good at the social protocol of the Sematuse.

"It is a fine day, my Chief," Bent Grass responded in a manner showing the proper respect with which to address a chief.

Ta-keen Eagle, as was his custom, got right to the point. "Star Flower is very lonely. She is afraid Standing Wolf will not return." He looked to Warm Hands. When the medicine man said nothing, he continued, "Do your visions tell anything of his mission or his return?"

Frank opened his mouth to speak but one glance from Bent Grass's black eyes froze the words in his mouth.

"I, too, am troubled," she began. "I have had visions and I have come to realize that he who possesses the amulet walks with *Sunk Manitu Tanka*. He is protected by *Sunk Manitu Tanka*. I am not sure what the future holds when two men, with very different purposes, possess an amulet." Bent Grass sighed. "I made the amulet for Frank so he could be of help to Standing Wolf and so he could take care of his trap line. Those two would have been as one, but with one amulet in the possession of a horse soldier I am concerned."

"Do you fear for his life?" Warm Hands interjected, showing as much respect for the seer as for their chief.

"No, he is protected. I am afraid the soldier will find out he has the power of *Sunk Manitu Tanka* and will use it to bring soldiers back to our valley while Standing Wolf is gone." She looked toward the big mountain, *Chopaka*, its top shrouded in a misty fog and said, "Without Standing Wolf we are not safe from the soldiers."

Again Fire-hair Frank opened his mouth to speak but Bent Grass stopped him. "This is no one's fault but mine," she said, placing her hand on his arm. "Frank wanted only to help. No one could have expected that soldier to react the way he did. I wish I knew what to do. There is no way to bring Standing Wolf back until he finds that amulet."

Frank finally managed to speak. "If only I could go after him, I could find him and explain why he needs to return, amulet or not."

"What makes you think you can find him?" Ta-keen Eagle asked, dubious.

"Don't know that I could, Chief," Frank stated. "Just wish I could do something besides sit around and worry."

Spotted Fawn and Little Beaver approached the group in a high-spirited mood.

"Father," Spotted Fawn exuberantly announced, "we are going to the river of rainbows to see if the big fish are here yet. Would you like to come with us?" She quickly covered her mouth in apology for her interruption.

Bent Grass waved a delicate hand at Frank. "Go, enjoy this time with your daughter. There is nothing to be done about this matter now."

Little Beaver held out a new spear he had carved from the stock of a young yew wood tree. Porcupine quills, inserted into the pointed end, were wrapped with horsehair to secure the quills. The butt-end was notched and a braided horsehair rope was attached; the coiled rope allowed the thrower to pull a speared fish to the bank, where a quick jerk of the spear would release the fish.

Little Beaver waited patiently for the proper accolades before flashing a proud smile and taking Spotted Fawn's hand, leaving a question in the minds of those watching whether his pride was for the spear or his lovely young wife.

As the trio walked away, Spotted Fawn hand-in-hand with her husband and her father, Ta-keen Eagle spoke. "There go three reasons why we must not fail in keeping this valley sacred and our people free."

Chapter Twelve

Noisy Waters

Standing Wolf studied the scene of the apparent panic with renewed determination.

"This has to be were Sam and his companions parted ways," he muttered.

However, after leading Whiskey up and down both sides of the small tributary, he found no sign where a single rider broke away from the band.

He continued mumbling to himself, which reminded him of Lone Frank. "There is only one possibility; he had to break free of the band and leave the river-bend by riding in the water."

Satisfied that he had reached the only logical conclusion he now needed only to decide which way Sam went…up stream or down?

He is not going to follow the Indians, he concluded. But there was a new problem. With the water so low, Sam could follow the river, never having to leave the water until the river ended. Unless Standing Wolf watched each bank very carefully, he could miss a departure from the watery trail.

He can't camp in the river.

"I will feel a whole better if I find where he has camped."

Moving slowly downstream along the river for several days, Standing Wolf finally found a single set of tracks and the remains of a small fire. Confident he was on Sam's trail, Standing Wolf felt a twinge of excitement tempered by stark reality. If Sam camped there his first night after separating from the Indian band, it meant the distance he had traveled in several days, Sam had covered in one.

"I am not going to catch him unless he stops someplace."

Standing Wolf accessed the situation while he prepared to camp for the night. His progress thus far was slow because he had to watch both banks, and he could not travel at night for fear he would miss Sam's tracks leaving the river. His only choice was to continue what he was doing and hope Sam found a reason to slow down.

His thoughts returned to Janis Crossing and the unexplained killing of soldiers and settlers. What ever happened there cost him his best chance of catching Sam and getting the amulet back. While Standing Wolf regreted that diversion more with each passing day, he was intrigued by the ghastly scene, who had died and who or what had killed them?

His initial thought was that one of the tribes from the northern *Okinakane*, angry over attempts to move them to the Sand Flats, had attacked a wagon train of settlers escorted by a company of cavalrymen. However, he found no sign of women among the dead.

An advance party?

From his experience with Custer's 7th along the Missouri and in the Powder River country, Standing Wolf knew settlers got one chance for a military escort, which meant everything, including women and children, were part of the wagon train. He pondered who could secure a military escort.

Politicians or prospectors?

Not unless they were rich prospectors. That thought made him smile and his mind turned to Lone Frank, Star Flower and the valley.

"Now there is another mystery," he exclaimed to his non-speaking partner. "How do Frank, his daughter and I wind up in a hidden valley where entry is only granted by the sacred black wolf or the amulet?"

He left the question hanging for a moment, then with no response from Whiskey, continued, "And what about Roy? He led the colonel and his troops into the valley through the black wolf's spirit trail. How could he have known about it? Did the wolf show him and if so why?"

Standing Wolf shook his head and began preparing for another night on the trail. There were more immediate concerns than the mysteries surrounding the valley and Roy. He had to stay on Sam's trail and he needed to eat. He found a patch of huckleberries along the riverbank.

"Now, if I got a grouse or a rabbit I would have dinner and desert."

The trail was slow and tedious but a pattern was emerging. With the constant checking along both sides of the river, and the occasional backtrack to be sure he hadn't missed anything, Standing Wolf was camping three nights to Sam's one. It was apparent Sam was using the river to put as much distance between him and his past as possible.

Does he know where he is going?

Not much chance, he thought. The 5th Cavalry under Colonel Wolard's Command came west from Kansas so it was unlikely anyone in his command was familiar with the upper Columbia River country.

The trail was growing older and colder with each passing day and when the river he was following narrowed into a deep rock cut, Standing Wolf left it to ride around the gorge. Soon the river merged with another larger river, and the trail ended. He could find no sign beyond a few faint tracks leading into the larger river. There was no way to know if Sam went upstream, downstream or even if he crossed to the other side.

Standing Wolf slid off Whiskey, knelt, picked up a rock and flung it into the water. The rock hit the surface with a ka-plunk and sank to the bottom, much like Standing Wolf's hopes of finding Sam and retrieving the amulet. He was disappointed and fast becoming disillusioned. He grasped the amulet hanging around his neck and held it the way he did when doing the Ghost Dance.

"I could use a little help here," he whispered to whatever power might be listening. "Probably couldn't hear me anyhow," he muttered, his words muffled by a distant roar coming from downstream.

The words no more than slipped from his lips and he saw the buildings across the river.

"What do we have here?" he questioned. "Could be a military outpost, could be a trading post." He was thinking out-loud. "We better take a closer look."

He guided Whiskey into the water and after a short swim, moved quickly into the cover of a conifer forest. Dismounting and leaving Whiskey ground tied, Standing Wolf worked his way through the forest undergrowth toward the nearest building. The roar he had been hearing since reaching the river became increasingly louder as he neared the log structure. There, he saw men, white men in black robes.

Missionaries.

Next, he saw Indians, bare-chested with only loin-clothes around their waists. Some were entering the building carrying large fish, others were milling around with long-handled spears and bucket-type devices. Satisfied that there was no military presence, Standing Wolf decided to mingle and see if anyone knew anything about Sam.

Moving closer, the roar became deafening until it finally registered; waterfall. There was a large group of Indians busy with spears and unusual shaped baskets, balanced precariously on planks jutting out from the rock formations along the falls. He watched, fascinated, as they caught the big fish attempting to navigate the falls.

Standing Wolf learned the place was called *Shonitkwu,* meaning roaring or noisy waters. He was amazed to discover there were Indians who came from a place beyond the Pasayten called *Nootka.* The *Nootka* spoke Chinook and were said to have carried their 'fishing planks' all the way from the ocean. There were also Sioux and Cheyenne from the Black Hills and Flathead country, even a few Arapaho from the Tongue River but most of them were Nespelems.

Standing Wolf learned how to stand on a plank, and with a spear given to him by a Nootka Indian, he was able to spear several fish for himself. After much celebrating and back-slapping he took his fish to the small trading outpost, where he learned that he was back on the Columbia River and about a five-day ride upstream of Long Rapids. He also learned that the river he spent days tracking Sam on was known as *Ne-hoi-al-pit-kwu,* meaning Kettle or Kettle River, because of the kettle-shaped valley at its headwaters.

No one knew anything of a lone, horse soldier anywhere near the falls, though some Nespelems told a story of a headless soldier who rode with a band of much feared Indians called *Sarsapkins.* They told how this band, led by the headless horse soldier, had killed many white men and drove the soldiers from a fort they called Okanogan. No one actually knew where the *Sarsapkins* came from, but it was believed they were from somewhere in the mountains of the upper *Okinakane* where they were called *Choo-pin-it-pa-loo,* meaning People of the Mountains.

Standing Wolf listened to the stories attentively and with some interest but chuckled inside. This is how stories get started, he thought. He had not heard of the *Sarsapkins* before and thought he had contacted nearly all of the tribes and bands of the *Okinakane*. Could there be another hidden valley? He found that thought intriguing.

When he asked about Chief Little Moses, Standing Wolf was told the chief had gone to meet with many other chiefs along the Okanogan and Columbia Rivers to speak about reservations and the treatment of Indians including the Yakimas, Walla Wallas, Wenatchees and Chelans. The Nespelems believed the chiefs were planning to drive the white settlers, prospectors and horse soldiers out of the land and reclaim what the white man called 'reservations.' It was clear the verdict was not yet in on the missionaries. Some wanted to rid the land of all whites, while others wanted the 'God Speaking' people to stay because they brought the traders with whom the Indians bartered for guns, blankets and even wagons.

Standing Wolf remembered, while speaking with these people, finding Sam and the amulet was only part of his mission. As the Messiah, he carried the responsibility of spreading word of the Ghost Dance among the Native People. He began to speak first in Salish then in Siouan, and a large, if disbelieving, crowd gathered. He told the story of the white buffalo, the black wolf, his mother, the amulet, the Ghost Dance and the proclamation by *Ogle Wa Nagi*, Great Spirit of the Sematuse,

As the story continued the fishing stopped and Indians, packing spears and dragging baskets, joined the growing crowd. Some listened wide-eyed and open mouthed, others smiled and laughed among themselves. When he ran out of story, the Indians returned to fishing with few comments and little reaction.

That went well, he thought sarcastically.

So there is trouble brewing in the *Okinakane*, he thought. That was what the Colonel and Roy had been most concerned about. It is not going to matter to them now. "Damn shame," he muttered, feeling a twinge of sadness. He had liked Roy, if only the scoundrel had listened to the shaman.

Standing Wolf knew from his experience in the white man's world, the only way for Indians to continue to live in the 'old ways' was to rid the land of the whites. Before the apocalyptic event in the valley, he would not have believed such a thing to be possible, but after seeing the power of the Ghost Dance he was definitely a believer. He was also a believer in the power of the amulet; though created by his mother, he was sure it was an earthly totem, a gift from the Great Spirit.

What he was less sure about was the power of the amulet when in the possession of a white man. The fact that Sam was not at the trading post, which he must have seen, told StandingWolf the man was still running scared.

Can you blame him?

He began to wonder if Sam was just lucky or if the amulet, assuming the he still had it, was providing some kind of spiritual guidance. Did the charm work for a white man as well as an Indian? Did it work for any Indian? His mother believed it would work for Frank and it worked when his father left the valley, but StandingWolf was with his father back then, even though he was only a boy…with the blood of Bent Grass running through his veins. Standing Wolf was not with Sam when he fled the valley so he was apparently protected by the sacred black wolf. That thought was a chilling one because Sam could pose a far greater threat to the Sematuse than Colonel Wolard or Generals Custer, Crook or Terry or any other military men he had known, all put together.

Another consideration Standing Wolf was becoming painfully aware of was that he was no longer in country he was familiar with. His mind drifted back in time to when he left the army on the Rosebud in the Montana Territory and headed west. He had wandered for uncounted days with absolutely no idea where he was; of course it was several days before he ran out of army whisky. Because he spoke *Siouan*, the language of the Sioux and Great Basin tribes, and *Salish*, the language spoken by most of the Inland Northwest tribes, he was able to make his way to the Columbia River and on to Vancouver, where he ultimately met Roy.

Standing Wolf was confident Sam had gone up the Columbia River from here, but even if he followed the river upstream he knew the chance of finding Sam's trail was remote at best. He decided to camp with the Indian fisherman for the night and see what he could find out about the upper Columbia, not sure how it might help but at this moment he had no better plan…in fact he had no plan at all.

He returned to the falls and enjoyed a few hours of fishing and conversation although communicating over the roar of the falls was difficult. He was thrilled by the challenge of throwing a spear and hitting a leaping salmon in mid-air. He was also fascinated by the efficient use of the *Ilth koy ape,* or J shaped baskets used to catch the leaping salmon as they fell back toward the water below the falls. The Nespelems and Flatheads seemed to be particularly astute with the use of the basket contraption.

He also spent some time speaking with the priests at the mission near the Hudson Bay Outpost. He was somewhat surprised to discover they had no knowledge of Bishop Donneli or a mission or reservation on the *Okinakane,* though they were aware of discussions concerning the establishment of a reservation to be called Colville, which would include the falls so the Indians could continue their traditional fishing.

When a French priest attempted to explain that though he was of the Catholic persuasion he was actually a Jesuit with little or no knowledge of the business of the Catholic Church, Standing Wolf stopped him.

"Father," he said, extending an outstretched palm, "I was sent to a Catholic school as a boy, I already know more about the church than I care to admit."

He quickly left the mission before being engaged in a conversation he had no interest in having. The next morning he shared a fish breakfast with a group calling themselves Coeur d' Alenes, which he enjoyed immensely. Then with his mind busy as a bear in a bee-hive and carrying a bag full of dried meat, fish and venison, two canteens and a bag of oats for Whiskey, Standing Wolf returned to his horse and headed up river along the left bank.

As the shadows grew longer and darkness began sliding from the surrounding mountains into the river valley, Standing Wolf camped at the mouth of a small tributary to the Columbia. There were many big fish in the stream and using his newly acquired spear he skewered one and cooked it. He very much liked the taste of these fish and was beginning to understand why some of the tribes along the Columbia were referred to as 'fish eaters'.

Spearing the fish took his mind back to the valley and Little Beaver and, of course, to Star Flower. Standing Wolf was having second thoughts about his mission. He remembered the nuns at his boyhood school spoke of losing faith; that if you lost your faith you were damned to the fires of hell. Even if you eventually returned to believing, your soul was eternally lost. That was one of many ways the nuns scared hell out of, or into, kids at the school.

With his belly full, he licked his lips and savored the lingering taste of fish. He had eaten half and decided to save the rest for breakfast. It was nearly dark when he was startled by approaching horsemen. As they drew within clear view he could see they were Indian, four of them on well-bred pinto ponies.

Dismounting, they approached Standing Wolf with much excitement. They had heard him speak of the Ghost Dance at the falls and very much wanted to hear more. They spoke the language of the Sioux but with a slightly different dialect which was difficult for him to understand.

The most outspoken of the group called himself *Wodziwob* (Gray Hair) and said he and two of his companions were Paiutes who came from a land two full moons toward the sun from this place and were, like some other tribes along the Columbia, called 'fish eaters'.

The fourth Indian, whose name Standing Wolf could not quite understand but thought it was Long Foot or Big Foot, said he was chief of a band of Minneconjous. Long Foot said many of his people shared a reservation with the Paiutes and that they were not happy. They had little game or fish on the reservation and given little food from the army.

Gray Hair interjected that the food was not enough for their people and was often rotten or spoiled. He then told a story that left Standing Wolf stunned.

"I had a vision in which I traveled to a beautiful valley where the forest was full of game and the lakes and streams full of fish. There, a giant black wolf instructed me to tell my people to do a dance of circles called a round dance and a Messiah would come to us and drive the white man off the land and the Native People would again be free to live in the old ways."

Gray Hair was very excited making it more difficult for Standing Wolf to understand all he said.

"When you told the story of your valley and that the Great Spirit of your people spoke to your mother and told her she had born the Chosen One; one the Spirit called *Waboka*, I knew you were the answer to my vision. Your story is as I saw it in my vision. It was as if my vision was speaking to me."

For the first time since leaving the valley, Standing Wolf felt the enormity of his gift, his blessing and his responsibility. Had he not been a part of the revelation in the valley of the Sematuse, he would not believe the power granted him by *Ogle Wa Nagi*. However, he was not without concern. Were *Ogle Wa Nagi*, Great Spirit of the Sematuse and *Wakan Tanka*, Great Spirit of the Sioux Nation the same, or was there only one Great Spirit and the rest imposters? What of the Minneconjous and Paiutes, did they have there own Great Spirit? Would the power given him by *Ogle Wa Nagi* work outside the valley? The proof it should be believed was that the Ghost Dance did not bring only the ancestors of the Sematuse to their defense, but those of many other tribes.

Never did it occurr to StandingWolf that anyone outside the valley would have any knowledge of the Ghost Dance or the Messiah. These people, maybe all Native People were looking to him for deliverance from the control of the white man; to hunt and fish again without the constraints of imposed and erroneous reservation boundaries.

"We want you to come with us to free our people so they can again live in the old ways." Gray Hair spoke with a hint of desperation and hope.

Standing Wolf felt a twinge of panic and uncertainty. To guarantee the safety of the Sematuse he must find Sam and return the amulet to his mother, but as the Messiah his responsibility was to all Native People. He proceeded to explain the importance of his finding the runaway soldier and retrieving the amulet, identical to the one around his neck, and returning it to his people.

They talked long into the night, but nothing would dissuade the visitor's determination that he must accompany them to Nevada and the reservation at Walker Lake.

"We must leave before the big fish stop coming to the falls because there are mountains we must cross before the snow comes. It will take two full moons to reach our people with the good news," Long Foot proclaimed.

If only my mother were here, Standing Wolf thought. She is the one to whom the Great Spirit speaks. I must call upon her wisdom to make the right choice.

By morning the sky was cloudy and the small group was awakened not by the smile of Sister Sun but by the sprinkling of raindrops. Standing Wolf realized Sam's trail was already lost and with rain coming the chances were slim to none of picking it up again.

Standing Wolf knew the army had no tolerance for deserters. When that desertion involved abandoning fellow soldiers during a battle, it meant a firing squad or hanging with no questions asked. He reminded himself that he, too, was a deserter…twice, sort of. It was clear that Sam was running scared, probably more from the army than the fear of being pursued by Indians, which was a comforting thought to Standing Wolf. Sam was not likely to pose a threat to the Sematuse if he was running from a court martial.

The problem was Standing Wolf could not be sure the soldier still had the amulet. The band of Indians with whom Sam rode for many days, whether as a captive or companion may have it, or he could have sold or traded it.

I will never know unless I find him.

Eating breakfast under the protection of a large spruce, Standing Wolf spoke. "I can not go to Nevada. You must take the word of this meeting with you and tell your people to spread the word of the round dance and the Messiah to all who will listen beyond the members of your tribes and your reservation. I will return to *Shonitkwu* with you and show your band how the dance must be done."

Standing Wolf looked hard into the eyes of his four visitors. "Tell your people they must practice the dance so they are sure to do it right when the sign is given. Tell your people to be peaceful, do not complain or cause trouble and do not fight the white soldiers. You can not win! If your lives are threatened, dance until the sky spits out ancient warriors and the aspen leaves explode releasing the souls of Native People of the past, then fight with your ancestors with all the bravery and skill you possess. Only then will the white man be driven from your midst and swallowed up by Mother Earth!"

When Standing Wolf finished speaking, the woods were silent except for the gurgle of the stream and the chirp of a lone chickadee. Their ride back to the Noisy Waters was a quiet one, each Indian lost in his own thoughts. Each believing this marked a new beginning for the Native People and their long running struggle against the white man.

At a time when the last of the American Indians were being moved onto reservations and their children sent to white mission schools determined to destroy their culture, four Indians from three different tribes rode quietly along a wild river with a renewed spirit and filled with the audacity of hope.

Chapter Thirteen

Finders Keepers

Lieutenant William Radcliff's anxiety level was rising with each day as he and his patrol backtracked toward Fort Okanogan. When they reached Janis Crossing he halted the patrol. It was early in the day but he was not in a hurry to return to the fort and the ass chewing he was certain to get from Major Denton. Besides, they had all heard the screeching and squawking on there way upriver and William decided now was a good time to satisfy his curiosity.

"Sergeant," he addressed the buck-sergeant on the big bay next to him. "We will camp here tonight, but first I need a few volunteers to cross the river with me to see what the fuss we heard on the way up was all about."

Corporal Daniel Bone, a couple of privates and the buck-sergeant quickly volunteered while the remainder of the troop stayed behind to set up camp and get a little R&R.

Finding the source of their curiosity turned out to be at matter of following their senses. When they reached the far bank of the river, the faint screeching of carrion feeders reached their ears. They rode in the direction of the sound and were soon acutely aware of a second… smell; the stench of something very dead invaded their nostrils.

Will's first thought was of the colonel, a thought he quickly dismissed as impossible. Corporal Bone thought of guard duty and if there was one Indian who could move about in the darkness like a ghost, there might be more.

"Must be a dead animal up in them rocks, Sir, but that's a mighty powerful stench for one dead animal," Bone tentatively commented. "Doncha think?"

"Might be," the pot-bellied buck-sergeant replied but then uncharacteristically added, "Ah smelled uh lot uh dead animals in mah time but I ain't never smelled none like that."

The lieutenant was struggling with the need to know what was stinking up in those rocks, and a real fear of throwing up in front of his men. He was swallowing frequently to fight back the taste of bile rising in his throat, but moving closer to the source of the smell that battle was becoming more difficult to win.

As they approached a number of large boulders strewn about the narrow canyon floor, a gust of warm wind blowing in their faces overwhelmed their senses. Will heard the wrenching sound of men vomiting as the two privates and Daniel lost a battle none would have admitted they were fighting. Will was next and finally the sergeant spilled his guts as the garish scene appeared before them. With a wave of his hand, Will ordered the small contingent back the way they came. When they reached the river he pulled his mount up and stepped down.

"We have to take a closer look at what happened up there," he stated. "Soak your caps in the water and hold them over your face, it will help cut the smell. What ever happened up there was no accident."

Returning to the ghoulish site of half-eaten rotting human bodies, water-soaked caps held firmly over nose and mouth, the soldiers began prodding and poking human remains and scratching and digging in nearby soil with sturdy sticks. Arrows lay in the morbid remains of most of the corpses, proof of manner of death. Rotting horses were scattered about the canyon bottom, their bellies torn open and intestines, except for the packed legumes of stomach content, were mostly gone or scattered.

Working their way though the gory scene the soldiers, sickened by the carnage around them, rounded a bend to find more men and horses decomposing in the late summer heat.

"Over here," called a private, his voice weak and trembling.

He stood over a pile of clothing that had been set on fire but only partially burned. Amid the blackened mess were the remains of cavalry uniforms and civilian clothing. Daniel Bone pulled a set of saddlebags free of a decaying horse and threw them over his shoulder. Other's found soldier's handbooks, some with currency stuffed between the pages, and pockets with gold and silver coins. Though certainly not a treasure, the loot probably totaled nearly one hundred dollars. Some of the handbooks contained identification papers, last will and testaments and journals but no one wanted to take the time to look through them here. Their water soaked caps were drying fast and the stench was nearing unbearable again.

Lieutenant Radcliff judiciously collected all the money, determined there would be no grave robbing on his watch, even if the poor bastards didn't have the benefit of a proper burial.

After removing everything of value they could find from the burn pile, Will instructed the men to continue searching the site. He was struck by the fact that while this was an obvious Indian attack, they found no evidence of any dead Indians.

The buck-sergeant exclaimed, "Lieutenant, ah'd set in uh pile uh buffalo guts an' eat mah lunch but ah cain't take no more uh this dead people smell. Ah gotta git out ah here…Sir."

"We'll all go, Sergeant," Will said, sounding almost relieved. "The major will probably want to send a patrol back to investigate this further." Will hoped he would not be part of that patrol, but knew better.

Back at camp none of the soldiers who went into the canyon with Will were in the mood for food or conversation. Each man was processing what he had seen in his own way. What was apparent to each of them was that they had witnessed the site of a brutal killing, one that appeared to have been planned and carried out with the efficiency of a highly skilled military operation. Yet the victims were soldiers and civilians, the attackers Indian, a very skilled, very angry band of Indians, killing, apparently, out of hatred or vengeance.

Corporal Bone thought of the naked Indian at the fort who disarmed Joe Wright, took his clothes and left the private unconscious without his even knowing what happened. If that Indian was on some kind of recon mission for this angry band, the fort and everyone in it was in deep shit. Daniel remained silent about the incident with every intention of staying that way as long as Joe said nothing.

Really, what could he say? Daniel thought. All he knows is that he had a headache.

Bone threw out his bedroll and decided to try getting some sleep. If only I can keep my mind off that canyon, he thought. While getting settled, he remembered the saddlebags he'd pulled from the dead horse. Picking up the leather bags, he was surprised by the weight. They did not seem so heavy when he threw them over his shoulder amidst the carnage. He undid the buckles and looked inside.

There were several small pouches in one bag, in the other a waxed container of matches, a pint of Kentucky Whiskey with the seal unbroken and a wooden box with a metal clasp. Daniel removed a pouch from the first bag and opened it. It was nearly full of brownish-yellow flakes…gold dust! He quickly opened two more filled with the same precious metal. He pulled out and opened another pouch, much larger than the rest.

Nuggets!

It was full of gold nuggets ranging in size from a matchstick head to thumbnail size.

Daniel Bone quickly replaced the contents in the saddlebags and sat silently, considering his discovery. He knew he had to tell the lieutenant but for the moment, he savored the feeling.

So this is how it feels to be rich.

There must be thousands of dollars in gold here. I could quit the army, buy a ranch, get married, oh yeah, find a girl then get married. His mind was firing dreams at him like a red-hot Gatling gun.

Looking around the camp, Daniel saw everyone was fussing with their bedrolls while three privates moved to their lookout posts around the camp perimeter. Daniel placed the treasure-laden saddlebags on the ground and covered them with his military issue horse blanket, then he lay out his bedroll, folded the blanket over him and with his head on the horse blanket fell asleep, knowing how it felt to be rich.

With morning came a sinking feeling, Bone knew he should tell Lieutenant Radcliff about the gold but as the camp came to life, he began to re-evalutist the situation. Horses were retrieved from their tethers, and bridles, saddles and gear were put into place. The lieutenant was talking with the privates who came in from guard duty.

Holding his breath, Daniel untied his rain slicker from the back of his saddle and threw the contraband saddlebags over the military bags. He replaced his slicker and bedroll at the back of the saddle and taking a deep breath looked around. Maybe no one saw him pick up the bags. But didn't the lieutenant see him carry them back from the canyon? Maybe he forgot about them, or was waiting to see if he was going to do the right thing. Pulling his cinch tight and buckled, Daniel realized his hands were shaking.

Convinced he would tell the lieutenant about the gold soon, at least before they reached the fort, or whenever Will asked about the bags, Daniel set about the business of readying for the day's ride.

"Ain't cha fergittin' somthin' corporal?" The red-faced, buck-sergeant's voice cut through the cool morning air, and Daniel's gut.

Desperately trying to find his voice, Daniel responded weakly, "What?"

"Yer rifle, that is yer rifle ain't it, Corporal?" The sergeant pointed to the carbine lying near where Daniel's bedroll had been.

"Might be," Daniel managed with a smile.

The ride down river was mostly quiet, each man apparently caught up in his own thoughts. Will was rehearsing what he was going to say to Major Denton about the colonel and about the massacre at Janis.

Daniel was concerned that the Indian who threatened him on guard duty might have something to do with the Indians in the canyon. If he did, then they already knew about the fort and probably were just waiting for small patrols, like this one, to attack. Mostly he was thinking about the gold tied to the back of his saddle. He wanted to ride up to the lieutenant and tell him about it but he kept making excuses for why it was alright to wait. The worst part was, he was starting to feel like a thief.

Another thought wormed its way into Daniel's head. The Indians who killed those people had taken enough time to strip the victims of their clothes and set them on fire, yet they took no money from the pockets or the stash of gold. He wondered how many more saddlebags full of gold were in that canyon.

Don't even think it.

He wasn't going back there for all the gold in the Okanogan, and he was pretty sure there was a lot.

By time they reached the big meadow and began preparing for another bivouac in Indian country, Daniel was a mess. He had spent the whole day dreaming about what he could do with all that gold.

It didn't belong to anyone, the man was dead.

Hell, he didn't even know which man's horse he took it from. He didn't speak to Lieutenant Radcliff all day. Guilt, he thought.

"Corporal Bone, I'd like to speak with you," the lieutenant said.

Daniel's body felt suddenly cool and clammy despite it being late summer and warm.

"Yes Sir," he responded, finding it difficult to swallow.

"Corporal, I have a couple of sick privates on my hands, I need you to fill in on sentry duty tonight. Any reason you can't help me out?" Will inquired, more as a courtesy than a question.

"No, Sir, none at all."

Daniel felt as if the weight of a sack full of gold was lifted from his shoulders only to be replaced by the weight of a guilty conscience. He was actually glad to be on guard duty, he knew he wouldn't have been able to sleep, and the night watch gave him a chance to try and think this thing through. By morning he'd made a decision.

He mentally pondered a dozen different ways to tell the lieutenant about the gold but in the end, he settled on the truth. After telling his story, Bone expected to be placed under guard then in the brig when they reached the fort.

Instead, Will said, "No one knows about that gold but us. Let's keep it that way until we get back to the fort. Then we'll turn everything over to the major with you and me as witnesses. Most of the soldiers carried handbooks, those we can identify. We may never know who the civilians were but that will be the army's problem."

Daniel walked away feeling both relieved and ill. He just gave away enough gold to have changed his life forever. At least he now knew what it felt like to be rich for a couple of days. The lieutenant might have known he had the bags, but he could not have known what was in them. No matter, Bone learned a few things about himself during those last few days. He was inherently honest and could not live with a guilty conscience…and he wasn't going to stay in this man's army.

He had put his year in and he was going to resign as soon as he could convince the major it would not be a detriment to the command. Daniel Bone was willing to give up a dollar, even two a day in pay, to find a woman, get married and have a home…maybe even children. Unfortunately, the ranch would have to wait a while.

When the patrol arrived back at the fort, Major Denton was as nervous as a long-tailed cat in a room filled with rocking chairs. There was still no sign of Colonel Wolard and he was convinced the fort was going to be attacked most any time. Nothing Lieutenant Radcliff told him made him feel any better.

The story of a trail leading into a rock wall made about as much sense as the story that rat-bastard-deserter DeSoto told. A renegade band of blood- thirsty Indians as close as Janis Crossing nearly sent Denton over the edge.

Much to Lieutenant Radcliff's relief, the major decided not to send a patrol back to Janis. If there was an outlaw band of Indians intent on killing whites, out of revenge or otherwise, Denton was not going to risk anymore of this brigade chasing some elusive enemy. If he didn't get some direction from his superiors in the next week, he was prepared to leave Fort Okanogan and lead his troops back to Vancouver. Denton was not sure what the punishment for abandoning a fort was but as far as military protocol was concerned, he was in charge. With the colonel MIA, he was willing to make a judgment call based on the perceived threat to his men at this isolated outpost.

There was much to do; including rounding up enough beef from the colonel's brother's ranch to feed two thousand men for the thirty days it would take to reach Fort Vancouver. Roy was raising the beef for the army anyway and if he happened to turn up after they were gone, he could settle up with the army.

Corporal Bone and Private Joe Wright, who had recovered from an ordeal he retained no memory of, volunteered for the detail to round up twenty-five or thirty steers for the trip. The major wanted enough to feed the troops and a few to trade to tribes they might encounter along the way if need be. When they rode past the magnificent ranch house Roy built, Daniel was struck by two things: the house, auspicious as it was, looked sad…and if he had kept the gold in the saddlebags, it could have been his.

If Daniel had regrets about turning over the gold, his attitude was not improved when he and the other soldiers-turned-cow-punchers returned to the fort.

Lieutenant Radcliff took him aside. "Just thought you would like to know that small wooden box in the saddlebags you found contained a deed to a gold mine, somewhere on the Fraser River in Canada. The man who owned the claim's name is, or was, Francis Wolff. We can only assume he was one of the dead men. When we get the personal items retrieved from the canyon back to Fort Vancouver, the army will attempt to find the next of kin."

Will watched for a reaction from the corporal and seeing none continued, "Everything taken from the scene is the property of the army until next of kin can be located. In the case of the soldiers with handbooks, this should be easy. With civilians, the chances are not as good. I have suggested to Major Denton that if Mr. Wolff's next of kin can't be found, the contents of his bags should belong to you…. finders keepers, or something like that."

Daniel was speechless for a moment as he replayed the lieutenant's words in his head. "But Sir, doncha think they'll find a next uh kin… some relative somewhere?"

"That's hard to say, Corporal. If Colonel Wolard and his regiment don't show up pretty soon the army is going to be awfully busy just contacting soldier's next of kin."

"How long does the army look for relatives before they make a decision?" Daniel was trying very hard to stay calm and convince himself that whatever property the man had should go to his next of kin. "I don't mean ta sound greedy Sir, but that much gold could change a man's life."

"I'm not a barrister, Corporal, but I think the army gives next of kin a year to come forward with proof. I doubt there is a statute of limitations for a relative to come forward with a claim before a judge though."

Corporal Daniel Bone was riding an emotional bucking horse with the unexpected highs and lows, twists and turns, when sometimes the best you can hope for is to land on your feet.

Chapter Fourteen

Nine Pipes

Clarence Hobbs was pissed. After returning to town, he told his boss at the bar he was kicked by a horse and took the night off. His face felt like he'd been hit with a sledge hammer; his nose was on fire and probably broken, in fact his whole head hurt from the pounding that asshole gave him. His back hurt, his arms hurt but mostly his goddamn balls ached!

What should have been a night of lustful thrills had turned into a night of limping back to his room behind the saloon and nursing his wounds and his pride.

"I'll find that bitch," he whispered to the baying of coyotes that could be heard in the distance through his half-open window. "I'll find out who she is an' where she lives an' she won't be so lucky next time. She's way to fine to just forget about."

She probably recognized me from the saloon, he thought.

That concerned him a little but his experience was that most women would not say anything.

"To embarrassed or guilty about likin' the feel of ol' Clarence," he whispered with a grin. "Course that blond babe never got the pleasure," he growled, the grin turning to a scowl.

He would have to be careful, clever even, in asking about her. Hobbs was sure people around town knew who she was but *he* had no reason to be asking about her.

"The bastard that saved her…shit, I never even got a look at him, but don't worry," he told the darkness and coyotes. "Ol' Clarence has his ways."

He closed his eyes and pictured her mostly naked body. At least he had his memories for now.

Following a tearful good-bye to her parents, Lillian marched to the barn with a purpose.

"Sam," she said, forcefully.

He was digging a bucket of grain from a metal-lined bin.

"You don't need to worry about the chores. I'll have plenty of time to do them. You can go in the house, take a bath if you'd like and pick out some of my brother's clothes. Then you can go wherever you were headed. I'll be just fine here by myself."

"The bath and clothes sound good Miss, but I promised your father I would wait here till he returns."

"So what's he going to do if you're gone when he gets back, hunt you down and flog you for breaking a promise?"

"Lo siento, Señorita, I will not be in your way but I promised I would stay." Sam was a bit surprised by his own assertiveness.

"I have no idea how you know my mom or what you told my dad, but if you insist on remaining here you're going to take that bath and you're still sleeping in the barn!"

Lillian tossed her red hair over her shoulder with a jerk of her head and took the grain bucket out of his hand, scowling at his back as he walked toward the house.

For the second time in less than twenty-four hours, Sam was sure he'd gone to heaven. He reluctantly pulled the leather cord holding the amulet over his head and placed it on a nearby dresser. After lathering his face, he began shaving, a task that was a little tedious and a bit painful. The straightedge razor was not the best instrument for removing his thick shaggy growth.

When he finished, leaving a horseshoe mustache, because he was simply tired of shaving, he stood in front of the mirror feeling his face. He long since passed through the itchy stage of beard growth, now to feel water and air on his cheeks was like standing under a waterfall. He ran hot water into the deep four-legged bathtub. Though he had tried to clean himself in river water on occasion, sliding into hot water and lathering his body in soap was like being given a new life. It was heavenly to be able to wash his hair and scrubbed his scalp until his fingers began to cramp. He sat in the tub, scouring body parts he almost forgot he owned, until the water began to transform from hot to cold and from cleansing to disgusting.

Pulling the drain plug and stepping out of the tub, Sam wondered what it would be like to be able to do this once a week or however often you wanted. Even drying his body with a clean towel was a nearly spiritual experience.

Larry's jeans were a little snug but the length was good and the pale-green short-sleeve shirt fit well enough, though it was thread-stretching tight across his back when he crossed his arms over his chest. With his transformation complete, Sam couldn't resist a quick look in the mirror. A safe, comfortable feeling swept over him.

"Even I don't recognize my Spanish ass, so how could Major Denton ever find me?" he said, smiling, and slid the amulet back over his head.

He now thought of it as a good luck charm and a reminder of who he was and what he had witnessed.

Lillian was in the garden when she saw Sam open the gate and felt a lump in her throat followed by a fuzzy, tingly feeling in her belly.

"Who are…?"

The frightened words fell from her lips before she recognized her brother's shirt. Her mouth remained open but no more words escaped as her eyes quickly took in Sam's dark skin in contrast with the pale shirt, his muscular arms and broad shoulders stretching the fabric. The too-tight jeans also caught her eyes but she averted them with a sudden rush of embarrassment, her freckled cheeks flushed.

"I don't mean to bother, Miss, but since I'm going to be here anyway I sure would like to be of some help." His voice was deep, husky with a slight accent she did not noticed before.

Born in California, Sam talked more like an American than a Spaniard or Mexican, however, being bi-lingual and raised by Spanish speaking parents, he did have a hint of an accent, which gave away his heritage…that and the occasional slip of the tongue. He was not ashamed of his heritage, but the part about his ancestors being among the conquistadors was not something he wanted to brag about.

"I don't need any….help," Lilly stammered.

I have no reason to be rude, she thought. He has done nothing to me and besides he's a friend of mom's.

"Wait," she almost shouted. Taking a deep breath she said more calmly, "How do you know my mother and what is your last name… Sam?"

Sam remained standing in the open gate. "DeSoto, Miss, Samuel DeSoto," he said.

"Well, Mr. DeSoto," Lillian said curtly, "how do you know my mother and where are you from?"

If he doesn't want to talk, fine, but I need some answers, Lillian thought, softening a little.

Sam on the other hand found himself getting tense. He just met the most beautiful girl he had ever seen and already he was going to have to lie to her. "Miss…"

Lilly interrupted, "Enough with the 'Miss' already…my name is Lillian." She then awkwardly apologized, "Sorry, but just call me Lillian, okay?"

"All right, Lillian," he said softly, trying to gather his composure. "I am from California." So far, he was satisfied to be telling the truth. "Have you heard of it?" he asked, stalling for an answer to the other question.

"Of course, I've heard of it, I'm not stupid," she said defensively.

I'm not lying, she thought. She was pretty sure she'd heard her mom or dad mention California sometime although she had no clue where it was.

Still stalling, Sam said, "I lived on a ranch there a little bit like this one. It was called Destino. In the language of my padre, my father, it means fate."

"We call this ranch the Running R and that's our brand. It's because of my mom and dad…Ross and Ruth. Well, really my grandparents,

Ralph and Rose, but it's our brand now. My brother, Larry, and I said we were going to start our own ranch and call it the Lazy L." She paused for a moment then said, "You say words I don't understand sometimes, is that because you're from California?"

She smiled and Sam's mouth went dry and his palms turned sweaty.

"It is rude of me. Sometimes I forget and speak in the language of my father's people."

He made his way through the gate and was not more than four feet away from what he considered was an angel. He touched the amulet under his open shirt. For a fleeting moment, he thought of all that had happened since he grabbed the strange leather circlet.

Am I dead? Is this some kind of heaven?

He promptly remembered what the man was doing to this girl's mother and dropped the thought of heaven like a hot horseshoe.

"So what can I do to help?"

He wanted to get past this question and answer thing, not because he didn't have questions but because he didn't have answers.

"Do you know how to hitch up a team? There's hay shocked in the meadow and my dad would be real happy if we had it in the stack when he gets back."

Lilly was slowly deciding Sam was not such a bad guy and if he was willing to work, it would be great to have some help. She was still feeling guilty about Larry's ear and worried too. Her folks would never consider taking the buckboard all the way to Horse Plain unless it was serious. In the end, they decided to ride and take Drifter along for Larry. Ruth was determined to be optimistic, that Larry would be well enough to ride home by the end of the week.

"Show me the team, the harness, a wagon and the meadow and consider it done."

Sam would do anything to see this girl smile again and it would feel really good to be doing ranch work one more time.

Lillian put down the hoe she was weeding the tomatoes with and motioned for Sam to follow. "Are you in the army, it looked like a uniform you were wearing?" Lillian asked, as they walked toward the barn.

"I was but I am not anymore," Sam answered, evading the truth but not telling a lie.

"My brother has a couple of friends who joined the army to fight Indians. We thought they were dumb. We should leave the Indians alone. They were here before we were. My dad is friends with some Indians. He says they're just like us; they want to take care of their families and be happy. Like the wolves, some of the ranchers want to kill them. I think we should quit worrying about wolves and take better care of our cattle."

Lillian was relaxing around Sam, and becoming her self-confident opinionated self. Besides, he was kind of good looking now that he was clean.

"I never killed Indians," Sam said. "That is why I am not in the army anymore." He was growing very uncomfortable with all this dancing around the truth.

Lillian opened the door to the tack room and pointed at the heavy leather harnesses. "This is Jake's and this is Jim's," she said, patting first one harness, then the other.

"Jake and Jim?" Sam asked, puzzled.

"The horses, silly," Lillian laughed. "The team is Jake and Jim. You need to know that if you want them to work for you."

Sam spent the day talking to Jake and Jim, pitching shocks, stacking hay and sweating. He could not remember ever feeling better, he felt empowered the way he did back home on Destino when his mom and dad were alive, and like he just awoke from a nightmare. As the sun settled into the western sky, he was tired but sorry the day was ending.

"We can finish this job tomorrow," he told a less enthusiastic Jake and Jim.

Returning to the barn, he pulled the harness from the horses, made sure they had clean water and hay in their stalls then gave each a small bucket of oats. He pulled off his shirt and was cleaning up in a stock tank when he was startled by the sound of his name.

"Sam, when you're finished up there, come on over to the house for supper."

Sam turned to face her, water dripping from his face and hair and running down his muscular chest and taunt rippling belly.

"It's...." Her words stuck in her throat and she looked away. This time the embarrassment started in her face and washed over her whole body, causing a slight tremor. "It is chicken and dumplings," she managed, after regaining her composure. "Unless you don't like chicken and dumplings, then I guess you'll have to wait and see what breakfast brings."

It is a dream, he thought.

Sam's mother used to fix chicken and dumplings every Friday. It was his dad's favorite, along with sweet peas and onions.

The chicken and dumplings were even better than Sam remembered, though the dinner conversation was awkward. Sam was so nervous and excited he could barely talk at all. It was more than two years since he'd eaten at a table with anyone except a bunch of uncouth soldiers. He hoped he remembered most of the manners his mother taught him. *'Don't chew with your mouth open'* lodged firmly in his brain.

"You still haven't told me how you know my mom," Lillian said, watching him take a second helping.

Sam felt a twinge of panic. It was the question he hoped she had forgotten about.

"There was some trouble on the road and I was able to help her," he began, weighing his words carefully. "She was worried about your brother and asked if I would mind staying here for a few days while she and your father went to be with him."

"What kind of trouble?" Lillian pressed.

Give me a break here, Sam thought. His mind searched for words to explain without sharing the ugly truth.

"She was attacked by an animal and I was nearby and ran it off."

"I was chased by a bear once," Lillian stated. "My horse, Buttercup, outran it. I'll show you Buttercup tomorrow. She's real pretty and fast. Hey, maybe we can go for a ride tomorrow. I'll drive Jake and Jim and you can load the wagon, when we get the hay stacked we could go, you could ride Weasel. He's a good horse, pretty fast but not as fast as Buttercup. He is a brown and white pinto and Buttercup is a Palomino."

Sam was captivated as he listened to this beautiful girl ramble on. The sound of her voice was like listening to silver bells in a light summer breeze. Her blue eyes danced and sparkled when she talked about her horse and going for a ride.

"You have a horse named Weasel?" he blurted.

After doing nothing but riding since running from the Indians in the valley, Sam couldn't think of anything he wanted to do less, but to be with this girl he knew he would ride anywhere and like it.

"My horse is named Major," Sam said defensively, then flustered at his ungracious response, muttered, "How old are you, Lillian?"

"Why Samuel DeSoto, a gentleman never asks a lady her age," she retorted with mock disdain. "How old are you, Sam?" she asked, returning the question almost flirtatiously.

Sam's dark-brown cheeks turned rose-red and his tongue refused to function. He was trying very hard to see the lovely Lillian as an impetuous young girl because the thought of her as a gorgeous young lady was a one he would rather not have.

"I will tell you when you tell me," he said, feeling a little foolish but liking the light-hearted banter.

"By the way, who would name a horse Weasel and why?" he asked, genuinely curious.

"He is my brother's horse and who knows why Larry does anything? You'd have to know my brother," Lillian said, giggling. "He says it's because Weasel is pinto and doesn't know if it's summer or winter…I don't get it."

With supper finished, Sam thanked Lillian in excess. She handed him a dishtowel and said, "Here, I'll wash, you dry and enough with the thanks, okay?"

With that chore done, Sam headed for the door and his bed of straw.

"Wait," Lillian said softly. "I'll show you the bunkhouse. Mom wants you to sleep there."

Walking together through the soft night air, Sam wrestled with the thought of how much his life changed over night.

The bunkhouse sat behind an aspen grove about a hundred yards from the main house. It was log with a prow front, inside was a cook stove in a small living area with a leather couch and chair, and a rock fireplace took up most of one wall. There were four small bedrooms, each with a cot, a dresser and a mirror. It even had a bathroom with a shower, sink and toilet. In many ways it was a miniature replica of the main house.

It was becoming apparent to Sam that these people were not simply ranchers, they were very successful ranchers, and he began to formulate a plan. He didn't see any hands around and no one was living in the bunkhouse. If their son was sick, maybe they would need extra help until he got better.

"You do not have any hired hands?" he asked while Lillian showed him where to get his bedding. "Does no one else live here?"

"Sometimes we do," she answered. "Our neighbor worked here for a while but he kept going to the house asking mom things that he could have asked my dad. Dad said he didn't like the way the man looked at my mom so he told him we didn't need him anymore. We usually hire a few cowboys in the spring to help with branding and sometimes in the fall to help move the cattle in closer to home." Lillian took a deep breath, cocked her pretty head a little to the right and continued, "You looking for a job? My dad would probably hire you. He's pretty worried about getting the cattle home, especially the cows and calves since my brother saw the wolves up at Wild Horse Creek."

Sam was awestruck. This girl could talk the peel off a potato and he loved hearing every word; her voice mesmerized him.

Lillian knew she talked when she was nervous and right now, she was all nerves. It wasn't a bad nervous, there was just something about this guy that made her chatter. Maybe it was because he seemed so interested; maybe because he was kind of quiet and just let her talk without always interrupting or maybe it was because he really was good looking. The more she was around him the better looking he seemed to get.

Wolves!

Sam's mind was yanked back to the river and that huge black wolf. It was hard to believe it really happened; that he was freed from the Indian band by a huge wolf that almost spoke to him. The whole thing seemed like a lifetime ago and he could have convinced himself it was all a dream if it were not for the amulet hanging around his neck.

"Someday, if you do not let me forget, I will tell you a story about a special wolf," he said, hoping she would take the bait.

"I'd like that," she said, and nearly ran out of the bunkhouse.

He wished he could tell her everything.

The trip to Horse Plain was slow and Ross wanted to know more about the attack but mostly he wanted to know if Ruth knew her attacker.

Ruth didn't want to talk about it. "I already told you, I didn't know him."

It wasn't a total lie, he was the bartender she spoke to about Doc Jensen, but she didn't know him. She didn't want to talk about it because she wanted to forget what he did, and she wanted to concentrate on Larry and being positive, but the main reason was, Ruth knew if she told Ross where she her attacker worked, he would go there and kill the man. It wasn't that she didn't wish he was dead. She would kill him herself if she got the chance, but she did not want Ross to kill him.

They spent the night at a boarding house in Paradise that belonged to friends. After a lengthy discussion, concerning Larry's condition over a fine meal and a generous serving of raspberry brandy, they retired for the night.

Watching Ruth slip out of her shirt, brasserie and riding pants and slide into bed, Ross felt the familiar tightness in his groin but knew this was neither the time nor the place. He was content to feel the warmth of her breasts against his back, her right arm draped over his side and her hand placed lightly against his stomach.

It was late morning when Ross and Ruth rode into Horse Plain. They went directly to Doc Jensen's office.

"Oh good, Mr. and Mrs. Riley," he said, as they stepped through the wooden door. "I am glad you're here, you have a very sick boy."

He had learned over the years that sugar coating the truth was bad medicine.

A gasp escaped Ruth's lips and Ross' face turned ashen.

"He's getting better isn't he?" Ruth asked, weakly.

"No Ma'am, he isn't. I seem to be able to keep up with the infection but I can't seem to get ahead of it. I don't think it is tetanus and it isn't gangrene but it seems to be some kind of blood poisoning. I wish I had thought to have you bring the trap that cut him with you."

"You think something on the trap might have poisoned him?" Ross asked, puzzled.

"I'm not sure, Mr. Riley, but I have soaked his ear in iodine and Epson salt and washed it with alcohol. The wound is clean, in fact, the color is getting better and the swelling is going down but his fever is getting worse. With most blood poisoning, once the wound is clean the body will cleanse itself of the infection, the fever drops and the patient gets well."

"Can we see him?" Ruth asked, tears welling up in her green eyes.

"Of course," Doc Jensen said.

He turned and led them down a hallway with whitewashed doors partially open on either side then stopped next to the third door on the right.

When he pushed it open Ruth stepped in side, choking back her tears as she went to her son. Ross followed close on her heals. Larry was flushed and sweating, there were wet rags on his shoulders, chest and forehead. He smiled feebly when Ruth took his hand.

"How're you doing, Son?" She knew it was a dumb question but it just fell out.

"My ear feels better but otherwise I feel pretty crappy," Larry said and took a deep breath. "Hear any more about the wolves?" he asked, not wanting to talk about how miserable he felt.

"The wolves will keep, Son," Ross declared. "Right now we're only concerned about you." Then he reconsidered; it would probably be good to talk about the wolves, they were important to Larry and would get his mind off being sick. "I'm sure they're still around," he added quickly, "When you get out of here, we'll go look for the one that made that big track."

"Where's Lilly?" Larry asked, surprised by her absence.

"We weren't sure how long we might need to be here," Ross said. "We needed her to look after things."

"She's home alone!?" Larry exclaimed. "Dad, she's only sixteen."

"That's enough for now," Doc Jensen intervened. "I don't want his blood pressure going up right now." He ushered the reluctant mother and father from the room.

"What can we do, Doc? How can we help?" Ross was shaken at the sight of Larry's fevered condition.

"Well, I suggested prayer, but your wife didn't seem to cotton much to that idea," Doc Jensen said, hoping to lighten the moment a little.

"But I do believe in the power of positive thinking," Ruth interjected. "I don't see much point in asking God for help when if there is a God and if he is all powerful, and if he cared, he could have prevented the problem to began with."

Doc Jensen knew this was not an argument he wanted to engage in, especially not now. He was too busy trying to find a way to save a young man's life.

After spending the last twenty-four hours in his room behind the saloon, with a wet cloth on his face, Hobb's nose was still swollen, just not quite as much, and both of his eyes were the color of old liver.

"I'd kill the son-of-a-bitch that did this to me but I don't even know what the bastard looks like," he growled.

He was pissed and worried about his nose. He was certain that it was broken and wondered if he should see Doc Jensen. It was Friday and the Doc wouldn't be back until the middle of next week, providing there were no emergencies in Horse Plain. Hobbs could ride there in two or three hours but what the hell do you do for a broken nose?

"Sure cain't put it in a cast," he spat at the dreadful looking image in the mirror.

As dark shadows invaded his room, Clarence decided he needed some pain reliever.

"Jesus-help-me-Christ!" Hobb's replacement behind the bar exclaimed. "The boss said you was kicked by a horse, didn't say you was nearly stomped ta death. You see a doctor yet?"

"Just gimme uh Wild Turkey an' keep em comin' 'till I fall off uh this stool," Clarence mumbled and breathing the only way he could; through his mouth.

After two or three shots he began to feel a little better, at least the sharp throbbing in his nose was replaced with a dull pain. After a couple more shots, he bought a bottle and went back to his room.

When the first rays of light drifted into his room, Clarence opened his eyes and quickly closed them. He had a headache that would drop a buffalo to its knees. Slowly opening his eyes again, he looked around the room; a half empty bottle of Wild Turkey sat on the small wooden table in the middle of the room. He quickly looked away, tasting puke halfway up his throat. Unsure if he was suffering from the whisky or the beating, he chose not to look at the bottle until he was sure.

By noon Hobbs was feeling better, his headache was mostly gone and he could breathe somewhat through his nose. It still looked like summer sausage and his eyes were black as axle grease but he felt better. He began thinking about the blonde beauty, he didn't care who she was, but wanted to find out where she lived.

It was two days since he last ate and Hobbs's stomach growled loudly in protest. He suddenly realized he was hungry, closer to starving, and headed for the boarding house, confident he could make it in time for lunch.

"What's for lunch?" he squawked to the woman clearing dirty dishes from an empty table.

"What happened to you?" she replied, stopping for a moment to stare.

"Got kicked by a horse," he lied. If it worked for his boss it would work for this broad.

"Looks painful."

If you only knew, he thought silently and repeated, "What's for lunch?"

"Meatloaf sandwich, mashed potatoes and gravy for 50 cents, piece of hot apple pie for a dime more."

"I can hardly wait," Hobbs retorted, feeling more like hisself.

"You own this place?" he asked, when she brought his steaming meal.

"No, I just help out sometimes. The owners are in Horse Plain today. Their friend's son is sick," the woman pleasantly replied.

"Not the boy with the bad ear?" he asked with renewed interest.

"Why, I think they did say something about an injured ear. Do you know him?"

"Nope, but I heard they was good people an' it was too bad 'bout the boy." Hobbs was fishing now.

"The Riley's, they're great people, got a big ranch out by Nine Pipes. Sure hope the boy gets better. They've only got him and the girl."

"So are they all in Horse Plain with the boy?"

This is like shooting fish in a barrel.

"Now, that I don't know," she answered, thinking. *This guy seems nice enough but he sure asks a lot of questions.*

"You don't want to let that meatloaf get cold," she said, and turned to leave.

"One last question, I'm new 'round here. What is Nine Pipes?" He was pushing it but he may never have a better chance.

"Not exactly sure," she replied. "I think there was a big treaty signed there years ago. Guess they smoked nine pipes or something, nothing there now but the Riley's ranch."

Sure is a curious fellow, she thought as she continued walking toward the kitchen.

The meal was excellent and Clarence had garnered some very interesting information. Now he had to find out where this ranch was. When the woman returned with the apple pie, he took one last shot.

"Do ya know where the Riley's ranch is? I'm kind uh looking for work an' might stop by there in a few days, see if they can use any help."

How cool am I? He smugly thought.

"Oh sure, it's the Running R, about forty miles from here up the Flathead River. How was lunch?" she asked, changing the subject abruptly.

"Perfect," he replied, "just perfect."

Leaving the boarding house Hobbs was feeling like a hunter again, a predator.

"I need a plan," he stated. A familiar itch returned to a place deep inside his belly.

Up early and after the best bacon and eggs he could remember ever eating, Sam and Lillian hooked up Jake and Jim and set out to bring in the rest of the meadow hay. Lillian was delighted she would be able to surprise her mom and dad with an important job done.

Sam was ecstatic spending the day with this beautiful girl. After a couple good nights' sleep and food in his belly, he was feeling good and enjoying the hard work. He never felt so alive since before he lost his parents. He tried not to think about how he got here or the serious realities of his situation. When those thoughts crossed his mind, Sam worked harder, focusing on *now*.

By mid-afternoon, the hay was stacked, Jake and Jim were happily munching oats in their stalls and Sam had taken another half-bath in a stock tank.

"You want to take a ride up toward Wild Horse? I can show you the lake and we can check on the cattle at Big Arm. I'll make a lunch and we can have a picnic." Lillian was exuberant. The hay was in, her folks would be proud and she couldn't have done it without Sam.

"Si, I will go for a ride," Sam replied with his heart in his throat.

It felt like a date.

The thought made his stomach tickle.

"While I make a lunch you could saddle the horses. I think you should ride Weasel and let your mare rest. She looks like she could stand to put on a little weight."

Lillian was concerned about the little sorrel mare but she had a more devious purpose. Weasel was the most high-strung and unpredictable horse in their herd. Larry was the only one who ever rode him and since her folks had taken the gentle Drifter to Paradise, Weasel was available. She wasn't sure if it was her mischievous nature or a more sinister purpose she wasn't willing to accept, but she wanted to see how Sam would handle a spirited horse like Weasel. Lillian pointed out the pinto grazing with a few other horses fenced in a pasture.

"I'll ride the Palomino," she said.

She was beaming as she walked toward the ranch house and out of Sam's view.

"Larry can handle Weasel," she giggled impishly. "I'll see if Sam can."

Turning back she said, "They should be easy to catch but if you have any trouble get some oats and you won't be able to fight them off."

With lunches stuffed into saddlebags, Sam and Lillian rode along the river toward Big Arm and the lake Lillian wanted him to see. It was clear from the start that Weasel was aware of a different rider. Prancing and throwing his head, the horse was so light in the front end Sam thought it felt like he was like dancing on egg shells.

Now this is riding.

He felt like he was back at Destino training the high-spirited Arabians and Thoroughbreds his father raised.

Gripping the reins tightly in his left hand, Sam stayed light on the horse's mouth. As the two danced and darted up the trail, getting accustomed to each other, Sam was in utopia…the ranch, the horse, the girl, then he remembered how he got here and the abuse inflicted on Lillian's mother by that perverted animal.

The irony and incongruity…I should have killed him while I had the chance, he thought, and tried to understand Ruth's suffering leading to his good fortune.

Lillian, oblivious to the events that brought Sam to the Running R was enjoying watching him and Weasel.

This guy can ride.

She smiled at the silly thought…of course he can ride, everybody can ride or they'd never get anywhere but the way he was handling Weasel told her Sam knew more than how to ride…he knew horses.

"You learn how to ride in the army?"

She kept a tight rein on Buttercup; the Palomino horse always sensed a race when traveling alongside Weasel, a condition Lilly knew she and Larry were to blame for.

"No, I was in the cavalry and of course I rode a lot, but I learned to ride before I left home. We raised horses and it was my job to train them."

"How long ago was that?"

I'd still like to know how old he is, she thought.

"A lifetime ago, a whole lifetime ago," he answered.

And I am only twenty-two, he thought.

A sharp-tailed grouse broke from the dense snowberry and wild rose, making a noisy escape. Weasel went straight in the air, landed stiffly on all fours, reared, spun and leaped into the brush along the trail. He jerked his head down and made one jump before Sam got control and pulled the horse in. Weasel shook his head and fought for the bit, Sam patted him on the neck, talking softly.

"Samuel DeSoto, did you do that to impress a lady?" Lillian was laughing loudly but there was a spark of admiration in her blue eyes.

Lady, he mused, I must keep thinking girl, little girl.

"The name Weasel is beginning to sound more appropriate," Sam retorted, focusing on the bundle of nerves he was riding.

When they reached the lake, Lillian pulled Buttercup to a halt, stepped off and said, "We better have our picnic and head back. I wanted to show you where my brother saw the wolves but we're not going to have time."

Dismounting, Sam watched Lillian lay down a blanket and set out lunch. He felt his mouth go dry when he got a good look at the way her cute bottom filled out her jeans, not to mention the obvious development of breasts under her loose fitting shirt.

"What about these lobos…er, wolves? I would think they would be common in these parts." He didn't know where 'these parts' were but believed it was somewhere in Canada.

"I guess they used to be a long time ago. My dad and some of the other ranchers killed most of them so we don't see them much anymore. We can hear them up in the Cabinets and over on the Thompson but not around here."

"Do the ranchers always kill them when they see them?"

"Most do, but Larry and I are trying to convince dad there is no need to kill them. Did you know wolves mate for life?" Lillian abrutpty asked, handing Sam a piece of fried chicken.

"No, but if you promise not to laugh, I will tell you a wolf story."

Lilly promised, but the gleam in her eyes caused him to question her sincerity. No matter, he really wanted to tell someone about the giant black wolf, maybe telling the story would somehow make it all more believable.

Downplaying his time in captivity with the rogue Indian band, Sam told in great detail about the appearance of a black wolf the size of a bear and how it caused much excitement and fear among the Indians, so much fear that they ran away, leaving him alone with the wolf.

"It was as though that lobo's eyes looked right into my corazon, my heart, and then he was gone. I did not see where he went."

Lillian sat sober-faced and quiet, seriously considering Sam's story. She shook her pretty head, her orange-red hair creating a halo effect in the fading sunlight.

"First dad and now you," she said, perplexed. "My dad saw a track over by the Thompson River he said looked like a wolf but was the size of a bear track. Mom saw it too. Dad thinks there might be a wolf with a deformed foot running around." She paused for a moment then smiling brightly said, "Wouldn't it be cool if it's the same wolf?"

The thought sent a chill up and down Sam's spine. Could that giant wolf be following me? He pulled the amulet from inside his shirt and lifted it over his head then handed it to Lillian.

Somewhat reluctantly, she took it and lightly ran her fingers over the painted surface. Transfixed, she said, "It's remarkable. Where did you get it?"

Sam's mind shot back to the valley and he swallowed hard. That was a story he was not yet ready to tell.

Night came and went and Larry's condition was not improved. His fever remained high but he complained of being cold and he was suffering from stomach craps and vomiting. Ross and Ruth were worried, exhausted and perplexed. How could this have happened?

Ross was kicking himself for not bringing the trap with him. "I should have known it could be important," he told a badly shaken Ruth. "I just expected him to be fine when we got here, and complaining about having to ride Drifter all the way home."

Larry didn't feel much like talking so Ross and Ruth spent a lot of time talking to each other, staring at their very sick son. When he did speak, Larry seemed most concerned about Lillian being home alone. Neither Ross nor Ruth told him they left her with a young man they barely knew; a reality not setting well with Ross either. He questioned the decision from the beginning but Ruth assured him it would be fine.

"We should've kept her with us," Ross complained. "Now I feel like both the kids are at risk. I don't know how you can be so sure about this Sam guy when you only met him a few hours before you brought him home."

Ruth detected a note of jealousy in his voice. Not surprising, she thought, it's his male pride. All the more reason I can't tell him what really happened.

"I know Sam is a good man because he went out of his way to help me when I was in trouble. Trust me…if it weren't for Sam we'd both be sorry," she said in her I-don't-want-to-hear-another-word-about-it tone.

"What are you guys talking about?" Larry asked, rousing from what they hoped was a restful sleep.

"It's nothing. We're just worried about you. Are you feeling any better?" Ruth quickly inquired.

Horrified and humiliated at the abuse she had been subjected to, Ruth wished there was someone she could confide in, but knew that would not be her husband or her son. Only Sam knew her secret and she wished he was there to talk to.

Larry's stomach cramps were getting more violent, causing him to arch off the bed in painful convulsions.

"My head and shoulders really hurt…my stomach, too," he moaned, breathlessly.

Ruth was distraught and went in search Doc Jensen. She found him setting the broken arm of a six-year-old boy.

"Doc, please come as soon as you can, Larry seems to be getting worse."

"How is he getting worse?" Jensen asked.

"He's having convulsions or something and says he's really hurting."

"I'll be there as soon as I finish patching up this young cowboy. He was practicing his roping on some steers at his ranch and accidentally caught one." Doc Jensen smiled. "He didn't want to lose his rope so he tried to hang on."

"Sounds like Larry when he was that age," Ruth said, trying to be cheerful, but broke into tears.

"Give me just a minute, Mrs. Riley, and I'll see what I can do."

The doctor was out of good guesses when it came to Larry's condition. The ear was clean and healing so what could be causing his problem? When he walked into Larry's room even he was shocked. The young man was shaking violently, his legs and arms were thrashing about and his head was jerking spastically.

"I'm going to need some help here," Jensen stated, looking squarely at Larry's shaken father.

Together, they held Larry on the bed while Ruth brought in more blankets, at the doctor's request.

"Try to keep him as quiet as possible," he said to the two frantic parents. "I have to cram for a life and death exam."

Leaving the room, Doc Jensen quickly returned to his office and began perusing a lifetime of medical books and journals neatly stacked on wooden shelves.

"What can poison the body other than an infection?" he questioned the silent assemblage of knowledge bound in leather and paper. "What am I missing?" He was desperate but knew he must remain calm. "Look for poisons." He searched along the shelves from left to right, bottom to top. "This could take some time and I'm afraid I have… Larry has, very little. "

A thought struck him and he rushed back into Larry's room. Ross and Ruth were ashen and tears filled their eyes while they fought to keep Larry calm and their emotions in check.

"Do you folks do any mining?" Jensen asked. "Do you have gold on your property? Would Larry have any reason to be around cyanide?"

"There could be gold," Ross said in a trembling voice. "I never have looked for it. What does that have to do with cyanide?" He was bewildered.

"Miners sometimes use cyanide to extract gold from rock," the doctor said. "I thought Larry might have been doing some work around a mine and gotten some on his hands. It will go through the pours of the skin into the bloodstream. I hate to say this, but I'm grasping at straws. You're certain there is no way he could have been around a gold mining operation?"

Ross was in a panic. "There are some gold mines in the Cabinets and on the Thompson but I don't know how Larry could have been involved."

He took Larry's jaw in his powerful hand, holding the twitching head still and looking directly into Larry's eyes asked emphatically, "Larry, have you been around a gold mine lately?"

The frightened boy shook his head from side to side and between gasping breathes forced out, "No."

"It was a shot," Doc Jensen muttered before leaving the room and striding resolutely back to his office and his books.

What would I have done if he'd said 'yes'? He asked himself. The only treatment he was aware of for poisoning was to induce vomiting. Larry had taken care of that himself and it obviously was not working.

Doc Jensen was stumped and rifling through book after journal, he searched for anything that might produce a clue or jar a memory of some past experience in his long career. He had treated everything from lockjaw to smallpox over the years, sometimes with lives saved and sometimes not. *This boy is young, strong and not dying from the injury to his ear, something else is going on.*

As a doctor, Jensen had watched a lot of patients die in his lifetime but it was always more difficult when the patient was young. He was not always able to prevent death, but almost always he knew what caused it. That was what made this case so frustrating.

I'm a doctor for God's sake; I'm supposed to know what to do!

While Ross and Ruth tried to comfort Larry as best they could, Ross struggled with what Doc Jensen said about cyanide and gold mining, racking his brain for any way Larry could have come in contact with cyanide.

Water!

The epiphany struck him like a mule kick. What if there were miners using cyanide in the headwaters of one of the many creeks that flow into Flathead Lake or the river? Could Larry have drunk from one of those streams and gotten poisoned? It was a paralyzing thought. What about Lilly? She was with Larry the day before he got sick, but she seemed fine. What if she was home sick and they didn't even know?

"I have to talk to the doc!" he told Ruth and bolted from the room, leaving her open-mouthed and wide-eyed.

After laying out his theory for Doc Jensen, Ross asked, "Could he be sick from drinking cyanide contaminated water?"

Doc Jensen knew there was no simple answer to that question and they didn't have time for a lengthy dissertation.

"Depends how close he was to the source and how much the cyanide was diluted. It's an interesting idea, Ross, but I doubt if that's our problem. Larry was fine before he hurt his ear, right?" He continued, not waiting for a response, "That was only a few days ago, cyanide usually builds up in your system over a long period of time, or kills you within minutes."

What Doc Jensen wasn't telling Ross was; if it was cyanide poisoning he had no idea how to treat it. He'd read up on it in the one article he could find and the only treatment recommendation was to remove the source… and allow the patient to breathe…duh.

Disheartened, Ross returned to the room where Larry clung to life. His convulsions were more frequent and more intense.

"He's getting worse," Ruth stated. "It's getting harder for him to breathe."

Ross looked into his wife's pleading eyes and felt weak and helpless.

As Larry's labored respirations rattled in his throat, Ruth was suddenly angry.

"This is all because some asshole rancher wanted to kill a few wolves!" She knew it was an illogical statement but she wanted… needed…to blame someone.

Ross was shocked out of his self-obsessed grief by his wife's outburst. He rarely heard a swear word get past her pretty lips, much less 'asshole'. Suddenly, the full impact of her words hit him like hard left hook.

Ranchers, wolves, traps… **Strychnine!**

Ranchers sometimes used strychnine to kill wolves and coyotes and though outlawed by mutual agreement because of unintended consequences, it was still readily available. Could the traps Larry and Lilly found have been laced with strychnine? Who would do that?

Who cares… right now?

Ross sprinted out of Larry's room and down the hall to the doctor's office.

"You could be onto something," Doc Jensen said, his voice controlled but with an edge of excitement.

He swiftly ran his finger down a row of books until he reached the one he wanted and pulled it off the shelf, flipped through pages, turned back then flipped some more.

"Come with me," he said.

Whether it was an order or a request didn't matter, Ross was right on his heels when they went through a back door into a small shed.

"Grab an axe."

Again the command was quiet but no nonsense. They went into a brushy field, axes in hand, Doc Jensen carrying a small metal bucket. They went less than fifty feet when Doc Jensen stopped at a burned out log.

"Whittle away as much of the burned charcoal as you can and put it in this bucket."

Ross continued to do what he was told but clearly confused, he asked, "What are we doing?"

"We're trying to save your boys life," the doctor declared. "I have no idea if this will work but if you're right about the strychnine it's probably our only chance."

With the bucket full of charcoal, hands and faces streaked with black smudges, the two rushed back into the doctor's office. There Doc Jensen ground the charcoal in to a fine grain and stirred it into a large pitcher of water and handed it, along with a glass, to Ross.

"Take this to Larry's room. I'll be right behind you."

He reached into the back of a cabinet and removed a small bottle and a rag then followed Ross down the hall.

Trying to get the thick, black charcoal concoction down Larry was like trying to push a rope up a waterfall, but eventually, Doc Jensen was satisfied that enough of the thick substance was forced down and into the boy's stomach. The trick now would be to keep it there. Doc Jensen soaked the rag with chloroform from the bottle and placed it over the Larry's nose and mouth.

Within minutes the convulsing stopped, Larry quit gagging and lay quietly. The doctor held the chloroformed rag in place for another minute. This is all guess work, he thought.

"Now we wait," he said in a somber tone. "I don't know how long he will be out, but if this works he should wake up in a couple of hours and on his way to recovery. If it doesn't, I have done all I know to do… it will be between him and God."

Chapter Fifteen

Shaman

At Noisy Waters, Standing Wolf directed Gray Hair, the Paiute and Long Foot, the Minniconjous, to gather their people at a place down river of the fishing falls at the confluence of the Colville River with the Columbia. Once there, Standing Wolf danced for the gathering and spoke at length with Gray Hair and Long Foot. He told the story of the amulet and that the wolf painted on it was a sacred symbol of the Great Spirit of the Sematuse.

He told them it would be good if each people, Paiute, Minniconjous, Sioux, Cheyenne, Crow or Chippewa made their own symbol as a totem or talisman and carried it with them on their quivers or on their person.

The more he spoke of the dance and its powers, the more Standing Wolf was aware that it was his mother, Bent Grass, who truly understood the power of the amulet and the spirits. He also knew from his experience as a soldier, a scout and a Sematuse, most tribes would not believe or accept that a woman could speak directly to the Great Spirit. Such an honor could only belong to a chief, a medicine man or a shaman.

Gray Hair, Long Foot and their followers were very excited and anxious to return to the reservation to spread the good news. While listening to Standing Wolf describing the events that took place in the valley of the Sematuse, Gray Hair was convinced this buckskin-clad half-breed was a messenger from the place he traveled to in his vision, a place he believed to be of another world.

Two days later an edified group of thirty-five Paiute and Minniconjous left the fishing falls of Noisy Waters and started their journey back to Nevada State and Walker Lake. With them they carried six pack-boxes of dried fish, two pack-boxes of pemmican, ten .50 caliber Spencer carbines and a belief that the land and the buffalo would soon be returned to the Native People.

Standing Wolf, however, was troubled, he had begun one part of what he believed his mission to be; spreading the word of the Messiah and bringing hope to the Native People. The other part; to find and retrieve the amulet and return it to the Valley of rainbows, was cause for despair. What began as simple matter of tracking down a lone soldier and taking back the amulet by whatever means necessary, was now a string of missed leads and lost trails.

He did not doubt his skill as a tracker. As far as he was concerned, no man, Indian, white, mountain man, or Methodist could have followed the trail left by the elusive Sam. The intangible factor in this chase seemed to be what a gambler called, 'lady luck'. Soldier Sam, as Standing Wolf thought of him, was just downright lucky, and more and more Standing Wolf was beginning to wonder how much was because of the amulet.

Luck or not, the trail was stone cold and even if he could pick it up again, he was so far behind there was a good chance the snows of winter would fall before he caught up with Sam and the amulet.

If he still had it?

At least I know where I am, he thought.

He could be back in the valley in a couple of weeks. Though he was raised white, he was surprised to be thinking like a white man… only in the valley was he 'all Indian'. Standing Wolf was saddened by that thought and wondered how long it would be before Indians on reservations would no longer be 'all Indian'. He guessed one generation, maybe two, if the government, the Indian Bureau and the churches had there way.

After spending the night on the south bank of the Columbia, down stream from where he met with Gray Hair and the others, Standing

Wolf decided to change his strategy. He had chased Sam long enough and saw no evidence that the army was after Sam, and if they were they either lost his trail or were even farther behind then he.

The only way Sam was a threat to the Sematuse was if he led soldiers back to the valley. If he intended to do that, Standing Wolf believed Sam would not have run. Should the army catch him they would either court martial him, meaning death, or offer him his freedom if he took them to Colonel Wolard and his men.

Before employing a new tact, Standing Wolf wanted to be sure he considered all the possibilities. Try as he might to console himself, rationalizing that losing Sam and the amulet was not such big a deal, he failed. The real issue was the amulet, not Sam. The amulet was a sacred symbol of the Sematuse and must be returned to restore the balance of Mother Earth among all things.

His longing, and love for Star Flower and his mother, were clouding his resolve to do what he believed he must; continue his search until he could return the amulet to Bent Grass.

Sitting on the point of a small granite outcrop, he watched the rushing waters of the Columbia and wondered; if the river could talk, could it tell me where the amulet is and who has it? Touching his own amulet and rubbing it between thumb and forefinger, his thoughts drifted toward the river and its waters…older than time itself.

The morning was cool but he felt a gush of warm air envelope him as if carried by a warm current on the river. In the clear light of day a pale-gray moon hovered over the water. In the distance, Standing Wolf heard the unmistakable howl of a lone wolf, its long mournful wail leaving him shuddering and covered in small, tingling bumps. He rubbed the back of his neck in an effort to curb the chills and regain his composure…both failed.

Then he saw a man sitting astride a large bay horse, rising up from the dark waters of the Columbia. He was wearing blue jeans and a green Pendleton shirt; an ivory-handled Colt .45 rested in an ornately tooled leather holster on his hip and a black Stetson with a Texas roll sat on his head. The big bay stood **on** the water and stomped his front foot, which was clearly visible on the water's surface.

Standing Wolf's dark-tanned skin turned the color of the pale morning moon hovering above the black Stetson. He mouthed the word "Roy" but no sound came out. After all he had seen, the white buffalo spirit of the Sioux, the great black spirit wolf of the Sematuse, the golden-haired shaman and his ghostly-white stallion, the apocalyptic event in the valley, Standing Wolf would not have believed anything could happen that would leave him paralyzed, unable to stand, run or even blink! He even stopped breathing!

"Sombitch! The man on the bay horse said, twirling his mustache. "Breed, is that you? For Christsake, ya look like sheeit!"

The sound of Roy's voice rang in Standing Wolf's ears like the sound of death. His normally quick mind was simply unable to function.

"Ain't ya even gonna say hello? Ya gotta be surprised ta see me."

Roy swung a spur-laden boot over the bay's neck and hooked his knee around the saddle horn.

"If ya don't wanna talk ta me, ya could at least say 'hi' ta Bastard, here. Ah'm sure he's glad ta see ya."

Though he had not regained the power of speech, Standing Wolf's mind was struggling to process the sight before him. He saw the man and horse emerge from the river yet neither appeared to be wet. He did not actually seen Roy die in the valley, but was convinced Soldier Sam was the only survivor of that fateful day. Besides, Bastard might be a good horse but he damn sure could not walk on water.

"Ah know yer wonderin' Breed, so ah'll tell ya. Ah'm dead as a sack a door knobs… so's Bastard but it ain't that bad. Only complaint ah got is, far as ah can tell, there ain't no whores here, but ah ain't done lookin' yet. One more thing, Breed, the Injuns are right…there ain't no hell cause if there was ah'd damn sure be there. Now ah got ta talk ta ya 'bout some serious sheeit!"

Roy removed his leg from its casual, draped position and kicked it back into the stirrup. Sitting stovepipe straight in the saddle, feet pushed forward and toes turned out as if ready for any unexpected leap or sidestep; he twirled his mustache with a gloved hand.

Scary shit!

Standing Wolf thought, nothing can be scarier than this. He desperately wanted to speak, to talk to Roy. He had so many questions but his tongue flopped like a fish on a stick.

"Ah know yer lookin' for a missin' symbol of yer people ya call an amulet. Ya once told me, 'ya don't find the shaman, the shaman finds you'…yer missin' symbol is the same. It's drawn ta its creator an' draws its bearer with it. That's how ya found that cave an' yer mother, because of that amulet hangin' 'round yer neck."

Roy grasp the saddle horn with both hands and leaned back is if trying to free the horn from its pommel.

Standing Wolf stood mesmerized, incapable of independent thought, able only to look and listen to the ghostly image of his old friend. His forefinger and thumb were subconsciously squeezing the amulet as though it was all he had left to hold onto.

While Roy sat silently atop his recalcitrant bay, the wail of the lone wolf again drifted over the river.

"Only people an' animals have souls, a fact ta which ah have only recently become aware, but that symbol on yer amulet, has a *spirit*. It is a gift from its maker. Betcha didn't know that, Breed."

Roy smoothed his mustache and smiled as if speaking from a newly elevated status of 'sage'.

"The amulet is pulled ta its likeness an' its likeness ta it. Like other spiritual totems, yer's has a *transcendental association* with its life form; eagle ta eagle or otter ta otter, but the wolf…he's the guardian of yer people."

Roy paused, removed his gloves, grasped his hat by its crown, lifted it, and ran his fingers through his curly-blond hair then sat his Stetson back on his head.

"As the buffalo is ta the Sioux, so is the wolf ta the Sematuse. The missing symbol can be found among the fateful ruins of a lost dream."

The rawboned bay was becoming agitated and his legs were melting into the black whirlpools of the river currents. Standing Wolf's desire to speak was drowned in a sea of questions.

"The symbol is one with its bearer an' the purity of purpose depends on it. Without the lost amulet, the spirit of the symbol is divided, powerful but not unified. Ya gotta fix that Breed or what yer fixin' ta do is gonna fail!"

As he spoke, Roy and Bastard sank slowly into the murky waters of the mighty Columbia.

"Ah wish ah could stay an' chat but mah window is closin'…"

Standing Wolf did not know how long he stood staring at the river after Roy and Bastard disappeared. That had to be a vision, he thought. After what happened in the valley, Standing Wolf was positive there was nothing left that could surprise him, until this! He struggled desperately to remember every word Roy had spoken. Roy, his unrepentant bastard of a friend talked like a shaman, a spirit of the people he so often ridiculed, even feared.

Roy, a shaman? Ridiculous!

Eventually, Standing Wolf slowly walked to the river and as if spiritually possessed, removed his moccasins and waded into the water. Stooping, he cupped his hands and splashed the refreshing liquid over his face and head. Like John the Babtist, waiting for the anointing of the Holy Water, he was seeking a baptism of knowledge from the cold waters of the Columbia, a metaphysical connection to his cantankerous dead friend; a friend who seemed empowered with knowledge of the ages…even Native culture. What he got was cold feet and a sense of sadness for opportunity lost. He returned to his camp site, and a slightly agitated Whiskey, with a firestorm of thoughts raging through his head.

"I know that was not Roy," he told Whiskey. "It was a vision, like the white buffalo or the black wolf. Roy would never talk like that, and what did he mean about a symbol divided?"

The mornful howl of a wolf reached his ears again, nearer this time and unmistakeably the same one he heard across the river right before his vision.

Oowooooooh. The wailing seemed to be coming from a small island in the river. Oowooooooh. The third cry was definitely closer and the morning air seemed to vibrate. Whiskey's head was high, his ears aimed directly at the sound then he snorted and stomped.

Standing Wolf spun around and saw it…the sacred black wolf of the Sematuse! The animal shook and water sprayed from its ebony coat, creating a rainbow-like halo above its huge form, his yellow eyes glowing like two harvest moons.

Standing Wolf's hand went to his amulet.

"Now I will get some answers," he said, and sank to the ground to sit cross-legged in humble appreciation of this revered beast.

Chapter Sixteen

Talking on the Wind

When Ta-keen Eagle neared the teepee he shared with his wife he heard the disturbing squeals and giggles of feminine laughter. It was disturbing because it usually meant his wife, her friend Willow and his sister, Star Flower, along with a few of the other more mischievous young females, were up to something that almost always ended in grief for him.

He was returning from his first grouse hunt of the fall, proud that he, Little Beaver and Three Feathers had done exceptionally well. He was anxious to boast a little to Laughing Doe because such boasting often ended with her rewarding the 'great hunter' with a special treat. That thought caused a tightening in his loins and he quickly cleared his mind to avoid what could be an embarrassing condition.

When the women saw Ta-keen Eagle approaching, they scattered, except for Laughing Doe, Willow and Star Flower. Greeting the trio with a suspicious grin, he placed the half-dozen blue grouse on the ground.

"I have provided food for much of the village, now my nymphs, what can you do for your chief?"

Ta-keen Eagle knew this group well enough that trying to get a straight answer about their little joke would be like putting feathers back on a goose.

Willow's flirtatious gray eyes beamed at the chance to tease the chief, her unrepentant sexual desires always boiling just below the surface of her gloriously sensual body.

"While these servants prepare our meal, I could reward you for your hunting skills with a few skills of my own," she teased, and motioned for Laughing Doe and Star Flower to leave.

Ta-keen Eagle smiled. He liked the light-hearted and frivolous Willow, as did all of the braves and *most* of the women of the village. A few thought her sexual openness threatening, though jealousy was unknown to the people of the valley.

The banter continued until Star Flower broke the frivolous mood. "My brother, I am sad to be without Standing Wolf, and Bent Grass is troubled that her son may be lost."

"Lost?" Ta-keen Eagle questioned. "Fire-hair Frank speaks of Standing Wolf being one who knows more of the world outside this valley than any man. How could he be lost?"

"Not lost because he does not know how to return home but misguided in his mission," Star Flower corrected then left in search of Spotted Fawn.

Star Flower became friends with Spotted Fawn while she was recovering from an attack by the white humpback. Since discovering Fire-hair Frank was her father, Spotted Fawn spent a lot of time with him. Spotted Fawn also knew Standing Wolf outside the valley, a little-known fact among the Sematuse. She found Spotted Fawn at the river cleaning the grouse her husband, Little Beaver brought from his hunt.

When Spotted Fawn saw Star Flower, she dropped a partially cleaned bird, quickly rinsed her hands in the water, and rushed to Star Flower, giving her a hug. If Star Flower thought of Spotted Fawn as her friend, the girl thought of Star Flower as the big sister she never had. With the exception of Warm Hands, her mentor and self-proclaimed father, there was no one in the valley Spotted Fawn admired more than Star Flower.

"It is so good to see you," Spotted Fawn said, after releasing the woman from the heart-felt hug.

Although graced with extraordinary beauty, as were most of the women in the valley of rainbows, Star Flower was best known for her kind heart and gentle nature. Anyone who had faced any kind of adversity would quickly confirm that as a truth.

"Spotted Fawn, my heart soars to see you so healthy and happy after the awful ordeal you endured. You are a gift to my people and to Little Beaver. He is well named as his teeth have not stopped showing since you took him into your heart and your body."

"You have kind words but none of that would matter if not for Standing Wolf and Bent Grass. All of the True People may have died from the soldier's bullets. You saw the good in Standing Wolf when many, including me, did not." Her brown eyes sparkled.

"How much has your father told you of his life with Standing Wolf outside our valley?"

"Not a lot. A long time ago they fought in a war where brothers fought brothers and they formed a special bond. My father said Standing Wolf, who was then called by a white man name, saved his life." Spotted Fawn picked up the grouse and resumed her task. "He did not say how and I did not ask. I believe there are many things my father knows but has not shared with me."

"Do you not wonder why he would keep things from you after losing you for so long?" Star Flower asked out of curiosity, not to pry.

"Sometime, but when it is time for me to know, he will tell me. I think he may be protecting me from hurtful things. I can not fault him for that, even if they are things I have a right to know." Spotted Fawn looked toward the village. "Speak of my father and like a woodpecker to wood, there he is."

Star Flower turned to see the odd-looking man ambling toward them. It was not that he was ugly like the bear, just that his fire-colored hair always surprised her. After greetings and hugs between father and daughter, his attention turned to Star Flower.

"Are you hearing anything about Standing Wolf?" he asked, knowing she could not have actually heard from the half-breed, but believing more and more in the Indian way of 'talking on the wind'. He did not know how it worked, not even Bent Grass could explain it, but he was sure it was real.

"Only that he is feeling conflicted," Star Flower replied as if saying the words brought her pain. "I feel him seeking guidance. That is what I wish to speak with you about, you and Bent Grass."

Frank wondered if she had just used the 'talking on the wind' thing on him. She wanted to talk to me and guess what, here I am, he thought. There was a time, not so long ago, when he would have found it all pretty spooky, but now he expected this kind of thing from these people.

"I think a lot of people are troubled over Standing Wolf and whatever he is trying to do. I say you, me, the chief and his bride, Bent Grass and my daughter here have a powwow. She can help translate whatever I might have to say. Not that I'm likely to say anything all that important."

Frank, too, was concerned about his friend and with a twinge of excitement thought, it will give me another chance to talk to the seer. He fought to block the hot springs image from forming a picture in his mind…and failed.

It was a warm, early fall, evening when the impromptu council was called to meet in Warm Hands cupola. Ta-keen Eagle wanted Warm Hands included, and his long-house provided an excellent place to gather.

Bent Grass spoke mostly about what she felt, not what she knew. She did not have a vision from the Great Spirit to guide her, only the transcendental connection she held with the amulet and the sacred black wolf. That message was confusing and somewhat troubling.

Each participant expressed their concern that Standing Wolf's mission outside the valley was somehow becoming distorted, even misguided. No one was concerned for Standing Wolf's safety, but there was a general sense, an intuitive uneasiness that something was not as it should be. All agreed it would be best if Standing Wolf would return to the valley to have a full council regarding his mission, and the missing amulet.

At the urging of everyone present, and especially Star Flower, Bent Grass agreed to enter the cave of spirits to seek council or a vision from *Ogle Wa Nagi*, and to inform this group of any message or enlightenment she received.

When they exited the cupola, a bright Brother Moon greeted them, casting eerie shadows over the mysterious valley. As they went their separate ways, Frank spoke to Bent Grass in his best Salish brogue.

"It is a fine night. Could we walk for a while?"

"Just walk, or would you like to talk as well?" Bent Grass replied lightheartedly. The council meeting raised her spirits and she was enjoying the moment.

"Yes, talking would be a nice if I can keep from tripping over my words," Frank said, trying to be funny.

Bent Grass laughed, actually laughed. Frank tried to remember if he ever heard her laugh before.

"You made *hoyake*, a joke, and I get it! Your Salish is much improved."

The seer smiled and Frank was surprised by a warm wave that swept through his body and lingered as a warm tingle beneath his red whiskers.

"When will you go back to the cave to speak with *Ogle Wa Nagi*?" he asked, disappointed that he could not think of another joke. He wanted to hear her laugh again.

"I could go now and you can come with me if you are not afraid." She was in a playful mood, something she found both perplexing and pleasurable.

A different kind of flush rushed through Frank's veins. He'd been in that cave a few times, mostly when he was still crazy, and that was bad enough. To go in there sane was, well…insane.

"Last time I went in there I was a crazy mountain man and I came out a father, a friend and seriously sane. I go in there again I could come out as something awful…like a wood rat. I hate wood rats," he stammered.

Some things you never get over.

Bent Grass found herself enjoying the company of this friend of Standing Wolf's. He was funny looking with his red hair and whiskers, but she found something about him comforting. She wondered if perhaps it was because he was a trapper. The only man she ever loved, Standing Wolf's father, French, was a trapper. This walk and talk was sparking feelings long since forgotten. Maybe it was because trappers have a connection and respect for the animals who gave their lives to be made into warm coats or moccasins or blankets. She believed trappers are more like Indians than like white men.

"Be brave," she said, suddenly inspired. "Come to the cave of *tlchachies* with me, I promise to protect you from the wood rats."

She is having fun with me, he thought, I have never seen this side of her. That thought reminded him of the side of her he *had* seen in the hot springs, and he was glad the moonlight was dim and his whiskers were already red. As unnerving as the notion of going back in the spirit cave was he enjoyed being with Bent Grass too much to let a little thing like paralyzing fear stand in his way.

"I am brave," he quipped. "But what will happen if your Great Spirit comes to visit you? Something tells me he is not going to be real happy see a white man in such a sacred place."

"It is not sacred only to the Sematuse. It is sacred to all who believe in the old ways. The color of your skin means nothing; red, white, black, brown, yellow…it is all the same to *Ogle Wa Nagi*. It is what is in your heart that matters. Of course, *Ogle Wa Nagi* would not strike down one who is loco or ignorant. Of course you are neither, but you could pretend," she added quickly and again Bent Grass smiled at Frank.

"Thanks for the reassurance," he replied good-naturedly.

Stepping through the small opening into the sacred cave, Bend Grass held out her hand for Frank, who grasped it and held it firmly. Taking that first step, he expected some strange phenomenon like sinking into the stone or turning upside down to occur. When nothing unusual happened he took a breath but did not release Bent Grass' hand. It was very dark and his head filled with the many mysteries this place held.

"Shouldn't we have a torch?" he asked, hopeful, while his eyes probed the darkness. "How do you see to paint in here?" He saw a faint glow from the painted ceiling and walls, giving an eerie illumination to the already daunting place. "And how do you make paints that glow in the dark?"

"I have my ways," she responded coyly. "Those secrets I have not even shared with our chief."

Frank felt foolish, realizing how presumptuous that question was. He mentally scolded himself then asked, "Why did you want me to come into this place with you? It is so dark in here we could not see wood rats if they had us surrounded."

Again, Bent Grass laughed and Frank felt he was witnessing something spiritual. With her hand firmly gripped by his, she tugged.

"Come with me, we will try to speak with Standing Wolf through the amulet."

Frank followed, feeling blind, the light so dim he could see nothing except the faint glow of Bent Grass' paintings.

She can see in the dark.

That must be her secret! The idea struck him as obvious, though he had no idea how she could do it. Maybe she was nocturnal, like an owl or a cat, or the Great Spirit guided her through the darkness like a bat.

Bats!

Frank didn't like them any better than wood rats.

Moving deeper into the cave, Frank concentrated on the hand leading him though the darkness. To him, it felt like there was a connection through their hands and she was drawing him to her. While he was savoring her touch, a rush of soft warm air encompassed them. They were entering a narrow passage, the walls so close he had to turn sideways to avoid bumping them with his shoulders. His thoughts raced back to the life-changing experiences encountered in this labyrinth.

Sweat began running down his nose and dripping onto his hairy face and into his mouth, tasting like salty brine. He was having difficulty breathing, and began to feel the vice-like grip of claustrophobia. He swallowed hard and fought the wave of panic threatening to overtake him.

Bent Grass felt his hand turn cold and sweaty, unsure of the reason but realized her partner was in trouble.

"Frank!" she said, sharply, pulling his hand against her chest. "Listen to me, concentrate on my voice, we will be through this passage very soon and there will be light. Put your other hand on my shoulder and think of something else, something pleasurable, we will soon be in a special place and I will give you light."

She held his right hand against her breast with his arm under her right elbow, his left hand was on her left shoulder, her back pressed against him so he had to move his feet very carefully to avoid stepping on her heels. Slowly they inched forward, Frank completely enamored by the feel of holding this delicate woman so close.

It's like holding a goddess in my arms, he thought…But then in this world she's as close to a goddess as there is.

Without warning, they broke out of the narrow confines of the passage and Bent Grass pulled free of his embrace. Frank was relieved and disappointed. He could breathe again, although he still could not see but he missed the feel of her closeness.

Releasing his hand, Bent Grass touched his arm lightly and said, "Stay here, there will soon be light."

Frank prepared himself for some unearthly bolt of lightning or a ball of fire thrown by the unseen hand of some supreme being, instead he heard the pounding of rock on rock and dripping water followed by a clicking noise, then silence and more rapid clicking. As his eyes sought the source of the sound there was a small spark, then a flash, and he found himself standing in a cavity approximately ten by twenty with an eight-foot ceiling. A small, intensely bright white light illuminated the entire area.

Bent Grass smiled at him.

Frank's eyes darted from her radiant smile to the glare of the flame. He noticed three small bowls setting on a small ledge, each filled with a grayish, powdery substance. A gourd pitcher sat under a small waterfall that seeped from the rock wall. As his eyes adjusted to the brightness, he made out a small canister with a reflective shield.

"Carbide light! My God, it's a goddamn carbide lamp!" he blurted in disbelief.

Frank knew the military used caride lanterns, but how could this seer of people who did not even understand gunpowder know how to make this kind of light?

"Do you like my light?" Bent Grass asked proudly.

Speechless, he looked around the cavernous opening. As in the main entrance, this part of the cave was adorned with Bent Grass' paintings; birds, fish, horses and deer…all life-like and colorful. There was even a painting of him, red hair and whiskers, wild-eyed and dressed in the mukluks and parka he was wearing when discovered by the village children. Standing Wolf was there, too, mounted on his big black Arab. He sat in a fancy western saddle, his Bowie knife resting against his thigh above the knee.

Frank opened his mouth to speak but only an assortment of grunts and groans came out. On the far wall, he saw a painted, life-sized image of a man dressed in fringed buckskins, a beaver-pelt hat, complete with its flat hairless tail, sitting on the man's head. A black beard covered his face, and long curly black hair flowed from under the hat.

Bent Grass quietly explained, "That is French, *achteway kin* of Standing Wolf…his father and *mihakin,* my husband. Was my husband," she corrected.

Frank was not only speechless but did not know what to say if he could speak. Finally he managed to force "how" from somewhere deep in his throat. It wasn't even a question, rather more a statement of his astonishment.

"How?" Bent Grass repeated, puzzled but slightly amused. "How do you like my lair?" she interpolated.

Frank was overwhelmed. Questions invaded his mind like locust in a cornfield. He began to laugh, starting with a chuckle, then a giggle, swelling into a gut wrenching, side-splitting close to rolling-on-the-floor laughter.

Startled, Bent Grass rushed to where he lay writhing in apparent pain but laughing like a crazed river otter. She felt a touch of panic. The cave of spirits turned him from loco to sane…had it now turn him back?

"Frank, Frank," she said, grabbing his shoulders, then out of desperation slapped his bearded face.

The laughter stopped abruptly, Frank was stunned and apologetically tried to explain. "I came here looking for answers, ways to help Standing Wolf, ways to help you and your people, and now this…" He motioned to the light, the painting of French and himself, to everything around him. "I have not found answers, only more questions, many more questions. I cannot help you. You have answers, I have only questions." Scrambling to his feet, he looked deeply into her brown eyes and smiled. "I am sorry for laughing like a fool. The whole thing struck me as outrageously funny. How in the name of heaven did you learn to make carbide light?"

"Heaven?" She looked puzzled. "I do not know heaven."

"Never mind," Frank said with a wave of his hand. "Tell me how you make the light."

"The light is a gift from French. He found rocks near *no-wha hee* that caused him much excitement. "It is his spirit light. He called it 'magic' and promised me as long as his spirit lived the light would burn." A tear rolled down her cheek, "Standing Wolf told me French is dead, but still his light burns." She sounded sad and confused.

Oh boy, thought Frank…How am I going to explain this?

He said, "Is it not like the warriors who came when Standing Wolf danced? They were dead, some for many winters, but their spirits live in the aspen leaves and thunder clouds. The spirit of French might live here in this cave."

Makes sense to me, he thought; first proud at his insight then dismayed at the prospect.

"If he is here, why can I not talk to him? I talk on the wind to many spirits from many strange place; places I have only seen from this cave. Even *Ogle Wa Nagi* speaks to me…why not French?"

I hope she doesn't expect an answer from me, Frank thought. She was the one who speaks to the Great Spirit, he couldn't even hold on to a sacred symbol when given one.

"Perhaps the one you call French does not speak because he has nothing to say. You can not hold his words in your arms or caress his thoughts with your fingers. His spirit might live but can not move from its world to yours."

Frank was not at all comfortable talking about spirits and the spirit-world with Bent Grass. She knew far more about that kind of thing than he could even imagine.

"Tell me about the light," he said, hoping to change the subject.

Besides, he really wanted to know what she knew about carbide light. He'd seen them used by the military but didn't understand how they worked and realized he should have asked them.

"I have told you, the light is the spirit of French." Bent Grass seemed a little annoyed. "He showed me how to make the black and white stones into powder and to put the powder in this thing he called 'lamp' then to pour in water, flick the striker with my thumb and the spirit of French gives me magic light." A quizzical look slid over her face, "Do you like magic?" she asked.

*I think I liked it better when I thought it **was** magic.*

"So this is how you painted the pictures in here," he confirmed. "Are there other places where you have painted, or only here and in the cave opening?"

"There are many, but I have not shared the light with anyone. Come, I will show you another."

Grabbing a handle at the top of the canister with one hand, she took Frank's with the other and led him though a maze of passages and tunnels.

No wonder Standing Wolf and I were lost in here. He thought... *This place is amazing.*

"You could hide in here forever," he murmured. "No one knows this cave like you. When standing Wolf and I were lost and I found my sanity, we fell into a hole and landed in an underground lake or river. Do you know that place?" It seemed unlikely, but he had learned never to underestimate this woman.

"I will take you there, it is not far," she said, tugging his hand. "It is a place of talking on the wind. It is how I know what happens outside the walls of our valley. It is also a place where strange things happen that I do not understand."

The cave was not as frightening to Frank, walking with Bent Grass and the carbide lantern, as it was with Standing Wolf, especially after their torch blew out, but it was still plenty spooky.

"Do you ever get lost in here?" he tentatively asked, while marveling at the spider web of underground passageways.

"Without the voice of *Chopaka* I am always lost, it is He who guides me."

Frank smiled. Even these people with no contact with the outside world or Christian missionaries have beliefs that ring of Christianity. They call Standing Wolf *Waboka,* which means Messiah. The Great Spirit speaks to Bent Grass from the mountain, as God did to Moses, and just like the desert, you could wander for forty years in this cave without divine guidance. The difference being, the Sematuse Messiah was already delivered, while the Jews and Christians were still waiting.

Frank was yanked from his reverie by the sound of voices. They were muffled, distant and unintelligible but clearly voices. Bent Grass turned to him.

•

"This is far enough," she said softly. "Beyond here it is not safe. It is where you and Standing Wolf fell into the waters of hope."

In the shadows of the light, Frank could see the tunnel floor descend at what he presumed to be a deceptive grade. The sound of running water was barley audible above the din of voices. When Bent Grass placed a finger to her lips, a sign for him to remain quiet, his mind was spinning. Now I know what it is like to be schizophrenic, he thought, and put his hands over his ears.

Bent Grass led him into a small alcove and the muffled jumble of words unscrambled like chicks on a nest. He heard different voices speaking an Indian language but not Sematuse, although he did occasionally understand a word or two. Bent Grass listened intently for what seemed like a millennium before she again took his hand, and led him back to what she earlier referred to as her lair.

"What did you hear back there?" Frank asked excitedly. "I heard their words! I could not understand them but I did hear them," he added, emphatically.

"They speak of trouble. A chief of the Yakima, Quil-tin-e-nock, has been killed by horse soldiers and many chiefs are gathering to avenge his death. Some white men and horse soldiers have already been killed. There is much anger among the Native People. The Sarsapkin Chief Ching-ga-skook has decided no more whites will have safe passage through the land of the *Okinakane*. The *Choo-pin-it-pa-loo,* are angry too, but they are always angry. The horse soldiers from the place Standing Wolf called 'fort' are leaving, fearing for their lives."

"Then they will not be coming back to the valley," Frank stated. "Is that not a good thing?"

"It is good for now, but I am concerned if many whites are killed by angry Natives, will they not send more horse soldiers to fight back? Will they not want to kill all Indians to make their people safe?" Bent Grass touched Frank's arm. "I do not believe we are safe until Standing Wolf does the Dance of *Tlchachie* and removes all white men…all **evil** white men from the land."

"Could you hear Standing Wolf, was he talking on the wind?" Frank was getting anxious.

"I did not hear him but I could feel him on the river web. He is trying to send his words but there is too much anger among many chiefs for his words to be heard. I know he is not angry or afraid, but he is troubled."

Frank's awe and admiration for this woman was nearing worship. Before the Ghost Dance he would not have believed any of this, not even the crazy trapper he used to be would have, but he had seen what she prophesied come to pass. Maybe the secret of the light and the cave paintings were not magic, but he did not doubt she knew things no mortal should know. Nothing about this valley was normal yet Spotted Fawn, Standing Wolf and he came there from outside. Why could they not leave without the amulet?

Or can we?

The questions were fighting to escape from his head like salmon up a waterfall.

"Troubled, how, and what is a river web?" he asked.

"I do not know what troubles him, maybe the anger on the river, maybe because he has not yet found the missing amulet, or maybe he is uncertain about his mission to save the Native People from losing the old ways." She looked up at Frank and continued to explain, "All the waters of the land are joined like the web of a spider and the wind on the water carries the words of the people to those who know how to listen. You heard the words…you know this to be true."

"So you have to go to the water to hear the words?" Frank asked sheepishly.

"Yes, but some waters are better for listening and some are better for sending."

Frank was faced with a dichotomy; he felt incredibly privileged to be in this sacred place with such a special, spiritual woman, yet he was feeling an intense need to get out of this cave and back into the open air…soon!

"Bent Grass," he said, sheepishly, "Could we go back to the village, I need some air." He hoped she didn't take that the wrong way, and flushed at the thought.

"Of course," she said, hearing the distress in his voice. She reached down and turned a lever on top of the canister and the light went out.

Again, Frank was open-mouthed and speechless. The entire chamber in which they stood glowed with a soft mix of greens, blues, yellows and other colors he could not begin to describe. Each painting was glowing and the combined light produced a sensation he could only compare to being inside a kaleidoscope. He realized that the paints must have absorbed the light to be able to glow in the dark, but wondered what kind of paint could do that?

Another gift from French I suppose, he thought. Who was this guy…a trapper or a geologist? Frank felt an unwelcome pang of jealousy but quickly recovered and simply said, "This is like living in a rainbow."

Bent Grass took his hand and led him from the spirit cave where the night air was so sweet he could taste it. He took two deep breaths and savored them. They walked under a starry sky, with the half-face of Brother Moon watching their progress, until they neared the village and the small teepee where Bent Grass slept when not in the spirit cave.

Frank stopped and waited for Bent Grass to turn back. "I thank you for this night," he said sincerely. "I have never felt as privileged as I do now. I do not know why you shared your secrets with me and fear I do not have the words to make you know how grateful and humbled I am."

Bent Grass stood erect in the moonlight, shoulders back, head tilted, brown eyes looking up at him.

My God, has she always been this beautiful, he thought…or is that cave magic too?

"I have always been a seer," she said. "When French came to this valley I was a young girl. I had never seen anyone like him and I was intrigued. He liked me from the beginning and when he saw how I could paint, he believed it to be a gift from what he called 'God'. He showed me many things; how to make light and the paint that glows in the dark.

"When Chief Chewaken offered French a woman, he chose me. I was honored and we loved each another until Standing Wolf was born, then French began to worry about his soul and that of his son. I understood none of this but was shown in a vision that I must paint the image of the sacred black wolf on stiff leather. With that symbol, French would be free to do whatever his God wanted of him.

"That was the last I saw of him, except for the painting in the cave. After that, with every vision I was given of a white-clay human,

I thought of French and our son…until the night after we sat in the *no-wha hee*. French came to me in a vision. He told me his spirit still loves me, but he can never return to this place or to me. He told me these things because he felt my desire and wanted to set my spirit free."

She turned and slowly walked a few short steps, stopped and turned back, facing Frank.

"You have been in the valley for many moons, yet you have not chosen a woman for your bed. Do you not like women?"

The question caught Frank completely of guard, his mind flashed back to the hot springs and his brief glimpse of her nude body. After an uncomfortably long pause he said, "I do like women, but there is a long sad story I can never tell anyone, not even you. I will tell you that for a very long time I have not felt any desire for a woman. I was content to catch cats and skin mink and muskrats. Even after I regained my senses I did not think of a woman, except for my daughter."

His hands started sweating and his mouth felt dry as a sand pit. He didn't know where his next words came from; he barely heard them but knew he spoke them.

"I do want a woman, for the first time since Spotted Fawn's mother, I want a woman to make love with, to hold, to touch, to laugh and cry with; I want you, Bent Grass, I want you."

Frank reached out to gently grip her shoulders then pulled her to him. To his surprise, she came willingly. He stooped and placed his lips on hers. Her arms reached around his back, one hand moving up his neck under his long hair, and she pressed her lips tighter against his. He slid his hands from her shoulders and engulfed her in an embrace that seemed like a thousand years in the making. Bent Grass again took his hand, this time to lead him into her shelter, her womanhood and her soul.

Chapter Seventeen

Apparition

"C'mon Sam," Lillian pleaded with exaggerated pain. "Tell me how you got this. A girl gave it to you didn't she?" She handed the amulet back to him but the teasing continued. "You have an Indian girlfriend don't you? Is this like an engagement ring or something?"

Sam was very uncomfortable with the way this conversation was going.

"I do not have an Indian girl friend and never did," he said, defensively. "If you must know, I stole it. That is why I do not want to talk about it. I know I should give it back but I can not, I would be killed if I tried." At least that was the truth.

"We better head back," Lillian said, thinking it was a joke and 'don't have a cow over it'.

Once mounted and headed back toward the Running R Sam broke the silence. "How far are we from where your brother saw the wolf pack?"

He hoped Lillian was not mad about the amulet.

"About ten miles, they were north of here on Wild Horse Creek. That's where Larry found the trap that cut his ear, too."

Sam was relieved, she sounded normal, if the sound of a voice from heaven could be considered normal.

"How did that happen? I do not see how you get your ear cut by a trap without sticking your head right into the jaws."

It was Lillian's turn to get defensive.

"He was riding Weasel and you know how he can be. He was jumping around and the trap flew up and hit Larry in the ear." Tears welled up in her eyes. "Okay," she blurted without provocation, "It was my fault. We were racing, I started it, and Weasel jumped and the trap hit Larry. It was my fault, Sam, I started the race!"

Sam was startled but was quickly overcome with empathy.

"It isn't your fault," he responded with compassion. "I do not know your brother but I am sure he is a big boy and capable of taking care of himself."

"He wanted me to carry the traps because my horse is gentler and I wouldn't do it because the traps stunk." She looked at Sam with water-filled lake-blue eyes. "If I had packed the traps we wouldn't have raced and Larry wouldn't be hurt."

Again, Sam saw the irony; first he was here because of the horrible thing that happened to Lillian's mother, now, because of careless horseplay he was here to help out and make sure nothing happened to Lillian. A couple of days ago he was running scared, hungry and with no idea what to do next. Now, because of bad things that happened to other people, he had new clothes, maybe a job, and hope for a future life.

It was dark when Sam and Lillian rode through the massive log-arch-gate of the Running R. Once their horses were put away Lillian asked, "You want to come up to the house for a piece of apple pie before you go to bed?"

"Just try to stop me," Sam joked, happy over his good fortune.

The pie was good and the company better, the more time he spent around Lillian the more infatuated he was becoming. I must admit, I don't have much to compare to, he thought, but watching her sun-colored hair drape over her shoulders, her blue eyes sparkling when he said something funny, and the fluid movements of her shapely body as she scurried about the kitchen picking up plates and putting things away, he was convinced there was no more beautiful girl on earth.

Chica! Girl!

He mentally slapped himself. That was what he had to remember.

With the pie eaten and the dishes washed and put away, Sam was out of reasons to stay at the house. He thanked Lillian for everything, ad nauseam, and retired to the bunkhouse. He fell asleep with images of the lovely Lillian occupying his thoughts.

Lobo and Lola hovered under the dense conifer canopy at the edge of the meadow. A large black bear was grunting and groaning as he pulled on the hind-leg of bloated white-faced cow. A loud snap startled the pair as the hip-socket broke, freeing the leg from the carcass. The rest of the pack, a dozen in all, was a couple hundred yards deeper into the forest cover, distracted by a snowshoe hare scurrying for cover under a burned out stump.

The alpha male and female were intrigued by the prey the big bear was devouring. The scent of the prey gave them no real clue as to what the bear found so appealing. They knew it was not a deer or elk, maybe a buffalo. It had been a long time since they fed on a buffalo carcass and the idea made Lobo's belly growl in anticipation.

They were on the southwestern part of their loop between the Cabinet Mountains and the Whitefish Range but they had never drifted this far south before. They had been distracted by a powerful, pungent scent of a lone male traveling through their territory. Lobo found it annoying and obtrusive while Lola was less annoyed and a little intrigued by the strong male odor.

When the rest of the pack tired of chasing the hare and joined the alpha pair, Lobo and Lola decided they had allowed the bear to feed long enough. With a flurry of growls, nips, yelps and whimpers the plan was communicated and the command to initiate was given.

It was a basic and time tested plan; the six yearling pups took turns slashing and dashing and generally irritated and aggravated the big bear into repeated attempts to rip them to shreds. With each failed attempt the bear grew more exhausted and less interested in food.

At Lobo's command, the entire pack charged growling, snapping, retreating and charging again until the frustrated bear decided to seek a little solitude, leaving the remainder of the cow to the irritating wolf pack.

Ah, the sweet smell of success, thought Lobo as he shoved his head into the chest cavity in search of the heart and lungs.

It's not buffalo, but it's not bad.

Lola fed contentedly on the fleshy hindquarters while the pups flitted from one exposed morsel to another. When even the smallest and most timid of the pups had eaten their fill, Lobo led the pack into the woods and a rock overhang within sight of the kill. From there they would guard against any intruder who might think the kill was abandoned while they spent some time playing and frolicking until once again they felt the urge to eat.

As daylight seeped on the meadow, darkness lingered in the forest. Lobo and Lola lay next to each other, their noses tucked into the other's flank. Whimpers and murmurs crawled from their throats as each dreamed of bringing down a mule deer as it fled on stiff-legged stotts, or a time not far away when they would again be driven by undeniable lust to mate and seek a den to restart the cycle of life in the wilds.

Lobo was jerked awake by the same annoying scent that had drawn him and the pack off course. Quietly slipping away from the sleeping Lola, he followed the scent on a light breeze. He made a couple wide circles around the kill to make certain the intruder was not planning a share of the meal they so cleverly acquired. The scent was becoming stronger, raising the hackles on the back of his neck.

When he hit a track in the dusty game trail he paused, sniffing and looking curiously, circling around the track several times. Something was not right, the track looked like his own and the smell was that of another wolf, but this paw print was twice the size of his. He was puzzled and followed the trail cautiously as it led into a timbered ravine and along a dry creek bed.

The gully grew steeper and became choked with dense underbrush until eventually, the dry bed changed to a few isolated pools; he stopped and lapped up the cool, sweet liquid. Farther on, the streambed was filled with flowing water and the trail was gone, the intruders scent faint. Again he stopped and realized he had lost the scent of Lola and the pack. He'd come too far, it was time to go back. Milling around, he found a rotting cedar stump and lifted his leg, the mark increasing the pack's home range by another few miles to the south. Satisfied the intruder was outside their territory, Lobo headed back toward Lola and his clan.

He traveled only a short distance when a shift in the wind brought a new scent to his sensitive nostrils. He stopped and with nose to the wind, sniffed repeatedly. This was a new smell, not the annoying scent of a possible adversary, but a sweet smell, the smell of food similar to the current fare they had taken from the bear. It was the kind of smell that compelled him to find the source.

If the breeze held, it would take him right to it. The terrain flattened and the cover became sparse as he came upon a well-used game trail and the smell grew stronger, then faded. He circled around puzzled but determined. *It is here somewhere.*

Sam woke to the incessant crowing of a proud rooster and the prospect of spending another day with Lillian. *I haven't been this happy since before my mother died,* he thought as he crawled out of bed and looked around the bunkhouse.

"Don't get stupid," he said. "She is still a chica, a very pretty girl but still a girl, probably not more than fourteen."

He took extra time shaving, trimming around his newly acquired horseshoe mustache and combing his thick black hair, grown longer since his escape from the fort. Acknowledging his motivation for taking extra care with his appearance, he silently admonished himself for his vanity. Leaving the bunkhouse and heading toward the barn, he was ready for a day of chores and whatever the 'boss lady' wanted done. He smiled at the thought as he entered the stall where Major was kept. The little mare was being pampered since arriving at the Running R. She had lost considerable weight and was on the verge of going lame the day he arrived at the ranch.

Ten yards from her stall, Sam stopped short.

Ahhroooooo....

Turning his head, he listened carefully.

Ahhrooooooo...

It was the distant but unmistakable sound of a wolf and seemed to coming from the direction he and Lillian had ridden yesterday.

Remembering Lilly's apparent interest in wolves, he headed for the ranch house.

"I hope the howling doesn't stop before I get there," he mumbled.

Mounting the log steps, he hurried across the porch and grasped the cowbell hanging from a leather cord. He rang it, waited and rang it again.

"Who is it?" Lillian asked, from behind the heavy wooden door.

"Sam, who else would **it** be?" he answered, anxious for her to open the door.

"What do you want, Sam?" she persisted.

"I heard wolves up toward the lake. I thought you might want to hear them."

"Just a minute."

The big door swung open and Lillian stepped out wrapped in a terry-cloth robe, wet hair dripping.

"They better be howling or you're a dead man," she said, serious as sour milk.

Sam tried to swallow the lump in his throat but failed. He was desperate for the wolf to redeem him and stunned by the wet-haired beauty standing before him. Her face was so shiny and clean, and there was something about her wet hair that aroused him, which flusterd him even more.

Ahhrrooooh....

Thank God, he thought, finally able to swallow the lump. He looked away toward the distant howling, hoping to control the unwelcome arousal.

"Cool," Lillian's responsed to the mournful cry. "Sounds like only one, that's a little odd."

"How far away do you think it is?" Sam asked.

"Hard to say…sounds like it's up by the lake, maybe farther." She stepped back inside. "I have to get some clothes on. If you want to take care of the chores, I'll make us some breakfast then we can discuss a wolf hunt."

Sam was halfway done with the chores before all of him got over the sight of Lillian in her robe, wet hair and all. His mind had runaway with his body or maybe the other way around. In any case, he was flustered, embarrassed and a little concerned.

"I can not be thinking of her that way," he admonished.

When Lillian set biscuits and sausage gravy on the table, Sam touched the amulet hanging around his neck. He was positive it was a good luck charm. I could spend the rest of my life living like this, he thought. Then he felt a pang of regret; unless Lillian's dad hired him, he would have to be on his way when her parents returned.

"When do you think your parents will be back?" He asked but didn't know what day of the week it was or how long they had been gone.

Lillian's face went ashen.

"I don't know but I'm getting worried. They've been gone for five days and if Larry was okay they should be home by now." Tears filled her eyes and she wiped them away with the back of her hand. "I'm scared Sam, I'm really scared." Gaining her composure she said, "I think they should be home today unless they had to wait a while for Larry's infection to go away. If they take their time it's a two day ride to Horse Plain."

Five days.

Sam thought, My God I must have missed a couple of days somewhere.

Not wanting to upset Lillian more than she already was and not wanting to think about her folks getting home and his stay in heaven ending, he changed the subject.

"What do you have for me to do today boss-lady?" He hoped she would see some humor in the question.

"I was thinking it would be fun to ride up north and see if we could find any sign of wolves. I kind of hate to leave the ranch in case mom, dad and Larry get back but I can't stand to wait around here either. So, if you'll saddle the horses I'll fix us a lunch and we'll go on a little wolf hunt. If we find any stray cows we can move them to the Big Arm pasture. That will make Dad happy." Lillian got up from the table and started gathering up dishes. "Go," she said with a sweeping motion of her hand. "You think you can just sit around and chat all day? We have work to do."

As Sam and Lillian rode north from the Running R toward the Big Arm and the fall pasture they were surprised and curious. Though it was very early morning it was certainly broad daylight the sound of the wolf had grown increasingly vocal.

"I'm no wolf expert but it seems like pretty unusual behavior to me. I thought wolves only hunted at night and slept during the day," Sam said. He knew Lillian would have an opinion or two where wolves were concerned.

"Larry says wolves will hunt whenever they're hungry, daylight or dark, they usually travel more at night though. I haven't heard wolves all that much but these do sound strange."

The clear howl of a singular wolf was punctuated by coyote-like barks and yips with an occasional drawn-out howl as more wolves joined the chorus.

When the riders drew closer to the raucous sound of the wolves, Sam touched the amulet resting on his chest and thought of the black wolf and its unnerving yellow eyes. They rode in silence for a while, Sam letting his mind wander, surprised at the mix of emotions the eerie wailing generated, continuing to touch the amulet; Lillian focused on narrowing down the location of this unlikely reveille.

By lunch time Lillian was convinced the incessant commotion was coming from Wild Horse Creek.

"It's only a couple more miles to where Larry found the traps and that sounds like about where the wolves are. I think we should wait 'till we get there before we eat lunch. That okay with you?" Lillian was getting tense. "I know I'm young, Sam, but I've got a bad feeling, something is not right."

"Wolves do not make that kind of a ruckus in the same spot for such a long time. It is not normal…ahora no. Lo siento, I am sorry, I meant to say not now…not during the day."

Sam had been on his best behavior and trying to speak the correct English he was taught as a boy, not the army jargon he'd become used to, however, he couldn't help occasionally falling back on his father's native tongue. His army buddies used to tease him unmercifully about his accent and even more so when a Spanish word slipped out. He feared the lovely Lilly might find his manner of speech offensive.

"You're not normal, Sam, most of Larry's friends talk as if they'd never seen the inside of a school even though they have. I don't mean to be impolite but I find your accent quite pleasing, not to mention how nice it is to hear to a man speak like he has a brain in his head."

Sam could hardly believe his ears. She actually liked the way he talked!

A man.

Lillian played the words over in her head and a warm rush swept through her body. Well he is. She thought…not like Larry's stupid friends who were always saying dumb things and trying to get her alone.

Sam smiled, pleased that Lilly was not offended by his Spanish heritage.

Ahhrrooooo…

Sam's hand went to the butt of the carbine in his saddle scabbard, glad he had decided to ride Major today. The high-strung Weasel was a fun ride but Sam had a feeling he was going to have enough excitement today without trying to out-guess that unpredictable pinto. Besides, he noticed Major was starting to pout about being left behind.

The first wolves they sighted were like a mirage; three or four ghostly gray wolves trotting stealthily through the sage. Sam and Lilly pulled their mounts to a halt and with their eyes fixed on the tall sage and holding their breath, they scanned the gentle slope for any movement. Suddenly there was an explosion of barks, yips, yelps and vocal pandemonium. It was apparent the wolves were worked into a frenzy by whatever was in a ravine that veered off to their left.

Sam slowly removed the carbine from his scabbard then seeing Lillian's blue eyes boring into him said, "Don't worry, I'm not planning to shoot any wolves but I want to be ready for what ever is up that canyon."

He had a hunch this might be a quarrel between wolves and a grizzly over a kill, and he did not want to be caught off guard by a riled up griz.

Lillian had a hunch of her own. She pictured a pack of wolves feeding on a couple Running R calves or even a big cow. That would not be good news to deliver when her folks got home. However, she did not want Sam to start shooting wolves, they couldn't be sure if the wolves did the killing.

When the riders broke free of a strip of timber, neither could have imagined the sight before them. Less than fifty yards away in a small grassy swale, a dozen wolves were circling, feigning charges then retreating rapidly with tails tucked between their legs. In the center of the commotion stood a black wolf, double the size of those rallying around it!

Lobo closed in on the strange sweet smell but was confounded by slight changes in the light breeze. When his nose led him into a small fescue-filled swale his heart rate increased.

I think I have it.

Another scent invaded his nostrils, the annoying scent of a lone dominant male wolf, the same annoying scent he and his mate encountered before. Lobo curtailed his pursuit of the sweet smell to locate the invader.

As if emerging from Mother Earth herself, a giant black wolf appeared within pouncing distance to his right. Lobo immediately knew he was being confronted by another alpha male and braced his front feet in a wide stance. He lowered his head, hackles bristling on his neck and prepared to fight for his mate, his pride and his pack.

Poised for an eminent attack, Lobo emitted an ominous growl from deep in his throat. The big wolf moved closer, measuring his opponent while Lobo crouched, ready to spring.

SNAP!

Lobo jumped high in the air and with the quickness of a frightened snowshoe hare switched ends, retreating several yards from the sound. The huge wolf leaped straight up like a coyote playfully pursuing a mouse. But this was no game.

The black wolf made no sound, merely backed away from the source of the sudden noise; his entrapped front leg extended before him. This large intruder was intimidating and clearly a threat to Lobo's domain, yet the animal made no aggressive move or sound. He simply stood, unmoving, with one leg extended in an odd position with a strange object seemingly attached to it.

Lobo continued to snarl and snap at his adversary but the big animal made no attempt to engage in battle. He was confused by the sweet smell of food and the disturbing smell of this alpha male. Then the comforting scent of Lola and the rest of the pack wafted to his nose.

Lola, after awakening to find Lobo gone, had rousted the younger members of the pack and followed his scent to this strange scene. Lobo quickly retreated from the strange-acting male and met Lola and the pack a safe distance away. He began howling, unsure if the intruder was a threat or merely an irritation, but announcing his supreme reign over his mate and extended family.

Encouraged by Lobo's show of confidence, the remaining members of the pack began taunting the black wolf while taking great care not to get to close to the seeemingly immobile beast. Try as they might they could not insight the intruder into attacking or frighten him away. He simply stood or moved marginally from side to side and glared at them with piercing yellow eyes. Lobo would never show it outwardly, but inwardly he harbored considerable relief this huge wolf did not seem interested in a fight.

As the standoff continued, Lobo grew weary of a foe that would neither fight nor flee and began to think this distant cousin was actually trying to warn him, telling him there was danger in this place.

Lobo paused and returned the yellow-eyed stare, curiously trying to decipher any message contained in those intense amber eyes. The stare-down was broken when the big wolf abruptly jerked his head in the direction of a timbered rise. The sight and scent hit Lobo like a bullet to the brain. He froze momentarily, his mind processing the strange looking beasts coming toward him.

They were big, even larger than the huge black wolf, the scent, one he could not identify although it did seem vaguely familiar. It was too much for him. With a bark and a burst of speed he bolted for the distant cover, Lola and the pack snapping at his heels every step of the way.

Sam could not have fired off a shot if he wanted to. In fact, the pack of gray wolves barely registered in his mind. His focus was squarely on the big black animal in their midst. He fought to rein in his thoughts, along with his normally acquiescent mount.

Could it be the same wolf?

He couldn't imagine another wolf that size anywhere and why didn't it run with the others?

Lillian was likewise occupied. Buttercup, startled by the sudden appearance and departure of the wolf pack, continued to be more than mildly disturbed by the remaining black wolf. She also thought of the black wolf in Sam's story and the huge track her parents saw, but mostly she was puzzled because the wolf remained fixed, making no attempt to run.

She stole a glance at Sam and was surprised to see his dark-brown face as pale as desert sand. The carbine was in Sam's right hand and resting across the saddle in front of him, his left hand firmly gripping Major's reins. It was clear he was not planning to shoot and Lillian took a brief sigh of relief.

The black wolf moved but its left front leg was stretched out at an odd angle.

"TRAP!" Sam and Lillian reacted in chorus, stunned and bewildered.

Lillian was outraged that such a magnificent animal should be caught in a trap…anyone's trap.

Sam was overwhelmed with sadness and disappointment. He had come to believe the amulet was some kind of legitimate Indian spirit charm and the wolf that saved him from his captors was some kind of spirit, looking over him like a guardian angel.

"You do not catch a spirit in a trap," he whispered.

"What can we do Sam?" Lillian recovered enough to speak. "Can we get him out of the trap?" She knew it was a stupid question.

"Not alive," Sam flatly stated.

Cautiously, they rode closer, desperately looking for an option other than putting this remarkable beast out of its misery. When they were within ten yards, the trap and drag chain were clearly visible, the jaws locked down on the extended leg just above the animal's foot.

"I've heard that coyotes will chew their leg off to escape from a trap," Lillian said quietly. "Do you think this wolf would do that? What if you could shoot his leg off, do think he would live?" She was grasping at straws.

Sam was also searching for solutions. Shooting the leg off seemed like the most plausible answer but he had serious doubts about the outcome, if he could even do it. The animal would be better off dead than crippled.

For the second time in his young life, Sam felt that eerie feeling this giant wolf wanted to speak to him. Without conscious thought, his right hand went to the amulet. The wolf's yellow eyes began to intensify until, even in the daylight, they resembled shimmering orbs of orange-yellow flame.

Sam and Lillian sat in mesmerized silence while the wolf rose on his hind legs, the trap and drag chain clearly visible. He shook his left front leg, rattling the chain then dropped back on all fours. Even more amazing, he lowered his huge head to his restrained foot and after a couple of tentative licks he grasp the long spring of the trap in his jaws and squeezed. The astonished couple watched with open mouths as the spring compressed and the trap's jaws fell open. With his paw removed from the jaws of death, the wolf again rose on his hind legs.

When the animal attained full vertical position, it was nearly seven feet tall, and slowly changed form. Human fingers began to protrude from the wolf's clawed toes and the fur peeled off its legs, revealing a dark-skinned person's muscular arms and legs. As the metamorphosis continued, the furry beast gave way to the features of a large Indian with long, sleek black hair that seemed to flare out from his head as if exploding. His cheeks were streaked with yellow, red and blue line as if he'd dipped his fingers in paint and dragged them down his face from temple to chin. He wore a breach-cloth of animal skin, a breastplate of bleached-white bone and could have passed for an Indian war chief, except for his slanted yellow eyes and hairy wolf-like ears.

Neither Sam nor Lillian looked at one another. They could not take their eyes off the unbelievable sight before them. Lillian wanted to whirl Buttercup around and run for her life but she was completely hypnotized by the apparition standing less than thirty feet away.

Sam was likewise transfixed but had no desire to flee. Ever since he escaped with the amulet, he felt an uncommon kinship with wolves. He didn't understand it and knew very little about them, but was never able to get that huge black one out of his head. Now here he was, not thirty feet away. Sam was convinced this was the same wolf...or whatever it was.

Even the horses were calm and quiet, anticipating the wolf-man's words. Instead, he reached down and picked up the trap, yanking the drag chain along with its steel stake from the ground, and threw it down. The trap fell near the nervous hooves of Buttercup who made a ten foot leap sideways out of the swail and landed with a series of crow hops onto the side of the trail. Fortunately, Lillian was an expert rider or she wouldn't have been able to stay aboard the frightened Palomino. Emitting a chilling cry that was a cross between a scream and a growl, the chimera creature dropped to all fours and disappeared into the nearby forest.

Major, stomping, snorting and acting generally unhappy about being there, did not bolt. Instead, she stood with her head high and pointy ears forward, looking intently into the forest where the wolf disappeared. The riders sat silent, trying to process what they saw, or thought they had seen. Sam was the first to speak.

"That was him...the black wolf I told you about but did you see what I think I saw or am I going loco?"

Lillian opened her mouth but she could not make words pass between her lips. Her young mind was struggling to comprehend what her eyes had witnessed. She grew up in the Montana wilds with the ever present dangers of grizzlies, mountain lions and rattlesnakes, but she never worried about them and was never as frightened as she was now. She also heard stories of a large hairy creature the Indians called Sasquatch...but this was different...or was it? To believe there was a huge wolf roaming around these woods was difficult enough, but one that was some kind of man-wolf was impossible.

I did see it, didn't I?

Sam dismounted but Lillian stayed aboard Buttercup, the fleet Palomino was her security, her lifeline if she needed to escape. He searched the area carefully but the creature left no tracks in the grass covered soil of the swale. With a gloved hand, Sam picked up the trap and studied it carefully. It was a Number 5 Bridger, single-spring leghold. He had seen these in California; the sheep ranchers in the Sierra Nevada's used number 3's for coyotes, the number 5's were for wolves.

Deciding not to pursue the question of what he had or had not seen, Sam focused on the undeniable.

"Whoever set this trap is definitely after wolves," he said to a shaken Lillian. "A coyote trap would be smaller and if he was after big cats the set would be much different. It would be in the rocks or the timber and there would be something to attract the cats, like a bird wing or strip of hide."

He thought for a moment before asking, "How far is this from where you and Larry found the traps?"

Lillian's voice returned, weak and quivering like a new actress with a bad case of stage fright but she said, "A quarter mile, maybe a half, north of here in Wild Horse Creek canyon." Reluctantly she continued, "Sam, did you see what I saw? Did that wolf turn into a man? Was that even a wolf?

She certainly hoped Sam had seen it, too.

"I saw it Lillian. I do not know what it was but I saw it," he assured her, "and I think I know where it came from." His mind flashed back to the mysterious valley, and he touched the amulet. "But I do not know what it is."

He made a couple of dallies around his saddle horn with the drag chain and punching his left foot into the stirrup, swung aboard Major.

"What about the other wolves? Were they together? Was there a pack running with that big wolf? There were other wolves, weren't there?" Sam asked.

"Sam, I'm scared," Lillian finally admitted. "Yes, there was a pack with that black one but that black one seemed human…and mad! What if he thinks we set that trap? He could kill us!" She was fighting back tears as she hesitantly continued, "Sam, the Indians have a story about a creature they call Sasquatch. It is suppose to be a huge hairy man-like beast. Do you think we saw a Sasquatch and not a wolf?" She was grasping at straws but dead serious.

"Lillian," Sam said. He felt obligated to tell Lilly his whole story. "I know that black wolf is the same one I told you about, and I am sure it is the one who made the track your parents saw. I am sure he is following me and you are right, he could kill us, but I do not think he will. I think he knows we did not set that trap or any others. I think he wants us to stop whoever is trapping **or** he is trying to warn us about the traps. What I do not understand is **why?** These mountains are full of traps and trappers, why would this be different?"

"I don't understand. Why would that wolf follow you and why do you think he knows we didn't set the trap?"

"Because of this," Sam replied, pulling the amulet from beneath his shirt. "There is a story behind this, one I never intended to tell anyone and one few people would believe, but a story that if retold could cost me my life."

Pulling the sorrel mare to a stop, Sam looked at the wide-eyed Lillian…he had her undivided attention.

"What do you say we eat lunch here? I will tell you why I do not think you need to be afraid of what we saw."

Sam looked at her intently, his dark eyes searching for acceptance and understanding. He saw a girl filled with fear and confusion, trying desperately to be brave.

Using a fallen log for a bench and a stump for a table, Lillian laid out their lunch while Sam began telling his story. The cavalry, the strange passage, the mysterious valley, the dancing Indian, the ghostly warriors, the attack and his escape all laid out for her to accept or reject.

"I have never been so afraid, not just of dying but of dying at the hands of some ungodly force intent on taking my life and my soul," he concluded.

He wanted to tell her why he couldn't go back to the army, why he left the fort and ran and why she could never tell anyone because if he was caught he would probably be executed, but he couldn't. That would be too much of a burden to place on a young girl already struggling to cope with what she had seen.

Lillian listened, completely absorbed in Sam's tale. She might not have believed it before, but after today, she knew there were things only those who had 'seen' would believe. Sam's story of a lost valley and Indians from the un-dead was fascinating and she didn't doubt a word of it…she just couldn't comprehend it. The giant wolf-Indian she had to believe, she not only saw it with her own eyes, she had a witness. She unexpectedly felt an uncommon bond with Sam. They had experienced something together that was unbelievably frightening yet almost spiritual.

Sam waited for a response from Lilly while she sat on the log with a chicken leg in her hand and a blank stare on her face. Finally, in a quiet voice, she said, "Sam, we better head back to the ranch. Mom, dad and Larry might be home and we don't want to be late."

As he mounted up, Sam realized he forgot about Lillian's parents and her brother. If they were home, it might mean he would have to move on. He had never met her brother but at this moment it seemed like his life, maybe his future was dependent on the speed of Larry's recovery.

Sam was convinced the amulet had brought him good fortune thus far. The question was; did his good luck mean bad luck for those around him? He also began to question what he saw. Was his obsession with the amulet beginning to play tricks on his mind? But Lillian saw it, too. Didn't she? She was certainly frightened of something.

Chapter Eighteen

Nightmare

Ruth wouldn't leave Larry's side and Ross felt like a one-legged man at an ass kicking contest…helpless. He couldn't stand to sit around and hope Larry kept breathing, but he couldn't stand to be gone in case his son woke up…or didn't.

He stepped outside for a moment to get some air and think. Of one thing Ross was certain; whatever happened he was going to take the traps Larry and Lilly found to Kalispell to be analyzed. It would be a three-day ride from the Running R but if someone was using poison traps he wanted to know about it and these would be the last traps they'd ever set!

Standing next to Larry's bed, Ruth took his hand in hers and his body jerked once, then twice in violent convulsions…then he lay quietly, not moving…dead.

"**No! No!**"

Ross reached for the doorknob. Before his hand touched the knob, his stomach was hit by an empty ache like nothing he ever experienced, his mind went numb. He grasped the knob and fell against the door. His response was triggered by the blood-curdling scream from Larry's room!

"**Nooooo!**"

He heard the heart-wrenching wail of a woman whose heart had been broken, her life shattered.

Ross could not feel his legs as they carried him down the hall toward the source of the horrible screams and the room where Larry lay. When he opened the door, Doc Jensen was right behind him. Ruth was on her knees, wailing, sobbing, holding Larry's hand and mumbling incoherently. Ross felt his knees give way and would have fallen had Doc Jensen not caught him and eased him into the chair abandon by Ruth.

The room was filled with the agonizing cries over the death of a son, the devastating heartache known only to a parent who has lost a child. Even Doc Jensen was brought to tears.

"I can get Reverend Brown or Father Williams if you'd like," he said. His words rang hollow in Ruth's ears.

"I prayed," Ruth said, "for all the good it did. Save your preachers for those who think there is a God!" Her words were cold as a Yukon night.

Doc Jensen left the room.

It was dark when John Grimm knocked on the door where Ruth and Ross remained at Larry's side, dazed and in disbelief. With leaden legs, Ross got up, crossed the room and opened the door to a thin man, a little over five-and-a-half feet tall, wearing wire-rimmed glasses, a gray felt hat and a black suit with a red handkerchief stuffed in the breast pocket.

"Name's John Grimm, Doc Jensen told me my services were needed. I don't mean to rush you none, I know these are hard times but my advise is to go home or the hotel if you're staying in town. Let me do my job and come by my place in the morning and let me know how you want to handle the burial."

Grimm was the undertaker for Horse Plain, Paradise and the farms and ranches along the upper Clark Fork and lower Flathead Rivers. He did most of his work at night, he liked it that way. He could move about in his specially designed wagon without attracting a gaggle of curious onlookers gawking and making a nuisance of themselves.

Ruth buried her head in her hands, sobbing. Ross stepped out into the hall, closing the door behind him. He struggled with the anger welling up inside of him at this thoughtless intrusion, while being forced to come to grips with a harsh reality.

Larry is dead.

"Give us an hour," Ross managed to utter. "We're not ready yet."

"Not a problem," John Grimm replied. "I'll be back in an hour-n-thirty minutes. It would probably be easier if ya'll were gone by then." The undertaker was polite but all business.

Later, Doc Jensen knocked lightly before opening the door where Ruth and Ross stood holding each other.

"Can I walk you folks back to the hotel?" he asked. "If there is anything I can do to help please don't hesitate to ask."

Ruth spoke in a weak quivering voice, trembling and choking back sobs. "Thank you Doctor Jensen for all you did, I know you tried, I just can't understand how a little cut…how this could happen.

"It wasn't infection and it wasn't gangrene. I believe he was poisoned somehow, with something." Doc Jensen said. "If he was poisoned then it's murder!"

"Murder!" Ross blurted.

"At least manslaughter," Doc Jensen asserted, "if the water was poisoned by miners that might be negligence but a trap laced with poison, to me that's murder. A marshal might call it manslaughter but either way somebody belongs in jail or hung."

Doc Jensen told Ross he was couldn't be sure what killed Larry but if he had to guess, it would be strychnine. According to the information he found in various journals, cyanide would most likely be in the water, and that would mean dead animals *and* people.

Ross's grief gradually gave way to rage.

"If somebody is responsible for this, I'll find them and I will kill them no matter what the sheriff says," he flatly stated, noting the fear registering on Ruth's grief-stricken face.

He felt a twinge of guilt for causing her more distress at this time, but he would stop at nothing to avenge Larry's death if someone was to blame, even if it meant giving up his own life in the process.

"I intend to contact the marshals in Kalispell and Thompson Falls and report a death with suspicious circumstances. I suggest you let them handle it from there." Doc Jensen told him. "I'm going to report the traps and the cut, so a marshal will likely come to your ranch.

He will want to take the trap that cut Larry's ear to be checked for strychnine."

"I was planning on taking it to Kalispell myself," Ross declared.

"Why don't you let the marshal handle it Ross? You need to stay with Ruth, she shouldn't be alone."

"She wouldn't be….alone." Ross's face turned the color of egg whites and Ruth gasped.

"Lilly!" she screamed, "Oh my God, how can we tell Lilly?"

It took both Ross and Doc Jensen to drag Ruth away from Larry's lifeless body and help her to the hotel, her legs were simply too weak to support her. Once in the room, Ross helped her to the bed and lay down next to her where they fell asleep sobbing, wrapped in each other's arms.

Ruth was sleeping with her head resting on his arm that felt like it was full of needles from his shoulder to his fingertips. It took less than a minute for the cruel reality of Larry's death to douse any pleasure he may have felt from the feel of his beautiful wife's body lying next to him.

Ross refused to move, accepting the intense discomfort in his arm as preferable to the agonizing pain Ruth would feel when she woke from her grief-induced sleep.

Ross realized his whole body was numb, he couldn't move. How could he have lost his son to a freak accident…or was it an accident? The words of Doc Jensen flashed back…*murder*. Did some rancher's hatred of wolves lead to his son's death?

White hot anger shot though him but was quickly replaced by a feeling of panic. He thought of Lilly and a profound sadness settled in. How could this have happened? They were all so happy only a week ago.

He wanted to run, to hit something but he couldn't move. It was like something heavy was holding him down and he fought frantically against it, to free himself, to cry out for help.

"Ross, Ross!"

He could hear Ruth's voice calling to him from far away then felt her gentle hand on his shoulder.

Ruth had opened her eyes, sore and swollen from days of unbridled tears and turned her head to look at Ross. He was jerking and twitching, his face contorted and looked as if he were about to scream or burst into tears.

"Ross!" she called.

She shook him softly at first then more incessantly as he mumbled incoherently. His eyes jerked open and he had the wild look of a man possessed.

"Ross, wake up!" she shouted. "You were having a bad dream, a nightmare, my God, Ross, you're soaking wet."

He raised his head, blinking his eyes in an attempt to focus. Then he remembered, his head dropped back on the pillow and he sighed deeply. That afternoon, Larry had come out of the chloroform induced coma and even spoken to Ruth. He and Doc Jensen had heard her scream, surprised by Larry's sudden return to consciousness but when he and the doc reached the room Larry had slipped back into a restful sleep that Doc Jensen figured would last eight hours. He was optimistic that Larry was out of the woods…so to speak.

The doctor managed to convince Ross and Ruth that the best thing they could do was go back to the hotel and get some sleep. Neither of them had caught more than a short doze here and there for the last several days.

Ross tearfully took Ruth in his arms.

"My God I had an awful dream! Larry really is alright isn't he? I dreamed he died, Ruth! It was the worst dream I have ever had!" he told her. "I even dreamed I was awake and you were asleep. God, dreams can be bizarre."

Ruth said, "We need to get dressed and find out how Larry is. Doc Jensen thought he would be alright but I want to see for myself, especially after your awful dream."

It took less than an hour for Ruth and Ross to freshen up, throw on some clothes and reach Doc Jensen's office. The doc was sitting behind his old, scratched wooden desk when they walked in.

"Morning folks," he said, holding a cup of coffee in his hand. "I hope you two were able to get some sleep."

"How is Larry?" Ruth was in no mood for idle chatter.

Ross felt obliged to share the details of his nightmare with her and now she was anxious for some good news.

"He is awake, weak from his ordeal but I have no reason to think he won't make a full recovery. I'd like to keep him here for a couple more days just to be sure. Beside, it's going to take that long before he's strong enough to make the trip back home."

"Can we see him?" Ruth anxiously asked.

"Of course, just don't stay too long and remember his body has been through a lot. He came as close to dying as possible…and still be alive. He may be a little confused and not make a lot of sense. Don't let that concern you, it's natural to be disoriented and confused until his mind and body, learn to work together again."

Doc Jensen led Ruth down the hall toward the room where Larry had spent the last week. Ross followed at a distance trying to come to grips with that damned horrible nightmare.

It was so real, even Doc Jensen and John Grimm.

When Ruth walked into the room, Larry turned his head and the corners of his lips curled up slightly.

"Now that is a pitiful smile to welcome your mother with," she joked while her heart soared at the site of her son even trying to smile. "How are you feeling?" she asked, immediately biting her lower lip for asking such a stupid question again.

Larry didn't answer but his eyes told her all she needed to know. She quickly rephrased the question into a statement. "It looks like you're feeling better." He nodded his head in the affirmative.

Ross didn't speak but stood behind his wife and wrapped his arms around her, kissing her on the cheek. She covered his hands with hers and squeezed, both of them heaved a great sigh of relief.

Two days later, Doctor Jensen felt Larry was well enough to travel but to be sure he wanted to accompany the Riley's as far as Paradise.

The usually talkative Larry was uncommonly quite when he left Doc Jensen's office. But as they prepared to leave Horse Plain, his sense of humor was present when he asked, "You want me to ride Drifter? I might as well be in the doc's buckboard. Where's Weasel?" Then he asked, "Where's Lilly? You guys didn't leave her home alone, did you? Why isn't she here?"

Ross gave Ruth a don't-ask-me look and she responded.

"Lilly is fine, she has someone with her at the ranch. It is a little complicated and you're still a little fuzzy. I'll explain everything on the way home."

Doc Jensen suggested they stay at the boarding house in Paradise so Larry could rest one more night before the long ride to the ranch but Larry declared that he was okay.

"We can save a whole day by going and camping along the way," he insisted.

Though Ross and Ruth were convinced that Larry was going to be alright, Doc Jensen's wishes won out and the Riley family spent the night in Paradise. Ross and Ruth made love, something they had not done since a few days before Larry's injury. Their lovemaking was the combination of tender relief and lustful release. They fell asleep with Ruth snuggled against Ross's back where she goosed him at the slightest hint he might be dreaming. The next morning they made love again, this time simply because it seemed like the thing to do while they were still in Paradise.

After a bath, breakfast and best wishes from their friends at the boarding house, they met Doc Jensen for final directions and advice. He was as confident as was possible that Larry would recover completely and that there was little or no risk of a relapse.

"I would take that trap to Kalispell and have it tested. If there is a trace of strychnine on it, someone came very close to killing your boy."

With that, the good doctor wished them well. They paid him and thanked him profusely for all he had done.

The ride home was uneventful and their only cause for concern was that Larry failed to complain about having to ride Drifter. He simply sat on the smooth-gaited gelding and watched the road, transfixed. The sun was settling low in the western Montana sky when they heard the long mournful howl of a lone wolf. They were back on Running R land and Larry became surprisingly agitated.

"There's something wrong, Dad!" he adamantly declared. "There is something wrong with that wolf. The howling sounds strange."

Ross and Ruth smiled. Larry was worrying about wolves again. He truly was going to be okay.

*

Earlier in the day, Lilly brought a couple two-year old colts in from the pasture that Larry had been planning to work with. She didn't think there would be anything wrong with having Sam start them. He certainly was good enough.

"I'm the boss on this here spread," she teased, "and it's my job to make sure the help stays busy."

Lilly was back in the house and Sam was on his way to the barn and the colts when he heard the wolf again. He felt the hair stand up on the back of his neck, partly because the howl of a wolf will do that to you but mostly because of what he and Lillian had seen up on Wild Horse Creek. The howling brought Lillian running out of the house.

"You hear that?" she called to Sam who was halfway between the bunkhouse and the barn.

"Si, I hear it and it makes me very nervous."

"It's him, isn't it? It's that wolf we saw in the trap. Why is he hanging around here Sam? Is it because of that thing hanging around your neck?" Lillian was walking toward Sam when she unexpectedly screeched and ran toward the log gate. He looked that way, saw the three riders and instantly recognized Ruth's chestnut mare; chocolate brown with her flaxen mane and tail catching the last rays of sunlight. He watched from a distance as Lillian hugged her mother and father and tried to hug her brother, who seemed a little uncomfortable with the outpouring of affection from his sister.

After they tied their mounts to the hitching rail at the front steps and headed into the house, Lillian approached Sam.

"They're really tired Sam, would you mind putting their horses away?"

The way she looked at him with those big blue eyes, he would have curried their whole herd if she'd asked.

"Sam, Larry almost died, that's why they were gone so long. I knew something was wrong. They thought he *was* going to die but he is going to be okay. I'll talk to you tomorrow…and Sam, thanks for being here while they were gone." She turned and walked to the house.

Watching her walk away was like losing his best friend, his only friend. Now that Larry was back and Lillian's parents were home there was no need for him here. His only hope was that Lillian's dad might hire him for a while until Larry was feeling better, but winter was not far away and they wouldn't need any hired help then.

When morning came Sam was not anxious to get out of bed. Where would he go from here? The last couple of weeks on the Running R was so normal, so good, such a change from months on the run. He continued to believe he was in Canada and found some comfort in that. At least the army won't be looking for me up here, he thought.

When he eventually crawled out of bed he wasn't sure what to do. Should he take care of the normal chores like he had for the last couple of weeks or should he start packing up his meager possessions and get ready to move on? Before he could do either there was a knock on the bunkhouse door; it was Ruth.

"Good Morning Sam," she said, when he opened the door. "Ross and Larry are still sleeping and Lilly is fixing breakfast. I wanted to make sure you knew you are welcome to eat with us. I also want to thank you for staying here with Lilly while we were gone. The last two weeks have been unbelievably stressful and I…we…were so thankful Lilly was safe here with you." Ruth was fidgeting with her apron and seemed genuinely nervous. "Sam, how much did you tell Lilly about how you and I met? I was so worried about Larry I have given no one, not even Ross any details, only that you chased off a man who was bothering me."

"Lillian asked how I knew you and I told her you were attacked by an animal on the road and I ran it off. I did not think it was my place to tell her what happened and fortunately she never pressed the issue." Sam was curious. "If you did not tell your husband what happened, how did you explain your sore wrists and your cut lip?"

"I told him a man grabbed me by the wrists and tried to kiss me and his tooth cut my lip. He trusts me, Sam, and I didn't lie; besides we were so concerned about Larry we never talked about my problem anymore. Now that Larry is okay, I know Ross will want to know more. If I told him everything that happened, it would make him crazy. As long as no one but you and I know the whole truth, I'd like to keep it that way…get on with living and forget about that awful man."

"I understand, but what about that man? He is still out there, are you not worried, do you not want him caught?"

Sam found himself feeling defensive of this beautiful woman. He thought of his mother and his inability to protect her from the evil sickness.

"That is another reason I wanted to talk to you Sam. I know who that man was. He is a bartender at the saloon in Paradise."

Sam was stunned and puzzled. "You know him? Why do you not go to the sheriff? That man belongs in jail."

"Because I would have to tell the sheriff the man tried to rape me; that he tied me up and took off my clothes and put his hands on me. The sheriff knows my husband, I'm afraid he would tell Ross and Ross would kill the man."

"Would that be so bad?" Sam asked.

"I'm afraid it would also kill my husband, men are funny that way. No man has ever touched me or seen me without clothes except for Ross. I'm afraid the whole truth would eat at him and make him crazy. Besides, even if Ross didn't kill him and he was arrested, there would be a trail and I would have to testify. That would make me feel like every man in the courtroom was trying to rape me."

Sam was nervous and embarrassed; no woman ever spoke to him so frankly about such personal things. "Why are you telling me this?" he managed to ask.

"I know you are a good man Sam, I would never have left Lilly with you if I didn't believe that completely. You could have done anything you wanted to me after you chased off my attacker. Instead, you treated me with more respect than I could ever have expected from a complete stranger. I watched you. You didn't even look at me, at my body, when I'm sure as a man you wanted to. I also know you're in some kind of trouble. You were wearing a uniform but it was filthy… you looked like a man on the run. What are you running from Sam and how can I help?"

"It is a long story Señora. I told Lillian a little bit but the whole story is hard even for me to believe. You have already helped me. You gave me a place to rest, clean clothes…you will want the clothes back, sí?" He hoped she didn't.

Ruth smiled and Sam felt like a warm ray of sunshine touched his face.

"No Sam, we don't want the clothes back, although you should buy some that fit you a little better. Lilly told us how much you did around here while we were gone. We're going to pay you for two week's work."

"No, Señora!" Sam emphatically replied. "You gave me board and room and I did the work just because I wanted to, not because anyone asked me…although Lillian did order me around a little."

He smiled hoping to make light of the subject. Do not let pride over power your brain, he told himself, though he needed money. These people had done so much already.

"I must ask a stupid question," he reluctantly admitted. "Where am I…exactly?"

Ruth laughed, thinking he was joking but abruptly became somber. "You're serious aren't you? Sam you're not leaving this ranch until you tell me what kind of trouble you're in. How long have you been on the run? Are you in trouble with the law or the army, or both?"

Before anything more could be said, the bunkhouse door swung open and Lillian stuck her head inside.

"Breakfast is ready guys. Larry is still sleeping but Dad is up and he's pretty hungry so come and get it!" She popped back out and was off like a butterfly in the wind.

"We better not keep Ross waiting," Ruth said. "He can be a bear when he's hungry." They headed for the house and Sam breathed a sigh of relief.

Breakfast was fried taters, bacon, eggs and bread fresh from the oven. They were eating when Larry came downstairs. He didn't say much and only ate a half-slice of bread.

"You could eat something! After all, I made it 'asspecially' for your homecoming," Lillian sarcastically told him.

Sam was slightly embarrassed until Ruth made sure he knew this was common banter between the two, only thing was, Larry wasn't bantering back.

Blandly, he said, "Sorry, Lilly, I don't feel hungry."

He quietly left the table and lay down on a sofa in the spacious living room.

When they were done eating Sam offered to help with the dishes but was quickly shooed out of the kitchen. He and Ross went into the living room where Larry was asleep on the couch.

"He had a pretty rough time, we damn near lost him," Ross said and motioned for Sam to follow him.

Opening a door he ushered Sam into another room. A heavy oak desk occupied one wall with a large mule deer head adorning the wall above it. Through a window on his left, Sam could see the gentle hills with steeper breaks leading to the river in the distance. To his right, a small leather couch and matching chair sat near a small rock fireplace.

"Have a seat Sam." Ross settled into a leather chair next to the desk. "Lilly tells me you're a hard worker and a good hand, especially with horses. I'd like you to stay on for a while if you don't have any place you have to be. We're going to be gathering cattle and moving them onto the home pastures and I don't think Larry is going to be much help this year."

Ross studied Sam for a moment. "Ruth says you're a good man and I have never had cause to doubt her judgment, although I will admit to being a little fuzzy on how she knows this."

Sam was uncomfortable but he was also anxious. He wanted to stay here, to hire on full time if it were possible. He sensed Ross knew he and Ruth had some kind of secret between them and wished he could explain.

"I do not have any plans, Senior…Sir, I would be glad to help out for a while. It is not necessary for you to pay me. I will be happy with board and room."

"A man has to have money, Sam, otherwise he can't feel like a man. 'I'll give you a fair wage for a day's work…and I'll pay you for the two weeks you worked here while we were with Larry."

Sam felt like the luckiest man in the world as he followed Ross out of the office and through the living room. He did wonder 'where' in the world he was.

"Now that you're on the Running R payroll I guess I should give you some things to do. I could let Lilly line you out but she's a lot harder to work for than I am."

A dish rag sailed out from the kitchen and fell just short of a laughing Ross Riley.

"It's Lillian….!" the voice from the kitchen sounded like the song of a meadow lark to Sam.

Clarence Hobbs sat on a log at the edge of the timber on a hill overlooking the Running R ranch house. It took most of a week for him to recover from the beating he'd taken. His nose was the biggest problem; the unintended pun brought on a weak smile. It was days before the swelling went down enough that he could even breathe through it. It was still a little swollen and plenty sore, a constant reminder of the asshole that beat up on him and ruined his fun.

When he was hired as bartender in Paradise he had no intentions of sticking around for long, but now he had a couple scores to settle. He figured the blond would know him from the saloon but he was counting on her being too embarrassed or ashamed to say anything. Clarence never got a look at the bastard who broke his nose and that could be a problem. The guy might go to the sheriff and he would have no way of knowing.

"Yep, that could be a real problem," he whispered under his breath.

Normally this would have been enough reason for him to move on. Trouble was he wasn't thinking clearly, he couldn't get the vision of the blond beauty out of his head. He came so close to showing her what he could do to a woman, just a little while longer and she would have been his, she'd be sneaking off looking for him, begging for more.

He stood and took a deep breath of the crisp mountain air. He had to breathe through his mouth but it still felt good.

Fall is in the air.

My favorite time of the year, he thought…brings out the hunter in me.

He walked the short distance to his cayuse and pulled a new telescope from his saddlebag. Returning to the log, he put the device to his eye and adjusted the focus, then jerked his head back like he'd just seen a rattler up close and personal. It was the first time he looked through a telescope and he was impressed.

"Ain't this just a bitch? I feel like a goddamn eagle," he muttered.

He was confident this was the ranch the woman at the boarding house in Paradise said was the Riley's. As he scoped out the barns, corrals, outbuildings and sprawling log ranch house he scoffed, "So the bitch is rich. That's all the better."

The familiar tingle returned to his groin and he cautioned himself. "Patience, good things come to those who wait."

Hobbs smiled, pleased with the possibilities.

For Sam the next few days were busy ones and he could not have been happier. There were stack fences to repair after elk had knocked them down, logs cut and skidded to the woodshed where they would be sawed into lengths, split and stacked. He only saw Lillian at meal time but just knowing she was nearby made him feel good. He was aware of a bite in the air and a breeze out of the north carried a hint of things to come. Fall, he thought, if I am in Canada I might be in for a tough winter but better here than going south…a thought he would rather forget.

Larry was feeling much better and anxious to start moving cattle in around the fenced haystacks.

"Snow can come in out of Canada without much warning," he said, over huckleberry pancakes and sausage.

Canada.

Sam thought…Did he say 'in' Canada or 'out of' Canada? Why don't I just ask where I am?'

He knew why; because then he would have to explain how he could not know where in the hell he was. He decided if he was ever alone with Lillian or Ruth again he would ask.

Ross was also antsy. There was something he needed to do and he'd put it off as long as he could.

"I have to take that trap to Kalispell," he blurted. "I can be there and back in a week. If the tests are going to show anything I can't wait till spring, besides, with Larry feeling better and with Sam here, they can start bringing the cattle in."

"I can help," Lillian offered, "as long a Larry doesn't want to race." It was a joke she wouldn't have made a few days ago.

Ruth didn't want Ross to go but she also wanted to know if someone was using poisoned traps on the Flathead. With Ross in

Kalispell and Sam and the kids moving cattle she would be home alone. The idea was frightening since her encounter with that creep from Paradise.

At least he doesn't know where I live.

There was comfort in that thought and besides she had a shotgun and she knew how to use it.

Chapter Nineteen

Promise

Spotted Fawn lay wide awake next to her husband. They had made love earlier and Little Beaver was lost in the deep sleep of spent passion. She usually slept soundly after lovemaking but tonight she was energized by it. Quietly, she slipped from beneath the assortment of furs and pulled a buckskin dress over her head. She wanted to talk to her father. Making her way in the moonlight to the lean-to where he spent his nights, she was surprised to find it empty. He had not wandered in the dark since finding his head again. Mildly concerned, she decided to check the teepee of Bend Grass. The two were spending a lot of time together since Standing Wolf left the valley.

I will peek in her teepee, she thought…and if she is awake perhaps she will know where father is.

Moving quietly through the night as only an Indian or one who lives with Indians can, she reached Bent Grass's abode and pulled the flap back slightly. She closed her eyes, shook her head and opened her eyes again.

Her first reaction was embarrassment, then guilt and finally joy. There, amidst fox, mink and coyote pelts lay her father and Bent Grass, wrapped in each others arms. A smile came to her lips and she slipped away as quietly as a nighthawk on the wing.

Returning to her teepee she whispered, "*Mihaken!*"

Unable to contain her happiness when he didn't respond, she shook her husband. Little Beaver leaped from his bed and reached for his bone-handled knife.

"What is it?" he quieried, confused, "a bear, a wolf?"

She grabbed his bulging bicep with both hands and laughing said, "Neither, *mihaken*, it is my father and Bent Grass! They are together!"

"So," he said, looking puzzled. "They are together a lot these days."

"No," she insisted. "I mean naked in bed together."

"Oh, you mean together, together," he said.

Falling back on the pile of furs, he made a loose fist and inserted his forefinger in and out repeatedly. Laughing, Spotted Fawn slapped his hand.

"I am sooo happy!" she exclaimed. "*Achteway kin* has found a woman…the perfect woman."

She jumped into Little Beaver's arms. He rolled on top of her and felt a surge of excitement course through his loins.

Why does this woman do this to me? He thought, all the while knowing the reason was obvious.

The village was a buzz with whispers and giggles, accompanied with approving smiles over the news. Spotted Fawn was incapable of keeping her discovery secret; first she told Laughing Doe who told Willow who told everyone.

Bent Grass and Frank were equally surprised by the spontaneity with which they found themselves in her bed. Surprised but delighted, now if only they could shake the nagging feeling her son, his friend, was somehow in trouble.

Many years of running a solitary trap line in the Pasayten instilled awareness in Frank, a sixth sense of sorts, and it was telling him that his friend was in trouble. Not the someone-has-you-in-their-rifle-sights kind of trouble, more like the feeling he had when they split up during the war, after they managed to escape two-thirds of the entire confederate army.

Bent Grass'was a double-barreled consternation; the anxious worry of a mother for her son, and perhaps more importantly the sense of a seer who knows something is askew, out of balance, not right with

Mother Nature. When Bent Grass had this kind of feeling everyone in the valley worried, including their chief.

Ta-keen Eagle and Laughing Doe reveled in the union of Fire-hair Frank and Bent Grass along with the rest of the Sematuse. Laughing Doe, Star Flower and Willow saw to it they had a proper *mihinaga,* marriage, with much dancing, singing, eating and drinking of elderberry wine.

The petite Bent Grass was dressed in a sleeveless robe made of ermine that hung to mid-thigh, the white fur in stunning contrast with her dark-skinned arms and legs and jet-black waist-length hair. Fire-hair Frank wore buckskin pants, a shawl made from the pelt of a red fox and a necklace of tiny mink skulls, a gift from Laughing Doe and Willow who took much pleasure in the presentation of the suggestive gift.

While Bent Grass and Frank made a good-looking couple, a lot of attention was given to the provocative Laughing Doe and Willow dressed in their cleavage revealing, thigh-exposing dresses crafted cleverly from mink and beaver hides. The women called them fertility-robes and there was little doubt of their effectiveness. In fact, Ta-keen Eagle and his carefree brother Red Fox were feeling more than fertile by the end of the ceremony, a fact which Laughing Doe and Willow would soon be well aware.

When Sister Sun rose the following morning, Bent Grass and Frank were quite possibly the only ones in the valley not holding their heads or stomachs due to excessive intake of food or drink. However, the joy of the ceremony and the fulfillment brought by their union did little to dissuade their uneasiness.

When once again Bent Grass took his hand and headed for the cave of spirits, Frank knew the purpose, she was going in search of words on the water, talking on the wind as she called it. The answers to her distress and therefore his, were riding the winds of change along the watery maze of lakes, streams and rivers within the home range of the sacred black wolf.

No one among the Sematuse, not even Chief Ta-keen Eagle knew what happened when Bent Grass entered the mysterious tunnels, shafts and caverns inside the cave of spirits. All believed she was visited by *Ogle Wa Nagi* or perhaps spirits from the great mountain *Chopaka*. The only humans to ever enter the cave with her were French, her husband of many winters ago and Fire-hair Frank, her husband as of today.

French never shared any knowledge regarding the cave and Frank only entered the cave once before, without Bent Grass. That was when he was as loco as Crazy Crow and came out as sane as Ta-Keen Eagle. That event said more about the power and mystery of the cave than any story Frank could have told. Only Bent Grass, French, Frank and Standing Wolf ever went beyond the cave opening, and returned; none of them could or would tell about it.

The only place Frank wanted to be right now was wherever Bent Grass was so he followed his wife into the cave for the second time, with slightly less trepidation than before. After all, his first trip could not have ended better. After being led through the maze of tunnels to the source of her secret light, he was feeling so confident he took her in his arms and kissed her gently.

"I have never done anything in my life to deserve such happiness," he whispered in her ear.

Bent Grass placed a single finger to her lips in the sign of silence. She turned her head toward the narrow entrance of the brightly lit cavern. From the passage emerged the form of a giant wolf. It slowly squeezed from the tight opening like a shape-shifter passing through a keyhole. A scream froze on Frank's lips, halted by the four fingers Bent Grass gently placed over his mouth.

Once inside the cavern the giant beast shook, sending a cascade of water from an unseen source in tiny drops and rivulets. Bent Grass cautiously removed her hand from Frank's mouth. He remained silent, mouth closed, eyes open. It was not the first time Frank had seen this huge black wolf and he knew it was not going to be the last. He also knew every time the wolf appeared his life changed.

It had led him into the Pasayten; he had seen it as he laid freezing in a snowstorm a moment before arriving in this mysterious valley. He saw it along with the rest of the village right before the soldiers foolishly entered the valley…and now.

What now?

As the compelling creature rose on its hind legs then settled into a sitting position Frank felt a hint of panic deep in his gut.

Am I going crazy again?

Settling into a seated pose the animal morphed from a beast of the wilds into a large Indian sitting cross-legged, eyes closed as if meditating. Black braids hung over his broad shoulders and rested on a breast plate of white bone. His loins were covered with what appeared to be a breach-cloth made from the pelt of a gray wolf. Except for his size, the Indian looked remarkably normal, his facial features were slightly feminine but his shoulders and arms were muscular.

When he opened its eyes, they were the same ones Frank had stared at through his buckhorn sight, what seemed like a lifetime ago. The glowing eyes again held him captive as they did in that mountain meadow. As those animal-eyes fixed on him from the bronzed face of the Indian deity, Frank's skin began to itch and tingle like he was a snake about to shed its hide.

He felt Bent Grass' hand on his arm, averting his eyes from the intense stare of the mystical creature, he looked at Bent Grass. Her big round eyes like smooth black stones polished by a mountain stream were soft, comforting and knowing.

The Indian with the eyes and ears of a wolf spoke. "You have taken a mate, it is good," he stated, clearly speaking to Bent Grass. "It is the way of things."

It was astounding to Frank that Bent Grass seemed neither alarmed nor surprised that until a moment ago, what had been a huge wolf was now a a very large Indian speaking to them.

Frank was all eyes and ears scarcely taking a breath, he knew exactly who this chimera was talking about. Bent Grass lowered herself to the ground, legs together and pointed toward the cavern then pulled Frank down beside her and leaned against him.

The Indian's intense gaze slowly shifted to Frank, causing him to gasp. Bent Grass squeezed his hand reassuringly. The eyes shifted back to Bent Grass and Frank sensed they were looking at an old friend.

"Many things must be right for the Native People to be free of the white-clay humans, things you cannot control. You saved the True People, now it is your time to enjoy the old ways with your mate."

The shape-shifting deity began to morph, but with the warmth and gentleness of a mother for her child he again spoke, now appearing to be more wolf than man.

"Do not waste a rising sun waiting for what might be, take what is and savor it."

The creature stood on its four feet, tail held high and proud before melting into a crevice and disappearing, leaving Frank speechless and Bent Grass in a state of pensive rumination. They remained seated in the cave for several minutes, surrounded by the beauty of Bent Grass's paintings and the magic of the carbide light.

Bent Grass was first to speak. "Come," she said, taking Frank's hand. "We have some living to do, let us return to the valley of rainbows and begin."

Life for the Sematuse was good, it was the season of hunting and many deer were taken for meat and pemmican. They were busy preparing for winter when new pelts would be harvested and made into robes, vests, dresses and leggings. There would be much story telling and drinking of wild-berry wines. It was also when couples spent much of the day in their dwellings by warming fires and in each others arms by smoldering coals at night.

Even Sparrow Song, who lost her husband to the savage claws of the white-humpback, found comfort in the company of Two Dogs. He was now a young hunter and warrior who thought of Sparrow Song as his adopted mother and visited her often.

Only Star Flower was not happy. She missed Standing Wolf and with the union of Bent Grass and Frank, there was no one to share her loneliness. Ta-keen Eagle and Laughing Doe were sympathetic, Bent Grass and Frank were understanding but curiously dismissive.

Most of her support came from the unlikely sources of Willow and Red Fox. She always suspected her brother was demented and there was no doubt about Willow. There was no doubt among the Sematuse those two were a good match, though not exclusive by any stretch. Willow's sexual promiscuity was well known, even envied by a few. Red Fox was simply seen as the free-spirited brother of Chief Ta-keen Eagle and Star Flower. Despite his care-free and uninhibited ways, Red Fox cared deeply for his sister.

He was not thrilled when she had fallen for Breed or Standing Wolf, or whatever he was called. The half-breed was an outsider and no one except Bent Grass knew anything about him. But Star Flower loved him and that was enough for Red Fox; especially after bearing witness to the power granted to him by the Great Spirit. If he was good enough for *Ogle Wa Nagi* he *might* be good enough for his sister.

Willow's interest in Star Flower was less honorable but not out of character for the incorrigible nymph. She was a sensual, sexual beauty who knew no boundaries and apologized to no one. Her shapely body, crowned with hair the color of pine bark and smoke-gray eyes made her a stunning sight. The buckskin dresses, always a little too short on the thigh and a little too low in the cleavage, only increased her allure. She liked men, make no mistake, but she was not beyond exploring the intimate charms of a female body other than her own.

Star Flower was blessed with large, firm breasts, small waist and flaring hips. Her bronze skin was like melted honey, her eyes soft and round and her lips full and warm but most of all, she was kind, gentle and naive; a trait Willow found irresistible.

Star Flower found the attention of the temptress entertaining, even amusing, but her desires were for Standing Wolf only. She spent a great deal of time under an ancient cedar tree on a ledge overlooking the river of rainbows. It was an especially warm fall day with the feathery needles of the big cedar reflecting the season with a mix of green and rust colors. Sister Sun warmed the ledge with a gentleness seemingly reserved for the gentle soul perched there. Star Flower was lonely but she found comfort in this place, special to her since she was a small girl, and where she and Standing Wolf first made love. Lost in thought she was startled by the sound of a voice.

"I knew I would find you here," Willow boasted joyfully then curious asked, "Are you listening for talk on the wind?"

"What are you doing here?" Star Flower asked, with a hint of agitation.

"I wanted to talk with you but when I could not find you in the village I remembered this place. I followed you and Standing Wolf here once so it seemed like a good place to look."

Star Flower felt a rush of embarrassment and a touch of irritation. "When did you follow us?"

She wished she could take the question back the instant it slipped from her lips. Her mind flashed to intimate moments she had shared with Standing Wolf in this place.

"It was only once, I do not remember when. That does not matter. It is how I knew where to look for you."

"What do you wish to speak about?" Star Flower decided to move on believing nothing good could come from her questions.

"I thought since you are lonesome while Standing Wolf is gone and since I am alone we could be friends. The time of falling leaves is here and the season of long nights is near. It is a good time to have a friend."

Willow was sincere, she liked Star Flower and wanted to be her friend, but for Willow, friendship could, and often did, have a double meaning.

Star Flower sighed; she did not appreciate being disturbed but conceded that pining for her man was neither healthy nor constructive.

"But we are friends," she countered.

Star Flower decided as long as Willow was there, it might feel good to share some of her thoughts and concerns.

"I am feeling sorry for myself because no one needs me. Spotted Fawn is healed and happy with Little Beaver, Fire-hair Frank is no longer loco and has Bent Grass, Crazy Crow can not be helped, and even Sparrow Song is better now that she has Two Dogs to lean on. Standing Wolf has many important matters to attend to. I can not expect him to stay here with me but I miss him."

This kind of self-pity was so out of character for Star Flower. She was always the one to offer comfort and encouragement, not to complain. Willow was like a velvet snake, quickly striking at any sign of vulnerability.

"I understand how you feel. Red Fox, Long Bow, Twisted Stick, even Wild Horse are all hunting. Can you believe they would rather chase after a big-eared deer than me?"

Willow was having fun, whimsical in nature, she chided until forcing a reluctant smile from Star Flower's lovely face.

"Am I getting ugly?" Willow continued. "I can not even turn Bird Legs' frail head anymore."

Bird Legs was older than the water in the river of rainbows and had not looked at a woman in a serious way since buffalo roamed the plains. Star Flower laughed, she could not help but like this beautiful, silly, sensuous woman. And she did feel better.

"Maybe I should see if *I* can turn Bird Legs' head," Star Flower joked.

"Now you leave that nice old man alone," Willow purred. "I am sure you could turn his head like that of an owl but his heart might not keep beating."

"Are you saying I am so ugly I would scare him to death?" Star Flower bantered back, knowing it was a mistake the moment the words left her mouth.

Willow knelt behind Star Flower, leaned against her back and whispered softly, "If you were ugly I would not worry, it is this kind of beauty I fear his heart could not take."

As Willow spoke, she placed her hands on Star Flower's shoulders then slowly slid them around the seated woman's neck. She massaged gently, briefly then slid her hands downward toward the buckskin top that covered Star Flower's firm, full breasts. Her fingers reached the top of the leather garment and slipped underneath.

If Star Flower had a fault, it was that she saw the best side of everyone and was always anxious to please. Now was no different. It was not until she felt Willow's fingers touch her taunt nipples that Star Flower pulled away.

"I really should get back to the village," she said, a nervous tremor in her voice. "I promised Laughing Doe I would go with her to gather elderberries."

She scrambled to her feet and started back toward the village. Willow quickly caught up to her.

"I am not busy and it is a fine day, maybe I will join you."

Star Flower looked at the precocious beauty. If Standing Wolf did not return soon, this is going to be a long winter, she thought…a real long winter.

Chapter Twenty
Messiah

Standing Wolf was disappointed and dismayed. After his old friend Roy mysteriously emerged from and melted back into the depths of the Columbia, the giant wolf appeared. It shook the cold water from its sleek black coat, stared intently at him for a brief moment then disappeared into the hawthorn and wildrose lining the river bank.

He knew it was the same wolf he saw when he first entered the valley beyond the spirit cave and the one Roy had seen with Spirit-walker. If this was a spirit sent by *Ogle Wa Nagi* to communicate with the True People, why didn't it speak to him, the Chosen One?

Standing Wolf believed the big wolf was sent by his mother to guide his way and to help him retrieve the lost amulet. But if it didn't have a message for him why was it there? Was it now following Roy the way it had Spirit-walker? Where was Spirit-walker? Was it simply checking on his well being, making sure he was still alive? Was the wolf, by not speaking, telling him he was on his own?

What had Roy said about a symbol divided, about the amulet being drawn to its likeness and its likeness to it?

Had Roy really been there?

"A lot of crazy things happen along the waters of the Columbia and *Okinakane*. No one should know that better than me," he chided himself.

He patted Whiskey on his arched neck. "If we are on our own big guy, what do you think we should do?"

Some things were clear to Standing Wolf. It was he who decided he must leave the valley in search of the soldier with the stolen amulet. It was he who decided, as the Chosen One, he bore the responsibility to save all Native People from oppression as he had the Sematuse. The Great Spirit did not interfere with his decisions, a fact Standing Wolf took to mean that he was doing what was expected, even required.

"That is why the sacred black wolf had no message," he confirmed to his attentive mount. "He is only an observer, a part of the Great Spirit…as am I."

Ogle Wa Nagi, Wakan Tanka, Ate and Tunkashils, all Supreme Beings of the Native Peoples had given him the power. He was now as sacred as the black wolf or Spirit-walker. He was a shaman, a spirit. There was no message because he had the power to choose and the Native People would bear the consequences of his choices, good or bad. He used that power wisely 'back then' but with with his mother's guidance and direction. She had told him what to do because he did not yet understand his power…and because they were in the valley. When he told her he must leave to fulfill his obligation as Messiah, she made no attempt to stop him. In fact, she seemed proud. He now understood though she supported him, it was his decision. He had not asked but told her he was leaving. There was no doubt, as a seer, she knew if he was doing the right thing. Spirit-walker had and now he, Standing Wolf, could but Bent Grass would not or could not interfere with things outside the walls of the valley of rainbows

"Well friend," he said, feeling apotheosized, "It is you and me and since we are in the white man's world, we get to play God, and we better be smart about it."

Since leaving the cave of spirits in search of the soldier with the amulet Standing Wolf had been waiting, expecting some kind of sign, a message or vision from his mother, from Spirit-walker or the Great Spirit. He believed the astonishing events resulting from his doing the Ghost Dance were an extension of his mother's gift. It was now his gift, his power and his decision how to use it.

He did not feel like a God of any kind, but there was no denying what happened in the valley. At first he blamed himself for the soldiers being there but decided it was more fate than fault.

Why him?...he wondered. But it made sense, if any of it did. He had gone to the white man's school, attended their church, and studied the culture of Indians on and off reservations. If he held the fate of whites **and** Natives in the power granted him and a judgment was to be made, why not have it made by one who was half-Indian and half-white?

However, Standing Wolf did not expect to be in this alone. But what had he expected? He expected to find the runaway soldier and retrieve the amulet within a few days, tell the story of the Ghost Dance up and down the *Okinakane* and Columbia then wait for a sign that it was time to return to the valley and Star Flower. He expected to be back in her arms before the cold winds of winter.

There was already a bite to the wind on the river and Sam's trail was stone cold. Standing Wolf had told his story to a few wandering fishermen but it was clear the only way he would be back in the valley before winter was if he abandoned all his reasons for leaving.

The breeze blowing up the Columbia was still cool by mid-day. Standing Wolf was on the brink of making what could be some colossal decisions. The first was his name. If he was a God or shaman, he needed to start believing it. He had gone by many names in his life, a fact he found perplexing. Born among the Sematuse as Standing Wolf, after returning to the white-man's world his father called him Charlie. When Charlie deserted Custer's 7th Cavalry he called himself Breed because of his mixed blood. Back in the valley he was once again Standing Wolf, but deemed by the Great Spirit to be *Waboka*.

He knew Christians believed in a Messiah but did not think they shared the same God. If Jesus Christ meant Messiah to them, and *Waboka* meant Messiah to the Sematuse, so be it. He would remain Standing Wolf so he could not be mistaken for the white man's God.

As for Sam and the amulet, it was time to admit he had lost his trail and had no way of knowing if Sam even still possessed the amulet. In his vision Roy told him, 'The amulet is pulled to its likeness and its likeness to it'. That could mean the spirit of the two amulets would draw them together, or perhaps that both were drawn to the sacred black wolf. Either way Standing Wolf believed the amulets would find each other.

"And the black wolf was right here this morning," he said, confirming his thoughts.

Roy also spoke about a 'symbol divided' and that he was 'fixin' ta fail'. Standing Wolf figured that problem would resolve itself, which left the Ghost Dance. He had told his story to the Indians at Noisy Waters and the Indians of the Columbia listened politely, showing moderate interest but the Indians living on reservations in far off places exibited much excitement. He had seen how the Sioux and Cheyenne lived on the reservations of the Dakotas and Wyoming. It was no surprise they would grasp at any hope of returning to the old ways.

Gray Hair and Long Foot very much wanted him to accompany them to Walker Lake in Nevada. They were very excited and promised to 'show the dance around' to all of their people, the Paiutes and Minneconjous.

Standing Wolf thought about what he had told the Paiutes, not so much about the dance but about the promise of deliverance from oppression by the Messiah. He replayed the teachings of his father and of his father's church in his mind, especially the part about Jesus and the resurrection.

He was beginning to get a bad feeling. But for the undeniable revelation in the valley, Standing Wolf might have reason to doubt his own story. Perhaps it was his sub-conscience replaying the teachings of his father and the Mother Church.

He played out the similarities in his mind; Jesus was said to have emerged from a cave and told his followers to spread his story so they might be saved from damnation. He said if his own people, the Jewish People, did not believe in Him, to tell his story to all creation so they might be saved.

Jesus told them to be compliant, generous and kind, and 'to do unto others,' to gather and worship and trust in Him. As He ascended to the heavens He promised to return and reward them with eternal life.

Standing Wolf also emerged from a cave and told his story to the people of the Columbia who were somewhat skeptical, and then to the Paiutes and Minneconjous who believed he came to them in a vision years earlier and were now believers.

He, too, told the Natives to be compliant and not to fight or rise up against the army or the government, to do the dance faithfully and wait for the Messiah to call up the spirits of the dead, a kind of rapture that would free them from oppression…

Finally, both had sacred symbols, the church with its chants, holy water, crosses, rosary, incense and wine: He had the amulet and the Dance of Ghosts.

'Is it pure coincidence?' he wondered…or did it mean something and if so, what?

Leaping effortlessly onto Whiskey's back, Standing Wolf pointed the proud animal downstream. His gut told him Sam was probably somewhere upstream and if he had the amulet, there was a good chance they would meet, sooner or later.   Right now Standing Wolf was more concerned about his newfound status and message. Comparing himself to Jesus was disconcerting and surely blasphemous. He had stopped believing in the teachings of the church a long time before his father's death, but he was baptized Catholic and lessons learned as a child die hard. It was time to stop over-thinking everything, time to let destiny be his guide.

What would Jesus do?

There is an ironic question, he thought…But what would Jesus do? Were Jesus's actions a matter of free will or controlled by destiny, by a higher power, by God?

Any sign from *Ogle Wa Nagi, Wakan Tanka* or even his mother would be much appreciated, but Standing Wolf knew he was on his own, in this case, he was the higher power.

"This is not how I imagined it," he muttered.

"Let this cup pass from me, not my will but thine be done."

Jesus made that plea to God when hanging on the cross. It was hardly a fair comparison, but if StandingWolf followed his own will it would take him home and back to Star Flower.

If destiny or God or the Great Spirit had other plans for him, now was the time to speak up or at least give him a sign. Jesus said there would be signs before His return.

Chapter Twenty-one
Sweet Duty

Standing Wolf rode down river for the next few days, at one point encountering another river spilling into the Columbia from the east. He was grateful that it was late fall and the flows were low. Had it been high flows he would have been trapped, stuck at the confluence of the two rivers with no choice but to backtrack until he found a place to ford the Columbia.

The chance you take when traveling in unfamiliar territory, he thought.

On the third day after fording the secondary river things began to look familiar, then he saw it. Across the river perched on a rise overlooking the majestic Columbia and nestled proudly at the mouth of a rim-rock canyon was a large log building, Roy's ranch house.

Things looked a little different to Standing Wolf because he was on the opposite side of the river, a place he had not been before but he knew it had to be Roy's house, and if he was right, he was back in the land of Chief Little Moses and the Nespelems.

"Only one way to find out," he said to Whiskey.

He was not sure if it was nostalgia, curiosity or some more meaningful purpose but he knew he had to see for himself, to make sure it was Roy's house and if it was, to go inside.

"Maybe that vision is haunting me," he told his horse.

He began searching for a likely place to cross the Columbia. Even in low water, fording the Columbia was risky business, currents were deceiving and deep-water channel cuts were hard to see. Whiskey took the dangerous crossing in stride. A couple of missed steps into deep water were easily overcome by the powerful Arab. Safely on the north bank Whiskey shook violently, nearly unseating his unsuspecting rider, even if he were a God.

Ascending the long gradual slope leading to the canyon and ranch house, Standing Wolf's heart began beating rapidly. Time had taught him to trust his instincts. He thought of the ghostly sight of Roy on the river and his anxiety level escalated. He heard voices! He was certain this was Roy's house but who could be there? Definitely not Roy, he thought, only partially convinced.

Topping the rise a hundred yards from the house, the sound of voices grew louder. He looked around for cover where he could get a closer look. Dismounting, he led Whiskey off the rise and out of sight of the house. Leaving the well-trained horse ground tied, Standing Wolf moved toward the talus bottom of the rimrock bluff near the back of the house. Moving through the Saskatoon, tall sage and greasewood he worked his way to within forty or fifty yards of the back door. He hunkered, trying to pinpoint the location of the voices, then moved carefully toward a better vantage point. The sound of wood being chopped was accompanied by a steady banter of what seemed to be only two people.

"I gotta thank ya Daniel." The voice was in clear ear shot. "The only way this could be better was if we had a couple uh womans here."

"You'd bitch if'n ya was hung with a new rope," another voice replied then added, "but good luck with that idea."

The voices were coming from the far end of the house along with the unmistakable 'whack' of wood being chopped. There was a nip in the air and the thought of the rock fireplace Standing Wolf knew was in the house was appealing.

Who would be living in Roy's house? Not Roy, he thought…that was for sure, or was it?

Corporal Daniel Bone and Private Joe Wright were enjoying what could only be called 'sweet duty'. When Major Denton decided to pull the 5th Cavalry out of Fort Okanogan and go back to Fort Vancouver there were some loose ends to be addressed. Among them was Roy Wolard's twenty thousand acre ranch along with his newly constructed log house that needed to be watched over, until the army changed his current status of missing to deceased. There would be a year to attempt to locate any possible heirs, if none could be found it would become the property of the US Government or part of the newly established Colville Indian Reservation.

Major Denton, at the recommendation of Lieutenant William Radcliff, gave the assignment of watching over the Wolard holdings to Corporal Bone, allowing him to select one soldier to share in the duty. Bone selected Private Wright for one reason; he didn't want word of the visit paid to him and Joe by the mysterious Indian while they were on guard duty to get back to Major Denton.

Daniel knew Joe didn't remember much about that night but any talk of an Indian so close to the fort would send the major into a rage. If the major learned that naked Indian claimed to have knowledge of the fate of Colonel Wolard and his men and he hadn't been told, it could mean a court martial. Daniel would not risk getting on the wrong side of the army as long as there was a chance of claiming the saddle bags he found at the massacre at Janis Crossing. Having Joe here with him and not back at Fort Vancouver where he could get drunk and shoot his mouth off was the perfect solution.

Daniel smiled. He might not be the smartest corporal in the 5th Cavalry but he was beginning to feel like the luckiest. Not only were he and Joe assigned to watch over this beautiful house and fifty head of cattle the major elected to leave behind, if no next of kin for Francis Wolff was found within a year he, Daniel Bone, would part ways with the army a rich man.

Because Roy had the foresight to make sure his crew gathered plenty of firewood while getting logs for his house, Daniel simply had to make sure there was enough wood split for the fireplace and stove and that the cows didn't starve to death.

Private Wright can do the wood splitting, I'll keep an eye on the cattle, Bone thought.

"That's enough wood for tonight," Daniel said, "unless yer plannin' on roastin' a pig."

"If we had a pig, I'd damn sure cook it," Joe responded, loading his arms with firewood. "I bet there ain't a pig within a couple hundred miles uh here." He sounded truly sorry.

What they did have was an ample supply of salted pork, a dozen chickens the major didn't want to haul back to Vancouver and all the beef they could eat. They even had a sack of seed potatoes, a few ears of seed corn and some dried beans.

"We better enjoy the hell outta this Joe, 'cause this might be as close ta rich as we'll ever git," Daniel said, as he pushed open the ornately carved wooden door and followed Joe inside.

While Joe torched off a log in the big rock fireplace, Daniel let his eyes wander over the splendid interior of the house. The ceilings were vaulted; something he never saw in a house before. A stairway with a smoothly polished handrail worked its way up to a loft overlooking the spacious living room with a few hand-made chairs and a couch with animal hides thrown over it for furnishings. Rugged-out bear, mountain lion, and smaller pelts like beaver and otter were scattered about on the floors. In the kitchen, a wood cook stove sat on a shiny granite floor.

"If'n this were mine," Joe cracked, as he rubbed his hands together admiring his fire, "I'd fill it with nice leather sofas and chairs an' I'd have a dining table big enough for twelve people." He paused and grinned. "Then I'd make sure eleven of 'em was womans."

"If ya owned a house like this ya might find eleven women willing ta be in the same house with ya," Daniel smirked, "but that'd be the only way."

Before Standing Wolf was able to find a vantage point where he could get a look at the source of the voices, the men were inside the house. What he could see were a couple of axes, a splitting maul and a woodshed stuffed full of wood.

As darkness fell, he looked longingly at the crimson glow of firelight through the house windows. It was the one and only thing he missed from his days living like a white man; his cabin at the fort and the warmth of the wood stove on a cold night.

Silently, cautiously, he inched closer to a window. Pressing his face to the glass, he could see two men, soldiers, one a corporal the other sporting the thin-yellow stripe of a private.

What are soldiers doing in Roy's house?

A corporal, he thought…could I have found Sam?

He felt a rush of adrenaline as he strained for a better look, concentrating on the corporal. "Its that damn stable guard," he muttered, "the same guard who told him Sam left the fort on the major's horse."

What is he doing here?

He backed away from the window. He never got a good look at the private he rendered unconscious that night but he had been a big guy. He was convinced they were the same two soldiers. Walking back to the patiently waiting Whiskey, Standing Wolf wrestled with why the two guards would be here in Roy's house. The light breeze was building into a wind that whistled over the rim-rock wall and swept down around him. He shivered involuntariy.

"We need to get out of this wind," he stated and Whiskey shook his head up and down in agreement.

About a half mile downstream Standing Wolf found a hollow with a few strategically placed pine trees standing guard like eternal sentries. The howling wind turned surprisingly warm and he rolled out a blanket, ready to settle in for the night.

As darkness slid up the river and settled over the hollow, his attention was drawn to a faint glow in the early evening sky. It was down river and to the west. It was not the moon coming up, it was too early and in the wrong place. He looked away to allow his eyes to focus then looked back, the light was still there. Unable to discern what it was, he dismissed it for the moment while he built a small fire to cook the prairie chicken he managed to kill earlier with a rock. He was not concerned about the wind, though the grass was tall because fall rains. The hollow provided enough shelter so the cook fire could burn quietly without fear of spreading, allowing Standing Wolf to relax and enjoy his dinner.

After complimenting himself on a perfectly cooked meal, he rolled up in his blanket and fell asleep to the sound of the high wind whistling over head.

It was well after midnight when Daniel Bone stepped out of the log house and searched the dark for a place not too close to the door to take a leak. There was a bathroom in the house but he could not get used to the idea of pissing in the house…it just seemed vulgar.

He'd pulled on his pants and boots and stood shirtless, draining his lizard and looking at the night sky and a million stars when he realized he was pissing up wind.

"Shit!" he exclaimed in disgust as his stream blew back onto his pants and boots.

He quickly turned his back to the howling wind.

"Sure is warm for November," he muttered, shaking his eel before stuffing it back into his pants.

Taking one last look at the starlit sky he was fascinated by a strange glow streaming over the canyon wall. It was faint at first but steadily grew brighter and seemed to dance across the sky like the northern lights he'd seen when stationed at Fort Abraham Lincoln in the Dakotas.

Daniel smelled smoke!

Looking at the house chimney he could see a pillar of white smoke blowing out along the roof line and away from him while the glow was growing brighter and higher in the sky.

Wildfire!

Daniel ran for the house. "Get yer ass outa bed, Joe!" he shouted. "We got 'rselves a problem!"

Standing Wolf awoke to the musty smell of smoke. His first thought was the house and that the wind must be blowing chimney smoke his way. It took only a moment to realize he was upwind from the house… then he saw the glowing sky. What he earlier saw as a curious light was now obvious. There was a fire down river…and it was a big one. He had experienced a lot of things but a wildfire was not among them. The thought was frightening and he wondered how it started.

"It was not lightening," he assured himself. "Which leaves man… but who and why?"

White man, Indian, wagon train, war party, the possibilities were numerous and unimportant. The wind was raging and Standing Wolf knew this was serious.

"Wish I knew which side of the river it is on," he muttered, studying the eerie glow.

He thought about Roy's house and felt a pang of sadness. The house had been Roy's dream and with it there, it seemed like his dream was still alive, even if he was not.

If the fire is coming this way and burning on this side of the river there would be no way to save the house and the two soldiers would be helpless. Their only chance of escape, like his, was to cross the river, unless the fire was on both sides. The last thought sent a chill through him.

It appeared to be a long way off but that was little comfort. Standing Wolf knew with a wind like this, a fire could travel faster than a man could run, even on a good horse. If he could get to higher ground he might be able to see which side of the river the fire was on.

With daybreak came evidence of the raging fire even more ominous than the glowing night sky. Bright orange-red flames mingled with black and gray smoke billowed high into the sky obliterating the distant horizon. Riding to the top of the rim, Standing Wolf looked out over the high prairie landscape. The fire was a long way off but appeared to span several miles in every direction.

He thought of Chief Little Moses and the Nespelems…even the good father's mission and school could be at risk…and what about the fort? It was impossible to tell exactly where the fire was but one thing was certain, it was big and getting bigger. The whistling wind was blowing right at him, causing his long-black hair to stand straight out from this head.

Sitting astride Whiskey Standing Wolf was confident he and the big Arab had plenty of time to run if need be, but he wanted to be sure on which side of the river to run. He watched the blackish-gray smoke turn an eerie orange as the sun rose above the horizon behind him. He was filled with a sense of urgency when gray burned-out cinders of grass, needles and other debris blew past him. None were flaming or glowing but he knew spot-fires could be flaring up far in advance of the main fire and on either side of the river. It was time to start back down toward the only possible safety…water.

Chaos would be a generous description of the scene playing out for Daniel Bone and Joe Wright. After being rudely awoken by an animated, cursing Daniel, Joe managed to get dressed and assess their predicament. It didn't take him long to share Daniel's excitement and concern. Daylight was even more alarming as the smoke rose like giant thunder clouds through tongues of fire, and gray burned-out particles blew around them like volcanic ash.

"We ain't got a chance uh savin' this house or them beeves if that fire's on this side uh the river," said Joe in a voice elevated in tone, unable to contain his rapidly approaching panic.

"We can round em up an' drive em to the river," Daniel countered. "Even if that fire's on the other side, we can always drive 'em back. First we need ta let the horses an' mules out uh the barn in case we cain't get back for 'em."

"I'll saddle us up a couple an' turn the rest loose. Ya think they'll be smart enough ta go to the river?" There was no mistaking the anxiety in Joe's voice.

"Hell, Joe, don't go gettin' all excited. That fire ain't likely ta even get here. It's uh damn long ways off an' if we get uh little change in the wind we'll be in good shape."

"Ya never been in a wildfire, have ya Daniel?" Joe asked. "Well, I have," he added without waiting for an answer. "When I was fourteen we got burned out by one. It was a Kansas prairie fire an' it's as close ta hell as I ever wanna get." Joe waited for a response. When none came he continued, "Killed my Pa and my little brother. He was eight." His voice was shaking and he shook his head to get control. "Ma and I survived in the root cellar, damn near baked us alive but it was movin' so fast the cellar cooled down 'fore we cooked."

"Jesus Joe, how come ya never said nothin' 'bout that before?" Daniel asked, sounding a little offended.

"Don't like talkin' 'bout it. A couple years later Ma was fixin' ta loose the farm an' some hot-shot banker come along an' took Ma an' the farm. That's when I joined the army, ain't too proud uh that decision neither."

Joe headed for the barn hollering at Daniel as he went. "Ya never said if ya ever been in a wildfire but I'm guessin' ya ain't. I'll get a couple saddle horses an' you let out the others an' mules an' that damn milk cow."

Should let the damn cow burn, Joe fussed. He was annoyed with her ever since she stuck her foot in a bucket of milk he had painstakingly extracted from her oversized bag.

They hustled around freeing livestock, saddling two good horses and trying to act calm but as burned out cinders fell around them, their urgency of motion increased.

"That fire must be fifty miles away but the wind's probably blowin' forty, fifty miles an hour. Don't leave us much time to gather cows an' get the hell out uh here." Joe was not anxious about spending time driving cows to the river but he knew they were too stupid to go there on their own.

Ain't nothin' dummer'n a cow.

He was relieved when they found all the cattle grazing near a small lake not far from the barn. As they began pushing them toward the river Joe had a new concern. What would happen to their 'sweet duty' if the house burned down?

It was a question Daniel had also thought of but was not ready to consider. He didn't know what he would do, it was a possibility they'd never discussed.

"We cain't very well guard somethin' that ain't there," he said, dejected.

Shit, Joe thought...I hate fire!

With the cattle delivered to the water's edge they were faced with another decision, push them across or leave them close until they could see which side the fire was on?

"I say we leave 'em here and get as much of our stuff out uh the house as we can," Joe proclaimed.

If they had to go back to Fort Vancouver they would need all the supplies and gear they could save. After a brief and somewhat animated discussion, Daniel agreed they would leave the cattle where they were, return to the house and barn and move what they could to the river as well. From there they would watch the fire and hope for the best, their greatest concern was that the fire might be on both sides of the Columbia.

By the time Standing Wolf returned to the river his thoughts labored over Roy's house and ranch. It seemed like everything that happened, the valley, his mother, Star Flower, was because of Roy's dream of having a magnificent ranch and beautiful house.

I wonder where his cattle are now.

They could all be lost along with the house which would mark the end of Roy's dream. Standing Wolf contemplated what Roy said in his vision; 'The missing symbol can be found among the fateful ruins of a lost dream'.

Standing Wolf felt a rush of excitement…did Roy mean **his** lost dream? Could the amulet be here, on the ranch Roy called Wishbone?

A flood of thoughts hit him and he began to feel like a fool. Had he been duped? Was the guard duty corporal who told him Sam ran off with Major Denton's horse, really Sam? He never considered the guard might not be telling the truth, he should have known better… white men lie all the time. The army made a habit of lying, breaking promises and disregarding treaties, but he had figured the guard was too scared to lie.

He tried to remember Sam in the valley. So much had happened very quickly and he was so intent on the dance he did not pay attention to the soldiers who were assigned to guard him and Frank.

Frank, he thought…He knew what Sam looked like for all the good that did. "Can't worry about that now," he scolded aloud. "I have to find out if Sam is there, in Roy's house."

Standing Wolf headed back up river until he spotted a large herd of cattle milling around along the bank.

"They did not get there on their own," he whispered. "I wonder if there are more than two soldiers around."

His ruminations were cut short when burning embers began falling around him. He felt a rush of regret, nothing but torrential rains could save Roy's ranch and the thought left him feeling sick. To say Roy had been a rascal would be too generous but the ranch seemed to be the one good thing in his life. If not for his brother and the priest, Roy would still be ranching rather than the sad conclusion his existence ended with.

Cutting away from the river, Standing Wolf headed toward the ranch house. From a point overlooking the house he saw two soldiers hurriedly carrying items from the house and loading it into pack boxes on three mules.

The house had a cedar shake roof and live embers were landing on it, flaring up briefly then fading out.

This hopeless, he thought, wishing there was something he could do.

Do I not have Godlike powers?

He touched the amulet and thought of the Ghost Dance.

"No!" he exclaimed with a ferocity that surprised him. "I can not use the spirits of my ancestors to save a white man's house. All we can do right now is hole up near the river and wait for the fire to play its hand. Then I will find out if that corporal has the amulet." He felt better informing Whiskey of his intentions."

At the house, the falling burned-out cinders became hot twigs and needles spiraling to earth like flaming arrows. The blaze remained out of view but the wind felt like the hot billows in a blacksmith shop while bits of fire fell all around the two soldiers.

"Its time we head for the river," Daniel stated. "This place is gonna blow up like a Confederate cannon."

Once they reached the river Daniel and Joe hunkered down, keeping their saddle horses close in the event they needed to make a run for it, although neither one had any idea where they would run to.

Standing Wolf worked his way back to the river and noticed the cattle were becoming restless. The smell of smoke was strong and the thick gray haze reduced visibility. Looking down river he was unable to see any flames but it was obvious the fire was getting closer…and fast. He was about a quarter-mile down river from the milling herd when he pulled Whiskey to a halt.

The soldiers are probably with the cows and are most certainly armed, he thought. "We will wait here until we see what this fire is going to do," he confided in the Arab.

When he eventaully saw the flames they were at least a mile away but seemed to be leaping and dancing, reaching out to hungrily consume grass and sage or anything else that lay in its path. Occasionally it would explode high into the air when an old growth pine or cluster of fir ignited. The flames spread from the river bank to beyond the northern horizon. The smoke was getting thicker, although the wind tossed it around creating open spots where he could see small blazes popping up well ahead of the raging inferno. Knowing Roy's dream would go up in smoke left him with an empty feeling. There should be something he could do.

"Like what?" he asked sarcastically. "Make it rain, move the river, move the house?"

As the fire drew closer the wind began swirling and gusting ferociously while burning projectiles fell like rain all around him. He looked up river, the cattle were no longer visible, either they stampeded or were obscured by smoke. He thought of Roy's prize mule deer head that would have been so proudly displayed inside the house. It was as though the huge buck was dying all over again.

A large hawthorn bush and a chokecherry tree exploded into flame less than a hundred yards from him. The fire was awe-inspiring and terrifying at the same time. He decided this would be a good time to cross and watch this show from the other side of the Columbia. A blast of stinging hot air hit him in the face and he knew it was now or never.

A quarter-mile upstream Corporal Daniel Bone and Private Joe Wright faced problems of their own. The herd of cattle including the milk cow, mules and spare horses were on the edge of unraveling. The two men considered pushing all the stock to the other side of the river but decided it might be wiser to drive them upstream away from the fire.

Living off the land with a steady diet of deer, grouse and fish was alright and they could live without eggs; they knew the chickens were already toast, but T-bone steaks and pot-roasts were another matter… they sure enjoyed their beef.

A hot blast of air shot around the end of the rim-rock wall and flames roared along the river bank like a blow torch. Though the soldiers didn't want to loose their beef supply, when they felt the intense heat of the fire, their thoughts quickly turned to saving themselves. It's hard to be rational when your ass is burning.

Without a word or hesitation they urged their mounts into the dark waters. The horses swam fervently toward the far bank, drifting downstream, pushed by a strong current even in low water. Once their thrashing hooves hit the soft ground of the river bed they began bucking and lunging toward the shore. They were in belly-deep water, within a stone's throw of dry ground, when both men abruptly pulled their mounts to a halt. Fifty feet away was an Indian dressed in buckskin leggings and a bright-colored shirt, seated on a magnificent, black stallion.

The blood drain from Daniel's head and his arms felt weak, he would know this Indian anywhere; it was the naked Indian from the fort, only now he wasn't naked…but he was every bit as terrifying.

Joe reached for his rifle but Daniel held out his hand to stop him, his instincts screaming a warning. The Indian appeared to be unarmed except for a knife tied to his leg.

It's like the devil and the deep blue sea, Daniel thought…except it's an Injun in the not-so-deep Columbia. He began to giggle like a school girl.

Joe glared at Daniel, thinking his friend had lost his mind.

"What's so damn funny, you know this Injun?" he asked impatiently, his hand moving closer to his rifle.

"Yeah, I know 'im an' so do you. Ya just ain't been formally introduced yet." Daniel's giggle broke into hysterical laughter.

Standing Wolf was as confused as Joe. What did this corporal whose life he'd threatened at the fort find so funny? If this soldier was the one who had taken the amulet from Frank, the joke would be over.

Daniel looked across the river…there was no going back; all he could see was a wall of flames. He no longer thought anything was funny. Slowly, he coaxed his horse toward the shore and the waiting Indian, Joe rode quietly along side with his hand resting on the stock of his rifle.

"We meet again," Standing Wolf stated.

"Only this time ya ain't got a rifle stuck in my face," Daniel replied.

"Why were you in Roy's house?"

"The major gave me an' Joe the detail uh watchin' over the place 'till the army figures out what ta do with it. Why do ya care what we're doin' here? What are you doin' here?" Daniel was agitated and anxious.

"I am still looking for the amulet you said Sam ran off with. I got to thinking you might be Sam!"

"Is that why you're here?" Daniel didn't like where this conversation was going.

Joe remained quite with his hand on his rifle, he'd heard enough to know he didn't like it.

"If you have the amulet, give it to me and I will be on my way. It is sacred to my people. You have no more use for it." Standing Wolf was speaking more forceful.

"Whoa there, wait just a goddamn minute, chief. I told ya Sam had that sacred thing you're talkin' 'bout an' he ran off with it. Took off in the middle uh the night like he was bein' chased by a ghost!" Daniel stated.

He was becoming unnerved he touched the butt of his rifle, looked at Joe and began to laugh again. "Looks ta me like ya brought a knife to a gun fight," he said flippantly. Somehow the wise crack didn't make him feel any better.

"So this is the Injun that left me ta die, naked!" Joe exclaimed, speaking to Daniel as though there was no one else there. "I owe ya, ya redskin son-of-a-bitch! Ya left me with a headache for a week." As he spoke Joe slowly removed his rifle from its scabbard.

"Don't do it Joe!" Daniel shouted.

"And why the hell not?" Joe responded, "This Injun mean somthin' ta ya? The bastard probably started this fire!"

"The amulet!" Standing Wolf demanded. "Are you telling me you do not have it?" There was finality to the question.

"Ain't ya been listenin', chief? Ah told ya more than once, Sam has what you're lookin' for. He's got it, I ain't!"

Joe run out of patience and raised his .50 caliber Spencer, leveling it at Standing Wolf.

Daniel never saw it coming…all he heard was the noise; a deafening roar like a stampede of ten thousand wild horses and it was behind them. Daniel turned his head to look. Joe turned his whole body dragging the rifle along with him. The wind had abruptly changed direction, blowing down river and directly into the onrushing fire, forcing flames high into the air. The sight was mesmerizing as red, orange and white flame mixed with black and gray smoke, creating a colossal wall of fire, smoke and debris three hundred feet high.

Joe and Daniel were spellbound, watching while the sight undulated, imploded then went silent. The back-draft created a whirlwind filled with tufts of smoke curling skyward in loose ringlets. It danced along the fire-line, tosssing burning embers into the sky. The pieces of smoldering wood and grass, their fire spent, floated harmlessly back to earth like tiny burned-out comets, leaving Roy's house completely untouched.

Remembering the Indian, both men looked back at the bank... he was gone. Their eyes searched up and down the river...he was not there. He had simply vanished.

"What happened ta that Injun?" Joe sounded disappointed to have lost a chance to even the score.

"He probably just saved your life," Daniel replied, not entirely sure what he meant.

Chapter Twenty-two
Ursus horribilis

Ross, Larry, Lillian and Sam were mounted and headed north toward Big Arm before daylight. Ross was on his way to Kalispell but wanted Larry and Lillian to show him where they found the trap that cut Larry's ear. Sam and Lillian told no one about their encounter with the giant wolf and its show of disdain for traps. Though Lillian was dying to tell her dad and Larry, she knew she would have to lie to make them believe her. She didn't want to lie so she said nothing.

Sam had way too much on his mind to worry about telling anyone about a wolf that displayed human characteristics. Besides, it was Lillian's place to tell her family what she wanted them to know.

Ruth didn't look forward to spending a long day alone but she had plans that would keep her busy. The last of the pumpkins and squash needed to be picked up and put in the root cellar. She wanted to get the last of the root vegetables out of the ground and there were still a few beans left to dry. There was also an elderberry patch down by the river she wanted to check and was hoping the bears had left a few berries for wine and jelly.

She was wearing a cotton dress and debated about changing into riding pants and shirt. She elected to stay with the dress, figuring if she rode out to check for berries later she could slip into pants then.

Right now another cup of coffee in front of the fireplace seemed like a perfect plan.

As she sipped the dark brew, she looked around the big house with its polished rail banisters, lofts overlooking the living area, the tall windows with a view of aspen thickets and the Flathead River in the distance, and reflected on her life.

"I am a very lucky woman," she said. "I have a wonderful husband and two great kids."

Her eyes grew moist at the thought of Larry and Lilly. She'd come so close to losing one of them.

"Another reason to count my blessing," she whispered, wiping her eyes. It was a stupid saying her mother always used, but sometimes it just seemed appropriate.

Ruth thought about Sam and how they met. She liked him. He had a strong gentleness about him. Lilly would called that an oxymoron; a word she found in the Encyclopedia Britannica, a set of twenty books Ross had ordered all the way from Scotland. Lilly read the encyclopedias the way some people read King James.

Ruth wasn't sure how Ross felt about Sam, for now he was abiding by her wishes. He was a good-looking young man once he was cleaned up and it wouldn't surprise her if Ross was a little jealous. He'd been jealous of some the hired hands in the past if they happened to be young and handsome. It was a little frustrating at times because she never had any interest in any of them but she guessed that was just how men were. She liked having Sam around, but mostly she felt she owed him. Without him saving her from that horrible man she might be dead, or wish she was. The problem was, every time she looked at him she remembered that day, it wasn't his fault it was just how it was.

What troubled her most was what she didn't know. The young man was a mystery. When they met he was wearing what was left of some kind of military uniform that looked like he'd been wearing for months without ever taking it off. She was sure he was running from something or someone and that troubled her.

'At least I know he isn't a rapist' was a thought she quickly cleared from her mind. That he might have killed someone was one she could not dismiss so easily.

"Well, he's not dangerous," she expounded aloud, surprising herself. "If he's running from the law or the military he probably has a very good reason," she confirmed, hoping she wasn't in denial.

The crisp November morning made fingers, toes and noses uncomfortable appendages. The sun peaking over the Mission Mountains was a welcome sight to the four riders, and an encouraging sign of the warmth to come.

Lilly's fingers were knotted into tiny fists inside her leather gloves and her toes refused to wiggle inside her boots. The only thing warm about her was her spirit, she would not have complained if her toes shattered like glass. This was the second year her dad had allowed her to come along on the fall cattle drives and she felt like she was finally grown up…earned her right of passage. She learned early that no matter how tough the conditions might be, to complain meant being sent home, and utter humiliation.

"It will warm up fast now kids," Ross said, hoping it wasn't an empty promise. November in Montana could be unpredictable.

"I'm fine Daddy," Lillian answered defensively. "My toes are just a little chilly." "Liar," Larry retorted. "I know you're cold. I bet even your nipples are frozen." "No more of that talk!" Ross scolded his son. "She might be your sister but Lilly is becoming a young woman and it's time you start showing some respect."

The banter between brother and sister continued as the four rode along sage-covered ridges, through grassy swales and timbered valleys. Ross smiled. It was good to have things back to normal. Larry was well enough to ride Weasel, Lilly looked at home on her Palomino and Sam rode the little sorrel mare he arrived at the ranch on.

But not everything was normal…Sam's arrival at the ranch, his slovenly appearance, his mysterious connection to Ruth…none of that was ordinary. Ross understood that some man had been bothering his wife and Sam intervened but that didn't tell the whole story. He wasn't sure if he wanted to know everything.

As they neared the Big Arm pasture, hundreds of Running R cattle littered the slopes, milling about in the tall grass. Years of routine taught some of the older cows to drift toward the Big Arm with the frosty mornings of fall.

"After you show me where you found the trap on Wild Horse, I think you better come back here and start moving these cows home," Ross assessed. "Also, keep your eyes peeled for that big wolf or at least his tracks, and Sam," he added, "If you see him, shoot him."

Sam was unable to muster a response and Larry and Lilly let the comment slide, but gave Sam a look that clearly meant the matter was not closed.

When the foursome reached Wild Horse Creek and the site where Larry had found the infamous trap, they dismounted and poked around the area in search of additional sets. Lillian and Sam exchanged knowing glances, uncomfortable even being near where they witnessed the unbelievable. Sam still had the trap in the bunkhouse that the chimera-like creature had thrown angrily to the ground. He felt a twinge of guilt for not giving the trap to Ross but that would have meant trying to explain how he found it. He agreed with Lillian…not telling wasn't lying.

Sam was relieved but not surprised when their search failed to produce anymore traps. The fact that he and Lillian found one in the next drainage over, more like it found them, told him that someone was systematically and cautiously setting wolf traps over the entire upper Flathead.

"You better head back if you're going to get home with any cattle tonight," Ross told Larry. "I'm going to spend the night at the Finley Sheep Ranch. I want to find out if they've heard about anyone trapping for wolves."

The Finley Ranch was on Flathead Lake south of the Yellow Bay Trading Post. Tomas Finley was the grandson of Irish immigrants, as was Ross. Tomas and his wife Elizabeth were the Riley's closest, maybe only real friends. Tomas called himself 'black Irish' because of his dark skin and contrasting blue eyes. Liz was a freckled, brown-eyed beauty with naturally curly, red hair that fell to her narrow waist.

Ross sometimes teased her saying, "I bet you have freckles on your butt," to which Liz would retort, "That is something you will never know, Ross Riley."

Their three kids, two boys and a girl were a little younger than Lilly and had little in common with her so they didn't spend much time in each other's company.

Tomas was a gregarious man who made frequent trips to Kalispell selling wool to merchants and weavers. There was not much that happened on the Flathead Tomas Finley didn't know about; and no one hated wolves more than sheep ranchers.

Lobo, Lola and the pack moved steadily away from the disturbing sights and smells. Lobo was especially glad to be rid of the huge alpha male. He was not afraid to fight for Lola and the pack but there was something about the scent of that male that unnerved him.

Once safely out of range of the intruding male, Lobo found a dense fir thicket littered with large logs rotting into the forest floor. A perfect place to hole up and wait for darkness, coaxing Lola away from the rest of the pack they curled up next to a three foot high log. It was soft from years of decay and advancing moss and mushrooms. He wrapped his long tongue around a gilled fungi protruding from the log and gobbled it down, licked his lips and grabbed another then looked at Lola who was already sound asleep. With a sigh and one last lick, he pushed his nose into Lola's flank and drifted off.

Lobo awoke with a start.

Why does that happen?

I can be sleeping so sound and then night drops and boom, I'm awake and hungry.

He nuzzled Lola's flank until she began to stir. One look into those yellow eyes told him she, too, was ready for food.

Soon the whole pack was awake and pacing around waiting for their alpha male to decide where and what they would eat tonight. Surrounded by the sights and sounds of the night the pack set off, trailing behind their leader, trotting at a leisurely but ground eating pace. The deep, resonant sound of the great gray owl were interrupted by the rapid trill of a screech owl. In the distance, a coyote yipped excitedly in pursuit of a snowshoe hare.

Lobo was looking for something significantly larger, a young elk or moose or even a yearling mule deer. He began to salivate at the thought, his white canines, polished on the bone of their most recent kill, gleamed in the moonlight. He stopped abruptly and caught a sniff.

There it is again…elk, not close but I'll find them.

He alerted Lola and she made certain the rest of the pack knew they were on the scent. They broke free of the timber and onto a long slope dominated by bunchgrass, sage and mountain mahogany. The scent of the elk was now mixed with a strange smell…one not familiar to Lobo or Lola.

The new scent reminded Lobo of a memory buried deep in his brain. He had not encountered this exact smell before but there was a hint of something, something good. He smelled water, lots of it. They must be close to a lake or river. Then he saw something odd, small and white.

Rabbits?

No, they were too big for rabbits.

The pack stopped, intrigued by the unusual looking and smelling animals spread about the hillside.

Looks like an easy kill but not much of a meal.

Lobo was not impressed with the find…an elk calf was a lot more appealing.

A couple of young males suddenly broke from the pack and charged one of the animals. It turned to run but was way too slow for the swift attackers. With fangs bared and snarling, they hit the wooly creature, sinking their teeth into its back. It was like biting into a rotten log, there was no taste or blood, just a mouthful of wool. Still, they believed they were about to score their first kill and excitement heated their blood.

Lobo threw his full weight into the recalcitrant pups. This fluffy animal might be easy prey but he was hungry for elk and the sooner they found a herd the better. He took time to mark three shrubs in a triangular pattern, if times got bad it would not hurt to remember this place.

It was late afternoon when Ross tied his blood-bay horse, Roy, to the hitching rail in front of the Finley house, walked up the board-walk and knocked on the heavy plank door. Elizabeth opened the door, gave a little squeal then hugged Ross with genuine affection.

A part of Ross was thankful for his thick coat, Elizabeth was a fine looking voluptuous woman and to feel the attributes of her shapely body so close to his could be unnerving.

"Tomas was concerned some of the sheep might be wandering to far into the mountains toward the south fork of the Flathead and headed off this morning to check on them. He should be back before long. You come right on in and wait," Elizabeth explained, and escorted Ross into her warm kitchen.

The coffee was always on at the Finley sheep farm and he and Liz enjoyed a cup as they discussed recent events. Larry's close call was a total shock to Liz and she struggled to contain her emotions. The discussion of wolf traps and strychnine came up but Liz quickly deferred that subject for Ross and Tomas to pursue later.

She did acknowledge they had heard wolves recently, a long way off toward the Cabinets and that Tomas was concerned but certainly was not setting traps anywhere.

When Ross told her he was headed for Kalispell, Liz suggested, "Tomas wants to make a trip into Kalispell before winter, maybe he'll want to go with you tomorrow."

Tomas returned an hour or so before dark and greeted Ross with a firm handshake and a slap on the back. Ross filled him in on the problems with Larry, the traps and the wolves.

"Can you think of anyone who might be setting out poisoned traps?" Ross asked.

"Not a clue," Tomas replied. "I'd like to think it's someone new to the valley but it sounds more like some bitter rancher who thinks he lost a prize calf or colt to wolves."

"But why poison a trap?" Ross pressed. "You catch a wolf in a trap and he's already dead."

"You're not positive the trap was poisoned, right?" Tomas asked. "Isn't that why you're going to Kalispell?"

"You're right Tom, but Doc Jensen was pretty convinced Larry had strychnine poisoning. Where else could he have gotten it?"

It was a question with no answer at the moment. Tomas decided to ride into Kalispell with Ross and the two men teased Elizabeth about the dangers of letting two successful, handsome ranchers loose in the big city.

"You two boys do anything stupid in town and Ruth and I will know about it the moment you get home," she firmly announced.

As the five Finley's and Ross sat down to a delicious meal of lamb chops and sweet taters, the mournful howl of wolves broke the reflective mood of the moment.

"Those wolves are in the Swans or the Mission Mountains, they're a hell-of-a-lot closer than the Cabinets," Tomas declared. "I gathered fifty or more sheep from the foothills of Swan Mountain and moved them closer to home just today."

A few more wails and yips prompted Liz to speak. "It sounds like they are a lot closer than the Swan Mountains to me, Tom, more like the Swan River."

Tomas didn't argue; the river was almost in their backyard and a cause for concern. After supper he debated about going to Kalispell, with wolves so close, but decided his boys, at thirteen and fourteen were old enough to keep an eye on the sheep for a few days. Besides, if need be, Liz could shoot a rifle as well as any man. It would be a sorry wolf that messed with her.

At the Running R, Ruth got an early start because Ross, Sam and the kids left before daylight. She was done with her chores by noon and after a light lunch, decided to slip into a pair of riding pants and check the elderberry patch.

Pulling her dress over her head, she took a moment to look in the full length mirror Ross had hauled all the way from Kalispell on a packhorse. It was a birthday gift for when she turned thirty. She'd been depressed, believing her youthful beauty would turn ugly automatically with the age.

She loved the mirror and eventually became convinced age had done little to change her shapely body. There were a few lines on her face she but considered them lines of intellect for lack of a better excuse.

In only a brassiere and panties she slowly turned, examining her body from all angles. She was not admiring her figure as much as she was looking for any lingering signs of her ordeal. Scratches on her back, and bruises on her thighs and buttock had been slow to heal and difficult to hide from Ross.

Relieved that all of the physical evidence was finally gone she took stock of her emotional state. The sight and feel of that horrible little man looking at her exposed body, running his hands over her breasts and belly left her feeling ill. The memory was fading, and now that the external evidence was gone she would be able to give herself to Ross without fear of exposing her and Sam's secret.

"Thank heaven for Sam," she whispered.

Clarence Hobbs spent the night on what was beginning to look like a permanent campsite. He was spending a night or two a week here depending on his schedule at the saloon and the weather. He had a bird's-eye view of the Running R but it was getting cold at night and he was rapidly losing his patience, and perhaps his opportunity.

His loins stirred every time he thought of the blonde babe, causing an uncomfortable situation whether at work or on the trail. He'd had a lot of women in his life, even a few virgins but there was something about this beauty that really got to him.

"Might be 'cause I came so close," he muttered but knew it was more than that.

Right now, he was puzzled and a little excited. After waking a little after daylight he had watched the house and barns from his perch, watched Ruth through his telescope as she gathered things from the garden and made a trip or two from the house to the barn. There was no sign of anyone else.

Could she be alone? He wondered…Is this it? Is this my chance? Get control of your self, Clarence, he admonished himself.

He learned the hard way that attacking a woman in her home was a bad idea. Too many things could go wrong, people had guns in their houses, and you never knew who might be in the house besides the woman. Just because she seemed to be alone was no guarantee, and you never knew when someone might come home or stop by to visit.

"Nope, not a good idea," he reiterated aloud.

Still, there was something odd. He'd watched this place for days hoping to see Ruth go somewhere alone. He knew there were at least three men around the ranch and one other woman or maybe a girl.

The first time he saw Lilly through his telescope he had squawked, "She'd do just fine in a pinch!"

Hobbs settled in with spy glass in hand. "Take your time Clarence," he muttered.

He assessed his situation. He liked his job at the saloon…it gave him a chance to see a lot of people, men and women. He could keep tabs on the gossip and rumors around town. He knew the Riley woman didn't go to the sheriff nor did the bastard who spoiled his fun.

"She's probably too embarrassed or scared. Or maybe she liked it," he gloated.

Clarence was yanked from his daydream by the sight of someone walking from the house toward the barn. Putting the telescope to his eye, he watched with bated breath as a woman disappeared into the barn and emerged astride a chestnut horse.

"Hot damn!" he exclaimed.

If there was ever any doubt about whether he had the right place and the right woman it was gone now.

"There cain't be more'n one gorgeous blond ridin' a chestnut horse this side of Tucson," he chuckled.

As he watched Ruth canter through the arched log gate and down a wagon road his breath became labored. Mounting his horse, Hobbs worked his way along the edge of the timber, hoping to drop in behind her once out of sight of the ranch house.

He waited until they were a mile or two north of the house before falling in behind her. The wagon road was torn up with horse tracks, a fact he found disappointing but not surprising. He wanted to stay far enough back to avoid alerting her or taking a chance she might see him, but with so many tracks it was difficult to trail her, he decided he would ride closer and keep her in sight.

He knew it was risky but risk excited him. The road took a slight bend to the right and he lost sight of her in a pocket of fir, when he got past the trees she was gone. Hobbs felt a rush of adrenaline wondering if she had seen him, if she carried a gun and was lying in wait. The brief panic attack passed when he spotted Ruth riding through tall sage away from the road.

Perfect.

He followed at a safe distance under the cover of tall sage and Saskatoon bushes.

Ruth circled the elderberry patch, she was in luck, there were a few broken limbs where bears had enjoyed a meal but plenty of berries still hung from the bushes like bluish-gray umbrellas. She dismounted, tied Cocoa to a sapling and began picking berries, one tuft at a time, dropping them into one of the six large flour sacks she brought along; four she could tie on behind her saddle and two she could drape over the front.

I might have wine and jelly by the time I get home, she mused.

Clarence pulled up short when he saw Ruth dismount. His main concern was staying far enough back so the horses didn't catch wind of each other. Pulling his trademark gear, a rag and piggin' string, from his saddlebags he began moving cautiously toward the berry picker. The sage made good cover and he worked his way to within thirty yards of her.

Watching Ruth stretch, reach and bend over picking berries and filling sacks, lusty thoughts threatened to over power caution.

"Don't get stupid," he muttered and forced himself to take stock of the situation.

He saw the butt of a gun protruding from a scabbard on the chestnut. The woman was probably fifty feet from her horse and the gun. He was about to thirty yards from the woman. He had to get closer, get between her and her horse then grab her.

Continuing to use sage for cover, Hobbs worked his way around until the chestnut was between them then carefully, using her horse for concealment, he sneaked closer. When he was thirty feet from the chestnut he weighed his chances of beating her to her horse and gun, to untie it and spook it, leaving her on foot and vulnerable?

Think this through.

If he attacked her and she got free she could get to the gun. If he ran her horse off it would return to the ranch and they would know something was wrong. He touched his sidearm but had no intention of using it on her...that would spoil all his fun.

Inching closer, Clarence let his mind wander as his eyes remained glued to the shapely form moving from bush to bush. He was close enough to really appreciate her beauty, to imagine how she looked when he came so close to having her; the full smooth breasts with nipples swollen, the sleek flat belly, tiny waist, and the golden-fleece leading the way to a treasure he intended to take his time claiming.

He loved the element of surprise; it had served him well in the past. He gauged the distance…twenty, fifteen just a few more feet and he would go for her. All of a sudden, the chestnut mare reared and spun, shaking her head as she attempted to pull the lead-rope free from the sapling. Clarence dropped flat on his belly trying to determine what spooked the animal and hoping to remain undetected.

Ruth dropped her bag of berries and ran to Cocoa.

"Whoa girl, whoa!" she shouted.

Ruth grasped the halter and struggled to untie the lead-rope while attempting to calm the wild-eyed horse. Finally succeeding in getting the rope loose, Ruth led the snorting, prancing mare away from the sapling and toward the partially filled sack of berries.

Clarence lay face down, afraid to even breathe. No matter what scared her horse, if this woman saw him he was a dead man. He was coming unwound like a cheap rope. Lying perfectly still, afraid to even raise his eyes, he heard her riding away.

Shit!

Lifting his head, all Hobbs saw were flaxen tail, blond hair and flying hooves. Dropping back to the ground he groaned in disappointment. Not again, he thought.

Shit!

He heard another groan, no more like a growl, a deep long rumble. Raising his head again he looked for the source of the noise.

"Oh my achin' balls!" he moaned.

An enormous hump-backed grizzly the color of a cinnamon stick stood no more than thirty feet away. Hobbs watched the bear lumber toward the bag of berries spilled on the ground.

"Don't even think of movin'," he told himself.

A steady rumble punctuated with an occasional 'woof' filled Clarence's ears while the big bear pawed at the sack, dumping more berries out on the ground then scooping them up with tongue and lips. Suddenly, the grizzly jerked its head up from the juicy dessert and looked around, its nose twitching as it searched for the source of a foreign scent.

Clarence pressed his face into the dirt, daring to barely opening one eye to watch the movement of the giant *Ursus horribilis*. He knows I'm here somewhere, Clarence thought, paralyzed with fear…If he sees me I'm dead. Dust and grass tickled his nose and he held his breath… If I sneeze that bastard'll be on me like slime on a slug.

The bear returned to his dessert, unable to locate what could have been the main course. Once he finished cleaning up all the berries he grasp the sack in his powerful jaws and shook it as if believing it was holding out on him. Convince the bag was empty he turned to the bushes, breaking limbs and sucking up berries. Again, he extended his nose and sniffed trying to get a better line on an irritating smell.

Clarence felt sweat running off his forehead and down the crease between his nose and cheek…it tickled.

Son-of-a-bitch! Hobbs mentally swore but willed himself to remain silent and still.

The grizzly stood upright, roared an ear-shattering challenge to the foul-smelling intruder then dropped back on all fours and sauntered away in search of food, fight or female.

Clarence never moved for what seemed like hours to him, even after the bear was out of sight. He'd heard stories of men mauled by grizzlies until they played dead, then when the bear left they tried to get away too quickly and the bear returned to finish the job.

When he was satisfied the grizzly was truly gone, he could barely stand, his arms and legs ached, he was stiff and freezing but most of all he was pissed!

"Son-of-a-whisky-drinkin' bastard!" he cursed under his breath.

He was still worried about the goddamn grizzly but as the fear subsided, his anger elevated. He almost had her and could damn near feel the soft, smooth silk like feel of her skin. In his mind's eye Hobbs could see the feminine secrets of her body that women kept so carefully hidden.

"Well, bullshit!" he exclaimed loudly.

All feeling of lust was gone as he headed back toward his waiting cayuse.

"It's like that bitch has a goddamn guardian angel or somethin'," he grumbled.

Larry, Lillian and Sam dropped off a hundred or so cows and calves at the first fenced haystack and returned to the ranch house feeling good about their day.

A slightly shaken Ruth recounted her close encounter with the grizzly over a meal of new potatoes, pot roast and mixed vegetables. She spoke to a captive audience as they considered yet another threat to livestock, only this time the threat also included people. No one at the table had first-hand knowledge of any human being killed by a grizzly but all believed the threat was very real.

Hot apple pie and cinnamon tea for dessert lightened the mood and the conversation changed into the brother-sister banter Ruth was so grateful to hear.

They filled Ruth in on the roundup, the failure to find anymore traps, the fact that they found no evidence of wolves killing cattle and that the roundup in general was off to a good start.

Ruth encouraged Lilly to stay in the living room with Larry and Sam while she moved the dishes to the kitchen, cleaned up the leftovers, put them in the ice box and tidied up. She wanted Larry and Sam to get comfortable with one another and thought Lilly might act as a catalyst in that process.

When Larry walked into the kitchen Ruth asked, "Where are Sam and Lilly?"

"Gone to bed," Larry replied.

Seeing Ruth's perplexed expression, he added playfully, "Not together Mom. Sam went to the bunkhouse."

Ruth frowned but did not respond.

"What's the deal with Sam?" Larry asked, trying to be nonchalant. "Dad says he came here with you looking like a bum and has been here ever since."

"What do you think of him?" Ruth probed.

"He seems okay. Lilly says he knows horses and he can ride but that's not the point. Are we going to hire him?"

"Do you think we should?"

"C'mon Mom, I'm trying to get some answers, not more questions."

"What did your dad say about him?" Ruth continued to dig.

"Not much but he acts like Sam's being here is your idea."

Ruth wiped her hands on her apron, took it off and hung it on a peg near the sink. Walking into the living room she settled into a rocker and motioned for Larry to sit.

"I will tell you all I know about Sam, but for now at least, it has to stay between us. I need you to promise."

Ruth told Larry her story about how she met Sam. She withheld some of the more salacious details she was attempting to rid from her memory but she included more than she told Ross or Lilly.

"Tell me who the bastard is Mom and I'll kill him! Larry said coldly. "I don't know who he is," she lied.

"So what about Sam?" Larry backtracked. "Do you want dad to hire him?"

"Well, he already has, at least for a while," Ruth confessed.

"So when was somebody going to tell me?" Larry fumed. "Does Lilly know?"

"Yes, Lilly knows but that's because he helped her while you were sick. When we returned Sam had done a lot of work around here and Ross and I thought we should pay him for that time. Then we decided to keep him on until you were recovered." Ruth hoped she didn't sound defensive.

"So now I'm well, so now what, do you want to keep Sam on?"

"Would that bother you, is there some reason you don't want us to hire him on steady?" Ruth was becoming anxious.

"Not really, Sam is a good hand but I think Lilly likes him."

Ruth was confused. "Well I hope she likes him, I know they were here together for the two weeks you were sick but what does that have to do with our hiring him or not?"

"No, Mom," Larry corrected. "I mean I think Lilly *really likes* him."

Ruth was totally blindsided. It never occurred to her Lilly and Sam might actually like each other. Her concern was that Lilly could tolerate having him around. She believed Sam was a fine young man but he was a man, Lilly was still her little girl even if she was sixteen.

"What makes you think that?" she managed to ask.

"You know Lilly, Mom," Larry began. "Strong willed, independent and generally a pain in the ass. I watched her and Sam today when they weren't aware, she was different around him and the way they looked at each other, it was like they share some kind of secret. I could be imagining things, Mom, but I think I know Lilly. There's something going on between them."

Ruth struggled with conflicting emotions. She believed she owed Sam for her life and that he was in some kind of trouble and she was determined to help, it was the only way she knew to pay him back. However, the thought of Sam and Lilly liking each other had never crossed her mind. She needed time to think on that, she needed to talk to Sam.

"What if you're right, how would you feel about that?"

"C'mon Mom, we don't know anything about this guy. I'm glad he helped you out of a sticky situation but he could be an outlaw, a gunfighter or a thief, maybe he just got out of prison. What do you know about him? It sounds like he did you a favor so you brought him home. Just because he stayed with Lilly while you and dad were gone and the guy is good with horses doesn't mean he's a good guy." Larry paused for a moment. "Mom, do you know more about Sam than you're telling?"

It was one of the things she loved about Larry, he had a way of cutting to the chase, but she felt trapped. She wondered if she should have told the whole story to begin with. No, she was sure Ross could not have handled it. She wasn't sure Larry could and she certainly didn't want either of them to strap on a gun to go after some monster they knew nothing about. Larry already wanted to kill the guy and he didn't know the half of it. Thoughts raced through Ruth's mind as Larry's question begged for an answer.

"I've told you all I can," she softly replied. "All I know about Sam is what my instincts tell me. I suspect he may be in some kind of trouble but I don't think it's serious and I don't think it's his fault, and I want to help him as much as I can."

"I don't get it Mom. This is not like you. Is this Sam blackmailing you or something?" Larry was getting agitated. "And one more thing, what is that thing he wears around his neck with the wolf painted on it? I've never seen him without it."

"Larry," Ruth spoke with a quiet firmness Larry knew meant it was time to leave it alone. "Some things happened while you were sick, things that would have been much worse were it not for Sam. I have said all I am going to say on that subject to you, to your dad or to Lilly…so get over it. I will ask Sam if there is anything going on between him and Lilly. I believe he will tell me the truth and Larry, thank you for caring but let me handle this. If there is something that needs to be dealt with I will do it, this is my doing."

This talk was over and Larry knew it.

"Okay Mom," Larry said and wrapped his arms around her in a big hug. "I love you Mom."

Ruth stood with tears rolling down her cheeks watching him head for the stairs and bed. It's not fair, she thought. She never asked for any of this but she couldn't tell them the sordid details of the attack.

She threw on a jacket. "I need to talk to Sam," she muttered and stepped out into the cold night air. "This is not only about me, it's also about Lillian."

Chapter Twenty-three
Dollar Bar

Ruth knocked on the bunkhouse door, quietly at first then with increased intensity.

"Just a minute, I'll be right there."

She knew Sam had probably been asleep but this couldn't wait. The door opened and Sam stood there shirtless, the leather amulet prominent on his chest, dressed only in tight jeans. Larry's tight jeans, she thought.

He looked good, broad shoulders, muscular chest and arms, narrow waist, tight butt. She thought of Lillian. *What have I done?*

"I am really sorry to wake you Sam but I need to talk to you, now." The last word punctuated the urgency she felt.

"Si Señora Ruth, no problem," Sam answered, a little groggy from sleep. "Que pasa? Is something wrong?"

"I don't know Sam. You tell me. If you're in some kind of trouble I have to know. Ross is gone for a few days and now is the time to come clean. I want to help you but I need to know the truth."

"Come in," Sam said. "I will stoke up the fire." He knew this day would come, now was probably a good a time. "This will be between us?" he asked cautiously.

"It can be if you want and if you tell me the truth," Ruth answered, feeling a touch of trepidation and wondering if the truth could be worse than not knowing.

"I will tell you the whole story Señora Riley, but I must warn you it will be hard to believe. I swear it is the truth but if I had not been there I would not believe it."

Sam told Ruth about the valley, the Indians, the dance and the ghostly warriors. He told her about the amulet, how he ran from the fort, deserted, fearing not only for his life but his soul, that he believed he was being pursued by the army and the Indians and if caught by either he would be executed or killed, as if there was somehow a difference. He told about the appearance of the black wolf and his escape from his Indain captors.

Ruth was transfixed and scarcely took a breath while Sam was talking. It took a leap of faith to believe the story but he was dead serious in the telling. It's either true or he's the best liar I ever met, she silently concluded.

Her thoughts returned to Lillian. "Sam, have you and Lilly done anything I need to know about?" She hated asking but could see no way around it.

"We did see the black lobo, wolf, I told you about, near where Larry found the trap that cut his ear. We agreed not to tell anyone because we thought no one would believe us. You will think I am loco but that wolf changed into part Indian and was really angry about the traps. He was caught in one and took it off his foot and threw it down. I have the trap here in the bunkhouse," he confessed. "I promised Lillian I would not tell because she did not want Larry to make fun of her and she was afraid Senior Ross would not see humor in it."

"So this is a secret the two of you have kept?" Ruth asked judiciously then added warily, "Is that the only secret you two have?"

"I did tell her about the amulet," he replied and touched the leather talisman. "I told her I think the black lobo is following it. That has been our secret."

Ruth felt a little chagrin and a lot relieved. Larry wasn't wrong…he just made an incorrect assumption.

Never assume.

She grinned at Sam. It's a good thing I'm nearly twice his age and in love with Ross, she thought.

"I would like to know something," Sam stated, assuming the inquisition was over. "Where am I? I have been running since the August before I met you and do not know where I am. I know it sounds very stupid, but am I in Canada?"

"No, Sam, this is Montana Territory. I don't know how far we are from the fort you ran away from but our ranch is about a hundred miles south of Canada. If you want to be in Canada it's another three or four day's ride. Head for Wild Horse Creek and keep on going north." Ruth looked at the floor then at the fire. "Is that were you want to be Sam? If it is, I'll make sure you have plenty of money and supplies to get there."

Sam absorbed the information. He'd heard of Montana, it seemed as far away from the fort as California but Canada was a different country; he would be safe there, at least from the army.

"Are you saying it is time for me to leave?" he asked with a touch of apprehension.

"I'm telling you that if you want to be in Canada I will make sure you have what you need to get there. Sam, I don't know what is best for you. If the army came here looking for you, I'm sure Ross wouldn't hide you. I would if it was up to me, but it isn't. I'll keep all you've told me between us but I can't risk the ranch and the future of our kids for you…I just can't."

Despair crowded Ruth's mind, if only her family knew how much they owe him. Then cynically she thought, maybe they don't owe him anything…it was my life he saved.

Sam was also emotionally tormented. He didn't want to leave. Working on this ranch was like having family again. He wanted to stay with Ruth and Lillian but knew he couldn't. They've helped me enough, now I am putting them at risk, he told himself.

Wanting to be pragmatic but succumbing to the desire in his gut he blurted, "Do you think Senior Ross would hire me on through winter? I would head for Canada in the spring. The army does not know where I am and I am not sure the Indians care." He touched the amulet to convince himself. "I will leave with the winter snow so you can stop worrying and get back to living."

"Sam, I want to make something very clear; as long as you want to stay here and work, I'll make sure you have a job. We can afford to pay you and besides, they tell me you're a good hand. I just won't hide you from the authorities if they come looking, not that I consider what you did criminal or cowardice. I don't think much of the army's mission to drive the Indians from their hunting and fishing grounds and killing them if they don't move. We can live with the Indians…the ranchers in this valley have proven that. They hunt and fish on land we call ours and we give them a few beef for letting us use the land they see as theirs. The only reason the Indians fight is because the army bullies them and expects them to stay on reservations when they don't understand boundaries. Shoot, they don't even know the difference between America and Canada…they don't care either!"

Ruth was becoming emotional, it was a sore subject with her and it angered her to think this fine young man was now a criminal because he left the army that was intent on killing Indians. He was definitely no coward either…she knew that first hand.

Clarence Hobbs was infuriated. He had the night off but he rode all the way back to town anyway.

"I had her, goddamn it! First she's saved by a damn human buzz-saw an' now a grizzly." He'd been talking to himself ever since he got far enough away from the bear to relax. "I should give it up but I'm damn mad now! I need a new plan 'cause what I'm doin' ain't workin'."

He stomped into the saloon, found a corner table and sat with his back to the wall, stroking his door-knocker mustache.

The bartender walked over. "Drinkin' on yer night off?" he joked. "That ain't like you, Clarence."

"I'll have whisky in a clean glass and you can keep your opinions."

Hobbs was in no mood for bar-talk or banter. He had an ache deep in his gut and had to find a way to cure it. The days were pretty nice if the sun was shining but winter weather was near and any chance of fun in the sun with that blond was rapidly slipping away.

"I sure as hell ain't plannin' on waitin' till spring ta get some uh that," he muttered after the bartender brought him his shot.

He threw back the whiskey, ordered another and looked around the saloon. There were a couple of local merchants who should have a table with their name on it. A few cowboys in dusty hats and boots and a half-dozen prospector-looking types were scattered around the room. He'd been seeing more prospectors lately, but hadn't heard about any new gold strikes in the area. "I got more important business than gold diggers ta think about," he muttered.

His second shot arrived and Hobbs leaned back into the corner and sighed deeply.

Another night in paradise.

If I'm gonna get ta her this winter it's gonna have ta be inside, maybe an abandon house or barn, something, he mused…and now she's carryin' a gun.

He silently cursed her male rescuer and the grizzly. Clarence also packed a sidearm and knew how to use it. Damned if he was going take a chance of getting beat up on again. Problem was a gun wouldn't do him much good when his pants were down. He ordered another drink.

"Somethin' botherin' ya ta night, Clarence?" the bartender asked, setting the shot down.

"Nothin' you can fix Clem," Hobbs responded in a surly tone.

When Ross and Tomas rode into Kalispell they went straight to the veterinarian. He had a laboratory and it was an animal trap, not a man trap. The vet said he would run some tests and should have the results in a day or two.

Tomas wanted to find a spinning wheel for Elizabeth and maybe a store-bought dress if he saw something he thought she would like. Ross cottoned on to the dress idea right away so the two men went shopping. Since the arrival of the railroad Kalispell had turned into a bustling town. There were saloons, livery stables, a claims office, banks, hotels, hardware and dry goods stores, and a huge house being built by the town's founder in clear view of the snow-covered mountains to the east.

By the time their shopping spree ended Ross was darn glad he brought along an extra packhorse. He'd found a green-calico dress and silk negligee for Ruth, a pair of boots and riding pants for Lilly and a leather vest for Larry, and he bought himself a black Stetson. That evening the men enjoyed a prime rib dinner, except for the eastern ale they ordered out of curiosity…it tasted like sheep dip.

Kalispell also had its share of fast-talking swindlers. Their favorite scam was selling bogus mining claims. Gold had been found along the Clark Fork south and west of Kalispell and some believed more money was made selling bogus claims than by those who actually found gold.

The next day Ross and Tomas checked at the claims office, after hearing stories that prospectors were staking claims on deeded land. There was some dispute between the Bureau of Mines and the Assessor's Office regarding to whom such a claim would actually belong.

Ross learned there were two claims on the Running R filed by one man, Clarence Hobbs from Tucson in the Arizona Territory. What he found most unusual was that the claims were filed on the same day two weeks ago.

Tomas found only one on his land, filed over a year ago by a Ronald Noland, with a last known address of Sacramento in the state of California. The Finley claim was consistent with the fuss caused by the Clark Fork rush, but the Running R claims were more curious.

Ross would get to the bottom of it if Mr. Hobbs was still around. Chances were he would be gone for sure by spring. Winter in Montana can come without warning and it can be unpredictable and unforgiving.

"One Montana winter and the streets of Tucson will probably look darn good," Ross laughed, as he and Tomas left the claims office in search of a good breakfast.

They stepped out into a frigid wind blowing out of the northeast. The sky that had been clear and sunny moments earlier was now the color of a gun barrel and scattered snow flakes danced on the wind. Ross wouldn't get the test results on the trap until afternoon so he would be spending another night in Kalispell.

"What do you think, Tomas, you going to stay another night or do you feel like you need to beat this storm home?"

"I'll stay another night, I wouldn't want Liz to get to thinking I miss her. Besides, I want to know what you find out about that trap."

The Finley ranch was only a day's ride from town, Tomas was not worried about the weather…not yet. Besides, if he was going to go home today he would have to leave now and he hadn't had breakfast yet.

After a healthy serving of, ham, eggs and red potatoes at a boarding house ran by a matronly middle-aged woman, the two men went about the mundane business of buying a few staples such as beans, flour, sugar, coffee, salt, and baking powder.

When they returned to the veterinary office, the tests were completed and the results not unexpected. Doc Jensen was right. The trap appeared to have been dipped in a mixture of lard and strychnine. When the trap cut Larry's ear the poisoned lard got into the cut and continued to release small amounts of strychnine into his blood stream until the cut was thoroughly cleaned by the doctor, but any amount of strychnine in the blood stream is deadly.

The veterinarian asked Ross a lot of questions regarding how Doc Jensen had treated the boy. He was fascinated by the use of an activated charcoal infusion but believed it was most likely the chloroform-induced coma-like state that saved Larry's life.

There was little doubt the traps were being set for wolves but Tomas was concerned about his herd dogs. Ross was livid and determined to find out who was setting them. As far as he was concerned the son-of-a-bitch had tried to murder his son.

The veterinarian was also concerned. Why would anyone go to the trouble of lacing traps with strychnine? If a wolf was caught in a trap the chances of escape or survival were virtually non-existent. Why not simply put out poison bait? Why not kill an elk or deer or even a cow and sprinkle it with strychnine which could kill an entire pack?

Only one thing was certain; this was the work of a maniac. Someone with such a homicidal hatred of wolves that he wanted to watch them suffer and die, one wolf at a time; or he was just plain crazy. If the later was true, what might he try next? People had dogs for pets and protection, would he trap them, too, knowing even if they were rescued from the trap they would die anyway?

Ross and Tomas left the vet's office angry and perplexed. They were happy to have proof the trap was poisoned but now what? How could they catch the jerk and how many more traps were there?

"Can you think of any rancher who could be doing this?" Ross asked.

"None," Tomas replied, "but it has to be someone who knows the country." He paused, thoughtful, then added, "Who knows the wolves are back?"

The sound of wolves on the Flathead had been absent for at least a couple of years until about the time of Larry's injury, yet the traps were already set. As they walked to a restaurant for their evening dinner, both men racked their brains in an effort to think of someone, anyone who might be suspicious.

"Who ever it is, it's going to be a little harder to sneak around with snow on the ground," Ross stated as flakes drifted around his ears. "Hope the kids are having good luck moving the cattle in around the feed stacks."

"Got most of my sheep in already," Tomas declared then added, "been a little worried about wolves."

"Did I tell you I have a new hired man?" Ross had nearly forgotten until he thought of the kids bringing in the cattle.

"Anybody I know?" queried Tomas.

"Not even anybody I know," Ross cracked. "He's somebody Ruth knows."

"Knows from where?" Tomas queried.

"Don't really know but I'll try and explain." After a brief run down of how Sam wound up on the Running R, Ross elaborated. "While Ruth and I were with Larry, Sam did a lot of work on the ranch. He didn't have to work, no one asked him to do anything but stay with Lilly. He doesn't have a buffalo nickel, we gave him some of Larry's clothes and burned the rags he was wearing, but he didn't want me to pay him for the work he did while we were gone."

"So how long are you going to keep him on?" Tomas quizzed.

"I guess I'm not sure, I was going to let him go as soon as I got back to the ranch. I kind of think Ruth would like me to keep him on through the winter, so I guess we'll see what happens when I get home."

"How old a man is he?" Tomas was looking for more information.

"He's just a kid, told me he's twenty two, looks about nineteen."

"How do your kids feel about him?" Tomas continued to probe.

"Don't know yet about Larry, Lilly seems to like him, she says he's good with horses. That makes him okay by her, besides, Ruth feels like she owes him for helping her out of a bad spot. So, as long as he's willing to work I suppose he'll have a job."

"Ross," Tomas said hesitantly, "how do you know this Sam has nothing to do with the poison traps? He showed up about the same time."

"I don't for sure. I'm mostly trusting Ruth but there is one thing. He wears a leather thing around his neck, looks like some kind of Indian charm or totem and it has the face of a wolf on it…a black wolf."

"Doesn't sound like something a guy who hates wolves would wear, just keep an eye on him for now, that's all I'm saying." Tomas felt like he was barefoot in a snake pit.

The two friends continued chatting over dinner and retired early, the ride back to the Finley sheep farm tomorrow could be a tough one.

When two cowboys walked into the saloon with snow on their hat brims, Clarence was struck with profound disappointment. From what people told him about winters in Montana, his chances of getting to the woman were not good for the next four or five months, a fact he found totally unacceptable.

"Snowin' ay?" he said as the men approached the bar.

"Yep," one of them replied. "If ya wanna remember what dirt looks like ya might wanna go out an' take a look. Ya might not see it again 'till April."

Clarence felt an empty spot in his belly. It was a craving, like needing a drink really bad and not having any money. Only it wasn't a drink or fresh apple pie or donuts that he craved, it was that blond beauty from the Running R. He'd gotten too close, seen too much of her, now he couldn't get her out of his head.

He wanted to think winter in Paradise couldn't be any worse than summer in Tucson but it was a full day's ride to the Running R, a ride he couldn't see happening in a snowstorm or in freezing temperatures. At least you could find shade in Tucson.

*

Ruth didn't bother to go back to the elderberry patch. She was sure the grizzly ate any berries she left in the sack and she had managed to get home with most of them. She didn't know how long the beast might hang around and grizzlies were so territorial she didn't want to risk making him think he had to protect his domain from her.

The kids were having good luck moving cattle onto the winter range and it looked like a good thing because the sky looked threatening. Sam and Larry seemed to get along okay and Lilly was unusually enthusiastic. She liked to help move the cattle but Ross was so protective she sometimes felt like he didn't appreciate her efforts.

Ruth was especially pleased with her talk with Sam. They'd been straight forward and honest with each other. She would see that Ross kept him on until spring, by that time Sam would have earned enough if he felt the need to head for Canada to start a new life, he could.

She slept well that night, but dreamed of the grizzly and her run for safety aboard Cocoa. It was a good dream compared to some of the nightmares she'd had of that horrible little man who tried to rape her.

Thankfully those dreams were becoming less frequent and sometimes she wondered if it actually happened. Of course, seeing Sam was a constant reminder that it had.

"You'd think that would be a bad thing," she whispered. Instead, it made her feel safe, and having someone to share the secret of her attack was somehow liberating.

The morning brought a snowstorm, not a Montana blizzard by any means but snow none the less. She worried about Ross, she expected him back within a day or two and the weather could turn ugly really fast this time of year. She would fret from now until she saw him ride through the gate on his big blood-bay.

At breakfast Larry looked out the window at the snowfall. "I don't think we need to go out today Mom. We got most of the cattle off Big Arm and a little weather will make the lead cows start heading for home. If we give them a day or two, the rest will be easy to find."

The routine was well established, the older cows knew it and the younger ones would follow.

"When's dad going to be home?" Lilly asked, wondering about her future with the cattle drive.

"When you see him ride Roy through that arched gate," Ruth replied, pointing out the window. "Then he'll be home," she added.

Sam was quiet during breakfast and Ruth wondered if it had anything to do with their talk. Not likely, she decided. He was always pretty quiet unless directly engaged. She also kept a wooly eye on him and Lilly, she wanted to believe his story about the strange wolf-like creature but she couldn't totally dismiss Larry's intuition.

What if there was something between Sam and Lilly? No, she really believed Sam would have told her, she had to.

Larry decided it would be a good day for him and Sam to work with the two colts Sam started while he was sick. Working with a high-strung colt could get your blood flowing and you wouldn't even notice a little cold wind or snow.

Sam had sacked the colts out good and thrown saddles on them but as of yet had not crawled on to see how they would react to a human on their backs. After a couple hours reinforcing what the colts already knew, it was time to see how they liked a man in the saddle.

The two colts were in a small round corral, both were saddled and ready for a rider. Sam and Larry were trying to decide who would ride which colt. Lilly, who observed the process from the beginning decided it was time to intervene.

"Men," she huffed in exasperation, "breaking a horse is a masterful art and there are a few rules that need to be followed." She was speaking with an exaggerated, self-righteous tone. "Before anyone gets on a colt for the first time, it must have a name. Only one colt may be mounted at a time, to do otherwise, diminishes the significance of the event and makes it more difficult for the observer to focus on the man who is getting bucked off. It is fortunate for you boys that I am here or you would have completely screwed this up."

Lilly jumped down from her perch on the corral rail and pointed at the bay colt with a white slash running from his forehead and bending smoothly under one eye. He was standing with his back bowed in resistance to the cinch around his girth.

"From this day forward you shall be known as Bodie," she declared.

"Why Bodie?" Larry asked curiously.

"Because of the white slash under his eye, you know, like a Jim Bodie knife."

Sam and Larry looked at each other momentarily then burst into spitting, sputtering laughter.

"What's so funny about that?" she asked, frowning suspiciously.

"It's Bowie, Lil…Jim Bowie," Larry managed with a straight face.

The two boys failed miserably in their attempt to remain serious and laughter erupted again.

"Whatever," Lilly said, smiling sheepishly. "Is somebody going to ride Bodie or do I have to show you cowboys how it's done?"

"You ride him," Larry said to Sam. "I'll ride…what's his name?"

Larry was looking at a stout Morgan-quarter horse mix.

"That's Bigfoot," Lilly stated, pointing to the over-sized hooves.

Bodie, in spite of his apparent dislike of the cinch around his belly behaved fairly well when, with Lilly and Larry holding him, Sam stuck his foot in a stirrup and carefully swung onboard. Once released the colt took a few careful steps, imitating someone walking on egg shells, his eyes wide and rolling nervously while he tried to figure out what this thing was on his back.

After watching a few moments from her kitchen window, Ruth tossed on a coat and joined Larry and Lilly…everyone enjoyed a good rodeo.

Bodie continued his light-footed walk around the small corral, shaking his head, baulked then dropped his head and leaped. Sam pulled the colt's head up after the first jump and the horse reared, spun and took a high-dive in a futile attempt to free itself of the pesky thing on its back. After a couple lofty, stiff-legged jumps Sam regained control, pulled Bodie up short and patted him a few times on the neck, talking all the while.

After a few more trips around the corral Sam motioned for Larry to open the gate and he and Bodie were free. If the horse started bucking now Sam better stick with him or the horse could wind up in Canada. But Bodie didn't buck. Having control of the horses's head, Sam urged him into a canter. The colt took a couple crow hops but he was a fast learner. Bodie was on his way toward being one more option in the Riley string. Sam rode Bodie back into the corral, carefully stepped off the horse and patted the bay on the butt.

"Good boy, I think you might turn into a cow horse." He laughed trying to picture what that might look like.

Then it was Larry's turn to ride the unusual silver-bronze colt with the big feet.

"Do you want Lilly to help Sam hold him?" Ruth asked from her seat alongside Lilly on the fence.

"Might be a good idea, he has kind of a mean eye," Larry assessed, rubbing the horse's nose.

You can tell a lot by looking a horse in the eye, some have a soft, gentle look and some don't; Larry Riley knew the difference.

Lilly crawled down from the top rail amid swirling snowflakes and stood next to Sam and held Bigfoot's halter while Larry vigilantly mounted the animal. Once on the colt's back, Larry squirmed around to secure his seat, then with a nod of his head signaled Sam and Lilly to turn him loose.

The colt stood, front feet spread apart as if unsure what to do next. With Larry's coaxing, Bigfoot took one tentative step and another. Then with a quickness belying the colt's awkward appearance, he dropped his head, spun to his left and leaped for the sky.

The sudden move threw Larry hard onto his right stirrup. He fought to gain control of the colt's head but his feet were out of position. The colt landed in a stiff-legged, bone-jarring, teeth-rattling crunch. Unable to absorb the landing through his legs, Larry felt the full impact from spine to eyelids, flashes of red and blue punctuated by tiny white lights illuminated a solid-black background.

The next jump sent Larry high into the air and he came down with a resounding thud, landing on his left side. Sam hurriedly gathered up Bigfoot's dangling reins while Ruth and Lillian rushed to Larry. He lay still, unable, or unwilling to move.

Kneeling at his head, Ruth asked, "Are you alright?"

Larry responded with a series of moans and a weak, "I don't think so."

With Bigfoot secured, Sam joined the women next to Larry's inert body.

"Can you move your arms and legs?" Sam solemnly asked.

Larry began by wiggling his feet then bending his legs, followed by the wiggling of fingers, he moved his right arm working the elbow then his left.

"Aaugh!" he shouted in pain. His right hand grabbed his left shoulder and very carefully he moved his left arm again. "Aaaaw... Jeesus!" he muttered in pain and disgust.

"Is it your shoulder?" Sam asked and without waiting for an answer added, "Maybe we better get you to the house."

Snow was beginning to accumulate on the ground, not a good place for an injured man to be lying.

Sam and Ruth got Larry to his feet and with Sam supporting him on his right side they moved slowly toward the house. Lilly picked up Larry's hat that had landed outside the corral. Back at the house Ruth removed Larry's jacket, vest and shirt, each with great care. Once the shirt was removed the injury was obvious, an egg-size lump protruded halfway between his neck and the point of his shoulder.

"Looks like you broke your collar bone," Sam said with a degree of certainty.

"Jeeesus," Larry muttered. "I'm not going back to the doctor." He was as much discouraged as in pain.

Sam moved in closer and began probing Larry's left side gently.

"Does that hurt?" he asked with each probe, knowing that asking was really not necessary; if it hurt Larry would let them all know. "Take a deep breath," he instructed. Satisfied that there were no broken ribs, Sam looked at Ruth and said, "Señora Riley, the only thing a doctor would do is put his arm in a sling for six weeks or so. You can do the same thing with an old apron."

"Are you sure Sam, how do you know?"

"My mother was a doctor," he replied.

"Larry in an apron, I can hardly wait," Lilly jibed.

A surly look from Larry made it clear he was in no mood for jokes.

"I will help you with a sling and keep an eye on his healing progress if you want," Sam offered, trying not to be presumptuous.

Ruth nodded approval through a multitude of thoughts. She hoped Ross got home soon but he was not going to be happy to find Larry laid up. Sam never ceased to amaze her; his mother, a doctor, he'd not told her but then she never asked about his parents. All she knew was what he told her about the Indians and the fort. She wondered if Lilly had known, after all she and Sam spent a lot of time together.

It was late afternoon and five inches of snow had already accumulated when Lilly yelled, "Mom, dad's home!"

Ruth threw on a coat and a pair of boots and hurried out to the barn to meet him. When they came into the house Ross hugged Lilly, nodded to Sam and gave Larry a long perplexed look. Larry was shirtless, his arm hanging in a flowered apron fashioned into a sling.

"I thought I raised a cowboy," he said with a touch of sarcasm. "Sounds like that Dollar Bar colt got the best of you."

The colt that threw Larry was out of a mare from a line of running quarter horses sired by Dollar Bar, infamous for being unpredictable and ferocious bucking stock. Ross had reasoned that mixing the Dollar Bar speed with the good disposition of his Morgan stud would produce an exceptional animal, though there was always a chance for a throwback.

This might be one of 'em.

Ross looked at Sam. "Ruth says you believe Larry will heal alright without going to a doctor. She also tells me your mother is a doctor. What else don't we know about you?" Ross asked, as he inspected the lump on Larry's shoulder.

"Was a doctor," Sam said flatly. "She died."

Ross looked at Ruth, Ruth looked at Lilly…no one knew.

"I'm sorry," Ross said. "I didn't know. In fact there's a lot I don't know about you." He was again looking at Sam. "With Larry hurt it looks like we need to keep you on for the winter, if you're willing. If so, we need to have a talk…all of us."

"What is there to talk about?" Ruth interjected. "We need help and Sam needs a job, we should be glad he's here."

"I say we hire Sam on one condition," Larry said quietly. "I want to see him try to ride that big-footed colt." He smiled slyly.

"Done," Sam quickly agreed.

"Men," Ruth whispered.

Pride goeth before a fall.

"The bible did get some things right," she sighed.

Chapter Twenty-four

Jack Wilson

Standing Wolf rode down river from where he had watched the wildfire explode in an awe inspiring crescendo. The great wind-spirit *Mariah* had intervened and saved Roy's dream house and his Wishbone Ranch from any serious damage. Some of the grasslands burned but they would come back better than before.

The two soldiers, still cranky over what Standing Wolf did to them back at the fort were itching for a fight, a fight only he knew they could not win. In the confusion of the moment he simply rode away, convinced the amulet was not here, he was more concerned about how and where the fire started than fooling with a couple of soldiers high on adrenaline.

He passed Long Rapids where he last visited Chief Little Moses; the village was gone but from the far side of the river he could not tell if the band escaped the fire or perished.

When he reached the delta that formed at the mouth of the *Okinakane* River where it converged with the Columbia, he crossed to the north bank of the Columbia and rode cautiously up the long slope leading to Fort Okanogan. Darkness was settling in and he was confident he could get close to the fort without being seen.

When he got within sight of the fort, what he saw left him shaken. Fort Okanogan was a glowing, smoldering pile of logs, doors and debris. Darkness was encroaching so he decided to retreat to the river, and settled in for the night under the cover of cottonwood, hawthorn, and choke-cheery. He wondered if the soldiers left the fort before the fire or if there had been a battle that perhaps caused it. He saw no evidence of any victims, soldier or Indian but he would take a closer look in the morning.

After a restless night, morning brought some answers and a new sense of purpose. The burning fort and high winds were the cause of the wildfire and the fort was apparently unoccupied at the time of the fire. There was no evidence of what or how the fire started but Standing Wolf believed Little Moses might have something to do with it.

If the 5th Cavalry abandoned the fort, it appeared they left no one behind to guard it. There were no bodies or bones to indicate anyone perished in the fire. Why would the army leave two guards at Roy's Wishbone ranch and none at the fort? Could they all have been captured and taken prisoner?

One thing was certain, no matter what caused the fire, the destruction of a military facility would not go unnoticed and Indians would get the blame. If the 5th returned to Vancouver after the loss of Colonel Wolard and his men, they would not return until after the snows of winter and the swollen rivers of spring, but they would return. Standing Wolf knew from his experience with Custer and the 7th that the cavalry suffered setbacks, not defeats.

He thought about the valley and his mother, Star Flower and Frank, would they again be in danger? Not before next summer… eight months or more, he thought…a virtual lifetime, time for all the uncertainty to end.

Time…it meant nothing to the Sematuse…the only thing that mattered to them was *now*. Time was not a way of measuring the distance between birth and death, a line beginning with an entry into and ending with an exit from this world. A circle has no beginning or end, only points of transformation from one life to the next.

It became clear to Standing Wolf what he must do. He rode Whiskey back across the Columbia and began the journey south, not so unlike the journey he made west with Custer and the 7th, except this time he would be alone on a mission to save the Indians and the old ways…not destroy them.

His destination was Nevada and the Walker Lake Reservation. The Paiute, Gray Hair, and the Minneconjous, Long Foot would be waiting; he knew it was so. The trip was nothing like Standing Wolf expected. He was rarely alone because he met Indians nearly every day, most living on reservations and all discouraged, despondent, depressed or simply angry.

He told them about the Ghost Dance, showed them the amulet and talked of the sacred black wolf and his mother, the seer. He spoke with tribes he knew, the Yakima, Chelan and Wenatchee, and many he did not; the Nez Perce, Lapwai and Kalamath.

By time he reached Walker Lake Standing Wolf had traveled nearly a thousand miles on the back of his faithful Arabian. He had been trapped in box canyons, detoured by impassable rivers, belly deep in mountains snow and parched in vast deserts. It was only with help from the various Indian tribes that he survived the arduous journey.

The most remarkable part of his travels was that from the time he left the land of the *Okinakane*, every tribe knew he was coming. He was welcomed with food, shelter, guides, and women, whom he declined although at times with much difficulty. Reluctant to offend and often tempted, Standing Wolf never forgot Star Flower. He believed her to be his chosen one with whom he was destined to spend eternity, she was the hub around which his circle revolved.

When he arrived at Walker Lake, Gray Hair and Long Foot were so excited to see Standing Wolf, after their brief meeting at Noisy Waters they showered him with gifts and food. They sent riders and runners to nearby reservations announcing the arrival of the Messiah. The remarkable Indian communication system, the miraculous 'talking on the wind' spread the word along the streams and rivers all the way to the Great Sioux Nation and back. Indians from many tribes gathered to meet him and hear about the Ghost Dance. There were Klamath, Miwok, Modoc and Yurok. Even people of the Hunkpapas and Lakoka Sioux, Blackfeet and Cheyenne gathered at Walker Lake.

Standing Wolf told the story of the Sematuse and Colonel Wolard, of Bent Grass and the sacred black wolf and its symbol, the amulet. He spoke with local missionaries and military leaders, all alarmed at the large number of Indians assembled in one place, on one reservation.

His assurance that he spoke only of peace and compliance was met with measured skepticism.

Days turned into weeks and the gatherings grew larger, with many Indians practicing the dance which often went from daylight through the night till daylight again, with some falling in exhaustion only to be replaced by dancers from a previous collapse. As word of the dance spread from reservation to reservation some, especially the Paiutes, began calling it the 'round dance' because it was done in a circle… and it was spreading 'round' among the tribes and often 'round' the clock, according to concerned whites. The Sioux, Cheyenne, Arapaho, Kiowa and Minneconjou continued steadfastly to call it the 'Dance of Ghosts', believing that to change the name given by the Messiah would weaken its powers. Standing Wolf resisted referring to himself as Messiah. Often, in his mind, he replayed the message from the Great Spirit of the Semautse.

"Listen carefully my children. There is one among you who shall be called Waboka. To others, he will be known as Messiah. Open your ears and hear me."

Standing Wolf believed the 'others' were the whites. Because he was delivering a message of hope and deliverance to a decimated, subjugated and imprisoned Native People, the whites would see him as a false prophet to their own Messiah, the one they called Jesus. The whites, led by the missionaries, would see his message as blasphemous and consider it a threat, not a message of peace. He did not want anyone referring to him as Jesus, or he and his followers could definitely be in danger.

Some who claimed to represent Red Cloud, Sitting Bull and the Sioux Nation wanted Standing Wolf to travel with them to the Rose Bud, Tongue River and Pine Ridge. Standing Wolf declined; it was on the Rose Bud that the white buffalo came to him in a vision that changed his life forever. He would not go back there.

Standing Wolf eventually believed his mission was accomplished, having told the story of the Ghost Dance to thousands of Indians from an innumerable number of tribes, and his instincts were telling him it was time to return to the valley of rainbows, the Sematuse and to Star Flower. Satisfied with his decision, he prepared for the long trip north.

Two days into his journey home, taking a different route at the advice of the well-traveled Gray Hair and Long Foot, he came to a large lake of great beauty. Camped on its eastern shore he was preparing to cook a sage grouse, a bird similar to those found in the northern mountains but larger. As the bird sizzled over a small fire, a rider approached from the south. He was dressed in white man's clothing and riding a western saddle. As the man drew closer, Standing Wolf could see he was an Indian.

"My name is Jack Wilson," the man said as a form of greeting. "I am on the trail of one known to my people as Messiah." After a thoughtful pause he asked, "Are you him?"

"I am but do I know you?"

After speaking with so many Indians and being approached by others, Standing Wolf was not surprised or alarmed by the visit.

"We have not before met," Jack replied.

Standing Wolf recognized the English words as those of one who learned the white man's language well but not as one who grown up speaking English, as he had.

"You say you are looking for me…might I ask why?"

"When I was a boy my father, Tavibo, spoke of a day when the Indians would rise up from the dead and reclaim all that was taken from them by the white man. The land on which to hunt, the rivers in which to fish and the freedom to live where we wish would once again be ours…the old ways would be returned to us."

Jack studied Standing Wolf as he spoke. "When my father died I believed his words to be false. I went to live with my white father. I was on his ranch when word of your visit to my Native People reached me. I thought Tavibo's vision died with him until I learned of the message you gave. I now believe you are the Messiah my father spoke of, sent to free all Indians from suppression by the white man and his ways."

"I too was born Indian and raised white, we have much to talk about, sit, we will eat and speak," Standing Wolf told him.

Their similarities were astonishing; Jack was born Indian, raised white and was acutely aware of the spiritual beliefs of both because his Indian father was a Paiute shaman and prophet, his adoptive father was a Methodist minister.

Standing Wolf though born Indian was raised white and studied both cultures extensively. He was educated in his father's Catholic religion and attended their private schools and his mother was a Sematuse seer. But there were differences as well, more in their message than in the men.

Standing Wolf retold the story of his life, the white buffalo, the black wolf, his mother and the valley. He told about the sacred amulet around his neck, careful to stress the Indians spirits and their cataclysmic powers when in balance with Mother Earth and Father Sky.

Jack told of his father's vision; the return of a Messiah who would free all Indians. "The Messiah came to earth a long time ago to live with the whites but they killed him!" he said. "You must beware and stay out of sight or the whites will kill you, too."

"I do not fear the white man. I believe my journey is coming to an end. My mission is complete. I now return to a most sacred place where Mother Earth and Father Sky live, a place beyond time, the home of my mother's people the Sematuse and the valley of rainbows."

"Surely, now that you have come you will not leave without driving the white man from our land so we can return to the old ways. Perhaps the whites do not have to be killed. Perhaps we allow them to live as long as they do not interfere with our ways."

Jack was convinced Standing Wolf was, in fact, the Messiah prophesied by his father and was determined not to lose him.

"I am no longer needed here," Standing Wolf explained. "Do the Ghost Dance as I have spoken, tell the shaman of all tribes to prepare a sacred symbol for their tribe to be worn by a chief, shaman or seer. Do not seek war with the white soldiers but be true to the ways of your ancestors. If the soldiers try to force you to abandon the old ways, resist. You will not have to fight because the mounted warriors from the days of the buffalo will defeat the whites and drive them from the land."

He is a good man, this Jack Wilson, Standing Wolf decided. He knows the ways of the whites and the Natives. He is fair-minded and compassionate. He knows the ways of the Great Spirit.

"Why must you go?" Jack insisted. "What could be more important than the reason you came here?"

Jack was not finished asking questions, the ones he most wanted to ask were about the place Standing Wolf called the valley of rainbows. To him it sounded a lot like what the whites called heaven. Of course it could not be heaven because apparently only Indians lived there, or could it?

Standing Wolf could not answer all Jack Wilson's questions. He knew about the white man's heaven, a place not of earth but somewhere 'out there' where one could only enter if baptized by a Holy Father and the acceptance of Jesus Christ. He was pretty sure there were no Indians there…at least not yet.

"I must go because I am not of this world. I come from a world within a world, a place where time is not as it is here, a time where buffalo still walk the plains, where there are no reservations and where horse soldiers are seen only in visions. The Great Spirit allowed me to leave to spread an important message. I have done so and now must return." Standing Wolf looked carefully at his new found friend. "Did you have a name before your white father called you Jack Wilson?"

"I was called Wovoka by my people until the death of my father. My mother died at my birth. Once given my new name of Jack, I was told never of speak of Wovoka again. I have not…until now." He paused, thoughtful, then proudly added, "As a boy, I was a good fisherman. I had a good eye and strong arm for spearing."

Their mystical talk continued for three days during which lightening flashed, thunder roared and a bond was formed, a bond so powerful that when Jack asked if he could accompany Standing Wolf to the valley of rainbows so he could see such a heavenly place, Standing Wolf agreed. Reluctant at first, he concluded that they could enter the valley through the cave of spirits if they grasped hands. Exiting could be accomplished by the same method.

The trip north took over a month in which the Indian and the half-breed became like blood brothers. Following the advice of Gray Hair, the return trip was much easier than what Standing Wolf experienced on the trip south. There were fewer river crossings and only one mountain range which was much lower in elevation and easier to navigate. It was the season of water grass, called so by the Indians because of its lack of nutrients.

Jack had never traveled anywhere beyond the desert southwest and was in awe of the snow-capped mountains that looked like fingers reaching for Father Sky. He was equally pleased they did not have to travel over any of the distant spires. They continued north, then west along the Snake River, traversed the Horse Heaven Hills, bringing back memories of Roy and what Standing Wolf liked to think of as his scoundrel days.

They passed the sight of the burned-out Fort Okanogan and traveled up river into the land of the *Okinakane*. The closer they got to Lost River the more anxious Standing Wolf became for Jack to see the spirit cave, the valley and meet his mother, his wife and the rest of the Sematuse. He thought of Frank and Spotted Fawn who, except for his father, were the only white people to enter the valley and live. He wondered if his mother played any part in that.

Standing Wolf explained his unusual name situation, the one given to him by his mother, the one by his father and finally one by the Great Spirit, and that it would be encountered to some degree once they were in the valley.

It was like preaching to the choir. Jack Wilson wanted to revert back to his given name, Wovoka, but decided to wait until he saw this valley his friend spoke about.

The two marveled at their physical similarities, a fact which drew them even closer. Both men were powerfully built, broad shoulders, strong arms and flat hard bellys. Jack was not gifted with the extraordinary hand speed of Standing Wolf but was compensated with powerful hands that could grip like bear traps. Jack's hair was long and braided Indian-style but his clothes were those of a white man, which would have to change once they were in the valley.

By time they reached the spirit cave they had grown to so close Standing Wolf considered sharing his woman with Jack but quickly dismissed the idea. If Jack desired a woman there were plenty in the village, he would not share Star Flower with anyone, not even Jack Wilson. It was becoming difficult to think of anything but Star Flower. He wondered how long he had been gone but realized it did not matter, once he was back in the valley it would be like he never left.

Inside the cave, Jack stared at the glowing paintings with wide-eyed amazement.

"Your mother painted this?"

It wasn't so much a question as a statement of disbelief and confirmation of their previous conversations.

Filled with pride, Standing Wolf answered, "This and much more."

They slowly moved through the painted cavern until they reached the opening leading into the valley. Jack's mouth dropped open and his eyes blinked as he tried to comprehend what he was seeing. He watched, dumfounded, when Sanding Wolf stepped through the opening and disappeared…not all at once; first a foot then his leg, an arm…then all of him!

The Paiute stared spellbound at the last place he saw his friend, chills ran down his spine raising the hair on his neck and arms as if caught in some kind of magnetic force field. He tried to call out but the sound never escaped his lips. What he saw caused his knees to buckle and an inaudible gurgle to fall from his mouth. Through the cave opening a hand reached out to him. Barely able to breathe, Jack reached out with a trembling hand and grasped the one Standing Wolf extended and held on tight. He took one step then two and found himself looking out over green meadows spattered by gleaming-white aspen. A sky-blue river stretched out before him like a giant serpent. In the distance a glorious array of purple, yellows, reds and greens hung in suspended glory over the entire scene.

It was then Jack realized he was standing next to Standing Wolf. Startled, he pulled his hand free from Standing Wolf's, who was smiling.

"Is it not all I said and more?" he asked, gazing over the magnificent valley.

"It is," Jack said weakly, struggling with a new sensation.

He felt a sense of euphoric well-being. He had been tired from the long trip when they reached the spirit cave. Now he felt strong, young and full of energy.

Standing Wolf turned away and disappeared back into the cave then soon re-emerged in the same eerie manner with his black Arab and Jack's dapple-gray mare.

Even my horse looks better, Jack thought as he swung onto her back. His mind was busy as a gravel bar in spawning season as they rode deeper into the valley. Heaven, he thought, albeit a far different heaven than the one his father preached about.

Riding through scattered aspen thickets a smile came to Jack's lips, he would never look at an aspen tree the same way again. He reached out and touched the leaves gently as if caressing an ancient ancestor. As they approached a village there was much excitement, men were yelling in a language Jack did not understand. Women rushed about and children hid in teepees and behind trees and bushes.

"Standing Wolf!"

Jack heard a loud squeal then saw a stunningly beautiful woman running straight toward the blaze-faced Arab and its rider. Standing Wolf slid from his mount and the woman leaped into his arms, they kissed, hugged, whispered then kissed some more. Jack watched as the couple was surrounded by many well-wishers. Soon there were murmurs and the attention of the group turned to the stranger on the gray mare. He stepped off his horse and the people gathered around to look at his white man's saddle.

Standing Wolf introduced him to the chief of the Sematuse, Ta-keen Eagle and his wife, Laughing Doe, to Little Beaver and Spotted Fawn, to Fire-hair Frank and Warm Hands and finally to his mother, Bent Grass, and his wife, Star Flower.

It was a joyous occasion and cause for celebration. There was elderberry wine, rose-hip tea, and a feast of salmon and venison.

"My body aches for you, Standing Wolf," Star Flower whispered. "Take me away and make me yours."

With his desire swelling, Standing Wolf led her to the teepee they shared and closed the flap. She pulled his legging down as he pulled her dress up, their eyes feasted on each other's naked bodies. With her eyes locked on his, she pulled him down on top of her, opened her thighs and welcomed him with wild abandon.

Jack was being abused by questions from Ta-keen Eagle and teased unmercifully by Laughing Doe, Spotted Fawn and Willow…especially Willow. He was a big man with strong arms and hands and despite his odd clothing Willow was on fire. Ta-keen Eagle wanted to know about the Paiutes, where and how they lived, what they ate. All wanted to know why he was dressed like a white man.

"Is the bird you call sage grouse really twice a large as a blue grouse?" Little Beaver asked and Spotted Fawn giggled.

"Maybe everything is twice as large in the land of the Paiutes," Willow purred suggestively.

Laughing Doe, in a playful mood, suggested they all go to her teepee and find out. Ta-keen Eagle, often on the receiving end of her and Willow's playful moods smiled but said nothing.

Jack was embarrassed, intrigued and overwhelmed. All his friend told him about the valley and the people was true. Not that he expected it wouldn't be, but never did he see such beautiful people so sensually open and provocative. This place was like none other on Mother Earth. He was sure of it, and it was a little frightening.

What if this really is heaven, he wondered. What if he could not leave no matter what Standing Wolf said? He could come and go but **he** was the Chosen One.

*There can't be but **one** Chosen One.*

As the night waned, it became very clear that Willow was more than casually interested in the oddly dressed stranger. Her demeanor was less aggressive and more submissive but her attention was clearly intended for him alone. No one would have to offer the newcomer a woman for the night, she would see to that.

Standing Wolf awoke to the sound of meadow larks, western bluebirds and the feel of Star Flower's shapely, firm bottom pressed against his loins. He slipped his arms around her and she twisted onto her back and turned her face to his.

"*Mihakin*," she whispered. "Lying with you brings much pleasure."

Spreading her thighs, she moaned in a voice filled with passion.

"Show me again that I am your woman."

His response was immediate and intense.

When Standing Wolf and Star Flower left the privacy of their teepee, Sister Sun was smiling down on the valley, her warm rays painting smiles on daisies, sunflowers and bluebells. They went directly to the teepee of Bent Grass. Star Flower already gave him the news of his mother's marriage to Fire-hair Frank. Standing Wolf was anxious to hear how such a thing happened, not that he was not pleased, just that he could not have been more surprised if Roy and his recalcitrant bay, Bastard, had risen out of the river of rainbows.

In fact, Standing Wolf could think of little that pleased him more. It was perfect for his mother who had lived alone far too long, and Frank who never expected to love again. As Bent Grass and Frank re-told their love story for her son and Star Flower, Ta-keen Eagle and Laughing Doe who stopped by.

"Tell the story again," Laughing Doe pleaded.

Two of her favorite stories involved Bent Grass. The first was when Bent Grass was reunited with her son, now this. Everyone laughed and smiled and hugged as Frank and Bent Grass told their story yet again. Sister Sun was directly overhead when Willow and Jack stepped out of her small teepee and looked around the way a rabbit looks for a fox. Jack was in a euphoric daze. Willow was not the only woman he was ever with but she was by far the most amazing. Then there was this valley, beyond anything he could have ever imagined. He silently questioned if it was a vision or a dream.

Can any of this be real?

Jack tried everything he knew to wake up but he was still there.

Willow was lost in a sexual abyss and clung to him like pitch to pine. He made her feel things she never felt before and yet she barely knew him. She knew that could be part of the reason, but only a small part. Star Flower and Laughing Doe happily agreed to help Williow make some appropriate clothing for him. Once he had leggings, a shirt and vest, the white man clothes would be burned in yet another celebration.

For days one joyous event followed another in the valley of rainbows. Love and laughter were everywhere, only Jack and the Messiah had a worry in the world, any world. Both men knew the day was near when Jack would have to return to the world outside. Before that could happen he and Standing Wolf would have to talk with his mother.

Standing Wolf had questions only his mother could answer; what about the amulet that was still missing? Could the gift and power he was granted be passed to Jack, whom he thought was worthy, and what would happen to Jack once he left the valley? He wantedto speak with his mother, the sooner the better.

The way Jack Wilson and Willow were clinging to each other, Standing Wolf was becoming concerned his friend might decide he wanted to stay in the valley.

Then what?

The Paiute mystic held little doubt that this was heaven and that meant he was having a vision. Not a dream where he could awaken but a vision where the only way out, was the way he got in. He was not sure when the vision began; was it when he caught up to the Sematuse Messiah on the trail or when he entered the valley through the spirit cave? It didn't matter; Jack knew he must leave this place soon and return to Walker Lake and his people, even though there was no place he would rather be than right here in the peaceful valley with these beautiful people, especially the amazing Willow.

A warm rain was falling and rainbows hung over the valley like the protective wings of a dove when the small group consisting of Standing Wolf, Jack, Ta-keen Eagle, Warm Hands and Bent Grass, met in the village long-house.

Ta-keen Eagle spoke first. "Since being led to this valley by the sacred black wolf the True People lived in peace unaware of the outside world, until recently. Contact began with the arrival of a trapper named French who fathered a child with our seer, Bent Grass. No one is sure how French made his way into the valley, but since that time white men and half-white men are coming and going like the salmon in the rivers."

Warm Hands smiled at the chief's apparent exasperation. "Do not forget the white girl who became my daughter and the first medicine woman of the Sematuse," he said.

It was Ta-keen Eagle's turn to smile as he fixed his attention on the medicine man, carefully considering his reply. "I have not forgotten the girl. I do forget she was ever white. She is as Indian as a burnt stump is black." "Bent Grass," he said, turning to address the diminutive seer. "You called this council to speak of another man, one brought here by your son. What do you wish to say on the matter?"

Bent Grass stood, having barely an ant's girth and stretching only five feet in height. "You know the man I speak of. He is called Wovoka by his people who live beyond this valley. He came here with my son to learn more of the power of the Dance of *Tlchachie*. Now it is time for him to leave and rejoin his people. He will carry the word of the dance with him and it will spread among the Native People like a prairie fire."

"Was it not your son, the one now called Standing Wolf who was chosen by *Ogle Wa Nagi* to speak of the Dance of *Tlchachie*, is that not why he left the valley?" Warm Hands asked.

"It was, and to recover the amulet taken from Fire-hair during the attack. My son and I have spoken of the amulet, I do not believe it can be recovered but I also believe it poses no danger to the Sematuse. The amulet carries the spirit of the sacred black wolf; therefore he who possesses the sacred symbol is controlled by the wolf and will do no harm to the True People, a fact I only recently was made aware of."

"So, as long as Standing Wolf remains in the valley he could again call on our ancestors to defeat the whites if the need arose?" Ta-keen Eagle was double-checking his hole card though he knew nothing of the white man's poker game.

"I believe the True People are safe, my Chief," Bent Grass assured him, "but there are many others who are suffering in places called reservations. They can no longer hunt or fish and are not allowed to live in the old ways or permitted to speak in their native tongue. Both my son and Jack told me these things and I believe them to be true." She momentarily focused her gaze on the Paiute then nodded to her son.

Jack did not understand the Sematuse words so Standing Wolf translated most of what was being said but the Paiute wore a look of bewilderment. He hoped to be able stay longer in this magical place with Willow whose language he did understand but realized that was not going to be an option.

On his mother's queue, Standing Wolf said, "It is time for my friend to return to the world outside this valley. Many bands and tribes have been separated, scattered and mixed by the white soldiers and the white man's government in hopes of stealing away their identity. They are being forced to learn the white man's religion and punished for believing in the old ways. They need something they can believe in, they need one of their own who can speak for all Indians, not just the Sematuse."

Standing Wolf put his hand on Jack's shoulder. "After the words from *Ogle Wa Nagi* I believed I was chosen to deliver **all** Native People from subjugation, I now know I was only the messenger. I was chosen to save only the Sematuse, Wovoka is chosen to save the others."

When the council ended so did the rain. Jack found Willow finishing a buckskin shirt she was making for him, with the help of Star Flower. Believing that he would be leaving the valley soon, she wanted to give him something besides memories to remember her. Struggling with the Sematuse language, Jack was able to make her understand he must leave.

"It makes my heart weep to leave you and this valley but I have no choice. I wish you could come with me but I fear that is also not a choice. If I could return here someday I would, but I fear that may also not be a choice."

Willow sternly told him, "I do not wish to speak about sad things. Come, let us find a hiding place and stay there until the time for you to go is upon on us."

She was determined not to lament over sad things when the opportunity to make love existed. When it was time to be sad, she would be sad and not a moment before.

Willow led him to one of her many secret places. Kneeling before him she looked up, her alluring gray eyes filled with love and passion. Her breath came in ragged gasps as she wrapped her arms around his legs and pulled him to her. By time their passion drove the lovers to the apex of desire, Brother Moon past overhead like a silent voyeur.

Their good-byes were heart-felt and painful, she could not offer to wait for his return and he could not promise to ever return. It was as though their souls met in some cosmic void leaving their hearts and minds to cope with the harsh realities.

When Standing Wolf and Jack reached the entrance to the cave, Standing Wolf grasped Jack's hand and they stepped inside.

"I believe the Great Spirit wishes you to leave Jack Wilson here, in the spirit cave, and return to your people as Wovoka," Standing Wolf told him. "Believe me…Jack Wilson will not be alone; there are many others here who will keep him company. Perhaps you will pass this way again and Wovoka and Jack can have a reunion."

With Jack clinging to Standing Wolf's hand they exited the cave. Wovoka released his grip and felt a pressure as if he had just been introduced to gravity. He felt slow and clumsy for a few dreadful minutes, his mind the only thing that seemed to be working at a high rate of speed.

He began talking to himself in an attempt to find some form of reality. "I have been to heaven," he muttered in disbelief, unaware of Standing Wolf's departure. "I have been to heaven and returned and it was not a dream, not a vision, it really happened."

He knew he would never be the same, never be Jack Wilson again, but of all the amazing things he experienced in that mysterious valley, the most remarkable was that he believed he had met God…and her name was Bent Grass.

Chapter Twenty-five
Famished

Sam's first Montana winter was a mild one according to the Riley family. He didn't doubt their assessment but it didn't leave him looking forward to experiencing a severe one. The most difficult part of the winter was listening to Larry fuss. His diminished capacity made him cranky and restless. Ross found a copy of the Hellgate Treaty in Kalispell and Larry spent much of his time reading the document while waiting for his collar bone to mend.

The treaty, originally signed in 1855, had been ratified and was one of the reasons the Riley's settled along the Flathead. It seemed every time gold was discovered or land was needed for a mission school the treaty would be modified to permit more of the reservation to be settled or used by white men.

Ross and Ruth always treated their ranch like they had a lifetime lease with the Flatheads. Even though several years ago the government passed a Congressional Act, making the ranch legally theirs, it wasn't until a couple years ago they were actually granted title through the Dawes Act.Influenced by his parents, Larry respected the Indians and believed even if the ranch belonged to the Riley's, the Indians should be allowed to hunt and fish on it. Studying the treaty gave Larry a way of passing the long winter days but did little for his attitude. He fussed about the government and the military and their mistreatment of the

Indians. He even threw a few tantrums over the missions and how the schools were stealing the Indians culture and beliefs.

By time the first buttercups of spring popped up on the slopes and spring grass began turning the hills green, everyone including Sam was relieved. Larry's shoulder was fully functional and there were calves to be tended, drift fences to be mended and preparations for driving cattle to their summer range. They also finished off the two colts. Sam kept his part of the bargain, much to Larry's chagrin, and managed to ride Bigfoot.

Ranch life on the Running R was almost normal with Larry fully recuperated, and Sam was worrying about how much longer he would be needed. His status with the military and the possible guilt by association being a risk for the Riley's weighed heavy on his mind. There was also trouble brewing on the reservation. Ross discovered from neighbors that a chief called Charlo was not happy with the treatment the Flatheads were receiving. In fact Charlo was not happy with some of the Flathead chiefs whom he believed were 'scared white' by the missionaries.

Word was spreading over the reservation brought by some of their cousins among the Lakota Sioux about a 'Dance of Ghosts'. They believed this dance would free them from the oppressive ways of the white man and give them back the land, even the buffalo. A council of chiefs, called a 'court' by the Indian Bureau and military leaders, was put in place to keep the Flatheads in line. Their first order banned the Ghost Dance as well as numerous ceremonial dances such as the sun, war and scalp dances that were a long-standing Flathead tradition. This so angered chiefs like Arlee and Charlo that talk of war was on the wind.

Spring warmed into summer and Ross decided that if Sam would stay on a little longer, he would ride to the Jocko Agency and try to see if he could get to the bottom of things.

"I'll be glad to stay on Senior Riley," Sam said, trying to mask his excitement. "But who am I working for while you are gone?" He smiled knowing Ross understood.

Sam found Lillian in the garden with Ruth, weeding the tomatoes and peppers and Lillian was pouting. She is beautiful even when she is frowning, he thought, as he opened the gate and approached them.

The two beauties were bent over, their loose summer dresses revealing enough cleavage to cause Sam to avert his eyes in near desperation. He blinked to erase the memory of Ruth's breasts exposed during her attack, then fought to convince himself that Lillian was still a girl; too young for breasts, though they celebrated her seventeenth birthday last month.

So much for not asking a lady her age.

That was another thought he didn't need.

"Senior Ross asked if I would stay on for a while longer," he said, watching for any reaction from Lillian. "He wants to go to the Indian Agency to see what the talk of war is about."

The frown on Lillian's lips curled up ever so slightly but she quickly wiped away any threat of a smile.

"Oh good," she casually replied, "I have some jobs I'd like to have done, this is one of them." She tossed a handful of weeds on the pile and adjusted her dress so the neckline was not quite so low. "Unless you're too busy doing man's work," she added with a touch of sarcasm.

Ruth rose slowly but Sam had no trouble focusing his eyes on Lillian's blue eyes and red hair and was more than thankful for the diversion.

"I'm glad you'll be here," she said, "so Ross can get this Indian problem off his chest. I know he's concerned there may be some kind of uprising, I just hope calmer heads will prevail." She, too, adjusted her neckline. "I believe we would support the Indians and I'm not sure how that would set with the boys at Fort Benton."

"Fort Benton?" Sam questioned. He had never heard anyone talk about Fort Benton or any other fort anywhere near.

"It's the closest fort, I think," Ruth said, aware of Sam's obvious concern, and quickly added, "It's in the upper Missouri River country and the only military anywhere closer are a few small outposts."

"So you think the Indians are being cheated out of their land?" Sam asked.

"Not so much their land, they don't want to own. It's really their way of life that's being taken. Of course it's easy for me to say. We already have the Running R so it's a little like saying 'we have ours, let the Indians have the rest'." In an attempt to justify her position, she said, "But we have always shared our land with the Indians and most of the time they are great neighbors."

"So are you going to do some work or are you here to talk to my mom?" Lillian asked, pointing at the weeds. "You can have that row," she laughed. To Sam it was like hearing the chimes of angels.

With talk of trouble on the reservation, Ross decided not to push the stock toward Big Arm or the Thompson this summer. He was interested in new summer pasture Tomas Finley told him about, located south of his sheep pasture in the Mission Mountains. It was closer to the Running R and this seemed like the perfect year to try it out.

It cut a week off the usual drive time and Ross was feeling good about his decision. The grass looked good, it was closer to home, and if trouble broke out with the Indians it would be easier to keep an eye on the cattle.

Things were tense on the Flathead and no one went anywhere without a sidearm on their hip and a carbine in their scabbard. Ross hoped it was much ado about nothing.

Sam took a liking to the Dollar Bar colt Bigfoot and was riding him as they moved the last of the cattle onto Mission Range. The livestock were well dispersed and all was well when Ross, Ruth, Sam, Larry and Lillian began the ride back home. Without warning, Bigfoot kicked ferociously with both hind feet then took one leap skyward before Sam got control of his head.

"Damn," Larry laughed, "thought I was going to see you bust you're collar bone for a minute."

"Silly boy," Lillian piped up. "For those of us who can ride, a little kick or buck doesn't hurt you."

"I like this colt but I must admit, he does not give you much chance to relax and enjoy the scenery." Sam finished his comment looking squarely at Lillian, suddenly embarrassed he quickly added, "Well, it is pretty country."

"The only pretty country you've seen all day has red hair, blue eyes and a nice butt," Larry quipped, grinning like a Cheshire cat.

"Alright kids," Ruth interjected. "Be nice."

"I said 'nice' butt," Larry proclaimed.

"To bad Bigfoot didn't kick you in the head and knock some sense into it," Lillian cracked, then suddenly inspired, added, "Let's call this our Kicking Horse pasture."

And so it was.

Ross smiled inwardly. He enjoyed having the family together riding the range, though he continued to be a little suspicious of how Sam fit into the picture. The young man was a good hand and certainly did come in handy during all of Larry's troubles.

"I'm sure glad Tomas told me about this pasture. With wolves and grizzlies up north, not to mention Indian troubles, it's going to be good having the cattle closer." He was mostly talking to Ruth but Lillian responded.

"I like this Kicking Horse pasture, it feels good."

"That's what Sam said about you."

Larry grinned again determined to get even for Sam riding Bigfoot.

Lillian grabbed a cone from a low hanging branch of a pine tree and threw it at Larry, hitting Weasel on the rump, resulting in Larry nearly losing his seat and breaking another bone.

"Enough," Ruth said, more emphatically.

Kids could be kids until someone got hurt. Then she had an even more frightening thought; they weren't kids anymore. Larry was soon to be eighteen, Lillian was seventeenth and Sam was twenty-something.

Back at the Running R, supper served and dishes done, Sam retired to the bunkhouse and thoughts of Lillian. Her seventeen birthday party had a profound effect on him. Until then, he didn't know how old she was and in spite of some obvious attributes to the contrary, tried to convince himself she was just an impetuous girl, fourteen or fifteen at most. It was a silly game but it kept his mind occupied.

The birthday party changed that. Seventeen was old enough to be married, even have a baby. That day in the garden he had never enjoyed weeding as much; in fact he had never weeded before… period. The glimpses down the front of her dress, despite his best intentions, were unnerving proof that she was a young woman. He was never completely successful at wiping out the memory of her mother's breasts. The reality of the phrase 'like mother, like daughter' left him too weak to stand and he settled onto his bunk in frustration.

Even more exasperating was the reality that his time on the Running R was running out and there was nothing he could do about it. He already managed to stay well beyond his greatest expectations, mostly thanks to Larry's misfortunes.

Winter for Clarence Hobbs was nothing short of a bitch. Not because of the cold or the snow but because he was thirty miles from the obsession that plagued him day and night. The craze for gold had died down a little but there were still enough hope-driven prospectors and greedy business men to keep the saloon busy.

"She probably thinks old Clarence done forgot about her," he fussed. "Well she's plum mistaken, I'm countin' on the third time bein' the charm."

Last fall, while scouting the Running R, he had found an old prospector's shack which gave him an idea and he began formulating a plan; it only needed a little modification.

The place was a shambles, wood rat infested, cloaked in spider webs and really old, but it was sound and would provide the perfect cover. He went to the trouble of riding to Kalispell and filing a claim on a couple of holes some old-timer had dug some years back into a vein of white quartz. Hobbs wasn't looking for gold but it gave him a defensible excuse for being on Running R land; a place he planned on being a lot.

With the arrival of summer, he began turning the cabin into his own hideaway out of sight of hungry grizzlies or passing heroes.

"All I got to do is figure out how to get her here," he mumbled as he tied his little gray cayuse and brown pack mule in the trees.

He proceeded to unload a mattress off the mule. It was thrown out of a saloon room after some drunk passed out and pissed on it but that didn't bother Hobbs, he wasn't planning on sleeping on it. After dumping the mattress on the floor inside, he returned to gather up the bindings, comprised of four hobbles with leather cuffs he had managed to get his hands on. These were strategically placed and securely nailed into the floor and wall around the mattress.

As he surveyed his handy work a rush of excitement and anticipation seeped through his body.

If this works out I just might have to drag that little red-headed girl out here too, he thought, salivating.

After breakfast Ross saddled Drifter, his stout Morgan gelding, and headed for the Jocko Agency. He knew a few of the Indians appointed to the court, like Grizzly Bear Stand Up, Spotted Foot and Red Owl. If things went well he should be gone one night, if not he intended to stay until he understood how real the threat of an uprising actually was.

With all the stock moved to summer pastures and hay crops growing, Sam figured the best use of his time was to ride Bigfoot. He was a smooth ride with speed to rival Buttercup or Weasel and he was smart. The only thing standing between being green broke and a good horse was a wet saddle blanket.

Anytime anyone on the Running R saddled up a horse Lillian had an uncanny knack of showing up.

"Whatcha' doin' Sam?" she inquired as she approached, fingers interlocked in front of her, a coy look on her face.

"Thought I'd give Bigfoot a little work out," Sam replied, pulling the latigo tight and slipping a half-hitch through the D-ring.

"You weren't planning on going without me were you, Sam?" She was teasing now.

He looked at the stunning girl, her hair reflecting like a beacon in the sunlight.

"You are going to ride in that?" he asked, pointing to the light summer dress she wore.

It was much like the loose-fitting one she wore while weeding but it caused him to imagine the firm, shapely form moving freely inside it.

"No," she replied. "If you can keep your horseshoes on for a few minutes I'll put on some riding clothes, unless of course you'd rather I didn't go with you."

He hated it when she did that, she seemed to take delight in putting him on the spot.

"I will wait, or you can ride in that if you want."

The thought of her sitting astride her horse with that dress bunched up around her waist caused him to fight for a breath.

"Yeah, I bet you'd like that," she snapped, "men!"

Sam was embarrassed and flustered. He hoped she didn't know what he was thinking but if she did, that was even worse. She is too young to know what I am thinking, he assured himself as she glided toward the house.

When Lillian returned in snug-fitting riding pants and a loose cotton shirt, Sam grinned. She could be wrapped up in a saddle blanket and still be gorgeous, he thought.

"Your mother told me there is a ranch not far from here that has buffalo. I would like to see one, how about you?"

"I know where that is. Larry says the owner is from Mexico or Spain. Maybe you know him since you're Spanish."

Sam shook his head. If she weren't so darn cute she'd be exasperating.

Lillian was enthralled when she saw the buffalo and wanted her dad to get some. Sam was also impressed. They are huge and Indians hunted them with spears and arrows, he thought…unbelievable.

"I have heard that the plains were once black with buffalo for as far as you could see, and white men killed them all," he said in disbelief.

"Why?" Lillian asked. "Nobody could eat that much meat."

"They did not eat them or even skin them. They were killed so the Indians could not have them."

"Makes me sick to be white," Lillian declared. "I'm glad you don't hate Indians, Sam. Mom and dad don't either, Indians saved their life before I was born. I've heard **that** story a few times."

Sam touched the amulet under his shirt.

"The only thing the Indians did wrong was believe in a different God," he said. "Funny thing is, their God was here first."

"You feel like a race?" Lilly impetuously quiped; it sounded more like a dare than a question.

She really is still a kid, he thought but he kind of wanted to know if Bigfoot could keep up with the fleet Palomino. "Only if I do not have to carry any traps," he retorted.

Buttercup took off, showering him and Bigfoot with clods of dirt and debris. Sam guided his black-legged bronze colt wide of the flying hooves of the Palomino. Lillian's red hair, trailing out behind her, looked like it was captured on canvas. Sam inched the colt along side

Buttercup until the horses were eye to eye, each seemingly determined to push at least a nose in front.

Sam looked at Lillian; she was smiling ear to ear in excitement and delight. Nose to nose, eye-ball to eye-ball, dirt flying, leather squeaking, they pounded down the old wagon road. Ever so slowly Buttercup gained the advantage, first a nose, a neck and then the mare moved her rider even with Bigfoot's nose.

Sam pulled in his determined mount with a series of light tugs on the reins until little by little the proud horse slowed. Lillian and Buttercup, victory in hand, eased up until Sam and Bigfoot were again alongside. Lillian was beaming.

"That was fun!" she squealed. "I think Bigfoot might be able to outrun Weasel but don't race him. Larry is upset enough because Bigfoot didn't buck you off."

Sam thought he detected a bit of pride in her voice; a puzzling thought.

"I hope he did not think I was showing off. I did not want to break my backside."

They reached a small stream that meandered down a fescue covered slope and cut a channel across their path.

"Looks like a good place for a drink," Sam said, swinging his leg over Bigfoot's rump. "What is Larry doing today?"

"Dad told him some guy filed a mining claim up by the old Ronan Mine. He's going to ride up that way and look around, doubt he'll find anything, there's nothing up there but a crappy old shack."   "Maybe I should have gone with him since I only wanted to give Bigfoot a little time under a saddle."

"You mean you'd rather be with him than me?" Surprised at her own remark she quickly added, "Actually I think he wanted to be alone, he's been acting a little funny lately. He says he feels fine but I'm not so sure."

She found a spot upstream of the drinking horses and knelt down, leaned forward and drank from the cool stream.

Sam closed his eyes. From his vantage point he feared to do otherwise would cause him to go blind or crazy. Stepping alongside her, he waited till she was finished drinking then offered his hand. Lilly reached out and he pulled her to her feet. She was slightly off balance and they found themselves pressed against one another. She looked up, their eyes met, then their lips. It was not a passionate kiss, rather a soft lingering kiss that left them both bewildered.

It may have lasted ten seconds or ten minutes, neither one knew, neither one cared. Sam wanted to speak but his tongue refused to cooperate. He half expected this red-haired beauty to knock half of his face off but she didn't move.

"Lillian, I…"

"Don't say anything, Sam," she whispered. "I liked it. I've never kissed anyone before, Sam, do it again."

She slid her arms around him, her eyes looking at his chest and the amulet that slipped out of his open shirt.

Struggling to contain his excitement he touched her chin with is fore- finger, turning her face upward then lowered his lips to hers, tentatively, cautiously but firmer, warmer. He put his arms around her and squeezed gently. For unmeasured time nothing existed but the feel of this amazingly beautiful creature in his arms. The stomping of horses and the rattle of bridles on shaking heads caused Sam to release his hold and break their reverie. The moment he released her he wanted her back in his arms, he reached out and took her hand.

"You are so beautiful."

The words were a spontaneous response to his thoughts the very first time he saw her. The feel of her hand in his thrilled him but he fought off the urge to pull her back into his arms and kiss her again and again.

Lillian tried to understand what she was feeling; weak, warm and giddy all at once. There was a tingling sensation in her tummy the first time she saw Sam without a shirt but the feeling now was so intensified she was breathing hard and could feel her heart pounding against the wall of her chest. Her face felt hot and flushed, she turned away for fear she was blushing.

"Are you angry?" Sam asked with a touch of concern and confusion.

"Have you kissed a girl…a woman before?" She answered his question with her own, quickly adding, "It's okay if you have."

Having slightly recovered his composure Sam joked, "Only my mother and only on the cheek."

"Do you really think I'm beautiful?" Lilly's voice was tinged with doubt.

Immediately dead serious, Sam said, "Si, yes, from the first time I saw you, when you were still a nina, a girl." He hoped to lighten the mood.

"No one ever said that except my mom and dad, until now…'till you. Larry says I look like a red fox."

Lillian smiled and Sam's stomach did another flip.

He got the fox part right, Sam thought.

He lightly stroked her long-red hair, then twined his fingers through the thick mane and gently pulled her to him and held her with her head resting on his chest. The feel of her against him ignited his senses to the edge of recklessness.

"We better head back," he said, knowing he was on the verge of doing or saying something he could regret.

After riding a short distance in silence Sam asked, "Are you going to tell your mother?"

"Should I?"

"I do not know, what do you think she will say?"

"I think she'd be okay, but she'll probably tell dad, I don't know what he'll say. We didn't do anything wrong." She sounded defensive.

Sam was silent for a bit then said, "That is good because I would like to do it again sometime."

"Me too," Lilly said.

She sank her heels into Buttercup's ribs and the Palomino shot forward. Sam smacked Bigfoot with his reins and once more the race was on. I hope this ends like the last one, he thought. It did, in that Lillian and Buttercup won again but the similarity stopped there.

The rest of the ride home was quiet, each in caught their private daydream. Only after the tack was put away and the horses rubbed down did Sam think of something to say, which he thought was pure genius.

"I think you should tell your mother what happened if you think we will do it again, if not we should forget it."

Lillian stopped dead in her tracks. "Do you want to forget it Sam? Can you forget it? If that's so, it will never happen again!"

Sam swallowed hard…so much for genius. "Si, I do want it to happen again! I meant if you did not…I mean I would kiss you right now if I could."

"And you can't because your afra…."

Sam pulled her to him, one hand on Lilly's trim waist, the other on the back of her neck. He lowered his head and his lips found hers. She had riled him just enough so that this time he was a little more forceful, a little more determined. Her soft, full lips didn't pull away, instead she responded by kissing him back and her body melted against him. He heard a soft moan escape from deep in her throat and he panicked. Slowly pulling his lips away he looked at her; her misty blue eyes were wide, full of promise.

"I think we better tell your madre," he said with conviction.

Ruth fixed mashed potatoes, beef gravy, pot roast and string beans for supper. Sam and Lillian sat across the wooden table from each other, both with heads down focused on their food appearing poised for escape. Larry was not back from his ride up to the old claim and Ruth was worried.

"With the kind of luck he's had lately, anything could have happened. I can't remember him ever being late for pot roast," she said.

"You know how Larry is around that old mine, Mom," Lilly said. "He always thinks he's going to find the Mother's Gold or Grandma's Stash or something."

"Mother Lode," Sam corrected, smiling at Lillian. "It is called Mother Lode."

"I know," Ruth agreed. "It's just that he's been so accident prone lately and he is riding that colt, Bodie."

"Bodie is a good horse Señora Riley. I do not think Larry will have trouble with him," Sam assured her.

"Mom," Lillian said. It seemed like a good time to change the subject. "I have, well, Sam and I have something to tell you."

There was something in her tone that caused Ruth to set her fork down.

"Is it about Larry?" Ruth asked.

"No, Mom, it's about me, me and Sam, we sort of, well we accidentally…"

Now she had Ruth's full attention, Lilly never balked at anything, what ever she was about to say could not be good.

You sort of accidentally, what?" she pressed.

Sam stopped chewing halfway into a bite of roast, his eyes drifted slowly toward Lillian, and he felt his cheeks flush.

"We kissed, Mom!" she blurted, then sounding more like her impetuous self added, "We kissed and we liked it."

Sam swallowed his meat without taking another chew. It slid down his throat like a snake swallowing a shrew; he knew his dark-brown face was either flaming scarlet or scared-stiff white.

Fortunately for everyone, Ruth's mouth was empty or it would not have been a pretty sight. She did not try to speak instead she struggled to hold back tears. Lillian gave Sam a 'say something' look of helplessness.

"Señora Riley," Sam said, mustering all the courage he could. "I do not know much about women, but I am pretty sure I am enamorado… in love…with your daughter."   It was a one-two punch that left Ruth open-mouthed and glassy-eyed. If Larry saw this coming, why hadn't she, even after he warned her? Her mind was filled with questions. What will Ross say or do? What about Sam's trouble with the army? What did Lilly want? She eventually found her voice.

"What about you Lilly, how do you feel about Sam?"

"I guess I love him, I know I sure like kissing him."

When Lilly looked at Sam, her face was as red as her hair.

Ruth took a pensive moment thinking, wondering. Is this my doing? I brought him here, I left them together but I wouldn't have a life were it not for him, he's become like a second son to me. So what's the problem? I should be overjoyed, but she's my baby, this is her first step toward becoming a woman. Ruth wiped a recalcitrant tear from her cheek and took her daughter's hand.

"Go slow. Be careful. Be sure," she whispered.

Looking at Sam she smiled and told him, "Be honest, about everything."   Picking up her fork, Ruth said, "I worked too hard on this dinner to waste it." She glanced at Larry's empty plate then looked at Lilly. "Do we tell dad about this or shall it be our secret for now?"

"Our secret," Lilly replied "For now."

Sam took another helping of meat and potatoes; he was suddenly famished.

Chapter Twenty-six
Evil

Larry pulled the bay colt to a stop.

"Interesting," he mumbled, regarding the little gray horse and mule tied to a tree near the old miner's cabin.

He touched the handle of his Colt .45. He wasn't sure why he'd decided to strap the pistol on before leaving the ranch, especially riding Bodie. The colt could be unpredictable, but he just had one of those feelings…what with the Indian tension and all.

It could be someone traveling between Thompson Falls and Kalispell who decided to hole up in the cabin over night, but it was pushing mid-day. They should be on their way by now.

Patting Bodie on the neck, Larry said, "A little chat never hurt anyone, let's see if we can find out what's going on."

He lightly nudged the colt with blunt rowels. As he approached the old cabin a small man emerged and jumped like a frightened cat when he saw Larry.

"Morning," Larry said, striving to sound nonchalant. "How's it going?"

"Not bad," the man responded.

Larry thought his voice and manner was rather nervous.

"Doing a little prospecting?" Larry asked, hoping to sound friendly, not nosey.

"Naw," the man replied, "just takin' a little break on my way to Kalispell."

Clarence was trying hard to stay calm. He recognized Larry as the kid with the cut ear…the blonde's boy and thought…He must not recognize me. He was kinda out of it that day.

"I was curious because someone filed a claim on this old mine. It's on my folk's land so I came out to check. It's kind of a coincidence to find you here." Larry's tone was still friendly but there was a hint of agitation. "My name is Larry, Larry Riley, what's yours?"

"My name is Clarence young fella, an' I ain't lookin' for no trouble an' I sure ain't lookin' for no gold. I'll just be on my way an' you can get on with what ever you need to." Don't push me kid or you'll regret it, he thought.

Clarence.

Larry remembered his dad telling him the guy's name who filed the claim was Clarence Hobbs.

This guy is lying.

"Where're you from Clarence?" Larry asked, trying to be casual.

"Not from around here. I'm just passin' through. Had a job in Thompson Falls an' got laid off…thought I'd see if I could find anything in Kalispell." Hobbs said, and thought…Let it go kid!

"Well, you have a good day and hope it works out for you in Kalispell," Larry replied. "I've got a few more things to do and need to be home for supper so I better get at it."

He rode off keeping an eye on Clarence until he was out of his sight. Something is not right with that guy, Larry thought….Why would he lie? He had to be the one who filed the claim.

"We'll just circle around and wait until he's gone then we'll take a look and see what he's got in the cabin," Larry confided in Bodie.

"Son-of-a-bitch!" Clarence exclaimed then chuckled at his unintended pun. "The goddamn kid could ruin everything if he looks in this cabin. I just ain't gonna let that happen," he assured himself.

Larry steered Bodie off the trail across a brushy draw and waited for Clarence to ride past on his way to Kalispell. After waiting impatiently for nearly an hour, Larry crossed back through the draw and worked his way around to the cabin. There was no horse, no mule and no Clarence, but where did he go? He hadn't taken the trail to Kalispell.

Why lie about where you're going? It's not like I care, Larry thought.

Clarence had found a place to watch the cabin from behind a dead log sheltered by low hanging branches and rested his Winchester Long Tom on the log. He shook his head when he saw Larry ride up to the cabin and dismount.

"I knew he couldn't leave it alone. Shit, now it gets complicated," he snorted.

Larry opened the cabin door, stepped inside and stopped dead in his tracks.

"What the …! What is this?" he exclaimed.

There was nothing in the cabin but an old mattress and what appeared to be some kind of hobbles or shackles nailed to the wall and floor. Larry took off his hat and scratched his head, baffled.

"What's this for?" Larry puzzled over the strange scene.

"You had to do it, didn't you kid? Now you're a dead man and you don't even know it yet," Clarence grumbled as he checked his sight trained on the cabin door.

Larry jerked on the strange hobbles; they were solid.

"A bear couldn't pull these loose," he muttered. "Dad will want to see this." He began to feel uneasy as he headed for the door, whispering, questioning. "If that Clarence guy did this, why lie about it? And if he didn't why wouldn't he have said something about it? I saw him come out of the cabin so he had to know what was in here."

Two steps short of the door Larry stopped. Bodie stood with head held high, eyes wide and alert, sharp-pointed ears aimed at an unseen object in the trees. There was no mistaking that look. Larry had seen it too many times. There was something in those trees; it could be a deer, a bear, another horse or it could be a man… Larry took two steps back.

"I'm probably being paranoid," he whispered, "but there was something about that guy that isn't right."

He looked around the interior of the small cabin. There were no windows…his only view was out the door where Bodie remained focused on something in the trees.

"Goddamn horse," Clarence swore. "I ought to shoot him."

The colt was looking right at him. Clarence remained motionless and focused, waiting for Larry to step through the door.

Larry watched Bodie, Bodie watched Clarence and Clarence watched the door. Bodie was the first to blink. He tired of the scent and sight that refused to move and began looking for stray tufts of fescue.

Larry, convinced the horse had been watching an animal, started back for the door. As he stepped through the opening Clarence squeezed the trigger…Larry never heard the shot.

By time supper was over and the dishes cleaned up, Ruth recovered from the shock of Lillian and Sam's announcement. If this worked out between them she would be thrilled. She wasn't sure she could say the same for Ross but they would deal with that when the time came. Right now Ruth was more concerned about Larry. It was getting late even for a summer evening, and it wasn't like him to miss supper, especially pot roast.

Sam had gone out to the bunkhouse and Ruth was rehearsing the mother-daughter talk with Lilly she'd been putting off for years. She kept going to the window, still no Larry. Scolding herself for waiting so long she went to Lilly's room and knocked.

"Who is it?" Lilly questioned.

"It's Mom, who else? We're the only ones in the house!" She was anxious and on edge.

"Come in Mother," Lilly replied. "You don't have to bite my head off, geez."

Ruth opened the door and looked around the room. There were paintings of horses, a vase filled with lilies and the quilt on Lilly's bed was a maze of water lilies, calla lilies, tiger lilies, mariposa lilies and more. Ruth made the quilt for her when Lilly was ten. It was like a bridge between past and present.

"Larry is still not home. I'm worried Lilly, where could he be?" Lilly rolled off the bed. Seeing the concern on her mom's face she said, "I can get Sam and we can go look for him but it's going to be dark soon."

"I know, Honey, but with the kind of luck he's been having lately I can't help worrying."

"If he got thrown, Bodie would come home. Maybe Bodie got hurt and Larry is walking home," Lilly said, exploring rational possibilities.

"Maybe they're both hurt and Larry is lying out there somewhere."

"What do you want to do Mother? Sam and I can go look until it gets dark. If we ride up toward the old mine we might find him." Ruth began to cry, softly, as tears rolled down her cheeks.

"Come on, Mom," Lilly pleaded. "I'm sure he's okay. He probably saw some wolves and followed them farther than he meant to. There could be a lot of reasons why he's late. Maybe some of the cows were coming back home and he pushed them back into the hills."

"I'm sorry, Lilly. I just have a bad feeling. Call it mother's intuition but I'm afraid something bad has happened."

"Let's go talk to Sam, Mom. Let's see what he thinks we should do."

Sam was still in a euphoric state, replaying the kiss and the feel of Lillian in his arms when he heard a knock at the bunkhouse door. He opened it and was surprised to see Lillian and Ruth standing there. He motioned for them to come in.

"What's going on?" he asked, noticing the strained look on the otherwise pretty faces.

"Larry isn't home yet and we're worried," Lillian said. "We're not sure what to do. It's going to be dark soon and we don't know if it would do any good to look for him in the dark."

"What do you think Sam, what should we do?" Ruth's voice was trembling and Sam felt a twinge of dread. With Larry it seemed there was always something.

"You said he was going up to some mine. Could we find it at night?" Sam asked Lillian.

"I think so, but there's nothing there, just an old cabin. There really is no mine, just a couple small holes in the ground."

"Nothing he could fall in?" Sam asked.

"Not even close. The holes are only three or four feet deep."

"We have an hour or so before dark, I say we head out toward the mine. We can holler, if he is hurt maybe he will hear us. We will look as long as we can and if we do not find him, or if he does not come home we will go back out in the morning." Sam was already pulling on his boots.

Ruth and Lilly headed for the house to get ready.

The Long Tom jumped in Clarence's hand, its butt kicking his shoulder. The bullet smashed into Larry, lifting him off his feet and throwing him against the door jamb.

Clarence swore, "Goddamn it kid, I tried ta warn ya! Now I got a problem ta take care of."

This wasn't the first time his 'hobby' had cost someone their life. The damn kid in Tucson wouldn't leave it alone either but at least that was self defense.

"This is murder for Christ sake," he muttered.

A sharp pang of fear cut into his gut as his mind processed the situation.

"I gotta get rid of the body," he whispered. "If anybody finds him, it can't be anywhere near this cabin."

Hobbs thought about the claim he filed in Kalispell and swore again.

"Shit, I might as well have signed a confession. Goddamn it! It seemed like a good idea at the time."

He was talking to himself in earnest as he shoved the Winchester into the scabbard. As he led the cayuse and mule back to the cabin he was breathing heavy, his legs were shaking and his knees felt like they might give way.

"Stay calm, just get the kid on the mule an' get him the hell away from here."

He thought about the mattress and hobbles.

"I can't worry about that right now, I'll deal with it later."

When he reached the cabin, Larry was face down in the dirt; blood pooled on the ground near his right shoulder. Clarence rubbed his door-knocker mustache with both hands as if it contained a solution to his problem. He reached down and grabbed Larry's arm, pulling him away from the pool of blood and the cabin.

Snubbing the mule up short to one of the cabin logs, Clarence took hold of Larry's bloody arm pits and lifted, a new source of panic swept over him. He managed to lift the body waist-high but lost his grip when he tried to hoist it up onto the mule…it dropped with a sickening thud. The mule shied away wide-eyed and wary.

"Think, goddamn it!" Clarence admonished his himself.

He looked around fighting the urge to panic. He looked up, the cabin ridge pole extended four or five feet beyond the door and wall.

"If I can hoist him up with a rope an' if the damn mule will hold still I might get him loaded."

Hobbs was talking as he worked, hoping to give himself encouragement. He looped a noose around Larry's waist and tossed the rope over the ridge pole.

"Well shit!" he grumbled. "That ain't gonna work."

Clarence found himself pulling his hundred-and-fifty pounds off the ground without budging Larry's dead weight.

"You dumb shit, don't panic, think!" he scolded.

He had an epiphany. Tying the rope around his saddle horn he slowly led his gray cayuse away from the pole. The rope tightened and Larry's body slowly began to levitate. Clarence watched the ridge pole closely.

"Just don't break," he whispered, as close to a prayer as ever left his lips.

Larry hung bent at the waist, blood dripping from his fingers like some ghoulish predator surveying the ground beneath for some careless morsel. Again tying the gray, Clarence led the mule under the body then untied his horse and slowly lowered Larry onto the pack mule. It worked! He quickly tied the body securely and took the first breath he could remember since he pulled the trigger.

"Sorry kid," he muttered without a trace of sincerity. "It's all gonna be worth it once I get your mother shackled in that cabin. I might have ta nab your sister, too, for all the trouble ya caused me." A faint smile touched his thin lips. "My name is Clarence but friends call me Evil," he said with a chuckle to an unhearing Larry Riley.

He gathered up some duff from around a nearby tree and sprinkled it over the blood-soaked ground.

"Damn," he quietly swore.

There was blood smeared on the door jamb and all over the front of his shirt. He shoved his foot into his stirrup and swung on the little gray, cursing softly under his breath, and led the mule and Larry away from the cabin.

Somewhere in an aspen grove located on the Flathead Reservation, near a small Indian village, Clarence Hobbs untied the ropes binding the body to a pack saddle and dumped Larry Riley in his final resting place.

Ruth, Lillian and Sam rode in the direction of the Ronan Mine with Lillian leading the way. The farther they got away from the ranch house the less likely Sam deemed their chances of meeting up with Larry. He expected they would run into him within the first mile or so out.

By time they reached what Lillian said was halfway to the mine, Sam became as concerned as the women. Dusk was rapidly giving way to darkness and the belief that something must be very wrong was impossible to ignore. Dejected, all they could do was head back and hope Larry had somehow ridden in behind them.

Owoooooo.

The long plaintive cry of a wolf cut through the somber mood of the trio.

"Oh, wow!" Lillian exclaimed. "I hope Larry can hear that, he's such a wolf-lover."

Ruth began to sob quietly and Lillian bit her tongue.

"I'm sorry, Mom, I'm sure he's back at the house eating a roast beef sandwich and wondering where we are."

The howl of the lone wolf punctuated the night air several times before the night went quiet. An uneasy feeling spread over Sam.

It is only one wolf.

He reached in his shirt and touched the amulet…the feeling intensified. He wondered if Ruth felt the same urgency and rubbed the leather talisman lightly.

If only it could talk.

After a comfortable nap at the base of an uprooted pine, he and Lola were awakened by the familiar scent of the large alpha male that had invaded their range. Like before, Lobo was agitated and Lola was intrigued but there was something else, a new scent, a scent they could not identify. It was tangy and a little bitter, like the rare scent of humans but different, more pungent but sweet, like the smell of a fresh kill, a scent that could not be ignored.

Lobo rousted the adults, leaving spring pups with their mothers in their dens, and set out in search of the source of the new odor. Chasing scent on the wind can be tricky, especially when it is new and unusual. Although occasionally distracted by the smell of deer or elk or briefly chasing a frightened rabbit, the pack was intent on locating the object of this strange malodor. The scent of the intruding male was interacting with the other stench, creating some dissent between Lobo and Lola.

As the effluvium became stronger, the pace of the pack quickened. They rushed down brush-laden draws, raced around open hillsides and ran out spiny ridges, following the commands of their olfactory organs.

The wind shifted slightly and the undeniable scent of the invader struck Lobo's nostrils. It was mixed with the foreign fragrance but it was the big male that had been hanging around for way too long. A long mournful howl pierced their ears; it was close. The hackles on Lobo's neck bristled. Snarling, he circled the pack and brought them to a halt. The howling continued and soon members of the pack were responding…all but Lobo. He was intent on fixing the position of the lone wolf.

Adding to Lobo's irritation, his annoying cousins, the coyotes, began to join in on the night-time recital. Giving Lola a nip in the flank, making it clear who her alpha male was, he led the pack toward the location of the frowzy odor. The sight of the huge black wolf abruptly stopped Lobo and the rest of the pack…he stood legs straddled over a kill, head down but there was something odd about his behavior.

Lobo's first thought was to run off the intruder and take his kill. There was only one of him and a lot of them. But as he watched the big male's actions he became perplexed; he wasn't eating his kill, he was licking it.

Blood.

He must be licking up blood but why not just rip into the kill and get a mouth full? Lola and the rest of the pack where looking to Lobo for direction. Should they circle this big wolf, distract him and take over his kill?

The intruding male raised his head slightly and looked directly at Lobo with his lips peeled back revealing large, unusually white canines. The hair on his neck stood straight up; a clear challenge to Lobo and his band.

Fearing nothing, not even a challenger of unprecedented size, Lobo circled to the right and Lola circled to the left while the rest of the pack held back waiting for instructions. Lobo made a run past the black male to get a closer look at the kill and plan a strategy, but came away more confused than before. The kill did not smell like anything he'd ever sniffed and it didn't look like anything he ever killed or ate.

Instinct was telling him to use the pack, out-maneuver the intruder and claim his meal; show him and Lola who the real alpha male in this territory was. But there was something else; a sense of a higher power, an inner voice telling him to leave this one alone.

Lobo pulled back and looked at Lola and the pack. They stood poised, ready to respond to his command. He looked back at the gigantic male and the kill he was protecting like it was his own offspring. Lobo looked closely at the kill, it looked skinny, sickly. He could see little or no flesh. Even its belly was flat and empty…and it smelled bad.

They could find a far more appealing prey than this without having to fight what would clearly be a formidable opponent for it. This male may be big and no doubt a ferocious fighter but he was not very smart when it came to choosing a kill.

Lobo barked his instructions and Lola and the pack fell in behind as he spun and darted off, leaving the intruding alpha male to his puny, stinky prey. The wind was filled with the fragrnce of elk and deer along with several other heady scents he found interesting. Lobo was sure there was a fine meal just over the next ridge.

When the threatening pack moved on, the black wolf returned to licking the face and arms of the lifeless body. Eventually, the wolf moved away from the man, howled mournfully, then circled the body several times before returning to the inert form.

There was a slight motion, a blinking of eye lids, the licking of lips the clenching of a fist. The wolf licked his face again and Larry moaned. It was barely audible but loud and clear to the keen ears of the black wolf. He licked the man's shirt, coated in dried blood and listened to more groans. The big wolf seemed anxious and began pacing back and forth near the body.

After Ruth, Sam and Lillian returned to the ranch house their hope turned to despair. There was no Larry, no sign he might have returned and gone looking for them…nothing. Even the pot roast was not disturbed.

Ruth was sobbing quietly and Sam and Lillian looked helplessly at each another. Where could he be? Ruth went into the bathroom for tissue and Sam moved closer to Lillian.

"I know it sounds loco, crazy, but I think this is trying to tell me something," he said, pulling the amulet from inside his shirt. "You must stay with your madre and be strong. Tell her I went to bed. You must trust me. I will return before first light."

"Sam, do you know something about Larry, where he is, if he's alright?" Lillian quizzed excitedly.

"I do not know, Lillian. Lo siento, I am sorry, it is more like a powerful hunch that grows stronger every time I touch the amulet."

He hugged Lillian, gave her a comforting kiss on the cheek and walked out into the night. The soulful cry of a lone wolf greeted him, sending chills up and down his spine.

Quietly, he led Major, the little army mare, from her stall and saddled her. Almost trance-like Sam mounted the horse and slowly rode into the night, driven by a powerful need.

The black wolf stopped his incessant pacing and sat on his haunches near Larry's head. He lifted his head skyward and howled, sending a signal to all within ear shot that something miraculous was about to happen.

Led by an unseen force, Sam rode quietly, unaware of time or distance as though the world around him waited for his arrival at some cosmic intersection. When he pulled the sorrel to a stop, it was by sense not by sight. In the dark of the night only shadows and silhouettes were visible. He sat aboard Major, straining his eyes into the darkness, looking for something, anything that might explain why he was here.

He saw a pale-blue light glowing faintly. It took a moment for his eyes to adjust so he could see that at the edge of the glow stood the dark form of a large wolf with piercing yellow eyes. The glow began undulating with bursts of pink, yellow and green, illuminating the body of a man, prone and unmoving. Sam's eyes were burning from the intensity of his gaze and the splendorous brightness. He stepped off Major and sank to the ground, struggling to comprehend what was happening before him.

The brilliant light faded to a soft, blue glow and from the man's body there rose a thread-like white light. It hovered momentarily over the motionless form then began to transform, taking human shape. Sam was astounded; the feel of Major's reins his only contact with reality. His hand moved slowly to the mysterious Indian enchantment hanging around his neck.

The hovering light transformed into the human-like form of Larry Riley and stood beside the lifeless body of its likeness. Neither it nor the wolf spoke but a message was implanted on Sam's brain that threatened his sanity.

The message came from Larry's light-form as the gigantic black wolf watched like an eternal guardian.

"You hear me though I am of no substance or sound. Deliver this message to my family. Tell them I feel no pain and happily run with the pack, though I cannot be counted. They will not see or hear me but they must know I am very much alive and present.

Because you bear the amulet, when you see me again I will be a white wolf with green eyes, visible only through the amulet and to creatures of my totem.

All humans have a totem. Consider yours carefully for at some time you will be as one."

The black wolf moved closer to Larry's body, gave it one last lick on the face then it and the light were gone; only the lifeless shell remained.

Sam did not, could not move, a sickening panic melted into his belly, a lump welled up in his throat and his eyes moistened. He wanted to ignore what just happened, laugh it off…call it a bad dream. He would have had it not been for the body lying in the grass.

Forcing his legs into action, Sam moved closer to the body, dreading what he might find but knowing there was no choice. Kneeling next to the deathly still form, tears spilled from his eyes and coursed down his brown cheeks. This was Larry, not a dream. Sam dropped onto his butt with a thud and silently wept.

It was too dark to determine what might have happened, how or why he was dead but Larry was for sure dead. Sam ran his hands over Larry's face, head and shirt, stiff from dried blood, when his finger snagged on a tear in the shirt. He ripped it open and felt the small hole in Larry's chest.

"Madre de Dios! You have been shot!"

It was an obvious conclusion with no beneficial purpose. All Sam could think about was that Larry was with his beloved wolves. He replayed the chimeric event he and Lillian witnessed. His mind leaped back to his mother and father, the only other times he remembered crying, and was suddenly angry. Why did some telepathic force lead him to Larry if he was going to be too late to help? Or had he helped? Was the sole purpose of his being there to deliver Larry's message to his family? How could he ever make them believe it? Could he even tell them? Would it be pointless?

"What am I suppose to do?!" he screamed into the night, shocking himself and startling Major who snorted and stomped in displeasure.

No matter how it occurred, Sam felt the full weight of his discovery.

"I can not go back to the ranch with Larry thrown over my saddle like a bag of grain but I can not leave him here to be torn apart by predators."

He put his hands under Larry's arms and lifted, his body came off the ground stiff as a fence post.

"Rigor mortis," Sam shook his head in disbelief. "How long have I been here?" He questioned. He knew Rigor mortis took a couple of hours to set in and he was sure he'd actually witnessed Larry die.

Tears ran down his cheeks and he roughly wiped them away with the back of his hand.

"I can not bring Ruth or Lillian out here."

As soon as the words came out he realized he didn't know where 'here' was.

Give a horse his head and he will take you home.

Sometimes that is good and sometimes not, he thought, remembering a time a lifetime ago when that didn't seem like such a good Idea…now it was his only idea.

"I can not wait until daylight but I have no way to get you home."

He was talking to Larry as if he needed to know his plans. Stepping up onto Major he draped the reins loosely over the saddle horn.

"Let's go home, chica."

The little horse began walking, head down, retracing their trail while darkness hung around them like a shroud of death. By time Major delivered him back to the ranch Sam had made some decisions. It was still dark when he pulled the saddle off the mare and placed it on a rail above the stall manger. He knew Ruth and Lillian would want to look for Larry again in the morning.

He awoke to knocking on the bunkhouse door.

"Sam, Larry is not home yet, we need to have some breakfast and decide what to do. Mom is frantic."

Sam's eyes burned, he rubbed them and tried holding them open.

"Bueno, I will be right there," he managed to reply.

His eyelids felt like grain sacks as he struggled to wake up, wishing he could go back to sleep. Then he remembered last night, the light, the black wolf….and Larry. Sam was wide awake then, but was everything he remembered a dream, a vision… or was it real? He touched the amulet.

"I am not sure," he muttered as he walked from the bunkhouse. "Even if I were sure I do not know where I was. It had to be a dream; impossible things always happen in dreams," he assured himself as he climbed the steps to the house.

Breakfast was difficult at best. Sam and Lillian picked at their buttermilk pancakes and sausage, Ruth nursed a cup of coffee, unable to eat at all.

She was fighting back tears when she said, "Sam, I'm going to stay here in case Larry comes home or Ross gets back. Will you and Lilly go up to the Ronan Mine today and see if you can find any sign of Larry? He could be anywhere but that is the one place I know he was going."

"We will Mom," Lilly answered for Sam. "And when we find him I'll have Sam kick his butt for all the worry."

Before saddling Bigfoot, Sam checked for signs to prove what happened could have been real but other than his saddle not being where he thought he left it, he found none. Major showed no signs of having been ridden all night, there was no blood on his clothes and when he touched the amulet he felt nothing unusual.

After saying their goodbyes, Sam and Lillian rode north toward the mine.

Clarence Hobbs watched through his telescope from his hilltop perch. Before they rode far Sam told Lilliam about what he called a dream, though he believed it was some kind of vision, he did not want to needlessly alarm her.

"The part about the wolves I could believe," Lillian said after hearing Sam's tale. "But there is no way Larry could get shot. Who on earth would want to shoot him?"

Sam hated to bring it up but did anyway. "What if he happened onto the hombre setting poisoned wolf traps? I could see Larry getting plenty upset about that."

"That's true, but Larry is awfully good with a gun. I doubt he'd be the one shot in an argument. He'd have to be ambushed and I can't see anyone around here with a reason to do that. I don't like this conversation, Sam. Can't we talk about something else, like when you are going to kiss me again?"

Sam smiled, thinking Lilly looked like a woman but in many ways but she was still a girl in denial, refusing to believe bad things can happen to good people. He loved her for it.

If only it were true, he thought; the memory of that perverted creep and her mother a case in point. Steering Bigfoot alongside Buttercup he leaned over and touched her lips with his.

When they reached Ronan Mine they dismounted and Lillian showed Sam the two holes, nothing imposing, just two holes barely deep enough to bury a dog. They looked in the cabin, nothing remarkable there either. Who ever filed the claim last fall sure hadn't spent any time or done any work there.

"Somebody was here and not that long ago," Sam said pointing to the tracks. "More than one horse too, looks like at least three or four. Doesn't that seem odd?"

"Don't know why anyone but Larry would have been up here. I guess it could be the guy with the claim but he sure wasn't doing any work," Lilly replied.

"Lillian," Sam voice was tense and strained, "this looks like blood on the door jamb. I am not sure but I do not know what else it would be."

He examined the dark stain on the bleached wood. He rubbed it with his thumb but the stain was completely absorbed by the wood. He moved his hand slowly down the door jamb and at the bottom just outside the threshold he touched a dark spot in the dirt…it was wet. He pulled his hand back; his fingers were sticky and red with blood. Looking carefully they found more, large dark spots in the dirt, some under leaves and needles.

"I do not know if last night was a dream, a vision or a premonition but something is terribly wrong," he said, pulling Lillian into his arms.

"I don't know either, Sam, but I'm afraid something bad happened here." She was choking back tears as she spoke.

They followed the tracks a ways on foot, finding an occasional drop of blood on a leaf or blade of grass. The trail led away from the cabin and Sam and Lillian were fighting a sick feeling creeping into the pit of their stomachs. There were no drag marks so whatever was bleeding was on a horse…or *was* a horse. They soon lost any sign of blood and returned to their mounts.

"What do you want to do Lillian?" Sam asked, knowing it was a question with no good answer. "Shall we try following the horse tracks or go back to the ranch and let your mother know what we have found?"

"I say we follow the tracks. If Larry is bleeding we need to find him as soon as possible."

More than ever, Sam hoped last night was nothing more than a bad dream. For several hours the trail was easy to follow until they entered the tall grass of a meadow. The ground was soft but finding tracks in the deep lush grass was nearly impossible. Within an hour they lost the trail completely.

"Got any idea where they could be going?" Sam asked.

"Maybe Paradise or Horse Plain, kind of the hard way to get there but if somebody is hurt it might be the shortest way. The Johnston Ranch is over this way but I can't imagine Larry going there, besides he would have been closer to home." Lillian's voice quivered on the verge of collapse. "If Larry could ride from the mine he would have come home, unless someone wouldn't let him, or he couldn't ride at all." Tears were streaming down her freckled cheeks. "Let's go on the Johnston's. I think we can get there and back before dark."

"How do you know Larry is not there?" Sam asked. "I have not heard of the Johnston Ranch. Do they have any girls around his age?" He hoped to lighten the mood with his comment.

"Oh yeah, but trust me Larry wouldn't be there unless he was kidnapped and if he is, we need to rescue him." She smiled but it was obvious her heart was not in it. "I'll tell you all about the Johnston's on the way. They call their ranch Bountiful," she began, "but if you ask me the only thing bountiful is Missus Johnston."

As Ruth fussed around the house she was so distraught she could barely control her emotions. She wanted Ross to get home. He always had a way of comforting her no matter how bad she felt.

She kept a watchful eye out the window, hoping to see either Ross or Larry ride through the arched gate. Alone, she found herself feeling vulnerable for the first time since Sam saved her from that bartender creep. She had been so worried about Larry she'd almost managed to put that dreadful day out of her mind. She went into the den and pulled a shotgun down from the rack. Checking to make sure it was loaded, she set it in the corner between the dining room and the kitchen.

"Now, that is just plain silly," she muttered and sniffed. "But I do feel better."

Chapter Twenty-seven
Desperate

"The Johnston's are Mormon. Do you know anything about Mormons, Sam?"

"No," he replied, sensing that Lillian was on a subject for which she held strong opinions. One of many, he thought affectionately.

"Well then, let me tell you about Mormons." Her tone was clearly one of distain. "They believe a woman's place is in the kitchen, the nursery or occasionally the bedroom. I don't think Missus Johnston is thirty years old yet and she already has at least fourteen kids. They want boys because the more boys they have the more land they can work. Girls are just a nuisance, an inconvenience, but they have figured out a way to make them useful; get them pregnant at twelve or thirteen so they'll have kids…hopefully boys."

Sam listened as Lillian rambled on, clearly worked up over the Johnstons. He figured it was good for her to get her mind off Larry.

"Besides," she continued, "Mr. Johnston hates wolves, coyotes, bears, cougars and Indians. He thinks the land belongs to him and God, no one or nothing else. No, I promise you Larry would not be at the Johnston's on purpose."

As they rode into the Johnston's barnyard Sam was appalled and intrigued. There must have been a hundred chickens, plus turkeys, goats, sheep, free roaming pigs, even a burro.

Eehyaaa! Eehyaaa!

The burro sounded the alarm as they approached the house, which was really a shack, a big shack but a shack nonetheless. In contrast the barn, located in a far corner of the yard, reveled in a sleek coat of paint and was double the size of the house.

Sam looked at Lillian quizzically.

"The house is for the women," she simply stated.

Heads began popping out from inside the barn, behind the barn, inside the house; it was like riding into a prairie dog colony. A middle-aged man with graying hair stepped out of the barn and approached the riders.

"Name's Jim Johnston, who might you be?"

"I'm Lillian Riley. My folks own the Running R and this is Sam… he works for us."

"An' how can I help you two?" He was stoic but not unfriendly.

"We're looking for my brother Larry. He went out to check on some things yesterday and didn't come home last night. Have you seen him?" Lillian was determined to match his tone, what ever it might be. "Or have you seen his horse, a bay colt with a white slash under his eye?"

Sam was attempting to keep track of the heads that peered around every corner and out every window. Most were kids but some looked old enough to know how to use a gun. His hand briefly touched the butt of his .45 then settled it back to rest on his chap-covered thigh.

"No stray horses around here, Missy. Mighty fine lookin' horses you're ridin' though. Don't hardly look like you'd miss one."

"You know my brother Larry, don't you Mr. Johnston?" Lillian ignored his sarcasm.

"Yeah, we know him. Ain't seen much of him for a long time though, heard he was kinda sick for a while."

Sam thought Johnston sounded a little nervous, a little defensive.

"It's not like Larry to miss supper and mom and dad are worried sick." Lillian was playing it a little coy.

"We'll make sure to keep an eye out for him. If we find him on Bountiful we'll send him home with his tail tucked between his legs." Mr. Johnston laughed at his own joke…he was loosening up a little.

"You mind if we take a look in your barn?" Lillian's question caught Sam completely off guard.

"Yes, I do, Missy," Johnston retorted. "I told you, your brother ain't here an' his horse ain't here. You Riley's think you own all the Flathead country. Well you don't! That's my barn an' everything in it belongs to me an' God. If you're accusin' me of somethin' then spit it out." Johnston's face was red and his neck veins were bulging.

Sam looked at Lillian, unsure what she was up to.

"No need to get riled up Mr. Johnston," Lilly said. "I just figured if you weren't hiding anything you wouldn't care if we looked. We've ridden a long way."

Johnston looked at Sam then at Lillian.

"You've got quite a mouth on you, Missy. Your Pa oughta take a strap to that pretty little behind of yours. Your wolf-lovin' brother ain't here an' ain't been here, an' it's time you weren't here either, so take your gun-slingin' hired man an' get the hell off my property."

Lillian spun Buttercup around and looking at Sam with a sparkle and a grin said, "Come on Sam, I don't think they like us here."

Once they were well off Bountiful land Sam spoke up. "What was that all about? Were you trying to get us killed or do you know something I do not?"

"I'm sorry, Sam, I just don't like that guy. I don't like the way he treats his wife and I wouldn't be surprised if God arranged for him to *marry* some of his older daughters. That place is like a baby farm." Lillian angrily replied. "And I'm mad because I probably wasted our time going there."

"Then you do not think he knows anything about Larry?" Sam questioned. "I have to admit that isn't the first time I have been called a gunslinger but why would he say that?"

"Don't ask me. I think Mr. Johnston is crazy, but as far as Larry goes, I doubt he knows anything." She giggled and added, "He sure didn't want us to look in his barn."

"If you think he knows something maybe we should go after the sheriff."

Sam continued to struggle with the plausibility of last night's experience and whether Larry might really have been shot and killed.

He wished he knew if it was a dream or real and if real…where **it** was?

"What would we tell the sheriff; that Larry's been gone overnight and you had a dream that he was shot?"

Sam thought for a moment, wondering…What if it was not a dream but a premonition? What if nothing has happened yet?

"Lillian, let us go back to the ranch. I would like to play out a hunch, no, not even a hunch…a real long shot."

"At this point a long shot is better than no shot," Lillian said with a quivering voice.

Sam changed the subject. They had a long ride home and there was nothing to do about Larry until tomorrow unless they somehow got lucky.

"I know you do not think much of the Mormon ways but what about Catholics? They are the ones who have missions all over the reservations and are so intent on converting the Indians. I too am Catholic but have abandoned the church and their beliefs."

Lilly took the bait. "Larry says the government even pays the Catholic Church or their missions to convert the Indians to our ways and religious beliefs. I don't like it, that's why dad went to the agency. I guess the Indians don't like it much either."

"Do you think the Indians could be upset enough to start killing whites?" Sam asked.

"I think dad does, that's why he's so concerned. People like my folks who settled here a long time ago get along with the Indians just fine, but there are a lot of new settlers and prospectors who don't respect the Indians, some even hate them. Larry says they think the reservation is way too big and want it made smaller then force the Indians to stay on it."

Sam decided to get to the point. "Lillian, do you think Indians could have done something to Larry, taken him captive or maybe killed him?"

"There's never been trouble with Indians that I knew about. I have never been afraid of them. In fact, some of them who speak English have even been to our house. I don't know why they would want to hurt Larry, he's on their side." Lillian's pretty face was solemn.

"Maybe they thought he was someone else." Sam hated seeing Lillian sad and hurriedly said, "Maybe he is home eating a pot roast sandwich and itching to tell someone his story."

Lilly coaxed Buttercup into an easy lope and Sam drew Bigfoot alongside, hoping this whole thing had a happy ending.

Ruth baked two apple pies, put a stew on the stove to simmer, utilizing the left-over pot roast and did some tidying up around the house. No matter who got home first, Ross or Larry, they were going to be hungry. Her chores completed she was tired. She sat down to wait, and waiting was the hardest.

"Auugh…!" Ruth's scream was cut short. She flailed her arms but couldn't get leverage to turn on her assailant. A fresh, sweet smell filled her senses.

Chloroform!

She remembered the smell from Doc Jensen's office. The arm across her throat cut off her air supply and the tightly held rag began to smell good, her arms and legs were suddenly heavy.

Fighting to remain conscious, she felt herself being dragged toward the woods…then she saw the sneering face of that horrible bartender leering at her.

Where am I? What are you doing?

She looked away from the evil eyes staring down at her. She was lying on a dirty wooden floor, light from the open door revealed the aging walls of a small building. Through the door she saw the tailings from what had to be a mine shaft.

The Ronan Mine!

That was where Larry was going. The thought was ripped from her mind by the feel of hot hands on her breasts. Ruth began to struggle, her green eyes wide with fright as she fought to figure out where she was and what was happening. An icicle-cold pang of fear stabbed deep into her belly when she realized her hands and feet were bound. Her fear escalated as she fought to clear her head and focused on the man kneeling over her.

Why me, what does he want with me?

It was a question with a dreaded answer she knew all too well. She nearly lost control of her bladder as panic swept through her body, settling deep in her abdomen.

She tried to roll over but he put a hand on her throat and when she tried to strike him with her knees he squeezed her throat tighter and she lay still. She could taste bile rising in her throat as he undid the buttons of her prairie dress. She felt the cool air on her skin when he roughly worked the bodice over her shoulders and down her arms to her elbows. Her breasts covered only by the white brasserie she'd bought in Thompson Falls.

A sob stuck in her throat as she felt his hand slide under her brasserie. Fear turned to anger when his fingers slid over the nipple of her breast. She struggled to free herself from his touch but he rubbed her nipple harder until she felt like her entire breast was on fire.

If I get loose I'll kill you!

But she couldn't get loose, her wrists were aching and her arms felt like thousands of tiny needles were poking them. She saw the knife briefly before his hand left her throat, only to be replaced by the blade of the knife. For a moment she wished he would kill her then felt the blade slip between her breasts, cutting the brassiere in half and exposing her breasts to his lewd eyes.

Ruth looked into his face, searching for some hint of decency, some glint of compassion or even empathy. She saw only evil lust-filled coldness, a wild beast toying with its prey.

Her entire body ached from its awkward position on the hard floor. His hands squeezed, kneaded and pinched her breasts then slid down her stomach to the end of the opened bodice. One hand slipped under her dress onto her lower belly. When it reached the waistband of her panties she bucked and twisted wildly.

Again, she felt the cold sharp steel of the knife-blade on her neck. Ruth was in a tug-a-war between two kinds of fear, that of dying and being dead without the benefit of death.

He grabbed the hem of her dress and yanked it up around her waist. With the knife still at her throat he tried to force his free hand between her legs but she squeezed them together, desperate to stop his lustful advance.

Ruth shook her head in disbelief, Larry was kneeling beside her. He lifted her head and stroked her face. She felt a surge of comfort, quickly replaced by the humiliation and horror of him seeing her like this.

Then he was gone and she was left with only the humiliation and horror as the evil little man moved his knife from her throat to her belly. Raising her head she saw the blade slip beneath the waistband of her underpants. With a flicking motion he cut away the waistband then ripped the panties from her body.

Threatening her with the knife, he forced her to spread her knees apart while he slid his hand between her legs. She screamed and began sobbing in shear hopelessness. Desperate to avoid his touch she twisted and squirmed as she felt his fingers probe her most intimate place.

A gutwenching cry woke Ruth so violently she seemed to levitate off the soft cushion of the leather couch. Her emerald-green eyes, wide with panic, searched her surroundings for any sign of safety.

"I'm home!"

The words yanked her back to reality and she began weeping again, partly from relief and partly from anger, a white-hot-fury kind of anger. She had been been tormented by horrible dreams ever since her humiliating attack. They had become less frequent but they weren't gone and she didn't know how to get rid of them.

She quickly got to her feet, glad no one was home and surprised it wasn't later…she had lost track of time and had a splitting headache, which she concluded was from the worry over Larry and the glass of wine she'd had to try and relax. She felt like she needed a bath, she went to the bathroom and turned the water on in the tub. Undressing she looked in the mirror, assuring herself it had been a dream.

"How could I feel so defiled, so used, so abused and not have a single mark to show for it? You could never tell by looking at me that anything ever happened."

The body heals much faster than the mind, she thought…but the scars on the inside are deep and permanent. She was convinced her only hope of banishing the dreams was to get even.

"At least I don't have to tell Ross," she whispered.

That evil man can torment me in my dreams as long as he doesn't hurt my family.

Ruth washed herself thoroughly, surprised how much it helped. Then she thought about Lillian.

"That bastard better not touch her!"

Ruth was suddenly was angry; at Ross for leaving her alone, at the bastard of a bartender for the torment he caused, mad at everything. It was only a bad dream but it was too damned real. When the bath water cooled she drained the tub and filled it again, thankful that Ross had installed the hot water coils in the cook stove.

When Sam and Lillian rode into the barnyard, Ruth rushed out to meet them before they reached the barn.

"No Larry?" she stated.

"No, Mom, I think he was at the mine but something happened there."

The mine?

The words hit Ruth like a sledge-hammer, her knees felt weak. Something horrible happened at the mine.

My dream!

Ruth wondered if it could have been some kind of sign, a warning, a premonition?

"It looked like there had been three riders there. We found some blood but that does not mean it was Larry's," Sam quickly added.

"I think they might have been taking someone to the doctor in Horse Plain or Paradise," Lilly interjected. "They were headed toward the Johnston's but we rode over there. I don't think they went there but I made Mr. Johnston mad." She looked proud.

"Your father wants you to stay away from the Johnston's. You know that. He doesn't want trouble with the neighbors, no matter how you feel about them."

"I know, Mom, but the tracks were headed that way so I thought we should check. Someone should ride into Paradise and Horse Plain to check with Doc Jensen. I can't see why Larry would go to town from the mine though. It makes more sense to come home." Lillian's nerves were on edge and she was trying to calm them by talking.

"We do not know if one of the riders was Larry," Sam said. "Anybody could have stopped by that old cabin, but there was a lot of blood there. That is troubling."

Sam and Lillian kept his dream to themselves. It seemed pointless to worry Ruth anymore than she already was.

"Put the horses away and come and eat, I've been cooking all day," Ruth said.

The beef stew and fresh bread were exactly what Sam and Lillian needed and for a few minutes they ate in silence, savoring the flavor of the meal. Sam was feeling the stress; tension and anxiety hung in the air like fog on a cold morning. He knew Ruth and Lillian were struggling to hold it together, while he was plagued with what he hoped was a just a dream or at least a premonition, something that could possibly be averted, if acted on in time.

Sam wished everything had not been so dark in his dream and wondered why he would be given a premonition if Larry was already dead, what good was that? There was one thing he knew could not be misinterpreted…Rigor mortis…that was a pretty sure sign of dead, dream or not.

"You think Senior Ross will make it home tonight?" he asked, making conversation.

Tears welled up in Ruth's eyes and she shook her head from side to side, clearly not up to casual chatter. Sam looked at Lillian; her pretty freckled face was drawn and white. The situation was becoming desperate.

Chapter Twenty-eight
Fallen Leaves

A LATE-NIGHT thunder storm rolled across the Running R but the flashing of lightning and the cracking and rumbling of thunder was a welcome diversion for Ruth and Lillian who lay awake in their beds. Sam also found the distraction a relief from his persistent struggle to find some meaning out of the cruel trick his mind seemed to have played on him.

He replayed Larry's message over and over, hoping to find some clue to his location, dead or alive.

Running with the pack.

He thought perhaps if I could find the wolf pack I would also find Larry, but how? They only howled at night and could travel miles on a single hunt? Sam desperately wanted to help the Riley's who had been so good to him, and Lillian whom he loved at first sight. As much as he wanted to help, he dreaded most having to deliver bad news.

Whispering to himself, Sam said, "It has been two days. If Larry is hurt he is running out of time."

As rain pelted the bunkhouse roof and he thought about tomorrow, a feeling of trepidation consumed him.

"Larry's message clearly was about wolves, but how do I find them?" he questioned the night.

Sam had told Lillian he had a hunch, a long shot, on their way from the Johnston Ranch.

"I must play it tomorrow," he declared between claps of thunder, "or it will be too late."

Ruth and Lillian were up, though it was dark when Ross came home. He was tired but he beat the storm. Neither Ruth nor Lillian mentioned Larry; it was obvious Ross wanted to go to bed and sleep, a fact Ruth was more than thankful for.

At breakfast it was clear no one had slept much, they all looked like they had poached eggs for eyes…except for Ross who remained in bed. Sam was glad Ross was not up but he was equally glad to find out he was home. Sam needed Lillian's help to explore his hunch and he was much more comfortable discussing his plan with Ruth than with Ross.

Ruth was also glad Ross was sleeping in; it gave her a chance to discuss the best way to tell him about Larry and get her emotions in check before facing him. She had to focus on the task at hand…finding Larry.

"I think I might have a way to find Larry or at least find out what happened to him." Sam broached the subject to Ruth as if juggling dynamite caps. "I need Lillian to go with me. Do you think Senior Ross will be upset if we are gone when he gets up?" "Do you know something, Sam? What is it?" Ruth's face brightened a shade.

"That is the problem, Señora. I do not know anything, but you must trust me."

He ached for this beautiful woman who'd had more than her share of grief since he had known her. Sure she was rich and they owned a magnificent ranch but he had come to realize, since knowing her, money wasn't everything.

"Okay, Sam, you do what you need to. You can go along if you want," she said, looking at Lilly.

"Of course I'll go!" Lilly spouted. "Larry is a jerk sometimes but I'd rather have a jerk of a brother than no brother at all." She fought back the tears, hoping she'd made a joke.

Ruth found it comforting to discuss with Sam and Lilly how to tell Ross about Larry. Having been so obsessed with thoughts of revenge, she felt guilty to welcome the distraction over Larry. Feeling the love from Sam and Lilly helped her get herself together. She had to keep her anger and hatred in check until the time was right, then she would make that perverted bartender wish he was never born. For now she had to think about Larry and Ross. She was glad Sam and Lilly were so fond of each other but she refused to have a runaway with that wagon either. Sam was Lilly's first love, that didn't mean he would be her last.

Lillian asked Sam to ride Weasel. "He hasn't been ridden since you and Larry broke Bigfoot and Bodie. As high-strung as he is, if somebody doesn't ride him pretty soon you'll have to break him all over again," she explained.

"I do not mind riding him," Sam told her. "Maybe it will help with my hunch."

What could it hurt?

"We will ride back to the mine. It is the last place we are pretty sure Larry was…then we will see if my idea works or if I am plumb loco."

When they reached the cabin, Sam dismounted.

"This will look very stupid," Sam told her. "Please, try not to laugh."

Sam removed the amulet from his shirt, pulled it over his head and touched it to the blood-stained door jamb. Then holding it waist high in front of him, he moved it in slow circles over the blood-soaked ground.

"Hi, yi, yi, yi, hi, yi, yi."

He began a slow, shuffling kind of dance, trying to imitate what that Indian had done in the valley. Sam knew it was weird, he felt silly but like he told Lilly…it was a crazy hunch.

As he moved in small circles over the blood-stained dirt, Lillian looked away and bit her lip. She never thought it would be this crazy. Sam danced and chanted for what seemed like enough time to assemble the entire Flathead Nation. When he was finished he slipped the leather cord holding the amulet back over his head.

"What do we do now oh mighty chief?" Lillian asked, as serious as a slipped cinch.

"We wait," Sam replied, "We just wait."

Last night's storm left the air fresh, yet musty. Proof Mother Nature has a sense of humor, Sam thought. The squall had moved on and the morning sun was bright and warm while he waited for something to happen; a funnel cloud, a bolt of lightning, anything. They didn't see it but they heard the howling of a wolf pack…and it was close. Lillian grabbed Sam's arm.

"Wolves don't hunt in the daytime," she declared but lacked certainty.

"Depends on the wolves," Sam responded, "and what they are hunting."

The pack was circling the cabin, there was too much cover to see them but they were getting closer. First two, then four broke from the dense cover less than a hundred yards away. They darted out of the trees in pairs then ducked back like they were on some kind of elastic band, yipping excitedly.

"I wish Larry was here," Lillian blurted and held tightly to Sam's arm.

"Maybe he is!" Sam replied without thinking.

"What are they after?" Lillian asked, concerned about the horses.

She pulled her carbine from the scabbard lying against Buttercup's ribs. She didn't want to shoot a wolf but she would if they threatened her horse.

Sam's attention was riveted on the wolves as he searched for the alpha male but they were all small, last year's pups or maybe two-year olds. Inexplicably, the yapping stopped and the young pack milled a safe distance away. Immediately, one large wolf appeared then another, until there were twelve…then thirteen. The last to appear was the largest, and as white as fresh snow. Sam couldn't see its eyes. He didn't have to.

Lillian's eyes were like saucers and if she squeezed his arm any harder he would be an amputee.

"What are they doing here Sam? Does it have something to do with that thing around your neck?" she quiried.

"It has everything to do with it," Sam replied. "That was my hunch but I am afraid it is not good news. Lillian, how many wolves do you see?" It seemed like a silly question but Sam was as serious as sour milk.

She paused a moment to count.

"Twelve," she said, impertinently. "Why, how many do you see?"

Sam cautiously pulled the amulet over his head then carefully placed it around Lillian's neck.

"My God, Sam, there's one more; a big white one!"

He removed the necklace. "And now?" he asked.

"The white wolf is gone but I know it was there." Lillian was tightly squeezing his arm again.

"Lillian, that wolf is Larry," Sam stated.

The wolves continued to mill around at the edge of cover, apparently perplexed by the sight and smell of humans and horses. Sam put the amulet around Lillian's next three more times, each time she saw the white wolf; without it she did not.

On her last look, the white wolf had narrowed the distance between her and Sam and the pack by half, so they could clearly see the glowing green eyes, even in the bright light of day.

"What did you mean, 'that wolf is Larry'?" Lillian reluctantly asked.

"I am afraid it means Larry is dead," Sam said, wishing for a softer way to say it. "I think the wolves will lead us to his body. Lo siento, Lillian, I am very sorry."

"How does that thing do that?" Lillian asked, reeling from the magic-like effect of the amulet.

"I do not know," Sam replied. "What I am sure of, is that it is far more than an ordinary Indian charm necklace. Frankly it is beginning to frighten me."

"But I thought you believed it saved your life," her voice made the comment sound more like a question.

Their conversation was cut short when the pack bolted, disappearing into the dense forest and undergrowth. Sam and Lillian hurriedly mounted up hoping to keep the moving pack within sight or sound.

After following for some distance Lillian said, "They're leading us back toward Bountiful. This is where we lost the horse tracks yesterday."

The morning was difficult for Ruth. Ross slept past mid-morning and when he woke he had disturbing information from his visit to the Jocko Agency. The fact that the government did not live up to the promises of the Hellgate Treaty was not news but the current unrest among the Flatheads was. With a lack of military presence on or near the reservation, the army had made 'policemen' of some tribesmen.

This was creating animosity among the Flatheads. This, along with the establishing of the tribal court, left many believing some Flatheads were abandoning the old ways and culture of the tribe in favor of the white man's dollar. That belief was further enhanced by the fact that young Indians were being taught at the mission schools to proselytize their parents and elders.

Ross learned that, in apparent retaliation, a new religious movement was taking root not only among some of the Flatheads but tribes all across the south and west. While it seemed for the most part to be a peaceful movement, the Indian Bureau and military were greatly concerned and threatening to stop the movement with force, if necessary.

No less disturbing, but far more fascinating to Ross, was the fact that this movement was believed to have originated not more than a couple hundred miles west of the Flathead Country in a place called Pasayten.

"They should have seen this coming," Ross told Ruth. "They've been pushing Christianity at the Indians ever since they were moved onto reservations. The Indians have always had their own beliefs and they don't want to go to church anymore."

Ruth listened to him as he ate breakfast, waiting, dreading her chance to tell him Larry was missing.

"They do something called a Ghost Dance or Circle Dance," he continued. "Louison Red Owl, who doesn't believe in the dance, thinks it might lead to some kind of uprising. He says many Indians are tired of the government's broken promises, the mission's teachings, the bureau's indifference and reservation life. He thinks some settlers could get burned out or killed."

"Ross," Ruth interjected, when he forked a mouthful of eggs and proceeded to chew. "Larry is missing. He left two days ago to check on the claim at the Ronan Mine and we haven't seen him since. Sam and Lilly are out looking for him but I'm scared Ross. I think something awful has happened." Ruth blurted her bad news out like it was burning her tongue.

Ross looked at Ruth in disbelief. "What horse was he riding?" His first thought was apparent.

"One of the colts, Bodie, but Sam doesn't think anything happened with the colt. Besides, if something did, Bodie would've come home by now." Her voice belied her otherwise stoic behavior.

"Where are they looking, do you know?" Ross asked, agitated.

"They found some tracks at the mine yesterday but lost the trail somewhere off toward the Bountiful Ranch. By the way, I heard wolves while you were sleeping. They sounded like they might be up around the mine too."

The very mention of the mine made Ruth's skin crawl but she had more to worry about than a stupid dream, no matter how horrible or real it seemed.

"You don't suppose Indians could have done something to Larry?" Ruth asked, redirecting her rampant thoughts.

"I don't think so, but there are a lot of Flatheads we don't know. We'll just have to find Larry." Ross pushed back from the table, "Drifter needs a rest after yesterday. I'd better saddle up Roy and go help look."

Ruth was surprised at how well she was handling her emotions given what had happened over the last two days. Her dream had stirred up all the emotions of her attack, only worse in a way. What didn't surprise her was the extent of panic she felt when Ross mentioned leaving. She knew she couldn't stay home alone again.

"I'm going with you Ross. I can't stay here and wait any longer."

"But shouldn't you be here in case he comes home?" Ross inquired.

"I'll leave a note," she replied, leaving no room for discussion.

Maybe she would get over it but for now the thought of being alone was terrifying. She thought about women who had actually been raped and wondered how they ever lived with it.

The big white male was quickly accepted as a new member of the pack by both Lobo and Lola. It was one of those odd quirks of nature that sometimes happen without an explanation. Lola found the newcomer virile and appealing yet Lobo sensed no threat, finding his white coat compromising and non-aggressive. To the rest of the pack he was another powerful hunter, always a welcome addition.

The yearlings and two-year olds enjoyed the rare hunt in broad daylight. Though instinctively they felt a little vulnerable without the cover of darkness, there were so many curious things to explore which they had not noticed at night.

When the pack saw the humans and horses, the young thought they would be signaled to burst from the cover of the forest, startling the prey into running then systematically separate the weakest and bring it down for the kill. They were surprised when no sign was given. All they did was watch while the white newcomer ventured close to the humans, seeming to be deciding whether or not they would make a decent meal. They wondered why there was no interest in the larger animals that looked like the elk or moose that made a great meal.

Lobo and Lola were willing to let the newcomer decide if the strange-looking prey was worth attacking. When the humans followed them the alpha's appeared unconcerned. The young looked to their leaders with anticipation when they spooked a small herd of elk, with at least two calves that seemed to be yelling, "Eat me!"

It was clear Lobo and Lola and the big white male had something else in mind. After crossing numerous streams, passing fir thickets and brush-choked canyons and ignoring several herds of elk and deer, the pack came to a halt in a small aspen grove.

Lobo, Lola waited while the white newcomer wandered around in circles, intently sniffing the ground. Unexpectedly, the white wolf lay down, his chest and belly heaving as he took a deep breath, holding his head high and proud, like he was absorbing the majesty of the aspen. He then lay quietly as if in mourning, occasionally stretching his neck out and laying his chin on the bed of aspen leaves.

Lobo and Lola were content to stand by and watch while the white wolf appeared to be carrying out the rite of some unknown ritual.

Sam and Lillian saw the wolf pack in the aspen grove from two hundred yards away.

Lillian thought she could see something on the ground and shuddered. They were obviously gathered around a kill. Cautiously riding closer, hoping not to spook the aniimals, Sam was the first to speak.

"It is the white wolf!" he exclaimed, "It has led us to this place."

Lillian didn't reply. She was confused and exasperated. Without the amulet around her neck she couldn't see any white wolf.

Sam touched the amulet. When he escaped from the valley and the fort and anyone who might be chasing him, he thought it must be an Indian good luck charm. He certainly was fortunate to have found Ruth and the Running R, but it was looking more and more like it wasn't so lucky for those around him. His contemplation was cut short by the excited yapping of the pack.

"They are leaving," he said, pointing toward the aspen thicket and the fleeing pack, "except for the white one."

Moving closer, and with all the caution of a powder man approaching an unexploded charge, Sam and Lillian drew within ten feet of the strange-acting wolf. He took Lillian's hand and placed it on the amulet resting against his chest. They watched in amazement and confusion as the white wolf lowered its head onto the bed of leaves and looked up at the humans with green eyes that were more soulful than menacing.

Sam and Lillian watched spellbound as the animal began pawing at the leaves. It hit Sam first…these were freshly fallen leaves! Leaves don't fall in the summer but these had. Then they saw it! Under the freshly fallen leaves lay the body of Larry Riley. It was as though Mother Nature had covered him like a mountain lion covers a kill to hide it from other predators.

Neither Sam nor Lillian spoke, nor did they see the white wolf vanish into the forest in pursuit of the distant pack. Lillian could not hold back the tears running down her freckled cheeks while Sam tried desperately to make sense of this. He gently tried to pull Lillian away from the sight of her brother's dead body. It was too much for her and she broke into sobbing convulsions. Her knees buckled and she sank collapsed into Sam's arms. He held her tightly, protectively, until her body was still, her tears depleted. After minutes that seemed like hours Lillian eased out of Sam's arms.

"What do we do Sam? How do I tell mom and dad? We can't just leave Larry here but we have no way to get him home."

Her words came in ragged gasps as she struggled to compose herself, trying to be rational hoping that might somehow ease her pain and heartache.

"I will see if I can tell what happened to him," Sam said.

Pushing more leaves aside, he examined the blood-stained shirt. He found a small hole to the right of the left pocket. It told the whole story. Just like the dream, he thought.

"He was shot," Sam said to Lillian and to affirm his findings. "He might have been murdered, Lillian, but who would want to kill Larry?"

He didn't expect an answer.

With his two fingers, Sam pulled Larry's eye lids down, ending the vacant stare of death.

"I can't look Sam. I don't want to remember him like this."

Lillian again broke into tears.

"I wonder where Bodie is?" The thought escaped Sam's mouth while his mind searched for answers. "If Larry was shot, Bodie should have come home…unless someone found him. How far is the Johnston Ranch from here?"

"Too far," Lillian replied weakly.

"We have to find a way to get him back home." Sam said, and remembering the dream, he grasped Larry by the arms and lifted. If there had been Rigor mortis it was gone now, Larry's body was completely limp.

"I think I can load him on Buttercup if you can hold her still," Sam said, apologetically.

Lillian squared her shoulders and with the look of a determination nodded.

"I can hold her but I can't watch."

The sojourn back to the Running R was nothing short of brutal. Sam and Lillian tried riding double on the high-strung Weasel, but that effort combined with leading a very skeptical Buttercup with Larry's body draped over her saddle, proofed futile.

Sam ultimately resorted to walking and leading Buttercup while Lillian rode ahead on Weasel. The trip was made even worse for Lillian because she had to ride Larry's horse.

She leaped off Weasel at the sight of her parents who had rushed from the house the instant Sam and Lillian past under the arch gate. Mother and daughter fell to their knees; Ross rushed up behind them, knelt and wrapped his arms around both of them. Together the family wept.

Sam watched the scene unfold, holding the end of Buttercup's lead rope. A wave of sadness swept over him that threatened to make him sick. He felt helpless, an outsider, a witness to an event that should be private. He didn't know if he should approach the family and offer his condolences or if he should slip off to the barn and let them grieve. He did neither.

Eventually, Ross motioned for him to take Buttercup and Larry to the barn. Only slightly relieved, Sam tied the Palomino to a rail and debated about what to do with Larry. He couldn't leave him draped over the saddle and couldn't dump him on the ground like a sack of potatoes either. He needed to talk to Ross but that would obviously have to wait. Larry had a bullet hole in him; to Sam that meant they needed to contact the sheriff but where and when? A freight and mail wagon came by the ranch twice a week but Sam didn't know what day it was, he had completely lost track of time.

Ross might want him to go for the sheriff and maybe an undertaker. The thought of going into town was nerve-wracking enough but to look for a sheriff on purpose seemed insane. However, if Larry was murdered they needed to find out who did it and why. Sam thought Ross should stay with his family…so he would be the one to go.

Ruth and Lillian went into the house and Ross walked into the barn to Sam and Larry. His face was grim and his eyes were red as he looked at his son's body. It was beginning to bloat and though it didn't smell yet, he would have to be taken care of soon.

"I need a big favor from you," Ross said to Sam. "I'll make it up to you but I need you to help me put Larry on my horse, Roy. We'll cover him with a tarp then I need you to take him to John Grimm in Horse Plain. He's the undertaker there and everybody knows how to find him. Then I want you to look up Sheriff Baker and get him over to Grimm's place. I'm sorry Sam, but I really need you to do it tonight while it's cool, and I'd rather it be done under the cover of darkness."

Ross was trying to function but only going through the motions. As an after thought he added, "I can't have Larry laying out here in the barn like no one cares."

Sam was exhausted emotionally and physically but this was one request he knew he could not refuse. In fact, he quickly realized no matter how tired he was, he would rather be doing something useful, something to help, than to stay here feeling helpless.

With Larry respectfully secured to a pack saddle on Roy, and after a few brief words with Ruth and a tearful kiss on the cheek from Lillian, Sam started down the road leading to Paradise... a cruel joke, he thought.

He attempted to sort out the events of the last three days; Larry's failure to return home, his prophetic dream and now the gruesome package he must deliver. Once out of sight of the Running R, Sam inserted a long narrow tube-like blade he had found in the barn, into Larry's stomach to aspirate the gases and prevent further bloating.

You learn these things growing up the son of a doctor, he thought. This tube like knife was normally used to save the life of a cow suffering from eating an excess of legumes, but for Sam it was a desperate attempt to preserve the sanctity of Larry's life even in death.

A few days later, John Grimm arrived at the Running R in a black horse-drawn carriage with a black canvas top and shear-black curtains that seemed to mourn its lone occupant. Sheriff Luke Baker rode alongside as if guarding a treasure already lost.

While the men were in the house, Sam spent the time finding one odd job to do after another, anything to stay away. He ached for all of them but didn't know what to say. He hadn't known Larry very well and though he had experienced the pain and sorrow associated with death in his family, Sam dealt with his grief alone. The sun was setting when Lillian knocked on the door of the bunkhouse.

"Sam."

After knocking and calling out repeatedly she turned and walked toward the barn where she found him cleaning and oiling harnesses.

"What are you doing Sam?" she asked. "That's usually a winter-time job."

Sam looked up from his task and felt like he had taken a sucker punch to the solar plexus. Lillian's eyes were red from wiping away seemingly endless tears. Biting her lower lip, she fought for composure.

"We're going to take Larry to a spot he always liked. He was planning on building a house there someday. We'd like you to come, too."

Sam was struck with a panicky feeling.

"But I hardly knew your brother and this time should be private, only for familia, family."

He was trying to be respectful while at the same time wanting desperately to be included.

"Besides, I do not have anything to wear..." He stopped short, realizing that was a lame thing to say.

How bad is this? Sam wondered. He was wearing her brother's clothes which must be sacrilegious or worse.

"Don't worry about the clothes, Sam. Come with us, we want you there, I want you there."

"Bueno...all right," Sam replied, following Lillian from the barn to the house. There are some things you don't say 'no' to.

Larry's casket was hauled to a grassy knoll among scattered aspen. The hill over-looked a small valley and a blue-ribbon stream. A low frame-work was built out of lodgepole and Larry's pine casket was placed on the platform. John Grimm removed the casket lid and placed it back on his wagon.

One at a time and with heart-wrenching sobs, Ruth and Lillian put a personal item in the box with Larry; for Ruth it was a tiny pair of boots and spurs made by a cordwainer in Thompson Falls and given to the fearless young bronc-buster at the age of four. Lillian placed a deer antler, on which a much younger Larry had carved and painted a replica of the animal that had once worn the antlers with pride. He made it for her to teach his little sister respect for animals, a lesson she had taken to heart.

Ross stepped up to the open casket and placed a leather wallet with an ornately-carved wolf that was painted white with emerald-green eyes. It was crafted special made by a saddle-maker in Kalispell for Larry's fourteenth birthday. Ross had put a ten-dollar bill in it for what he called 'seed'.

Sam felt conspicuous as he stood back with nothing to offer or say. For a brief moment he thought of the leather talisman with its wolf likeness hanging around his neck. It would have been fitting but he could not bring himself to part with it.

I could give him back his shirt. He scolded himself for such a callous thought.

As John Grimm placed the lid back on the casket, Lillian turned to Sam and put her arms around him, and placing her head against his chest she hugged him…and hugged him…until he led her away, trailing Ross and Ruth by a few steps. The group rode solemnly back to the house with Ross leading Weasel, adorned with an empty saddle, a silent reminder of their loss.

Chapter Twenty-nine
Verdict

Wovoka remained motionless for what may have been minutes or hours. At that moment he had no concept of time, it was as though he had been in some type of vortex where time ceased to exist. He remembered entering and exiting a strange cave and he remembered all that happened in the valley. All of that could not have happened in the blink of an eye but that was all the longer he felt he was gone. He could not remember when his dapple-gray mare emerged from the cavern but there she stood, nostrils flared and sweating as if ridden hard but there none-the-less.

Three months later Wovoka arrived at Walker Lake in Nevada and judging by the temperature, one would have thought it to be the middle of July instead of September.

The Sematuse had taught him to 'talk on the wind', so he had thrown word of the Ghost Dance out on every stream and river he crossed from Lost River to the Humboldt. Even so, he was surprised to discover upon his arrival back on the Paiute Reservation, many Indians were waiting for him.

Somehow, word of the Ghost Dance had spread from the Pasayten in the land of the *Okinakane* to the Black Hills and Pine Ridge of the Lakota, Hunkpapas and Blackfoot Sioux, to the Tongue River and Big Horn Mountains of the Cheyenne and Crow and beyond. Two

Minneconjou, Kicking Bear and Short Bull, along with others were told to travel to Nevada by the well-known Sioux war chief, Sitting Bull, to seek council with Wovoka.

There were Indians from so many reservations that Wovoka soon learned he could not speak the languages many brought with them. Yet somehow the Ghost Dance spread across the west from California to the Dakota's, from Arizona to Idaho, Oregon to Montana from Washington to Wyoming.

Unrest was growing in Flathead country, the establishment of the reservation court angered many chiefs who felt its intent was to turn Indian against Indian.

They were right.

But the court's real purpose was to protect the Northern Pacific Railroad and its advance into Indian country as well as the many settlers moving onto reservation land. The Indian Bureau believed if Indians policed and punished Indians, a full-scale uprising would be less likely.

They were wrong.

Unrest reached a boiling point when the court, made up of chiefs who had long been on friendly terms with the whites, ordered the prohibition of the religiously motivated Ghost Dance and other ceremonial dances.

Some of the elder chiefs, including Arlee and Charlo of the Flathead, challenged the courts authority and its appointed judges, including Red Owl, Grizzly Bear Stand Up, and Spotted Foot. Tensions rose and there was a threat of war not only between the Indians and whites, but between Indian and Indian.

Two young *Kutenais* (Kootenai), Red Thunder and Marmot, with families living on the Flathead Reservation returned from a summer of hunting and chasing rumors of buffalo along the Missouri River. Failing to find the now seemingly mythical buffalo they wandered on to a primarily Sioux reservation called Pine Ridge, where they learned a war chief named Sitting Bull lived.

Even the greatest Sioux chief of all, Red Cloud, along with many great chiefs from other tribes, were gathering at Pine Ridge where, with the coming of the water grass (or spring), the Ghost Dance would mark the end of the white man's reign over Native People.

It was told that Sitting Bull and another great chief named Crazy Horse killed so many soldiers in one battle at a place called Little Big Horn that the army had to send back east for more soldiers.

It was also said that with the demise of the whites would come the resurgence of the buffalo and they would once again cover the prairies like wild flowers.

Such stories so excited Red Thunder and Marmot that after returning home, they convinced countless Flathead and Kootenai people to join in the dance. When the reservation court attempted to ban the dance Red Thunder, Marmot and others became very angry.

"I will not stop dancing because some white Indian at some agency says I must!" a riled Red Thunder told all who would listen. "We must dance if we want to be set free with our brothers at Pine Ridge!"

Up and down the Flathead, Clark Fork and Thompson Rivers the word spread. But that wasn't the only news traveling up and down those rivers. There was also word of the murder of a highly-respected rancher's son, and some were blaming angry Indians…a charge Marmot responded to.

"If I want to kill whites I will start at the bureau not with some rancher's kid."

This kind of talk spurred the bureau to contact the authorities at Fort Benton in hopes of having troops sent to the Flathead Reservation. Their response was not encouraging, there were bigger problems in the Dakotas and agencies at Cheyenne River, Rose Bud, Standing Rock and Pine Ridge were all making desperate requests for troops.

The answer was clear. The Flathead problems would have to be resolved by the Flatheads…not the army.

Sheriff Luke Baker was a thin man with a nose like that of a hawk and piercing blue eyes to match. He kept those eyes on Samuel DeSoto during the family's funeral for Larry Riley. There was something about DeSoto and the Riley girl's story that troubled him. He wasn't buying the part about wolves leading them to Larry's body after three days, or that the body was covered in aspen leaves to protect it from predators.

All Baker had were suspicions, no evidence, no motive, just suspicions. He couldn't find out much about Sam from the Riley's or from Sam. He had the feeling they were hiding something or at least holding something back, but Sam had apparently been with the girl when Larry disappeared and pretty much ever since.

Ross Riley had a lot of influence in the Flathead country from Kalispell to Thompson Falls and he was using it to bring Larry's killer to justice. He was even threatening to bring in a U.S. Marshal from Portland in the State of Oregon if progress wasn't made soon.

More and more talk was that Indians had killed Larry but Luke Baker had even less reason to suspect Indians than he did Samuel DeSoto. The Riley family had a long standing relationship with the local tribes. In fact, Ross considered many chiefs among his friends. However, Baker also heard what the rebellious Red Thunder said about 'killing whites at the bureau before some rancher's kid'.

If Ruth Riley had any suspicions about who killed her son she was keeping them to herself. She seemed evasive and even uncooperative when he questioned her about Sam and what she knew about him. How and why DeSoto was hired seemed to be something of a secret, but he had no reason to suspect any of the Riley family. He definitely was perplexed about why or what they might be covering up when it came to Samuel DeSoto.

He asked around plenty and most people, even ranchers close to the Riley's, knew little or nothing about the hired man. In fact, most didn't even know he existed, but here were a lot of people moving up and down the Flathead and Clark Fork shrouded in an air of mystery. It certainly didn't make them killers.

Luke Baker met with lawmen from Thompson Falls and Kalispell but they had nothing. Some favored the idea that the boy was shot by Indians worked into a frenzy by the Ghost Dance and attempts by the bureau and reservation court to outlaw it. The fact that Larry's body was found near the village where Red Thunder and Marmot lived was considered suspect.

Then there was Sam and Lillian's testimony that the body was covered in aspen leaves. Some saw that as further evidence of an Indian killing, as some ceremonial wakes included covering the dead in aspen leaves. It was believed to be a way of appeasing Mother Nature and passing from one life to the next without breaking the circle.

With Luke that theory didn't fly. If Larry Riley was killed out of anger or to fuel some kind of Indian uprising, why worry about breaking the circle or any other ritual? Besides, Larry Riley was white, none of it made sense to Luke Baker. But it did to an ever-growing number of ranchers, settlers and business men who felt the growing unrest on the reservation and saw it as a threat to their own families and well-being.

As pressure mounted Luke decided to bring Red Thunder and Marmot in for questioning. Each claimed to have been somewhere on the Missouri looking for sign of buffalo when Larry Riley was reported to have gone missing. Although they corroborated each other's stories, Luke found the whole exercise a frustration. They had all summer to fabricate a story and of course the families backed them up.

During questioning, the two young Indians revealed an unhealthy anger at both Indians and whites, and a profound belief that a day was soon coming when at most white men would be eradicated and Indians would again live free of reservation boundaries. Baker decided to hold the two for a couple of days, until the circuit court judge came to town.

Judge Blume was a short, bald, rotund man of fifty some years, many of those spent on the bench. He was a staunch believer in the system of criminal justice and a trial by a jury of the accused peers.

The judge was not at all comfortable with this case because it involved the killing of a white boy on an Indian reservation, though it appeared to be a clear cut case of murder.

John Grimm had recovered the slug from Larry Riley's spine, a .30 caliber, the type most likely fired by a rifle, not a pistol. He was convinced Larry died as the result of cold-blooded murder rather than self-defense in a gunfight.

Grimm recommended to Sheriff Baker that Red Thunder and Marmot be arrested and held without bond for trial, scheduled for thirty days hence. If Luke Baker held any belief that he'd seen or heard the end of this case he could not have been more wrong.

He was first visited by Red Thunder and Marmot's families, then members of the reservation court, fueled by angry reservation Indians, who came to his small jail intent on removing the boys to the Jocko Agency.

Small Eagle told Sheriff Baker, "If these boys are to be tried for murder they will be judged by Indians on the reservation. You have no jurisdiction over reservation Indians."

"I'm not going to argue with you, Small Eagle," Luke said. "You get an order from Judge Blume releasing Red Thunder and Marmot to you and I'll help you escort them to the agency."

The sheriff was concerned he might need to hire two or three extra deputies just to keep the two Indians safe until trial.

The reservation court took its complaint to the bureau, and through the magic of telegraph, sent a request all the way to congress and President Stephen Grover Cleveland. One week before the scheduled trial, a rider, along with ten horse soldiers, delivered the order releasing Red Thunder and Marmot to the Flathead Reservation court.

The trial began two weeks later without a jury but with nine court judges set to determine the outcome. After three days of testimony, in which both Sam and Lillian were called, a white prosecutor from Kalispell and an Indian lawyer from the agency gave the closing arguements.

"Red Thunder and Marmot are young and impetuous," the prosecutor began. "They have gotten caught up in the notion that by doing some silly dance, they will bring on an apocalypse freeing them from God's law and the laws under which citizens of this country must abide. Larry Riley's body was found not two miles from where the accused live. It was reportedly covered with aspen leaves, a practice Red Thunder and Marmot are familiar with, and Marmot owns a .30 caliber carbine like the one suspected to be the murder weapon. The accused were angered by the loss of familiar hunting grounds to settlers and prospectors and when they saw young Riley riding near their home, they recognized him and decided he was scouting for additional grazing land for Running R cattle. Drawing a comparison between the white man's growing cattle herds and the dwindling buffalo, they chose to make a statement on behalf of the buffalo. That statement meant the loss of a fine young man who ironically, along with his family, always had the best interest of Indians at heart." He looked directly at Ross, Ruth and Lillian who sat stoically in the front row.

The agency lawyer told a far different story.

"Red Thunder and Marmot were not even on this reservation at the time Larry Riley went missing or at the subsequent discovery of his death. They were miles away on the Missouri River, a fact supported by family and friends. No one in their village remembers seeing them during that time, not even the village bartender who would normally see them every day. Many Indians know of the ritual involving aspen leaves, and if owning a .30 caliber carbine is a crime most everyone in this court would be in jail. It is true that Red Thunder and Marmot, like many Indians today, believe in a movement called the Ghost Dance or Circle Dance, but that is all the more reason why they would not kill a white man. They believe the time of the white man is coming to an end, that a great exhumation is eminent and that the land will be returned to the Indian to live in the old ways. Why risk killing a white man you don't know…and there is no proof Red Thunder or Marmot knew Larry Riley…when you believe all white men are destined for eviction soon?"

The young lawyer, dressed in a tailored suit but sporting long black braids paused to point at the defendants.

"These men did not kill Larry Riley because of buffalo or cattle. They did not kill Larry Riley at all. A .30 caliber carbine, as good a gun as it is, can not shoot from the Dakota Territory to the Montana Territory…and these men were in the Dakotas when Larry Riley was killed!"

Again he paused, this time looking at Ross Riley.

"Like the prosecutor, I believe Larry Riley was a fine young man with a bright future and that his death is a loss to us all. But to convict two men of murder because they have a religious believe that gives them hope, even if not shared by all, would not bring justice or avenge Larry Riley's death. It would only be another injustice in a land already filled with injustice and broken promises!"

After Sam testified he returned to the ranch, relieved that neither side chose to delve into his past or how he came to be at the Running R. He and Lillian agreed not to mention the white wolf in their testimonies and he was a little troubled to learn that the piling on of aspen leaves was part of an Indian ritual. He had believed the leaves were an anomaly of Mother Nature and an act of preservation by the wolf pack and wondered if it would have an impact on the outcome of the trial.

Ross, Ruth and Lillian joined Tomas and Elizabeth Finley after closing arguments in a room set aside by the court.

"Forget about what the court finds Ross. Do you think they did it?" Tomas asked, as if Ross's opinion was all that mattered.

"I really don't know. I don't believe those two boys knew Larry and even if they did, they had no reason to want to shoot him. Maybe all killing is senseless but if they killed Larry it was out of pure stupidity!"

Ross's grief had long since turned to anger and he struggled to contain his emotions. He was angry over the loss of his son but he was also angry about the loss of his wife. Ruth had not been the same since Larry's death. It was understandable, of course, but he knew at some point they had to get on with living, for Lillian and for each other.

Liz Finley reminded Ross of Lillian, and looking at the two of them together, he almost smiled. Liz was a voluptuous red-head with scattered freckles and kind eyes. Ross sometimes imagined Lillian at Elizabeth's age; the eyes were the only difference. Liz's were a compassionate brown while Lillian's were sapphire or icicle-blue, depending on her mood.

"Did Larry ever talk about having any Indian friends?" Liz asked.

Ross looked to Ruth who simply shrugged that she didn't know. There were so many things she didn't know. Why would Larry have been half-way between Paradise and Horse Plain when he only went to check on the Ronan Mine? Where was Bodie, the horse he was riding?

Lillian wished Sam was here with her. Besides missing him, she was struggling with how and when to tell her parents about the wolves; especially the white one. She knew what she had seen, but without Sam's confirmation it was sometimes hard for her to believe. She wanted to believe it, and to be able to make her parents believe it. It helped so much when she thought about her brother. Lilly made up her mind to tell her mother when the time was right and let Ruth tell Ross.

After a couple of hours of eating potato salad, beef sandwiches with high-octane horseradish and nibbling on rutabagas, turnips and carrots, word came that a verdict was about to be announced.

The little reservation court was overflowing with Indians and whites. Word of Larry's murder and the trial was big news throughout the Flathead country. As stragglers scurried to find a place to sit or stand, the entrance of the judges was announced and a tense, eerie silence ended the bustle.

Baptiste Ka-Ka-She (Spotted Foot), a brilliant man educated in a mission school and well-learned in the culture of his Native People, addressed the courtroom occupants in English, then in Salish.

"On behalf of the court I thank all of you for your attentive cooperation during this trial. This is a matter of grave importance to the victim's family and that of the accused and all Indians and whites living on or near this reservation." After repeating his words in Salish, Spotted Foot continued, "After consideration of all evidence and testimony presented, it is the finding of this court that the defendants, Red Thunder and Marmot, are not guilty of the charge of murder. It is the order of this court that the accused be freed immediately."

The most obvious reaction to the verdict was whoops and hollers of relief and joy. The families and supporters of Red Thunder and Marmot were vocal and boisterous. Some whites applauded the decision, though most remained conspicuously silent, assessing where to go from here.

Ross Riley placed his head in his hands, appearing to be deep in thought. Ruth and Lillian hugged, though it was unclear if it was a hug of relief or despair.

Later, outside the courtroom, Tomas Finley asked Ross, "What now? Do you think they got away with it or is the real killer somebody else?"

"I respect the judge's decision. I think the trial was fair and the outcome was supported by the evidence I heard. I wanted to be convinced they were guilty, but quite honestly I never was. I'm worried about where we go from here. I wonder if the reservation court would try another Indian for Larry's murder. I guess I'm disappointed because this means starting over, but I want Larry's killer punished, not some innocent scapegoat."

"I never thought they were guilty," Ruth said, in uncharacteristic spontaneity. "It didn't make sense. If they wanted to start a war why kill him and then hide him."

In contrast, Lillian remained unusually quiet. She wanted to tell everyone about Sam's dream and about the white wolf, but she and Sam agreed not to tell a story no one would believe and would not help find Larry's killer. She would tell her mom about the white wolf when the time was right.

The Riley's and Finley's rode back to the Running R together. Tomas and Elizabeth would stay the night at the Riley Ranch before heading home. Daylight was fading into darkness when they rode through the log arch into the complex of out buildings, barns and corrals of the Riley home place.

Sam was in the bunkhouse when he heard the clatter of hooves the squeaking of saddles and the jingling of spurs and bridles. Anxious to hear the trial verdict, he pulled on his boots and sauntered toward the barn. He didn't want to appear overly nosy, nor did he want to seem too anxious to see Lillian.

He greeted them by saying, "I am sure you all are tired. Let me put the horses away while you go in the house and put your feet up."

"Why, thank you, Sam," Ruth said sincerely, then looking the Finelys added, "Let's go in. I'll round up something to eat."

The foursome strolled toward the house but Lillian stayed. Holding Buttercup's reins she slid her arms around Sam's waist and looked up with wide eyes.

"They were found not guilty," she said. Rising up on her toes she added, "I missed you…now kiss me."

The feel of her warm lips on his sent a familiar tingle fluttering up and down in his belly like butterfly wings.

After a couple more lingering kisses Sam asked, "How do your parents feel about the verdict?"

"Well, mom never thought they were guilty and dad accepts it. He just wants to find out who did it. I haven't told anyone about the wolf. Mom and dad are dealing with Larry's loss in their own way and I hate to stir things up with a story I know dad wouldn't believe anyway."

"If that white wolf is Larry's spirit, I wish there was some way it could tell us what happened…who killed him," Sam said.

He wished he could help, and couldn't shake the feeling that Larry's death had something to do with him…and the amulet hanging around his neck.

Impossible!

Sam could not believe the necklace had an evil side.

"Me too," Lillian replied. "I'm really tired Sam, I'll see you in the morning for breakfast."

He watched as she walked away thinking…She might be tired but she still floats like an angel.

"Hold the son-of-a-bitch while I get a rope!"

A big man with a black beard yelled at the gang of a dozen or more men struggling with a man they had pulled from his horse. The man fought gallantly, knocking first one and then another to the ground only to have someone else take their place.

"What is the matter with you, are you crazy?" he yelled at the men, swinging his fists and kicking until he was subdued by five men.

"Leave me alone, I never did anything to you!" a second frightened voice screamed as a rope tightened around his neck. "What the hell is wrong with you?!" he shouted, and kicked one assailant in the crotch causing the man to double over, groaning and swearing with pain.

"You're gonna hang for that, asshole!" the man holding his crotch bellowed.

The whirr of a rope thrown over a tree limb ignited a flurry of activity. Horses were led into place, the men were placed in the saddles, faceless men yelled meaningless obscenities; a whip cracked as it stung the butt of a startled horse.

The sound of galloping horses stirred the night air and then it was quiet; only the squawking sound of ropes twisting on tree limbs weighted down by victims of a crazed mob broke the silence. Vigilante Justice, the ugly stepsister of Law and Order had over ruled the verdict and brought a death sentence for two innocent men, Red Thunder and Marmot.

If the rebellious young Indians had hoped to start an uprising by protesting the prohibition of the Ghost Dance, the vigilante mob had just succeeded where Red Thunder and Marmot would likely have failed.

Chapter Thirty

Orders

Corporal Daniel Bone and Private Joe Wright might have been the luckiest soldiers in the entire U.S. Army. For more than a year, they had no duty other than to live in the log mansion Roy Wolard built before his mysterious disappearance.

They had enough supplies and fresh beef to last for at least another year. What they didn't have was money or women. For a long time neither seemed to matter much; they ate steak whenever they felt like it, tossed logs into the massive rock fireplace in the winter and swam in the cool river during the heat of summer.

Since the fire, they grew accustomed to their good fortune. They had tried to figure out what caused the fire last year; their best guess was Indians, maybe the naked one that scared the bee-Jesus out of them…twice.

Joe said, "I'm tellin' ya Daniel, there's gotta be some women somewhere 'round here. There's settlers movin' in an' they got daughters an' sisters. We need ta get some regular clothes. If'n they thought we was rich ranchers we might even get some women what ain't fat an' got all their teeth." He was getting excited over the idea.

Daniel replied, "Be just 'r luck ta bring home uh couple uh beauties an' have the army waitin' here for us, court martial us for bein' out uh uniform." He thought for a minute. "There's gotta be uh lot uh Injun women at the mission. Ya got uh problem with Injun women Joe?" He figured he was simply being practical.

It was hot in the Kartar Valley but Daniel and Joe knew winter was not that far off. They had enough wood for a mild winter but planned on skidding logs from a nearby mountain to supplement their supply.

"We better finish gettin' wood before we start lookin' for women," Daniel suggested.

It was hard to motivate Joe into gathering wood when it was ninety degrees in the shade, and there was damn little shade.

The thought of Francis Wolff's gold was never far from Daniel Bone's mind, either. He managed to keep the secret from Joe even though it was awfully tempting to tell him on some of those long winter nights. It was over a year now and he was getting anxious. If he didn't hear anything soon it would be late next spring, probably summer, before they could expect anyone from Fort Vancouver to return to the burned out fort. He knew the next stop would be here, at Roy's Wishbone Ranch.

"Goddamn it! How could I be so stupid?"

Daniel felt a cold chill invade his entire body as all hope of being rich was suddenly sucked out of him. He cussed, stomped, and swore for a good ten minutes while a perplexed and slightly amused Joe Wright watched.

"So what the hell bit you in the ass?" Joe eventually asked, giving in to curiosity.

Daniel, convinced he had been swindled, told Joe about the saddle bags filled with gold and the deed to a gold mine in Canada.

"Uh course the lieutenant didn't want me ta tell anyone!" Bone raved. "That way it was just between Lieutenant Radcliff, Major Denton an' me. An' I'm a piss-ant corporal stuck out here in Injun country in the middle uh nowhere! What ever made me think they would come all the way out here from Vancouver ta give that gold back ta me?"

Daniel continued to stomp around the log mansion.

"Take uh good look Joe, that way ya'll always know what uh first class idiot looks like!"

"Jesus, Daniel, ya mean ya was rich an' ya gave it ta the army? That don't seem to smart ta me."

"It ain't smart Joe! I ain't got no schoolin' an' don't know what made me think I'd be good at thinkin'!"

Daniel's ranting digressed to quiet disappointment. "I hope the army does forget about us an' this here ranch. At least we can pretend ta be rich," he said in a hollow voice.

"Well, at least we're still gettin' paid," Joe said, trying to be positive. "I say when we go ta get 'r pay we pick up uh bottle ah whisky at the post. I feel uh good drunk comin' on."

Bone had to admit the army did manage to regularly deliver their pay, conveyed by mail riders and freight wagons to the small trading post and mission, located near the lake that marked the west end of Wishbone. Once a month, Daniel and Joe rode to the post to pick up their pay; twenty-five dollars in coin for Daniel and a twenty dollar gold piece for Joe, plus a few staples, then returned to the ranch in one day. Maybe next time they would get drunk and look for an Injun woman who would be willing to cook, clean and take care of their other needs.

While Daniel continued to mope around, Joe was surprisingly upbeat. "Ya really think we can get uh woman ta come out here an' live? Maybe we could just get 'er drunk an' bring 'er here. By the time she wakes up she'd be stuck here."

"That's kidnappin' ya fool. They can hang ya for that," Daniel fussed.

"Not if'n it's just uh Injun," Joe retorted. "Besides we could treat 'er good, couldn't we?" He seemed to be almost begging.

The next ten days passed painfully slow. Daniel remained depressed while Joe seemed obsessed with the idea of finally bringing a woman to Roy's house. Both were relieved when the day came to break the routine and make the trip to the mission.

Their method of time keeping was crude but effective. On their pay day Daniel filled a bag with thirty pebbles, every morning he took a pebble from one bag and put it in another, when the first bag was empty it was time to get another month's pay. Since the army paid every thirty days the system worked perfectly. They even gained a bonus of five days pay at the end of the year. It wasn't much, but it beat a poke in the eye with a forked stick.

Today the bag was empty.

As they threw their McClellan saddles on their horses, all issued by the military, Daniel remained sullen but Joe could hardly contain his excitement.

"Let's put uh regular saddle on the packhorse, Daniel," he blurted. "If'n we find uh woman, we don't want ta make 'er ride uh pack-saddle back ta the ranch."

Daniel shrugged. "What the hell," he said, tossing a McClellan on the packhorse. "Might as well enjoy 'rselves while we can."

The trip to the mission was routine, or unnerving, as usual. Once they reached the turquoise waters of what Daniel called Warrior Lake, the mounted braves appeared on the rimrocks surrounding the lake. It happened every time they rode to the mission like some mysterious messenger was alerting the warriors in advance. The warriors never bothered them, they merely watched.

"Well it is their reservation," Daniel told the nervous Private Joe Wright…same as he did every trip.

Routine, he thought.

They dismounted in front of the rather elaborate parish, constructed for Bishop Donneli before he vanished with the 5th Cavalry Regiment. Father Francis Paul Mantier occupied the parish and had graciously agreed to sign for, and hold, Daniel's and Sam's pay each month when it arrived with the freight.

Father Francis, as everyone called him, was a handsome man, if a man could be considered handsome dressed in his clerical vestments. He had the muscular build of a lumber jack with piecing black eyes, black hair graying at the temples and unusually white teeth, which he frequently showed off with his disarming smile.

"Hello, gentlemen," Father Francis greeted them. "Things are good on the ranch I presume."

It seemed like a question but Daniel knew it was only conversation.

"Everythin's great, Father. 'R pays here, ain't it?" Daniel asked, struggling with a feeling of trepidation.

"Yes, Daniel, it is," the congenial priest replied in a soft tone. "And there is a sealed letter addressed to both of you. Looks like you boys might have some new orders, probably going back to Fort Vancouver I'd guess."

Father Francis handed Daniel and Joe two sealed envelopes containing their usual pay and one larger envelope with the stamp of Major Benjamin Denton in the upper left hand corner.

"Ah knew it was too good ta last," Daniel muttered to Joe. "I bet they're orderin' us back ta Fort Vancouver. We got just about enough time ta get there, if'n we left right away."

Shit!

"Fits right in with the way this day's goin'," he added.

Daniel broke Major Denton's seal and removed the papers. He felt a surge of adrenaline that settled into an acute sense of panic. The writing was in a cursive longhand. He could read a little if the letters were printed, but this was too much. He stared at the papers for long enough to cut the trees to make the paper.

Joe finally interrupted Bone's dilemma.

"What's it say Daniel?" he asked.

Daniel's sun-browned skin turned a little darker.

"Father, I can read uh little," he said defensively, "but this here's in some kind uh writin' I cain't make out. Do ya think ya could read it ta me?"

Daniel thought he knew what was in the letter and figured a priest would probably forgive a man for not knowing how to read much but it added embarrassment to disappointment.

"No problem," said Father Francis, "and don't feel bad about not being able to read. It's never too late to learn, and if you boys would spend a couple of days out of the month here at the school I could teach both of you."

"That sounds good Father but I got uh feelin' that letter's gonna be sendin' us back ta Vancouver," Daniel replied.

"Well let's read it and find out." Father Francis said.

He studied the page, scanning the letter's formalities and jumped to the text;

To; Corporal Daniel Bone

Private Joseph Wright

Be advised that regarding your assignment as guard and caretaker of

the property of Mr. Roy Wolard, hereafter referred to as Wishbone Ranch, the following shall occur as outlined below.

This is to inform you that next of kin to Mr. Roy Wolard have been identified. Contact of said kin is at this time pending. Upon notification of next of kin it is the expectation of The Department of the Army that said kin take possession of Wishbone Ranch in a timely manner.

Your orders are to remain in your current status until the next of kin, accompanied by a representative of the Department of the Army confirming their rightful ownership, contact you.

Once the rightful owners have taken possession, you will both report to Fort Vancouver in the Washington Territory within thirty (30) days of your release from your current duties.

Post Script: Corporal Bone, in the matter of property belonging to Mr. Francis Wolff (deceased) no next of kin have been located. Therefore, said property shall be turned over to you at the direction of Major Benjamin Denton and Lieutenant William Radcliff upon your request in person.

Regards,

Colonel Roland Roberts
5th Cavalry, US Army

Daniel was dumb-founded and asked the good Father to read the post script over several times.

"Eeeehaaa, kiss my ass an' call me religious!" he shouted, jumping up and down then abruptly stopped. "I'm sorry your holiness," he said to Father Francis. "I didn't mean ta curse in front of ya. I'm rich Father, I mean really rich!"

"You boys want to come in and sit a spell? I think you need to take a deep breath Daniel then tell me all about this good fortune."

"I was feelin' sorry for myself all day, Father," Daniel said, breathless. "Now I'm so ashamed. There really are some honorable people in the world. Uh fact ya couldn't uh sold me on uh few hours ago."

"I guess this means when we get back ta Vancouver you'll be leavin' the army, huh?"

It was Joe's turn to be depressed; their sweet duty was coming to an end and his best friend was going to go where ever rich people went.

"Come on in," Father Francis reiterated. "I have a bottle of wine imported from France I have been saving for a special occasion. This sounds like a perfect time to me. We'll have a sip or two to your good fortune and your future."

Daniel retold his tale of good luck and short-lived paranoia to the attentive priest and a disheartened Joe Wright.

The cleric listened, sipping from a small ornate glass. When Daniel concluded his tale, the priest responded. "I'm not sure if two or three thousand dollars in gold really makes a man rich, Daniel, but it certainly is enough to give a man a fresh start. If you spend it wisely you may be rich someday. Are you planning to look into the mining claim in Canada?"

Daniel and Joe swallowed their glass of expensive wine in one gulp like it was cheap whisky, and waited for the burn.

"Heck, Father," Daniel said, trying to clean up his language now that he was rich. "This might be imported from France but it ain't got the kick of uh good bottle uh rot-gut from Tennessee."

Father Francis smiled.

You can put a dress on a pig…

"It might not have the kick but if you develop a taste for fine wine you'll live a lot longer to enjoy your new-found wealth than you will sucking down Tennessee Whiskey."

"Ya know, Father, you're right. I need ta start thinkin' 'bout stuff like that." Daniel was already itching to get back to Fort Vancouver and start being rich. "I sure hope those kin folk uh Roy's 'r back at the ranch when we get there. We could get back ta Vancouver afore winter if'n we start right away." He was looking at Joe but Joe looked away.

"Another thing you might want to think about is investing in your future," the priest suggested.

"I don't know nothin' 'bout investin', Father, but since ah got uh gold mine now I reckon I'll be investin' in it."

"I don't mean that, Daniel," the handsome cleric smiled. "I mean your eternal future. A few dollars a week to a church or mission and you could guarantee yourself eternal life with God."

Daniel suddenly found himself feeling uncomfortable.

"Guess that's what happens when ya get rich," he said. "People start askin' ya for money. Well, Father, I ain't even got the gold yet so I cain't be buyin' no future with God 'r anybody else."

"Just friendly advice, Daniel, just friendly advice," Father Francis said, cajolingly.

"Thanks for the wine, Father," Daniel said, standing. "C'mon Joe, ah think it's time we pick up whatever we need an' head back ta the ranch."

He wasn't thinking about supplies.

Chapter Thirty-one

Vengeance

Bent Grass was becoming more anxious with each passing of Sister Sun. The words on the wind were many, and from near and far.

"You and Jack Wilson have done well, my son," she said, as she sat by the small fire with Standing Wolf and Star Flower. "Word of the Dance of *Tlchachie* has spread like a prairie fire during the time of the dry-grass moon." Her mood did not reflect the movement's success.

"Is this not a good thing?" questioned Star Flower.

"It is what we believe to be right, to be the destiny of Native Peoples, but something does not feel right. I am not sure what or why. The spirit wolf is pleased and I have seen no signs of impending doom. All seems good outside this valley, yet I am troubled."

Bent Grass shook her lovely head, sending a cascade of blue-black hair over her shoulder and down her slender back.

Standing Wolf loved his mother. The miracle of finding her still gave him chills but as he learned more about her, he realized she was a worrier. Maybe it was the responsibility she felt as the Sematuse's seer. Maybe it was because she spent so much time in the cave of spirits. Maybe it started when his father took him and left her alone. Whatever it was, he hoped this time she was worrying needlessly.

"I believe Wovoka was chosen by the Great Spirit, as was I, to be a messenger. While the Great Spirit guided me here to live as a

Sematuse, Wovoka was brought here to learn so he might deliver the word of the Ghost Dance to all Indians, near and far," Standing Wolf and took his mother's hand. "When time outside the valley is right, he will be granted the power for all Native People as I was granted for the Sematuse."

"You are wise, *mono go kin,* my son. You know more of the world beyond this valley and of the thing they call 'time'. Perhaps I should be thinking about you and *mihakin* and wait to become *asile waktunk,* a grandmother." Bent Grass looked at Star Flower and flashed a heartwarming smile.

Standing Wolf's dark-brown face turned pink and his mouth dropped open like the entrance to the spirit cave. He looked at Star Flower.

"You knew?" he managed to say.

"Not for sure. I thought I was getting fat," she replied. Turning to Bent Grass she asked, "Are you sure?"

"I am a seer but this is no mystery," Bent Grass quipped and hugged the lovely woman with the kind eyes and nature to match.

Standing Wolf was overcome with emotion. Tears rolled down his bronze cheeks as he wrapped his arms around his wife and his mother. He felt weak, his mind raced back through his past. Never once in his entire life did he expect to have a wife, so having both a wife and child was unbelievable! All he ever wanted was to find his mother, never imagining what finding her might mean.

Pulling away from Star Flower, Bent Grass motioned for them to follow her.

"Come," she said, "I have some bragging to do."

A wave of panic swept over Standing Wolf.

"Should we not wait until the baby is more obvious?" he asked.

"Why wait? The seer has spoken," Bent Grass replied, already halfway out the door of the teepee.

The birth of a child in the valley of rainbows was not an uncommon occurrence so the news of a pregnancy should not have been cause for celebration. However, the prospect of the son of their seer and the chief's sister having a baby was another matter.

On their way to Warm Hand's cupola, Standing Wolf paused to take stock of all that had happened in what he knew to be only a little over a year's time. He raised his eyes to the deep-blue sky punctuated with bubbly gray-and-white thunderheads. A red-tailed hawk quarreled with a murder of crows for no apparent reason while a golden eagle soared above it all with regal majesty.

Inside the cupola, Ta-keen Eagle and Laughing Doe were listening to Warm Hands boast about his extraordinary powers as a grandfather. Everyone in the village knew of the bright-eyed, curly-haired baby boy born of Spotted Fawn and Little Beaver. A full Brother Moon had shown four times since the birth of Spotted Bear, named to honor his mother and the grizzly that brought her and Little Beaver together.

Frank, no longer Loco Frank or Lone Frank but a very happy Frank, caught up with Bent Grass, Star Flower and Standing Wolf outside the cupola.

"How are three of my favorite people?" he asked in his best Salish.

"You mean four," Bent Grass replied, laughing.

"I do?" Frank looked puzzled. "I been known to see double but I do not usually miss folks."

Bent Grass smiled at the blue-eyed man with the flowing fire-red hair. He may be sane but he is still a little loco, that is what I love about him, she thought.

Stepping into Warm Hands' cupola was like entering a witch doctor's lair. There were crow's feet, hawk skulls, gourds filled with blood from his *tah,* or totem - the otter. The shaman sat on a bench draped with fox and coyote hides, an otter skull hung from a cord around his neck. With his weather-blackened skin and long, prematurely silver-gray hair, he was an awe-inspiring sight.

Bent Grass wondered briefly why he never took a woman but a quick look around his cupola answered her question. His medicines were his life, only his *mini go kin,* or daughter (by proclamation), seemed comfortable among his menagerie of medicinal potions...and why not? Without them she would not be a mother or a wife...she would not be alive.

"Greetings my friends," Warm Hands softly greeted the four newcomers. "I hope none of you are suffering from *mantwiyan,* constipation," he said, laughing.

"Not exactly," Bent Grass spoke for the group, "but one of us has a condition that may require that you eventually give some relief."

He looked at them but not one of them looked the least bit sick to him.

"Who might that be, oh mighty seer?" he asked, knowing he was being toyed with.

"It is the chief's sister," Bent Grass replied.

She was having fun now. Ta-keen Eagle and Laughing Doe were suddenly were all ears.

"What is wrong with my sister?" Ta-keen Eagle asked, puzzled as he looked at the outrageously healthy looking Star Flower. She had played along for as long as she could.

"I am with child!" Star Flower happily declared.

"We are having a baby," she repeated, and threw her arms around Standing Wolf.

Laughing Doe hugged Star Flower then rushed from the cupola to spread the news. She was like the official village crier, but she stopped first to tell Spotted Fawn, Little Beaver and Willow who hurried to the cupola to join in the happy occasion. Soon there would be a celebration…the Sematuse loved a celebration.

Standing Wolf heaved a sigh of relief and understanding. Instinct had told him to return to the valley while he was in Nevada State. When he met Jack Wilson, instinct again told him to bring the man to the valley to be anointed with the gift only Bent Grass could give.

It is all part of my destiny, he thought.

It was his place to save the Sematuse then find the 'one' to free all Natives, and that destiny led Jack Wilson to him.

It was now up to Wovoka.

It was difficult for Jack to think of his friend, Standing Wolf, as the Son of God but difficult or not he had no doubt. Every night when he closed his eyes the image of that miraculous valley materialized.

"I am the only man alive to have traveled to heaven, spoke to God and returned."

It was an account he often told yet was always surprised when few questioned or doubted it.

The voice came to Jack in the middle of the night.

"You will be known as Wovoka." It was like a voice in his head, whether man or woman he could not tell, but he knew it was God or the Son of God speaking to him and he welcomed it.

Jack knew the time was near. The number of Indians traveling to the Walker Lake Reservation was staggering. He spoke in the agency long-house every day to hundreds of anxious Indians wanting to hear about the Ghost Dance. Many brought gifts and offerings.

Jack changed his name to Wovoka but never referred to himself as 'Messiah', adhering to the same concern expressed by Standing Wolf. However, more and more he was being called Messiah by the throngs of Indians to whom he spoke. He believed it was because they were confusing his message with that of the priests and parsons at the reservation missions and churches.

Rumors ran rampant. One Minneconjou, called Kicking Bear, gave Wovoka a brightly painted shirt and said, "Wear this ghost shirt and it will protect you from the white man's bullets. The shirt will cause their guns to shoot crooked, sending their bullets harmlessly across the prairie."

Stories of this kind were troubling to Wovoka. Neither God nor the Son of God had told him anything about ghost shirts. Others, mostly women who had lost fathers, husbands, sons or brothers in fights with the white soldiers, were dancing all day and night until they fainted from exhaustion. They refused to eat and drank little, convinced they must dance until their male relatives rose from the dead.

These are not my teachings.

At times a troubled Wovoka questioned the memory of his vision but it was so real he knew it to be true. The exhumation had already happened once and it would happen again. He was determined to believe, if not for himself then for his brothers. Many wanted Wovoka to travel to their respective reservations with them but he resisted.

"I am a Paiute, if I die I will die a Paiute, if I live I will live a Paiute until I see the white man disappear from our hunting and fishing grounds."

He insisted that any who yearned for his teaching knew where to find him. If he became a nomad, traveling from reservation to reservation, many who wanted to hear his message might not be able to find him.

"I will know through words from God what is happening across the land. If God tells me to leave Walker Lake then I shall, otherwise I will remain here."

It was a decree he verbalized over and over to anxious tribal leaders.

No one, Indian or white, knew or would have guessed that the God Wovoka spoke of, and believed in, was a beautiful Semtuse woman no more than five feet tall and called Bent Grass.

Word of unrest reached Wovoka from all across the land. From reservation after reservation came news of discontent, of disillusionment and despair, of anger over broken promises and even of bans on the Ghost Dance. The Indian telegraph, as the white man called it, was alive with the prospect of a new life and a return to the old ways.

Nowhere was the anger more prevalent than on the Flathead Reservation in the Montana Territory. Two young Indians, set free by an Indian court, had been lynched by whites. Revenge burned in the hearts of many Flatheads and full-scale war loomed on the horizon.

Such news concerned Wovoka greatly. He knew the Indians could never defeat the whites in battle. There were too many soldiers, too many weapons, besides it was not the way given to him in his vision.

He firmly repeated, "We must be compliant, obedient and peaceful. We must continue the dance until the Great Spirit chooses the time to exhume our ancestors so they can free us from subjugation."

He sent the word out among his followers who were many.

Blacktail, Stryker, and Whitefish were enraged. Stryker was a cousin of Red Thunder whom the white mob had lynched. He was determined to avenge his cousin's death and had little trouble finding young warriors with fire in their bellies willing to assist in such a noble cause.

"If we kill soldiers the army will send more," Stryker rationalized, "but if we kill settlers it will strike fear in their hearts and they will stay away." His logic seemed impeccable to those surrounding him in their clandestine meeting place.

Night comes early in the mountains of Montana even in September. It was already dark and a light rain fell as the small band proceeded to implement their retaliation. It was not a particularly well devised plan but rather one fueled by anger and opportunity. Less than ten miles from their meeting place, a family of settlers was moving in on a piece of bottomland. It appeared to be three generations of farmers, the grandchildren not more than eight years old.

They were going to sneak up close and set the two newly constructed houses on fire. They would kill the men as they fled the burning houses but not harm the women or children. The idea was that the survivors would be so terrified they would spread the word and others would think better of settling on the Flathead.

On their way to the targeted farm, the band of ten young warriors saw a campfire. Moving stealthily, they worked their way close enough to see three white men sitting around the fire. They were not close enough to hear what the men were saying but they could hear laughter and see what appeared to be a bottle, passing from man to man.

"These men are sitting ducks," Whitefish whispered to Stryker. "We could kill them and take their scalps to send a message. It would be better than taking a chance of hurting women and children."

"Have you ever taken a scalp?" Stryker asked mockingly.

"Never killed a man either," Whitefish retorted, "but there is a first time for everything."

"It does not seem right to kill them without giving them a fighting chance," another one of the young braves complained.

"The white men who hung my cousin never gave him or Marmot a chance. Would you rather be shot in the dark and never know what hit you or be hung and feel yourself die?" Stryker countered.

A brief discussion followed and an impulsive decision was made. They would each pick a target, thus each victim would be shot three or four times, assuring a quick death and no one would know exactly who fired the killing shot.

"Like the soldier's firing squad," rationalized Blacktail.

The three men sitting around the campfire were sharing a bottle of Wild Turkey they happily accepted from the bartender in Paradise. They'd pretty much been inebriated ever since they helped hang the two Indians the court had turned loose. They believed the Indians had it coming but they also had to admit they felt better about it when drunk then sober.

"It was like that bartender knew what we'd done and was wantin' ta thank us," one of the men slurred as he took another pull off the bottle.

"Maybe he could tell by lookin' at us we ain't the type ta take no bullshit off no Injuns," said another, reaching for his turn at the booze.

The night air exploded with a blinding flash as rifle muzzles shot flame into the darkness. Gunshots splintered the silence and echoed through the night and across the Flathead, announcing the message of revenge.

Bodies jerked and twisted as lead slugs hit their mark. Wild Turkey flew into the air as if the bird on the bottle had come to life. Slurred words hung in the darkness, suspended in time before all went deathly silent.

"You think they are dead?" Whitefish asked, as the warriors approached the bodies strewn around the campfire.

"They are if everyone did what they were supposed to," answered Stryker.

When they reached the grotesquely contorted bodies there was little doubt the men were dead.

"Are you still going to scalp them?" Blacktail asked, looking at Whitefish.

Whitefish looked a little pale even standing in the shadows away from the fire. Another warrior stepped forward into the light.

"I brought these arrows from home. I say we stick one in each of the white men. When they are found, everyone will know we are not afraid to fight for our brothers."

Word of the lynching and the campfire killings quickly spread throughout the Flathead country. No one was more disturbed by the news than Ross Riley. As angry and empty as he felt about Larry's murder, he was not convinced Indians had killed Larry and he sure didn't want his son's death to lead to war between Indians and whites.

"There's no telling where it will stop if each side keeps retaliating," He said, hovering over a bowl of split-pea soup and ham hocks.

"Do you think the army will send in troops to try and stop the killing?" Sam asked, always concerned about having the cavalry snooping around.

"More likely they will send in the cavalry to protect the settlers," Lillian quipped. "If the army sends troops here it will be to kill Indians, not talk to them."

"There's an odd irony," Ross said, becoming engaged in the conversation. "The mission schools are teaching young Indians to speak English, yet the only thing that has kept the Indians across the west from organizing and becoming a force as powerful as the Confederacy, is that most of the tribes have their own languages. If they all have a common language and realize their real enemy is the white man and not each other, things could be very different."

"But wouldn't that be bad for us?" Ruth asked, mildly interested.

"If things get worse on the reservation it will be bad for us anyway," Ross said. "To the whites we'll be seen as 'Indian lovers' and to the Indians we'll be 'whites'."

"But we've always been friends to the Indians. Do you really think they would burn us out or kill us?" There was a hint of sadness in Ruth's voice.

"I don't think we'd be among the first," Ross replied. "I think newer settlers are in more danger, unless some of the established places all ready have a history with the Flatheads."

"You mean like the Johnstons." Lillian interjected with a sense of satisfaction.

"Enough about the Johnstons," Ruth said with the first hint of a smile since Larry's death, "they are hard-working, god-fearing people."

"I'm sure Missus Johnston is hard working but I doubt its God she fears," Lillian stated with a grin.

"Is there anything we need to be doing to protect ourselves?" Sam asked, anxious to get Lillian off the subject of the Johnstons and feeling a sense of urgency as well.

"I don't think there's much we can do," Ross replied. "I think we need to stay close to the ranch for a while. I'm guessing the Flatheads will be looking more to ambush than attack."

The words were music to Ruth's ears. Ever since her devastating attack, she lived with fear, anger and guilt, not necessarily in that order. When she replayed the ordeal in her mind it only made her feel worse, from physically ill to uncontrollably angry and sometimes even guilty. The guilt came from the tormented belief that had she looked different or done something differently she would not have been attack. Deep down, she knew it wasn't her fault but that was little comfort to her.

And there were the dreams, the horrible dreams.

There were times when Ruth was alone that her desire for vengeance, the urge to take the shotgun and ride into Paradise and blow a hole in Clarence Hobbs, was nearly overwhelming. All that stopped her was the knowledge that killing Hobbs would mean everyone would know about her disgrace. She also knew some people would blame her, and she might even be charged with murder since there was no way to prove what he did. And there was Ross, she wasn't sure he could deal with it and even if he could, she didn't want him to have to.

At the Jocko Agency concern was growing. The Ghost Dance was becoming prevalent throughout the Flathead Reservation and violence was being driven by revenge killings and, some believed, the Ghost Dance. After all, the dance was a concern before the killing started. The council at Jocko knew the Ghost Dance was not a problem unique to the Flathead. It seemed every reservation west of the Missouri was experiencing the same revelation; Indians didn't want to work the farms, go to school or to church…they only wanted to dance.

Neither the council nor the reservation court could agree on what should be done. The court had already banned the dance on the reservation but the council believed, if left alone, most would soon tire of the dance.

"The Ghost Dance is a religion," Billy Condon, a council member expounded. "No different from Catholic or Methodist or Mormon… well, maybe a little different than Mormon," he added, smiling. "Religion is a belief and like any belief the more you oppose it the more people will believe in it," Billy continued. "We need to be concerned about the violence but I don't think one has anything to do with the other."

"I think we need to find out what other reservations are doing," said Tommy Rainwater. "I know they have problems on the Rose Bud, Cheyenne River and Pine Ridge reservations. There is some talk that Red Cloud and Sitting Bull are supporting the Ghost Dance."

The discussion within the council continued until it was agreed that as soon as the winter snow melted, they would send a delegation of three to Pine Ridge and the Sioux Nation. Billy Condon, who was most curious about the Ghost Dance, agreed to travel to Nevada and the Walker Lake Reservation where some believed the dance originated.

There was nothing to do now but try to control the vengeful mood on the reservation and wait for the time of water grass.

Chapter Thirty-two
Lost and Found

Daniel and Joe woke up the next morning at the Wishbone mansion with a hangover, in the same bed and with no memory of how they got there. Both felt a little better when they realized they were still fully dressed, less their boots. Still, the sight of the other's head lying on the next pillow sent the young soldiers clawing their way out of bed faster than a mongoose in a snake pit.

"What the hell are ya doin' in my bed, Daniel?!" Joe yelped, as he scrambled to his feet.

"Your bed my ass!" countered Daniel. "Look around ya, your room ain't been this clean since ya moved in."

They left the room grumbling, and started down the stairs stepping softly as if each step harbored a coiled rattler waiting to strike.

"I hate ta bring it up Daniel, but I think ya forgot your bedroom is on the main floor."

Daniel abruptly felt chagrin.

"Well, how'd your room get so clean?" he asked in defense.

"Ah cleaned it myself hopin' we'd find a woman at the post. Do ya think we did, Daniel?" Joe plaintively asked.

Indignant, Daniel said, "If'n we did I'd shor' like ta know why I was sleepin' with you?"

On the bottom step of the stairway, a bottle of Jack Daniels sat empty, a discarded cap lying next to it on the floor.

"I paid uh whole dollar for that bottle uh Tennessee Whiskey at the Tradin' Post. It said right on the bottle it was Daniel's so I felt compelled ta do so." Daniel realized he was still drunk. "But who drunk it all? There must be uh woman in this here house somewhere."

The whole conversation struck Joe's funny bone. Only slightly less drunk, he broke into laughter and every time Daniel added another comment the laughter grew more raucous, until Joe sat down in the middle of the floor and pounded his sides like a goose preparing for take off. Eventually, pulling himself to his feet Joe turned his head, sniffing like a blind dog in a butcher shop.

"If'n there's uh woman in this here house I'll find 'er," he declared and set off like a beagle after a bone, giggling like a maniac.

Together, they searched the sprawling log house, bedrooms, pantries, root cellar, behind couches and under tables. There was no woman.

"Goldarn Daniel," Joe moaned. "We done drunk that whole bottle 'rselves, no wonder we ain't feelin' to perky. Still don't explain what ya was doin' in my bed though."

It was the worst winter either Daniel or Joe experienced. Not because of deep snow or freezing cold, but because each were at the propinquity of change.

Daniel was anxious, almost desperate to get back to Vancouver and start his life as a rich man while Joe dreaded the coming of spring and the likely end to his 'sweet duty'.

Winter on the Flathead was long. The unrest continued and there were more isolated killings on both sides. No settlers were burned out, no families were slaughtered but there was growing anger. A company of 7th Cavalry troops was sent to the Jocko Agency from Fort Benton to keep a lid on things.

For the Riley's, winter was especially difficult. It was the first winter without Larry, and Sam agreed to stay on although no one ever said it was because of Larry's absence. Concern over Indian trouble was never far from Ross's mind and Ruth was dealing with her own private hell.

She hadn't had anymore bad dreams but then it's pretty hard to dream if you can't sleep.

In a selfish way she was glad for winter and even the Indian troubles. Both kept Ross and Sam close to home and each day that she didn't have to worry about 'that man' the more she was able to recover emotionally, and not live in constant fear.

Ruth tried to concentrate on what was good in her life. There was much to be thankful for and that, she decided, should be her focus. She loved her husband. Ross had always been there for her. From those early days when they were two kids who fell in lust to what, over the years, grew into a deep and comfortable love.

She had a beautiful home with a gravity flow water system she loved almost as much as her husband. They owned a lovely ranch with many well-bred cattle and horses. And there was something else in which she was finding a source of joy and entertainment, with only a touch of sadness.

Watching Sam and Lillian was like having her own private stage play, one with a constantly changing script and backdrop. Sam, so adoring, so respectful and treating Lillian as if she were a porcelain doll and Lillian, who seemed in awe of him, his masculine stature, his horsemanship, and his gentleness.

Ruth hadn't said a word to Ross about the relationship growing before his eyes. Men, she thought…If romance were a poisonous snake they'd all be dead. But even Ruth didn't know how far Sam and Lillian's romance had gone.

Lillian was never far from Sam's mind no matter where on the ranch he was or what task he was tending and she looked for any excuse to be with him. Wherever he was she wanted to be, what ever he was doing, she wanted to do.

It had been a typical Montana winter, cold, snowy and long, but Chinook winds were blowing out of the southwest promising change. Sam and Lillian were in the tack room cleaning and greasing harnesses. It was a tedious, dirty task and one Lillian would never have entertained had it not afforded the opportunity to be with Sam.

The smelly, sweaty harness, stained with streaks of gray and brown from the salty sweat of Jim and Jake, needed to be tended to every winter. Sam appreciated the job; it was out of the wind and weather and he liked the smell of boot oil and bear grease. Once finished with that job there were saddles and bridles to be soaped and cleaned. It was all part of ranch work, all part of what he loved, but to be able to do it next to the girl, who had grown before his eyes into the most beautiful woman he could imagine, was truly bliss. For Samuel DeSoto life was good. He touched the amulet under his flannel shirt.

"Hey boss, one more set of harness and we're ready to hook up Jake and Jim," he expounded.

Lilly's big blue eyes twinkled and her white teeth gleamed as she flashed him a smile that threatened to melt the nearest glacier.

"We're doing good….maybe one of us deserves a reward." Her eyes were saying what her words did not.

It was Sam's turn to smile. Setting down his cleaning rag he took her hands and pulled them up to the back of his neck.

"Maybe we both do," he said.

Lilly rose up on her toes as he wrapped his arms around her and lowered his lips to hers, their warm fullness inviting him for more. It was a long gentle kiss and she trembled at the feel of his rock-hard body. Her tummy felt like a hundred butterflies were fluttering around inside.

The kiss lingered, between nibbles, giggles, and gasps for air, and he was aware of every inch of her firm young body as she pressed against him. Gradually, his hands moved down her back toward her bubble-shaped buttocks. When he reached the rise at the small of her back he paused, raising his lips from hers and looked into her dreamy eyes. Lilly slowly turned away, never letting go of the bodily contact, and leaned back into him. Taking his hand in hers she slid them to her flat tummy then bit by bit upward, dragging the loose-fitting dress along with them. As she moved his hands closer to her firm young breasts, her dress was pulled to mid-thigh.

A rumble of hooves on frozen ground, the jangle of spurs and the snorting and blowing of horses interrupted their mid-day interlude. Looking out the tack room window, they were surprised to see a dozen or so mounted soldiers.

Cavalry!

To Sam, the sight was a rude reminder of his past…a past he had hoped was behind him. To Lillian it was frightening. She had never seen soldiers before and they looked foreboding, even imposing.

"What are soldiers doing here Sam?" she whispered, afraid they might hear her.

"No se, I do not know," Sam replied, but wondered if he did.

"Maybe it's about Larry," Lillian said, "or maybe they want to talk to Dad about the Indians."

I hope so, Sam thought.

Her curiosity piqued, Lillian asked, "Shall we go see?"

Sam felt sick.

"You go ahead. I think I will stay here and finish the harness."

He knew it was lame but it was the only thing he could do.

"If you're staying out here then I'm staying out here," she pouted.

Sam was nervous as a fly at a frog-jumping contest. He feverishly cleaned and polished the final harness as the cavalry mounts stomped and snorted at the hitching post in front of the house. The McClellan saddles reminded him of the officer's saddle with the initials of Ben Denton branded on the saddlebags stashed under his bed in the bunkhouse.

The longer the soldiers stayed in the house the more Sam recognized how foolish he was to think the army would forget about him, and to think he had almost worked up the courage to ask Lillian to marry him. This reality check confirmed to him how unfair such a proposal would be. Even if Lilly said 'yes' he couldn't give her a life. He was a deserter and they would never stop looking for him.

If only she would go in the house, he thought…I could make and run for it then when they come to get me they will find only an empty barn.

"We are almost done here Lillian. You go find out what the soldiers want while I finish up."

He was about as coy as a fox in a chicken coop.

Lillian never had a chance to answer before the soldiers emerged from the house. One with silver bars on his hat and shoulders shook hands with Ross and gave Ruth a formal hug.

Lillian gave Sam a perplexed look of confusion, which was absolutely nothing compared to what he was feeling.

"Why is a soldier hugging my mom?" she muttered.

Sam wanted to tell her to go find out but it was too late for him to run. The soldiers mounted up and rode back the way they came while Sam struggled to preserve his deteriorating composure.

"Let's go find out," Lillian said with the enthusiasm of a child on Christmas morning.

Sam was out of options and followed her toward the house, feeling more like a turkey on Thanksgiving day. Opening the door for Lillian, Sam followed her into the house to find Ross and Ruth sitting at the dining table engaged in a somber conversation. When Ross saw them, he motioned for them to sit.

"We have some bad news and we need to talk," he said, showing little emotion. "We just learned that your mother has suffered another loss. It isn't anyone you knew but it is quite a shock to your mother."

Ruth rubbed her eyes, blinking away the moisture that threatened to turn to tears.

"I had brothers," she began. "One left home when I was four or five. I hardly remember him but the other didn't leave until I was around twelve. After your dad and I got married and came west, I never expected to see or hear from them again. It turns out they're both dead, supposedly killed by Indians."

"When did they die, where are the buried?" Lillian asked, pensively.

"That seems to be a mystery," Ross said as Ruth sat passively. "It seems they went on patrol to check out some Indian problems and never returned.

Sam was suddenly all ears. This was sounding awfully familiar… too familiar.

"Do you know where this happened?" he asked.

"That's the crazy part," Ruth replied. "Apparently Lance, the oldest, was a colonel in command of a fort only a couple hundred miles west of here. It was called Fort Okanogan.

Sam felt the blood drain from his head….so they were here looking for him. Had the Riley's lied for him? His head was spinning. Colonel Wolard was Ruth Riley's brother.

It was too much.

"So both of your brothers were in the army and stationed at the same fort?" Lillian wondered.

"No," Ross interjected. "That's the part we need to talk to you and Sam about."

Sam opened his mouth to offer some explanation but no words could excuse the position he put them in…he remained silent.

"It seems," Ruth began, "that Roy -- by the way I named that bay horse after him -- was a rancher but was on some kind of special assignment with the army when he and Lance went missing. They've been gone for over a year and the army now considers them 'missing and presumed dead'.

Through a trace of Lance's records they found that my mother and father in Missouri are also dead and that I am the legal heir to Roy's ranch."

Ross looked directly at an obviously shaken Sam.

"It looks like we're going to be cutting the size of our herd on the Running R, Sam. That means we won't need you here any longer." Ross waited for the words to settle.

Lillian bristled, her dark-blue eyes fading to icicle-blue.

"Why, Daddy?" she blurted, her mouth one jump ahead of her brain. "I love him. I don't want him to lea…." She tried to swallow her words but it was too late.

"Then maybe you'll have to go with him, but we need Sam to run the Wishbone Ranch, at least for now if you're willing to take the job." Ross smiled. "We're going to cut our operation here because of the Indian problems, keep things a little closer to home and take the rest of the herd to Wishbone. It seems because Roy is 'presumed dead' the next of kin have to take possession of his ranch, or the army is obligated to auction it off. We're planning to go look at the place right away. From what the captain who delivered the papers says, it doesn't sound like a place we want to let go.

"The Wishbone is also on a reservation so we think it's smart to split the herd so we can keep the stock close. No decisions are final until we have a look at the place but it's over twenty thousand acres with a house and barns, apparently even a few cattle. It sounds pretty nice."

"It will be the only memory of my brothers I have," Ruth spoke as if in a trance.

Sam was not only speechless, his mind was like cold molasses. He couldn't get past the incongruity of it all. After running so far, trying so hard to put his past behind him, he finds himself in the home of the sister of the Colonel Wolard. Now he had an offer of a great job, one he knew he had to accept but it was back on the doorstep of the very fort he was running from. He thought about Major Denton.

"Who is in command of Fort Okanogan now?" Sam asked, trying to sound nonchalant.

"Captain said there is no longer a Fort Okanogan. He thought it was burned by Indians."

"It sounds like there is more Indian trouble there than here," Sam surmised. "If the fort was burned, did anyone get killed?"

Sam knew he was asking too many questions.

"There's Indian trouble everywhere but it will pass," Ross said. "I just hope it gets settled with as little killing as possible, as for killings at Fort Okanogan, he didn't say."

Lillian was playing catch-up.

"I can't believe I had a rich uncle and didn't even know it," she fussed.

"I can't believe my brothers were living within two hundred miles and I never knew it," Ruth lamented.

"So when do we leave?" Lillian asked, having returned to her feisty, energetic self. She hoped her dad had forgotten about her outburst.

"Well," Ross began, "your mom and I are going to go take a look while you and Sam watch over things here. But first, what is this about love? Is there something you want to tell me?" Ross was stern but not angry.

Lillian looked at Sam, they both looked at Ruth. Now Ross was looking at Ruth.

"Did you know? Was anyone ever going to talk to me?"

Ruth quietly replied, "They spoke to me, yes, but I was waiting to see if it was simply infatuation or if it might be more serious."

"And?" Ross hung the question.

"And," Ruth repeated, "I think it's time you talk to both of us," Ruth said, addressing Sam and Lillian.

Sam was caught in a personal tug-a-war.

"Before coming here the only woman I ever loved was my mother. I feel that same kind of love for you Señora Riley," Sam said and took a deep breath. "The love I feel for Lillian is much different, like what I think you and Señor Riley must feel for each other." He looked squarely at Ruth then Ross. "I love everything about your daughter. I love the way she walks, the way she talks, the sound of her voice, the way she thinks and what she believes in."

He looked at Lillian. "Estoy enamorado do ti, I'm in love with you, Lillian," he said. "I want to ask you to marry me," he said, taking her hand. "But I cannot, I am not good enough for you and can never give you the kind of life you deserve."

Lillian threw her arms around Sam's neck.

"I love you, too, Sam and if you ask me, I will marry you. I love you!"

Ruth's eyes filled with tears and Ross was looking at Lillian and Sam the way a horse trader might study the conformation of a new colt.

"Whoa," Ross said. "When did all of this happen?"

He didn't care who answered the question, he just wanted an answer.

Sam spoke first. "For me sir, it was the first time I saw Lillian. I knew she was just a girl but she looked like the most beautiful woman in the world to me."

Ross looked at Ruth. She puckered her lips and shot him a quizzical look.

"I didn't see it until Larry told me," she said with a bittersweet tone. "I think that was when his collar bone was broken."

"I don't know when I knew I loved you," Lillian said. She was looking at Sam but was clearly speaking for everyone's benefit.

"Maybe when you first told me about the black wolf and shared your secret about that strange valley in the Pasayten. Maybe when you kissed me the first time, the day Larry…," she paused, "went missing. All that matters to me is that I love you."

Ross was staring at Ruth. He knew this day would come but he never gave it much thought. He always expected Larry to marry first… proof that life is not played by any rules. He had thought at times how lucky the man would be who captured his daughter's heart, but he certainly never expected his wife would bring that man home with her after some altercation on the way home from town.

"I admit I was trying to have a little fun at your expense, Sam. The truth is, Ruth and I were planning to ask you if you wanted to stay on even before we knew about Wishbone," Ross said, his mood was serious. "With Larry gone we need help with the Running R, and now with the Indian issues I should spend time closer to home. You and Lillian seem to work well together, maybe now I know why, and we thought it could be a good deal for you and us."

Ross leaned back in his chair, lifting the two front legs off the floor, and his disposition seemed to lighten.

"Now it seems we have another matter to resolve," he said, then went silent for a moment, gathering thoughts or replaying past memories.

"If you two love each other and the only thing keeping you apart is you believing you're not good enough, let me give you a brief lesson in life and love."

Ruth was looking at her husband like she was seeing him for the very first time. She thought...He sounds sentimental, almost romantic.

"No man worth his salt ever believes he's good enough for the woman he wants to marry. If he did, he wouldn't be. What a woman deserves is to be loved, treated with respect and to always know there is no one in the world more important than her. Don't drop out of the race because you think someone else has a faster horse. Ride the race of your life like a winner and you will be." Ross dropped his chair back on four legs. "You have my permission to ask her, so do you want to marry the girl or not?"

Ruth was crying and laughing at the same time. Last year was easily the worst year of her life but she clung to the knowledge that gardens grow best when fertilized. It was spring, a time for last winter's dead grass to live again. Flowers would soon be blooming and the bleakness of winter not long remembered.

"Will you marry me?" Sam asked, looking into the bluest eyes he had ever seen.

"Yes, I will marry you, Sam, but there are two conditions." Lillian was smiling ear to ear.

"I agree to them…what are they?" Sam had never been so happy, but it was a scary happy.

"That you call me Lilly or freckles, or any other pet name you want and that you never again say you're not good enough for me."

"It is a deal…Freckles," Sam somberly replied.

The rest of the day was euphoric on the Running R. Ruth was happy for the first time since Larry died and probably for a while before that. She had lost Larry and nothing could take away the heartache of losing a child, but Sam had become like a son to her and the idea of his actually being part of the family went a long way toward filling that void. She was so pleased with the way Ross handled the whole 'proposal' situation. She was reminded of the sensitive, strong man she fell in love with so many years ago.

Ruth and Lillian began planning the wedding. There was no family to invite but they did have friends. It would be a small wedding right there on the Running R. They would go to Kalispell or Thompson Falls and buy a beautiful wedding dress, white with a long train that would be held up off the floor by the Polson twins, Peggy and Polly. They were so cute at four years old with long blond ringlets. The image made Lilly giddy.

Ross and Sam were talking business, ranching, Indians and other manly topics but were frequently interrupted by Ruth and Lillian, sometimes with questions about the wedding, and sometimes just to steal a touch or a kiss. Ross harbored questions about Sam's past, especially after he left California, but decided this wasn't the time to pursue the matter.

The wedding wasn't the only thing Ruth was planning. She was feeling great, like she hadn't felt for months. She was going to treat Ross the way a good man deserved to be treated…the way she had been unable to for way too long. She could hardly wait for bedtime.

Spring came and with it the buttercups, daisies and a contingent from the 7th Cavalry; the first soldiers Daniel or Joe had seen in over two years. It also brought the legal heirs to the Wishbone Ranch and the end to Joe and Daniel's 'sweet duty' tour.

After informal introductions, Corporal Bone took Ruth and Ross on a tour of the impressive ranch house. By the end of the tour, Ruth wanted to move. The house, while not quite a large as their home at the Running R, was unbelievably elegant, especially considering it was designed by Roy and built mostly by Indian laborers.

It had a lovely view of the river, a gravity flow water system similar to the one at the Running R, upstairs bedrooms, a master bedroom downstairs, lofts, and the most beautiful rock floor in the den she'd ever seen, made from flat slabs with an array of blues, greens and browns speckled with what looked like gold, and two river-rock fireplaces.

And it was two hundred miles from Paradise and Clarence Hobbs!

Ross was anxious to see the rest of the ranch so Daniel and Joe saddled a couple horses. They would be guides for Ross while Ruth opted to stay and familiarize herself with the house.

Part of the soldiers accompanied Daniel, Joe and Ross while the remainder stayed at the house with Ruth. She found little in the house that reminded her of the brother she remembered. It was obvious his tastes had improved since leaving the Missouri farm. She wasn't surprised there was not a lot of furniture, but there were some nice pieces…even dishes and wine goblets. She wondered where he found all the beautiful things. As much as she was impressed and a delighted with what she inherited, she was more curious about her brother. What did Roy do to own such a lovely house and ranch? There was obviously no wife, if there was any woman at all.

Ruth couldn't help wondering if Roy or Lance might still be alive. The army said no bodies were found and that they were with a thousand soldiers led by Lance who simply went out on patrol and never returned. The story itself was unbelievable.

Ross was enamored with the Kartar Valley with lush blue-bunch wheat grass and fescue and small ponds scattered about like sapphires tossed on a carpet of green. The valley was encased by imposing rock walls on two sides, a lake on one end and a river on the other.

A perfect ranch site, he thought. They found a few cattle scattered about but unfortunately, all of the male calves were now young bulls. Ross shook his head as he tried to imagine the mess that could mean.

He'd seen enough; this was definitely something he and Ruth would want to keep. Wishbone had a nice ring to it. He even thought he understood where the name came from. The valley was actually shaped like a wishbone with rimrock along either side, beginning at the lake, and fanning out to end near the river. Ross' smile faded when he considered how much Larry would have loved this place. For a moment he thought he heard the mournful howl of a distant wolf.

"Must be a high wind," he muttered, but the air was dead calm.

Daniel and Joe were relieved to get out of the house and away from Ruth Riley. Not because she was unkind or rude but because neither of them had been within a stones throw of a woman for over three years, and both men immediately recognized that Ruth Riley was not just a woman, she was the most beautiful woman either of them had ever seen.

It was unnerving, embarrassing and a bit ironic that they had given little thought to women while at Fort Okanogan or here at the Wishbone until the last few months. Being so close to a real woman, one with class, who smelled good and looked even better, was proving difficult. Neither Daniel nor Joe ever saw a woman in snug-fitting riding pants and the effect was obvious, too obvious. They spent a lot of time with their backs to her or holding their hats in front of them in what they hoped was seen as a show of respect.

By the time Ross and the group returned from looking over the ranch, Ruth had taken a bath and changed out of her riding pants. She had others with her but after a bath she always felt better in a dress. She was anxious to talk to Daniel and Joe about her brothers. However, though the two men had been stationed at Fort Okanogan under Lance's command and had seen Roy around, they didn't know him.

"Officers and enlisted men don't spend much time socializin', Ma'am," Daniel said nervously, "especially not a colonel. He was a good commander, though. Things kinda' went ta hell…'scuse me, Ma'am, went sideways after the colonel never come back."

Daniel was flustered and his red face was harder to hide than, well…, he was flustered.

What Ruth did learn was that Roy was simply known around the fort as 'the colonel's rich brother', and that he was raising beef for the army.

Daniel described Lance and Roy the best he could remember emphasizing that they were "proud and important men". He also told her of their attempt to find the colonel and his men and how the trail had ended at a huge rock bluff.

"Damn-dest thing ah ever seen, Ma'am, if'n ya'll pardon me. Shouldn't uh been too surprise though. We was up in them mountains what the Inju…Indians call Pasayten. Damn scary place that Pasayten! There's people in them mountains the Indians call *Choo-pin-it-pa-loo*. They say it means 'People of the Mountains' but ta me it means 'scary as hell', pardon my language, Ma'am."

When Ruth asked how he and Joe happened to stay behind to watch Roy's ranch, Daniel volunteered his story of how he found the saddle bags full of gold and that the major and lieutenant kept their word and now he would be rich once he got back to Fort Vancouver.

She was happy for Daniel, sad for Joe who was obviously going to be lost without him and sorry neither knew more about her brothers. However, it was more than she had known before. She silently questioned how her brothers could have left the farm years apart yet somehow ended up in this remote country together, one wealthy, the other a respected military officer.

"Is there an office or someplace my brother might have kept personal papers or belongings?" she aksed.

She had not seen an office but a splendid house like this surely had one.

Ross returned from the Kartar Valley tour with one question. "Either of you boys have any idea why Indians would burn down the fort but not this house? It is on the reservation, isn't it?"

"Well, Sir, they damn near did! Fire burned right ta the top uh that rim," Daniel said, pointing out the window. "Then the wind changed an' we was saved."

He purposely left out the part about the Indian at the river.

"But Indians never actually came here to set the house on fire," Ross pressed.

"No, sir, I think them Injuns kinda liked Roy. I know he gave 'em beeves."

"Sounds like a smart man," Ross said, smiling at Ruth. "I wish I'd known him."

"About that office, Ma'am," Daniel volunteered. "It's in the loft…it's locked. Me an' Joe got uh key but we never went in there. The lieutenant told us ta take care uh the house but stay out uh the office."

"I'd like to look in there if you don't mind," Ruth said.

She smiled and Daniel thought the rapid acceleration of his heart just took ten years off his life.

The office was no different from the rest of the house. The floors were the same type rock as in the den. There was an oak desk under a window that looked out over the valley. To the right of the door, mounted on the wall, was the biggest mule deer buck Ruth had ever seen.

"Ross," she called, "you're going to want to see this."

After a half-hour of oooh's and ahhh's and counting points on the huge antlers, Ross and the rest of the men who came to look departed, and Ruth turned her attention to the oak desk. Grasping a drawer handle she pulled. It was locked.

"I don't suppose you have a key for the desk." She queried Daniel, who lingered behind the other men.

"No, Ma'am, it wouldn't surprise me none if'n he had that with 'im when them Injuns got 'im."

"That would be *Indians*, Daniel, and you don't know for sure what or who got him, do you?" Ruth was a little stern and Daniel was sure he just lost another ten years.

"Keep this up an' I won't live long enough ta enjoy my wealth," he muttered under his breath.

Ruth went back over Daniel's story.

"So all the soldiers except you and Joe went back to Vancouver before Fort Okanogan was burned?"

"Yep," he replied.

"Is there anyone at the mission, or trading post you mentioned, who might have known either of my brothers?"

"I don't think so, Ma'am. That priest from the mission was with 'em when they vanished. But ya know what, Ma'am? There was one man who didn't vanish an' he come back ta the fort. Guess ya could say he was the sole survivor uh that massacre or whatever happened."

"Really? You mean he was with Lance and Roy when they vanished?!" Ruth asked. "Why haven't you mentioned this man before? How can I find him?"

She moved closer to Daniel and he felt beads of sweat popping out on his forehead. It began trickling down his cheeks and his hands got wet and clammy.

"Ain't nobody asked, an' I didn't know it would matter ta ya." Daniel was completely flustered. "There was uh Injun come ta the fort, too. Damn near killed Joe an' scared me uh inch short uh dead."

"Calm down," Ruth said, startled. Daniel was beginning to act rather oddly. "Take a deep breath and tell me what you know. If I don't believe you it will be my problem. If there is a chance there is someone alive who knows what happened to my brothers, I have to try and find him."

"I reckon he'll be plenty hard ta find, Ma'am. He came back from that patrol ridin' like the devil hisself was hot on his tail an told 'bout how Injuns come out uh the sky an' started killin' soldiers. Said they was all dead but him, that he got away an' never stopped runnin' 'til he got ta the fort."

Daniel was shaking when he finished his narrative, and when Ruth touched his hand he figured death must be right around the corner.

"It's alright Daniel, just take your time."

She was on the verge of jumping out of her skin.

"Where is this man now?" she asked anxiously.

"I don't know Ma'am, I doubt anyone does. The major wanted him ta take uh patrol back ta where he last seen the colonel. Reckon he didn't like that idea much 'cause that night he stole the major's horse an' took off, an' ain't no one seen 'r heard from 'im since."

"Did you know the man's name or anything about him?" Ruth was mesmerized.

"Didn't know him very well, kinda stuck ta hisself, never drank 'r nothin' with the rest uh us. He was uh corporal like me. We had guard duty uh few times together, seemed like uh reg'lar guy 'till that night. I reckon what ever it was he seen made 'im crazy. One thing I do know, if'n the major ever finds 'im, he'll be lookin' down the barrel of uh firin' squad."

"What was the man's name Daniel?" Ruth asked again impatiently.

"Sam, Corporal Samuel DeSoto."

It was Ruth's turn to sweat.

Chapter Thirty-three

Wishbone

"Lillian," Sam began tentatively. "I knew your uncles. Not well, but Lance was my commanding officer and I remember seeing Roy around the fort. I was with them when it happened. The story I told you about that valley, where I got this." He pulled the amulet from his shirt. "That was where your uncles died. I saw it happen."

It was all coming back to him like a giant wave, the fear, the guilt and shame, the unbelievable spectacle of mounted warriors descending from the clouds, the carnage. Lilly's uncles, Ruth's brothers, were among those killed by that ungodly Indian armada.

"Didn't you tell anyone? Didn't the army go back there to see if anyone was alive?" Lillian asked, puzzled.

"I did tell them, Lillian, but they wanted me to lead them back to the valley and I was afraid…I was a coward. I was certain they were all dead and I knew if I went back I would be dead, too."

Sam was feeling incredibly unworthy of the trust placed in him by the Riley's and undeserving of the love of this beautiful young woman and unable to do anything about it.

"From what you've told me, how could you be certain they were all dead? What if some were taken prisoner? They could still be alive." Her tone was not critical but anxious.

For Sam every question, every word was like swallowing the bitter taste of truth.

"Looking back more than two years later I can see I was wrong. I was running for my life and away from something that seemed worse than death. You have not heard the sound of a man's soul being ripped from his body and I can not explain it." Sam was defensive and remorseful.

"Did you actually see either of my uncles killed? Were they shot by guns or with arrows, were they killed with tomahawks or spears?" Lillian was pushing and Sam was more uncomfortable with each question.

"No," he admitted, "but those Indians had fire in their eyes and there were thousands of them, no one could have survived." His discomfort was bleeding into agitation.

"Sam," Lillian sensed it was time to steer the discussion in a different direction, "tell me again about the dance the Indian did. Do you think that dance and the dance the Flatheads are all worked up about could have any connection?"

"I do not know, I have not seen it, but maybe I should," Sam replied, struck with an epiphany. The thought that there could be a connection never occurred to him.

"Dad says they're dancing day and night at the agency."

"Do you want to take a little, ride? We can be to the agency and back before your parents, return."

Sam had to know…if the dance followed him from the valley, the Indians could not be far behind.

Ruth ushered Corporal Daniel Bone out of the office and closed the door, locked it and put the key in her pocket. She needed to get her thoughts and emotions sorted out. Sam had told her about the mysterious valley and how he snatched the amulet and ran for his life but it was only a story…until now…now, it was personal.

Sam was there when her brothers died…or disappeared. She had questions about his story and wanted explanations. She wanted to see for herself but even Daniel told her the trail ended at a rock wall.

"There's nothing I can do about it right now," she muttered as she descended the staircase, hand holding firmly to the polished lodgepole banister.

It was late and she was looking forward to her first night in this extraordinary house. The master bedroom was off the den, with its own bathroom and the biggest four-poster bed she had ever seen. It had a feather mattress Roy must have had hauled in from Portland or Seattle, or maybe Spokane…a town they had just discovered was rapidly becoming the rail-hub of the northwest.

Ross lay down on the bed and watched Ruth undress in the soft lamplight. He felt the familiar tightening in his groin as she removed her dress then undergarments, revealing more and more of her exquisite body. He hoped she was in the mood to make their first night at Wishbone a memorable one.

When Sam and Lillian arrived at the agency, they were surprised to see how many Indians were dancing.

"I thought the agency court banned the dance," Sam said.

"I guess telling somebody to stop and making them stop are two different things," Lillian replied. Then asked, "Does it look like the dance you saw in the valley?"

"No estoy seguro, I am not sure," Sam said. "In the valley there was solamente bailarin, one dancer, and what I remember most was the way that Indian held his amulet out like he was calling on God or the spirits."

Sam pulled the amulet from his shirt and concentrated on the occasional lone dancing Indian.

After a couple minutes, he said, "If I had to guess. I would say it is the same. It is hard to tell with those holding hands in a ring, but with the individuals it looks similar, except for the amulet."

"So what does that mean Sam? Are the Indians from that valley teaching these Indians to dance? Do you think they followed you here?"

Clearly, their trip to the Jocko Agency was producing more questions than answers.

"There were only two Indians and one white hombre who saw me in the valley. I have not seen either of them or believe me, I would know it. I see them clearly every time I close my eyes, but this is puzzling," Sam said, pointing to the dancers. "How can Indians here know about a dance I saw hundreds of miles away in a hidden valley. Maybe I am being paranoico, and only imagine it is the same dance." Sam sighed deeply. "One thing is for sure," he added. "This dance is not producing the same results."

Lillian's was puzzled.

"A white guy?" she questioned. "You never said anything about a white guy before. What would he be doing in some lost Indian village?"

"I do not know," Sam responded, chagrin. "I have been so concerned about the dancing Indian I forgot about the white hombre." Sam paused, "He is the one I took this amulet from."

"What made you so sure the white man wouldn't come after you?" Lillian wondered.

"I do not know. I guess because the dancing Indian looked like the one with the power. He was the one calling on God, or spirits…or something."

"And his amulet was just like yours?" Lillian asked.

"I guess," Sam said. "I did not see it up close but it was round and had a lobo painted on it. Now I am curious why the white hombre had this." He glanced down at the amulet. "I believe it is the only reason I escaped witih my life."

"If it got you out, maybe it could get you back in," Lillian surmised.

"That is a very bad idea!" Sam shuddered at the thought.

"Have you ever thought about what would happen if you did the dance? I mean, you do have the amulet, if that's what gave the dancing Indian his powers."

Another bad idea.

"I believe the amulet possesses powers I do not understand, but there is more than that. It scares me…I am afraid of having it and afraid to let it go."

"Could you find that valley again if you wanted to?"

"Maybe, but I do not want to!" Sam was emphatic on that score.

"But if you went back, maybe you could learn about the amulet and its powers?" Lillian was incorrigible. "Maybe you could find out what happened to my uncles."

"Maybe I would turn to stone or burst into flame or vanish into some unknown world."

Sam clearly had his spurs dug in on this whole line of thinking.

"Come on Sam," Lilly pressed. "I'd go with you."

A bad idea just got worse.

When morning came on the Wishbone, Ruth fixed biscuits and gravy for breakfast and Daniel and Joe thought they died overnight and woke up in heaven. It was partly the food and partly the idea of having a woman cook for them. Daniel decided what he was going to do with some of his gold….he was going to hire a wife.

Ross was also feeling chipper. After long months, Ruth was her sensuous, passionate self again and last night would be one he would remember for a while.

The lieutenant for Fort Benton was very interested in anything the two soldiers knew about the missing regiment. Unfortunately, all they knew was that the patrol sent out to find them lost the trail in a rock bluff.

"It was like they done rode right inta the mountain," Private Joe Wright insisted.

If either man knew more, they weren't saying.

"Is there any chance you might send out a patrol from Fort Benton to investigate?" Ross asked.

"No, it's really a matter for the 5th Cavalry to look into. After all this time I'd say it's been written off as an unsolved mystery. Trust me, it is not the only mystery the army has left unsolved.

The conversation ended and the detail from the 7th set about preparing for their return to Fort Benton. They would bivouac along the way, reaching the fort in five or six days if all went well.

Corporal Bone and Private Wright were also preparing for the long trip back to Fort Vancouver, but there were some details to be worked out. Ross and Ruth had a dilemma. Neither expected Wishbone to be so auspicious…especially the house, and they didn't want to leave it unattended yet they could only stay a few days. They had to get back home.

Home, Ruth thought, is where your heart is. It should be back on the Running R, my home for nearly twenty years, where we raised our family…and where we buried Larry.

She was in a quandary.

Her whole life was back at the Running R but there was something about this place. She could feel Roy's presence, especially in his office. Last night she awakened more than once expecting to see him standing over her. It wasn't a scary or creepy feeling, but warm and comforting. Of course she could only imagine what he might look like. Daniel gave her a rough description which was all she had to go on.

It didn't matter what he looked like. Ruth felt if she stayed here long enough, she would see him. It was perhaps the strangest feeling she'd ever had. It felt as if Roy's soul was near, searching for someone. And it was two hundred miles away from Clarence Hobbs. She wondered how much that was influencing her thinking.

"Is there an Indian agency somewhere on the reservation?" Ross asked Daniel.

"Yep, ya just missed it on your way here. It's 'bout ten miles from here. Ya go back up the river 'bout six 'r seven miles, then west 'bout three 'r four an' you're there. Cain't miss it, got uh wagon road right ta the front gate."

"You ever go there?" Ross asked.

"Nope, Injuns don't like whites much an' ah don't like them agency folks much neither."

Ross turned his attention to the lieutenant in charge of the detail.

"I'd like to request the army allow these two men to stay here for another month. It will take us that long to return to the Running R, move some of our stock here and get our hire…get our people here and set up."

"I don't see a problem," the lieutenant replied and informed an elated Private Wright and impatient Corporal Bone of the plan. "Your release date from this detail will be thirty days from today."

Ruth let the men talk and returned to Roy's office. She wanted to look around for a key to his desk. Where would he hide a key? Why would he hide a key? Maybe he did have it with him. She checked under the desk, under windowsills, above the door. It was too nice a desk to pry the drawers open, besides there might not be anything in there.

She sat in the high-backed leather chair and looked at the giant buck dominating one wall. Larry would have loved to hear the story behind that, she mused. Roy's presence was even stronger when she looked out the window over the Kartar Valley.

Ruth left the office, closed the door and made her way through the den into the large formal room then to the kitchen and finally outside. Bluebirds, robins and meadowlarks filled the soft air with chirps, tweets and warbles. The sweet smell of sage tickled her nostrils. It seemed so strange.

She never was close to her brothers. She didn't even remember Lance and Roy never seemed to notice she was alive. Now, after not thinking about him for fifteen years or more, Ruth was immersed in memories and it felt good. Ross was busy talking with the soldiers when Ruth decided to saddle Cocoa and take a short ride. It was time she saw more of Wishbone.

"And I don't have to worry about being alone," she whispered with a sigh of relief.

Riding through blanket of wildflowers and tall bunchgrass, Ruth was most impressed with the numerous ponds and small lakes she found. She would no more than lose sight of one and another would appear over the next rise.

Dropping into a hollow with yet another small lake offset by a half-dozen scattered aspen and a lone pine, Ruth decided to see if Cocoa wanted a drink. Riding into the shallow pond, she waited for the turbid water to settle. As the arch of gentle riffles subsided, her eyes were drawn to what appeared to be movement on the water's surface. At first, she thought it might be fish or some kind of floating vegetation. Letting the reins slide through her fingers, she gave Cocoa her head. As the chestnut drank, Ruth tried to focus on the image forming on the water.

She could see colors on the dark liquid surface that seemed to rise from beneath the still water. As the floating colors took shape, a bay horse and rider appeared. The horse looked like one of the raw-boned descendents of those left behind by the conquistadors. The rider looked small on the horse, his hair was blond and shoulder length; a handlebar mustache dominated his face. He seemed to stretch his legs and rock in the saddle then he looked directly at Ruth. His eyes were the color of robin eggs.

A shiver slithered down her back like a snake on a hot rock. She swallowed hard and gripped the saddle horn. Cocoa jerked her head up from drinking, her ears pointing intently toward the shimmering image.

It was gone!

Ruth sat shaken but not afraid.

"What was that?" she whispered to her alert mount. "I must be hallucinating."

Cocoa shook her head and returned to drinking. Ruth shuddered then laughed, scolding herself for an overactive imagination.

Chapter Thirty-four

Evidence

By time Sam and Lillian left the Jocko Agency Sam was convinced there was at least some connection between the dance he witnessed in the valley and what the Indians were doing, apparently all over. The only thing that seemed to be missing was the amulet...his amulet or one just like it.

"How could that dance get here?" he wondered out loud. "All the Indians in that valley would know about it. Maybe one of them is here on the Flathead."

Lillian didn't see what the big deal was about the dance. Indians were always dancing for some reason. Why was this any different?

Sam was rapidly becoming a wreck. This should be the happiest time of his life; he was engaged to marry the most beautiful girl he had ever seen, her parents were rich and he had a job. He might even get to run one of their ranches if things worked out in the Okanogan.

Maybe that was the problem...he was in denial. He had convinced himself he was no longer a wanted man, a fugitive, a deserter. The idea of moving back so close to that hidden valley of death and Fort Okanogan, from which he deserted, even if it was gone, was a grim reminder of his plight.

And there was something else...the amulet.

The strange piece of leather with the exquisite likeness of a black wolf painted on it was, at the very least, an uncommon display of artistic talent. At most...well, that was the troubling part. When he looked into its golden eyes he often felt like a sorcerer, that with a few magic words he might be capable of anything. But he didn't know the words. Perhaps they were hidden in the chants and songs of the dancing Indian.

"You've gotten awfully quiet."

Lillian's melodious voice startled Sam out of deep thought.

"I have been thinking," Sam responded.

"No kidding," Lillian acknowledged. "About me I hope," she teased.

"Si, sort of," he replied with a crooked grin.

"So whatchya' sorta' thinkin' about? Huh? huh?" She was playing with him now.

Sam was getting frustrated. Lilly wasn't taking any of this serious. Why should she? She was young and caefree, she just wanted to be happy. So do I, he thought, but I can not ignore reality. I have already done that for too long.

"I am thinking about this amulet," he finally replied. "This is going to sound loco, but what if that dance did follow the amulet here?"

He waited for a response from the red-haired beauty on the Palomino mare.

"Well, you're right, it sounds a little crazy. Besides, dad says this Ghost Dance is all over, on nearly all the reservations this side of the Missouri. You and that amulet haven't been to all of those places."

"You are right," Sam said, feeling relieved. "It was only a thought."

Still, he was convinced there was something he was missing. He was sure of it.

"I told you, I think you need to go back to that valley. It's where that thing came from. Maybe it scares you because it wants you to take it back. If it's as powerful as you think, somebody is surely missing it." Lillian's playful mood was gone.

Sam knew he was in trouble when that idea started making sense. He pondered her logic.

"You could be right, Freckles, but I sure would like to think of another way to unlock the mysteries of this little piece of leather."

"I told you...start dancing." She was grinning again.

"I have an idea but I will need your help," Sam hesitantly confided.

"I'll do anything you want, except return to the Bountiful Ranch," Lillian chirped.

"That is a thought I will spend some time on," he joked. "I can not make any promises about Bountiful."

Sam laid out his idea, and his theory, on the way back to the Running R while Lillian listened, skeptical but willing.

"It is not about me and it is only partly the amulet," he explained. "It is about that black wolf we saw. The one that rescued me from my captors, the one we saw in the trap. I believe what we saw was real, not an illusion, not an apparition but a powerful being. A god-like creature with powers unimaginable here on earth."

"So how do we find this monster wolf?"

"We do not, it will find us, but we must give it a chance."

"It sounds scary to me but I'm going to trust you…for now."

Sam was feeling much better about everything by time they reached the Running R. They unsaddled their horses and curried them, put away their gear and went to the house. It was late and they were both hungry; a late-night snack was in order.

Lillian fixed some corn fritters, fried some eggs and a couple slices of ham and they ate breakfast by moonlight. It was a warm night with a soft breeze as they ate, the resonant *whoo-whoo's* of a great gray owl reverberating under the porch roof. When they finished eating, they settled onto the porch swing. With one hand in her long hair and one on her cheek, Sam pulled her face gently toward his. The kiss was soft, gentle and lingering.

Lillian was filled with all the passion of a woman-child and Sam was, well, Sam was a hot-blooded Latino barely into his twenties. The kissing became more passionate, the touches more urgent. Lillian was wearing riding pants and a light summer top that buttoned up the front. Maneuvering for a comfortable position in the rocking swing, Sam's hand slipped over Lillian's breast, covered only by the thin material of her shirt and a lightweight brassiere.

He jerked his hand away as if it had just landed on a hot iron.

"Lo siento! I am sorry!" he blurted instinctively.

"Don't be sorry," she whispered. "It won't bite, but I probably should go in. We should save this for what happens later…after we're married."

"Absolutely," he said, scrambling out of the swing. "I am proud of you, of us. There is no one here to stop us yet we are doing the right thing. I think we will be very happy we waited."

Sam wondered who he was trying to convince.

"There hasn't been anyone here to stop us since the first time we met," Lilly cracked, "but I'm glad you understand. I really do want to wait but I don't think I could stop you if you wanted to now."

"Lilly, you know I would not force you," he said, almost hurt.

"Maybe what I mean is…I couldn't stop me if you really wanted to."

"Oh, I really want to but I can not and neither can you."

They left it at that.

When Sam walked to the bunkhouse, he savored the feel, the sensation of her breast. It was larger than he would have expected and soft, but he felt something hard too. He tried to picture what his hand had felt and concluded that it must have been part of her clothes.

Sleep was not a consideration. He was a twisting bundle of thoughts and feelings. He had a strange feeling his life was coming full circle; from nearly dying in that strange valley of ghostly warriors to unexpected and perhaps undeserved happiness back to apprehension for his happiness if not his life.

He didn't worry that anyone from his past would recognize him. His hair had grown from the close-cropped military cut to a shoulder-length mop of curls. His boyish, hairless face now sported the more un-kept look of a weeks worth of beard and a horseshoe mustache. He was twenty pounds heavier, thanks to the good cooking to which he had become accustomed. He wished he had changed his name. The thought never occurred to him when he first met Ruth, under the circumstances he was lucky to remember his.

It has to be all the talk about Wishbone and the unbelievable coincidence involving Ruth and her brothers, he surmised as he tossed and turned, unable to clear his mind.

The uncanny connection between the woman he'd come to think of as a second mother and the men with whom he witnessed the most chilling event of his life was, frankly, unnerving at best.

But there was more. Sam had a gnawing feeling that something very bad was about to happen. Without the benefit of an actual vision or dream he could only guess what the feeling might mean, an unwelcome meeting with a firing squad for desertion or a hanging tree for horse stealing were two possibilities he'd rather not envision.

Sam heard that men sometimes suffered serious doubts, even paranoia at the thought of getting married, but he was sure that was not the source of his anxiety. There was nothing he wanted more in this world than to marry Lillian.

"No, it is not that," he muttered, then cursed the moonlight seeping into the bunkhouse and his bedroom. "It always comes back to you." He was speaking to the amulet resting on his chest, willing it to speak to him. "What are you trying to tell me? Is it Ruth or Lillian? Is it something else?"

At breakfast, Sam enjoyed hash browns, scrabbled eggs and side-pork. He also took pleasure in the sight of his wife to be. Lillian was dressed in riding pants, a pullover top and her hair was pulled back into a waist-length ponytail. Her eyes this morning were that warm-blue that caused Sam's stomach to tingle.

"We must look inside that Bountiful barn," he said.

"And how do you propose we do that?" Lillian asked, as if she didn't want to know.

"I have not figured that out, but something is telling me there is information there that could help us find Larry's killer."

"Well, we can't just ask. We tried that and we don't have any evidence to go to the sheriff with." Lillian stated. "And it's not going to be easy to sneak in with a kid in every corner."

"You show me how to get there and I will find a way in."

Sam had an idea but no clue if it would work.

Once they passed onto Bountiful land, Sam pulled the unusual bronze colored Bigfoot to a halt. Pulling the amulet from around his neck, he began making small circles with it chest high in front of him. He didn't know any Indian chants but he hoped he wouldn't need them for what he had in mind. After ten minutes or more his confidence began to fade.

Bigfoot and Buttercup were the first to react. Their heads went up with ears aimed at a not yet visible target. Sam and Lillian looked hard in the direction the ears were pointing. At first they thought the sage was moving but it soon became clear there was a wolf pack, ten or fifteen strong, running through the mixed sage and grass and headed directly for them.

Sam continued to move the amulet in a circular motion while the pack kept its distance but moving at a steady pace. Lillian's eyes grew wide as Sam, while not chanting, did appear to be in some kind of trance.

"The wolves are headed toward Bountiful!" Lillian exclaimed.

Unexpectedly, the customary yipping and howling began. Maybe it was the mountains and meadow but to Lillian it sounded like the wolves were everywhere. As they neared the Bountiful ranch house, the pitiful bleeting of sheep joined the chorus of howling wolves. Sam pulled Bigfoot in and motioned for Lillian to hold up. They dismounted and tied their horses in the trees a couple hundred yard from the Johnston barn.

"Now we watch," he quietly stated.

They didn't have to wait long before an explosion of bodies, from young adults to a few barely old enough to run, burst into view. Some ran for the house, a few scurried into the barn and emerged with horses saddled while others delivered rifles to those already mounted. Finally, Jim Johnston rushed from the house, rifle in hand and climbed on a sorrel gelding.

The remaining Johnston's were ushered into the house like wayward chicks by Missus Johnston. When the door closed, Sam motioned to Lillian.

"Now is our chance. Look for Bodie or traps or anything that might have belonged to Larry."

Once inside the barn Sam was shocked. He had never seen such a menagerie. Rabbits, chickens, ducks, geese, goats, even pigs, but there was something else. In an obscure corner behind the pig pen was a wall about ten feet high with a single door…it was padlocked shut. Sam wondered why anyone would padlock a barn door, and looked around for a way over the wall. He found a sawhorse and placed it next to the wall. Standing on the horse, he could just see over the barrier. Inside was a ten-gallon wooden barrel with a copper tube extending up and leading outside through a hole in the barn wall.

At first glance, Sam thought it was some type of contraption used for making wine or moonshine. Working his way closer he could see there was a lid on the barrel and the pipes ran through tight-fitting holes on the side of the container near the top. He reached for the lid but Instinctively drew his hand back. To the right of the barrel a ladder led to a loft which he quickly ascended, and peaked into the loft.

Wolf hides were stacked in caped-out piles and forty or fifty traps were hung on the wall like silent harbingers of death. A half-dozen blue bottles sat on a shelf at eye level. Each bottle bore an imposing label; skull-and-crossbones painted in white.

Poison!

Sam hastily descended to the wooden barrel and cautiously lifting the lid, stared at its contents. Half-a-dozen traps were soaking in a clear odorless solution. Using a convenient wire hanging from a nail, he pulled a trap from the barrel and read the inscription…it was a number 5 Bridger spring leg-hold…like the one retrieved from the angry chimera, and poisoned Larry.

It was no surprise that Jim Johnston would hate wolves. He had a huge family to support and sheep contributed greatly to the family income. But why poison them? Sam did not doubt what was in the blue bottles and the wooden barrel.

Strychnine.

It was vented out of the barn because ingesting the fumes could kill you. Looking at the poison trap in his hand, Sam was glad he was wearing gloves.

"As long as I do not wipe my mouth or my eyes I am safe," he told himself to reinforce the thought.

Climbing back into the loft he worked his way over the wall and down onto the sawhorse. He looked around for Lillian who was exiting an enclosed room at the far end of the barn. Leaving the poison cask with evidence in hand he met Lillian part way.

"I found out who is setting the poisoned traps," he said in a loud whisper.

He noticed that Lillian was pale, her face so drawn and somber even her freckles looked white.

"What is the matter, Lilly? What did you find?"

"Larry's saddle is in there," she replied weakly, pointing to the room she just came out of. "How could he have Larry's saddle unless he killed him?"

Lilly was struggling to hold back her tears.

"Ivamos! Let's go! We must get out of here. This trap is enough evidence to bring the sheriff back. We do not want Senior Johnston to catch us here."

Leaving the way they entered, they ran to their waiting horses and swiftly mounted. Once safely off Bountiful land Sam asked, "Why would Senior Johnston want to kill Larry? It seems like he has enough trouble taking care of his family."

Lillian had successfully held back the tears and was now angry.

"The only thing that makes any sense is that Larry discovered who was putting out the poison traps and confronted Johnston. I don't think Johnston could have killed Larry face to face. One of his kids probably ambushed him from the barn. It's going to be hard to prove who actually murdered him."

"I do not think it will matter," Sam replied. "Senior Johnston should be responsible for anything that happens on his land. Even if one of the boys did the shooting it was probably at Johnston's direction."

Sam was no barrister but if logic meant anything, Jim Johnston was guilty of murder.

"I didn't see Bodie anywhere. What would he have done with Larry's horse?"

"Maybe sold him, or maybe one of them was riding Bodie when they went after the wolf pack."

Sam was sure they would know all the answers as soon as they got the sheriff to Bountiful.

"The wolves, Sam, how did that happen? How did you know they'd be here and how did you know Johnston and all his able-bodied off-spring would go running after them?" Lillian was regaining her composure, her anger now tempered by curiosity.

"It is the amulet," Sam replied. "I am beginning to understand its power, how it works. It is that big black wolf we saw in the trap. Its spirit is everywhere. I call on it, and it calls on what ever is needed. I have been afraid of it but I am now learning to respect it and how to use it."

I wish I would have figured it out sooner, I might have been able to save Larry, Sam thought sadly.

"So you're telling me you used the wolves as a decoy to get the Johnston's away from the house and barn? Do you think any of the wolves will be killed?"

"Johnston has been killing wolves. There were a bunch of hides in the loft above that locked room. But I do not think he will kill any of that pack. They are running with that big lobo and Larry's spirit. I do not think anyone will hurt them."

"So," Lillian said, trying to put the pieces together, "if Larry's spirit is in that white wolf and he's running with the same pack, can you call them anytime? Can Larry communicate with us?"

"I do not know about communicating. I only know I can summon the pack and they seem to know what I want."

"If we could talk to Larry he might be able to tell us who killed him."

And probably a whole lot more, Sam thought.

Chapter Thirty-five

Gunslinger

Ruth was deep in thought as the detail from the 7th Cavalry left Wishbone and escorted her and Ross back up the Columbia. Learning about the death of her brothers so close behind the murder of her son was shocking, but perhaps even more dreadful was the fact that Samuel DeSoto, her son-in-law to be, was a wanted man. Desertion during a time of war was punishable by death, a sentence the army would likely carry out if they ever found Sam.

And why hadn't he led the cavalry back to the valley? What if her brothers and others were not dead? What if they were prisoners of some angry band of Indians?

But Lillian loved him, and Ruth loved him. Sam was a good man who had acted instinctively. He was no coward even if he had been frightened by something he saw. It was one more secret she was afraid to share with Ross. She always felt she could tell her husband anything until Clarence Hobbs came along. Ironically, Sam came into their lives at the same time.

The group stopped by the Indian Agency at Nespelem, where the Riley's were very surprised to learn that Chief Joseph, a legend in the Montana and Idaho Territories, was residing. No longer a fierce chief, he was living quietly, accepting food and an occasional bottle from the Indian Agency.

The soldiers at the agency refused to discuss the plight of Joseph, and the Rileys left Nespelem feeling a sense of loss. In twenty years they had witnessed proud Indian Nations reduced to residents of reservations, dependent on the people who hated them the most to feed and cloth them.

"Maybe through this Ghost Dance they have regained a little of their dignity and hope," Ross said to Ruth.

They both remembered Wolf Chief, the Cheyenne warrior to whom they owed their lives and their ranch.

"I'm glad for their dignity," Ruth replied, "But I'm afraid their hope is a false one unless they have some powerful magic we haven't seen yet."

"If they do, I don't see much reason to wait, they ought to be using it right now." Ross was being flippant but not without an element of truth.

It felt odd traveling with a military escort. The group moved east over Cache Creek along the Sanpoil River then east over Bridge Creek Pass and back onto the Columbia. When the party reached Paradise, Ruth was grateful for the escort. She refused to think about the evil that was Clarence Hobbs when they rode through town and on toward the Running R. They were met by a serious Sam and excited Lilly who immediately shared the news of their visit to the Johnston's barn.

Ross was less than pleased with their illegal entry but was willing to overlook the means if Jim Johnston had Larry's bloody saddle in his barn.

Ross was livid. "I don't need the sheriff!" he raged. "I'll kill the bastard myself if he shot Larry over a few wolf traps."

"Is Larry's saddle proof that Jim Johnston killed him?" Ruth asked, always the rational one.

"It might not prove he did the shooting but it sure means he knows who did. He's going to pay either way!"

This is exactly why I can't tell Ross about Clarence Hobbs, Ruth thought. Ross would kill him and I have no way to prove the man ever touched me. If I had proof, I'd kill him myself.

"Senior Ross," Sam interjected, "if you go to Bountiful, I will go with you. If that hombre, Johnston, had anything to do with Larry's death I think I know how it happened. If I am right, you do not want to go there alone."

Ross ultimately agreed to take Sam with him to the Johnston's and the conversation turned to the Wishbone Ranch. Ruth was almost giddy when she described the house to Lilly.

"There are rock floors like nothing I've ever seen," she exclaimed.

An early breakfast found Ross agitated and ready to confront Jim Johnston. He and Sam left the Running R before the sun was above the horizon. Both were armed with Colt revolvers and carbines. Sam was convinced he was headed for a gunfight. He could see little chance to avoid it, Ross and Jim Johnston were both hot-headed and emotions were running high.

If Johnston hadn't killed Larry he would not take kindly to being accused, if he was guilty he had even more reason to fight. Ross was going to look in that barn if he had to shoot his way in. Sam hoped all his practice, all his shooting as a kid, would pay off now.

Ruth spent a goodly portion of the morning expounding the virtues of Wishbone to Lilly. Then seemingly out of the blue she declared, "I think you and Sam should get married right away. I have a surprise for you," she continued, leading Lilly into a spare bedroom. Pointing at a large box she said, "Open it and I hope you will forgive me for picking it out for you."

Lillian squealed and literally jumped up and down at the sight of the wedding gown. It was white with an embroidered bodice and lace sleeves with matching train. Pearls were stitched into a yoke-trim designed to accentuate her shapely form.

"Mother, it's beautiful! I love it…but will it fit?"

"It might need a nip here and a tuck there but it will fit fine. I saw it in the window of a seamstress' shop in Thompson Falls. The lady had just finished it and was so proud she put it in the window to show it off. Her husband has a photography shop and she offered his services for free, if you and Sam went to Thompson Falls for your honeymoon. All she asked was that you have the dress with you so she could get a picture of you in it."

"When are you thinking we should get married? I was expecting in a month or two, why such a hurry?" Lillian asked, excited and confused. "Something happened while we were looking at the ranch Roy left us. I will explain and hope you understand." Ruth's mood turned solemn. "There were two soldiers the army left to guard Roy's ranch. They knew about Sam."

Ross and Sam rode into the mess that was Bountiful. Chickens scurried, ducks flew and geese charged their horses like rabid dogs. Fortunately Sam was riding Major and Ross was on Roy or they might have had a rodeo and a couple dead geese.

When Jim Johnston emerged from the random pile of boards they called a house, he had a pistol strapped low on his leg and a rifle in his hand.

"Didn't figure I'd be seein' you Riley's again anytime soon." His voice was rough and raspy.

"I need to have a little talk with you, Jim." Ross' voice was steady and calm. "Talk around is, you've been setting out poisoned traps. One of those traps cut my boy's ear and almost killed him."

"Nobody on this ranch is settin' out poison wolf traps. In fact, any wolf comes around our stock we just shoot it, cleaner that way. Besides, what I hear is that your boy's dead, so why you worried about some trap that almost killed him?"

Sam caught a glimpse of movement in the barn, a brief glint of steel behind a tiny window. With one eye on the barn and one on Jim Johnston he waited nervously for Ross's reply.

"Never mentioned wolf traps, Jim, just poison traps," he said. "As for my boy being dead, you heard right and I got a feeling you might know something about that." Ross' voice had acquired a stinging edge.

Sam watched carefully as Johnston's eyes darted toward the barn then quickly back to Ross.

"If you wanted to talk man-to-man you should have come alone. I done told that gunslinger of yours I didn't want to see him on my property again!" Jim shouted.

"Take it easy, Jim." Ross was concerned that things might be reaching a boiling point. "I just want to take a look in your barn. If I don't find any traps or anything belonging to Larry I'll apologize and leave you alone."

"Take one step toward that barn and it'll be the last step you ever take in this life." There was nothing in Johnston's tone that hinted he was bluffing.

Ross pulled his right foot out of the stirrup, grasped the saddle horn with his left hand and made a move to dismount.

"If that foot touches the ground you're a dead man!" Johnston bellowed, glancing quickly at the barn.

Ross swung off Roy, placing the horse between him and the barn. The instant his foot hit the ground, Johnston pointed his rifle at Ross and pulled the hammer back, he never heard it click into firing position.

With a speed that defied time or measurement, the Colt .45 in Sam's hand exploded with a deafening roar, sending Jim Johnston's rifle flying through the air.

"Aaggh!"

Screaming in pain, Johnston grabbed for his pistol as another shot rang out. Wood and glass splintered and shattered as a bullet struck the barn window. Another yell was heard and a rifle tumbled from the window to the ground. As Johnston's hand found his side-arm a third shot sent the pistol flying in twisted pieces and Jim Johnston fell to his knees holding his bloody right hand. Wild cries of an injured child pierced ears already ringing from gun shots as a young boy, no more than thirteen or fourteen, ran from the barn, one arm hanging limply at his side. He ran directly into his father's arms.

"I quit! Jesus Jumpin' Joseph Smith, I quit!" Johnston screamed hysterically, and reached to hold the boy.

Blood dripped from the dangling arm and hand as the boy cried uncontrollably. A scream added to the chaos. The door of the house burst open and Missus Johnston, shotgun in hand, ran onto the porch.

"Don't!" Johnston yelled. "Don't! He'll kill you!"

She stopped, dropped the gun and ran to her husband and son.

"Did you shoot him? He's just a boy!" she shouted at Sam who sat on Major, pistol still in his hand.

"A boy with a gun, Ma'am," he corrected.

"Now I'll have a look in that barn if you don't mind," Ross said.

His eyes were wide and he had trouble finding his voice after what he just witnessed. No one was more stunned than Sam. He had acted on pure instinct, his actions seemed normal but everything else was in slow motion.

Am I really that fast?

Jim realized neither he nor his son was seriously hurt. His hand was burned and his thumb was bleeding where the hammer of his rifle tore the skin when it was blasted out of his hand. His son's arm and hand were bleeding from glass shards and splinters, not bullet wounds.

"Wait," he said, subdued, "Martha, take Johnny in the house and clean him up. I need to explain some things to these men." He slowly stood shaking his hand as he and Ross walked toward the barn.

Sam followed along behind, still mounted on Major. Ross looked back and thought…gunslinger..? Jim Johnston talked like a priest with his pants down when he tried to explain the poison traps and Larry's saddle.

"This guy came here more'n a year ago. Said he'd give me all the wolves he caught if he could trap on Bountiful…said he'd even do the skinin'…said he had a thing about wolves. He said it was personal an' sounded like I couldn't go wrong, so I agreed."

"But why poison the traps?" Sam questioned. He was dismounted and holding Major's reigns.

"He said he had trouble with people stealin' his traps, figured out a way to get even with the thieves."

Leading the way into the tack room, Jim pointed to a tan-colored saddle.

"Is this the saddle you think belonged to your boy?" Johnston's face was ashen as he rubbed his burnt, bleeding hand.

Ross stared at the saddle and pictured Larry on Weasel.

"Where did you get it?" he asked his voice almost gentle.

"That trapper stopped by a while back, not long before your daughter and this here gunfighter paid us a visit. He had a couple of wolf hides and this saddle on a pack mule. Wanted to know if I could use another saddle and of course I can always use another saddle."

"How am I supposed to know if I can believe you?" Ross became more accusatory.

"How do I know this saddle belonged to your son?"

"You sure that trapper didn't leave a bay horse here along with the saddle?" Ross was now elevated to anger.

"You callin' me a horse thief, Riley?"

Jim Johnston was apparently recovering from the shock of having two guns shot out of his hands.

"I never accused you of stealing the horse, just having a stolen horse in your possession."

Sam considered that while the gunfight was over the 'fight' might not be and interjected. "Since you admit you do not know where the saddle came from and since we are missing one, I would say that makes the chances pretty good the saddle belonged to Larry." He hoped a cooler head would prevail. He also decided to raise the stakes just a little. "Maybe we buy the saddle from you for ten dollars. That way we have Larry's saddle back and you are ten dollars ahead. The offer would have conditions; we look around here to make sure you do not have Larry's horse, and you give us the name of the trapper."

Jim Johnston was thinking, he looked at Ross and received a nod of agreement. He looked at Sam, a hint of fear betraying his stoic posture. This is a very dangerous man…that thought was imbedded deep in Jim Johnston's belly.

"Agreed," he said in a much quieter voice. "Trapper's name is Clarence and that's all I know, swear to God. He never gave a last name."

Ross and Sam looked in every corral, every pasture in view, and for any hidden stalls in the barn. The fact that they didn't find Bodie was not a surprise to Sam. He understood why Lillian didn't like Jim Johnston, the man was definitely undesirable but instinct told Sam he wasn't a liar and he wasn't a thief.

Ross gave the man a ten-dollar gold piece and tied Larry's saddle on behind his own. Once out of sight of Bountiful, Ross sighed with relief then filled with consternation, looked at Sam.

"There must be something you want to tell me," he began, "like what you and Lilly were doing at Bountiful, and where you learned to shoot like that, and why Jim Johnston called you a gunslinger. He was obviously right, but how did he know and why didn't I?"

Sam told Ross about his and Lillian's trip to the Johnston ranch in search of Larry adding, "That's how I knew there was a good chance someone would be hiding in the barn." It made sense to take the easy questions first. "We told Ruth about it but you were gone to the agency."

Sam opted to omit the story about the second trip to Bountiful.

"I know a little bit about guns," Ross said. "But no one would call me a gunslinger. I taught Larry all I know and he practiced a lot on his own. I would say he was good with a gun, probably better than most, but I never saw anything like what you did back there." Ross grabbed his hat with a big hand and wiped his brow. "I've never known much about your past, never needed to, I trust Ruth. But I think I just got a glimpse into a bit of your past and frankly, it looked a little troublesome."

Sam was as surprised as anyone when Johnston called him a gunslinger. "I am not a gunslinger, but I can assure you Senior Johnston is, or was a gunfighter. I have seen plenty of them and when you know what to look for you can spot one in an instant," he said and waited for some response from Ross, getting none he continued, "Senior Johnston knew the difference between a gunslinger and a gunfighter, only one or the other would know that."

"Both mean the same to me," Ross stated.

Now is not the time to argue semantics, Sam thought.

"I am a little out of practice but when I was a nino, a young boy, I had much natural ability with a handgun. I have never killed a man in a gunfight," he added quickly.

"Out of practice!" Ross yelped. "If that's out of practice I'm Jesse James. So what makes you think Jim Johnston is a gunfighter?" He was full of questions and ready to keep asking until he got answers to at least a few of them.

"The way he stood and the look in his eyes," Sam answered.

"I might as well be at the river talking to a clam," Ross cracked. "What about the way he stood and his eyes?" he pressed, a little frustrated.

"Well, Senior," Sam said, aware of the aggravation in Ross' tone. "When he talked to you he turned with his right side facing you. That way you had a much smaller target, and if he needed to pull his handgun it would be pointed at you the moment he cleared leather without having to take the gun around his body." Sam had Ross' full attention.

"The eyes are a little trickier but he had a cold, confident look…until he was tested. When he knew he was out-gunned he would have done anything to live and fight another day."

"You mean I didn't need to pay ten dollars for my own saddle?" Ross was starting to get the picture.

"No, but he needed to save face. Otherwise this thing would fester in his gut until he tried something stupid."

Fast and smart…very interesting young man, this future son-in-law of mine, Ross mused.

"By the way, did I tell you I was named Samuel after Samuel Colt? I must have looked like a gunslinger the day I was born," Sam jested, then changing the subject asked, "How do you think we will find this Clarence? He sounds like somebody we need to have a serious conversation with."

"Don't know how to find him but he could be the guy who filed on the Ronan claim. Clarence Hobbs is the name he filed under, said he was from Tucson in the Arizona Territory. There's got to be someone around who knows how to find him. I've got a feeling Johnston knows more than he told us. Never trust a man who says 'I swear to God'."

Chapter Thirty-six
Message

As excited as Bent Grass was at the prospect of being a grandmother she was almost as excited by a message that came to her on the wind. She hurried from the spirit cave in search of her son. The message spoke of the Ghost Dance and the resurrection of hope among Indians but it also carried a warning.

She was pleased her son's friend and spirit-brother, Wovoka, was fulfilling his promise to spread the message of the Ghost Dance among all Indians who would listen. Word of the dance was spreading over the highest mountains and across vast prairies and was being past among great chiefs.

The warning dealt with the matter of time, which was always confusing to Bent Grass because in the valley, the time was always right. If you thought of something, wanted to do something or to see someone, now was the time to do so. It seemed to Bent Grass that outside the valley time was never right. *Time*, not as it is but as it can be.

What was most confusing about the message was the messenger. The words rode the wind like the Great Spirit but they were not the words of *Ogle Wa Nagi* or *Wakan Tanka* or the black spirit-wolf. The words were those of someone she did not know, someone with whom she felt no connection, but the words were real and they spoke with great certainty of a time when The People would be free. The words were very old, as if they had been on the wind for a very, very long time. How could that be? Where had they been for so long and why was the message only now reaching the cave of spirits? She knew many spirits but not this one.

The message carried with it a strange vision unlike any she had seen or painted before.

Bent Grass found Standing Wolf along with Fire-hair, Little Beaver, Three Feathers, Red Fox and Ta-keen Eagle, spearing fish in the river of rainbows. Laughing Doe, Willow, Spotted Fawn and other women were cavorting in the not-so-warm waters, driving big fish upstream from the pools to the riffles where they were more easily speared.

All were soaking wet, naked and happy.

After a little frolicking of her own, Bent Grass told them about the strange message and its unknown sender. Standing Wolf was very interested and intrigued. Who, outside the valley, if not his spirit brother, Wovoka, could speak on the wind to his mother?

"Could this be a shaman you have not met yet?" Standing Wolf asked. "Is there no vision with this message, only words?" He thought of Roy and wondered if, perhaps, he could be the messenger, and smiled at the idea.

"There are visions and words," she answered, "and they are not like the words or visions spoken or seen by Natives yet the spirit is with them." Bent Grass cast her black eyes around the small assemblage. "They are the words of spirits, they warn of dangers but they are not threatening."

"Could they not be the words of Spirit-walker? Perhaps he has returned from delivering the horse soldiers to a place of no sleep." Ta-keen Eagle smiled at the prospect of Spirit-walker's return.

"I do not believe the words are those of a guardian but those of an informer. One who has searched for us ever since the spirit wolf guided The True People to this valley."

"How can that be?" asked Red Fox. "How can one be searching for us if they do not know we are here?"

"What are the words you hear? Can you tell us? Perhaps we can help you understand them. Spotted Fawn and Fire-hair know many words we do not." Little Beaver was always anxious for a challenge, any challenge.

"The words speak of time, of alignment and symbols. Words like andromeda, ascention, dorado, orion, lupus and Indus, of the many eyes of night looking upon a goat with satisfaction, of Brother Moon, Sister Sun, of lupus and little fox and knowledge of the ages." Bent Grass took a deep breath, "This message is not for us to fear, only to know." Bent Grass looked around but saw no enlightenment.

Little Beaver shook his head as if a bee flew in his ear. He looked at Spotted Fawn. She looked back with an expression she normally saved for his father, Crazy Crow.

"Do you think the message is for Wovoka?" Standing Wolf asked.

"I do not know, my son, but if it is, the spirit must think he is still here under Willow's spell." Bent Grass winked at the sensuous vixen.

"It was I who was under a spell," she purred. "And should that one ever return I shall lie under his spell again, and again." She smiled seductively.

Even Red Fox seemed amused by her provocative attitude. He said, "Until that day comes, you should be thankful to have such a fine lover as I to tend to your cravings."

"You are having another vision. Have I not told you many times the only reason I let you near me is because you are my chief's brother? If you were the brother of Three Feathers you would have to sleep with dogs." She placed a hand on his cheek then pinched it. "You lucky boy," she chirped.

Three Feathers looked at Chief Ta-keen Eagle and Laughing Doe. "Did she just call me a dog?"

Three Feathers barked like a dog chasing a bone.

Frank listened to the banter and watched as these beautiful people, engaged in verbal intercourse. Slipping an arm around his wife, he pulled her close. Her dark eyes sparkled like black diamonds as she snuggled against him.

I've come a long way from a crazy trapper in a rat-infested line shack, Frank thought.

But where had he come to? That remained a mystery to him. Was he in a valley hidden away within the sacred land of the Pasayten or was it something more. Now that his power of cognitive thinking had returned, Frank was not sure he could understand any of it. Did it really matter?

Frank accepted that he would never leave the valley. He did not need the gold he had hidden away. His daughter, Spotted Fawn, had no use for it. Even if he could go, there was no reason, he did not need to trap or file a claim on the mother lode he had found. He could live here forever and never be found, it was the perfect hideout where neither gold nor money had any meaning.

For Ta-keen Eagle and Laughing Doe, life had been great since the apocalyptic attack on the invading horse soldiers. He no longer worried about protecting the True People. He knew with protection from the Great Spirit and Standing Wolf, his people were safe.

No one was concerned about Bent Grass' latest enigma. As seer of the Sematuse, Bent Grass was often perplexed by visions and word received on the wind or from the Great Spirit. As long as she did not see anything posing a threat to the True People and their way of life, they looked upon her insight as enlightenment.

Ta-keen Eagle knew what happened outside their valley did matter since the coming of the horse soldiers. Standing Wolf, Spotted Fawn and Fire-hair Frank were proof that the words of Bent Grass were true.

"Our worlds are only a veil apart," she often said.

Since entry by the soldiers, the trail of the sacred black wolf had closed. That left only the spirit cave by which one could enter or exit the valley, and then only if you possessed the amulet. Even he, chief of the Sematuse, did not possess the amulet. As far as he was concerned the fact that there were two was one too many.

Chief Ta-keen Eagle had seen the great crevice in the towing bluff and questioned Bent Grass on how it could grow together.

"Perhaps it was only an illusion," she told him, "or a delusion."

She was learning the white man's words from Fire-hair and sometimes spoke them. Ta-keen Eagle wished she would just speak the language of the Sematuse.

As good as life was in the valley of the Sematuse, it was not without sadness. Bird Legs, who had been old since before water, was not well. Warm Hands was concerned the old man's circle was nearing completion. There was little he could do for him except feed him fish and willow tea and give him an occasional pipe filled with buds from the cannabis that grew near Chewaken Falls.

The valley elders were gathering and stories of past hunting and fishing adventures were being told. Cloud-on-Head, perhaps the oldest of the elders, along with the quiet mannered Turtle and the cheerful Stands-in-Water all shared tales of harrowing and hilarious events. Even Bird Legs who was frail, but on a good day joined in the celebration of his life…this one and the next.

Even the elders conceded that nothing they could remember compared to the events of the Ghost Dance and the return of the ancestral warriors.

"I believe Bird Legs is ready to go on because after seeing the Great Spirit and the Ghost Dance with his own eyes, there is nothing left here to see here." Cloud-on-Head stated. He shared those feeling but his body and mind was still too strong to go on to his next life.

As Bird Legs' body grew weaker his mind began to wander in search of new hunting and fishing grounds. After a particularly animated search in which his body seemed to be besieged with lightning bolts from his highly charged mind, he asked Spotted Fawn, who was tending him, to bring Bent Grass to him.

"I have come from outside the valley," Bird Legs told an attentive Bent Grass. "My body was here but I was soaring like the red-tailed hawk over vast mountains and plains. My eyes were keen like the eagle and I saw many things. I saw many Indians doing the Dance of *Tlchachie.* Their hearts soar and they sing with joy for they see a great victory over the white man when the Great Spirit gives the sign." Bird Legs took a huge labored breath. "It is the same dance but it is not the same place. The People believe but they are desperate. Desperate people are easily deceived. They do not choose the time to dance but instead they dance all the time."

"I hear your message, old wise one, but what can I do?" Bent Grass asked, frustrated.

Bird Legs' throat rattled as he spoke. "Perhaps there is nothing to be done. I only know a great sadness will come over The People if all hope is gone. I fear the loss of the old ways, the ways of our mothers and fathers." His faded brown eyes looked deeply into her onyx pools. "I have seen you from beyond the walls of this valley. I know your power. You can give them a sign telling them when to dance, but you must grant them the power."

Bent Grass smiled. "If you are so wise, old one, then tell me how I will know it is time."

"You will know," he asserted, "it will come to you out of the darkness."

If only I understood time.

How can one mark a place on the circle and call it the right place? Why would one mark be better than another? The circle knows no beginning and no end, so once you enter the circle 'time' is meaningless. Yet time is everything. Bent Grass closed her eyes as if attempting to clear her head.

"Tell me," she said to the frail old man. "Do you feel as though you are ending one life to begin another or do you believe you are only changing horses on the same endless ride?"

Bird Legs looked at her like she was an otter playing with a fish.

"What does that have to do with giving The People a sign?" he asked, showing irritation that was a privilege of his advanced age.

"There was once a saying among our people, 'hope is like the eternal spring'. Dancing gives them hope, I must never remove hope from The People," Bent Grass admonished.

Bird Legs continued to look at her with a mixture of awe and bewilderment.

"Beyond this valley the People do not have eternity. The thing called 'reservation' is stealing the old ways from them. Hope for those Indians must be soon, time is running out."

He would not normally have spoken so boldly to one so powerful… but for the privilege of his condition and his newly discovered insight.

"While you were traveling about outside the valley did you happen to see our missing amulet?" Bent Grass was being facetious but not without hope.

"I believe it is lost for eternity." Bird Legs was playing along with a conversation that was now more frivolous than serious.

Spotted Fawn sat wide-eyed and slightly amused as she listened to the discussion. The only thing she did not find entertaining was the part about reservations. She knew all about them and their mission schools and orphanages; they were about as funny as a dead buffalo.

"Is it dangerous, this amulet?" Spotted Fawn inquired.

Her father had worn the amulet very briefly before the soldier stole it, yet he found an unlikely love with Bent Grass, a woman who was to the Sematuse what the Virgin Mary was to Christians.

"Does the amulet bring good fortune to those who wear it?"

It seems to have worked for my father, she thought.

"As the symbol of the Sematuse, the amulet is very powerful. I do not believe it can be used to harm us but it has many mysterious powers I do not yet understand. I believe the day will come when it will return to our valley and to your father and me. Then we will see if the amulet controls its bearer or if the bearer controls the amulet. Then perhaps we will know its full power."

What Bent Grass did not tell Spotted Fawn was that the amulet, outside the valley, might be influenced by other forces…some could be evil.

Even she was still learning.

Chapter Thirty-seven
Suspect

They had a name. If Jim Johnston was telling the truth, Clarence Hobbs, the claim jumper from Tucson, was a prime suspect in the murder of Larry Riley. All they had to do was find him. Ross deduced that if Hobbs was this side of Tucson he was most likely in Kalispell where he filed the claim on the Ronan Mine.

The story of a gunslinger working on the Running R was quickly all over the Flathead country. Jim Johnston told everyone he knew and a lot of people he didn't, including Clarence Hobbs, who paid him another visit.

"I don't know where you got that saddle you gave me but if it had anything to do with that Riley kid's murder you better be lookin' for some place ta hide."

"I ain't afraid uh no gunslinger. I can take care uh myself," the cocky little man replied.

"I don't care who you are or who you think you are. You ain't got a chance against this guy. I've met up with a few gunfighters in my day an' this guy makes all of 'em look like old ladies."

"Maybe yer just gettin' old an' slow," Clarence jabbed.

"Let me put it this way," Jim retorted. "He ain't just fast, he's deadly accurate. I would bet my ranch there ain't never been a faster gun, alive or dead." Jim looked Clarence in the eye. "Just remember who told you, if this guy has a reason to come after you, you ain't got a chance unless you can ambush him, an' I wouldn't bet my life on that. Neither should you!"

"Why is nothin' ever easy?" Clarence mumbled, after leaving Jim Johnston and Bountiful.

He was perplexed over why the blond babe's husband would hire a gunfighter? And one good enough to make one-hell-of-an impression on Jim Johnston, a man Clarence knew was pretty damn good with a gun himself…at least he'd had quite a reputation around Tucson.

For Ruth Riley, the nightmare she didn't believe could possibly get worse was about to. She had found a way to live with what Clarence Hobbs had done to her and silently planned her revenge. No man was going to do to her what he did and get away with it. She didn't know how she was going to make him pay…with his life or worse.

But now everything changed. If Clarence Hobbs had murdered Larry it would no longer be up to her to decide his punishment, no longer up to her to make him pay. She knew where to find him but was afraid, if cornered, he would try to use her as an alibi or to blackmail.

It should have been a perfect summer for Ruth. Sam and Lillian were getting married and she was going to talk to Ross about moving to Wishbone and letting Sam and Lillian have the Running R. She loved the Kartar Valley, and the house. It was like having Roy's spirit with her.

But, Larry's saddle and Jim Johnston's story didn't make Clarence Hobbs Larry's killer. Withholding what she knew about the man's possible where-a-bouts only added to the guilt Ruth was already forced to live with. She had to be sure before she said anything.

She wanted Ross to tell everything he had learned to the sheriff and let him worry about Clarence Hobbs. She wanted to have a wedding for Sam and Lillian, go back to Wishbone and get her life back. However, now that Ross had a name he was determined to find the man. The only thing he seemed to be more excited about than finding Clarence Hobbs was telling the story of the confrontation with Jim Johnston.

"I'm telling you," he repeated over and over, "if I hadn't seen it I'd never believe it. Sam was so fast I never even saw his hand move until he was putting that Colt away."

Lillian had never seen her dad so impressed by anything and Ruth had to admit it was right up there with anything she'd ever shown him.

"And he never even hurt 'em," he raved on. "Shot the guns out of their hands…even that kid at forty yards away behind a window!"

If Sam wanted to imprint a place in Ross's mind, he had surely done that.

Without much warning things got exceptionally busy around the Running R. Ruth and Lillian were completely absorbed in planning a wedding. The fact that it was to be in two weeks instead of two months no longer concerned Lillian. She decided it was best for her and for Sam because it was becoming frustrating, even painful to keep their hands off each other.

Ross was thankful for Sam but he missed Larry. They needed to corral a small herd to move to Wishbone and Ross knew they were going to need to hire a few cow punchers for the journey. That meant a trip to Paradise and Horse Plain to roundup some hands. They would join the drive in Paradise and stay on all the way to Wishbone.

Sam agreed to stay at the Running R with the women while Ross was gone. There was a lot to do and it didn't take both of them to hire a few cowboys.

Clarence Hobbs was agitated. He had ridden out to the Running R several times but the blond babe was never alone. In fact a couple times he was pretty sure she wasn't even there.

He'd put his eye on that pretty little girl of hers through the magic of his telescope but she was never alone. She was a fine lookin' little snit and he was tempted to sneak up close and put a bullet in the hombre who was always hanging around her.

"Now ya ain't thinkin' with your head, Clarence," he admonished. "Montana's uh state now, two guys shot on the same ranch in less than uh year an' they'll have U.S. Marshal's an' the Pinkerton's snoopin' 'round here."

Besides, he hadn't completely forgotten what Jim Johnston told him about Riley's hired gun. He would never admit it but he had no desire to get within range of that guy's handgun. Standing behind the bar and pouring another drink for an already drunk cowboy, Clarence pondered his future.

"I gotta get at her before I leave an' I gotta be movin' on soon. Maybe I'll take her with me for uh ways. She gets ta be uh problem I'll kill her someplace uh long way from Montana."

Statehood was attracting more settlers and miners and that meant more lawmen…never a good thing in the eyes of Clarence Hobbs.

"Maybe I'll head back ta Tucson," he muttered, while patrons at the bar grinned at their bartender talking to no one but himself. "They'll never make that rattlesnake den uh state."

Truth was things were getting a little uncomfortable in Montana. Hobbs abandoned his plan of getting the Riley woman to the cabin after he killed the kid. It was risky enough going back to get rid of the mattress and shackles. If that wasn't enough, Jim Johnston paid him an unwelcome visit in Paradise.

"I told ya never ta contact me here," he seethed, ushering Jim from the saloon and into his room.

"I figured I'd better tell you. Riley is on to us," Jim complained. "He's got the kid's saddle an' I told him your name, just your first name," he emphasized apologetically.

"Ya what?!" Clarence was struggling to keep his voice down. "Ya lily-livered bastard!" Clarence was pissed and a little panicky. "Why in the hell would ya give 'em my name?" Clarence was pacing around the small room. "Why didn't ya tell me this the other day when I was out at Bountiful?"

"I didn't figure he'd ever find you. Then I got to thinkin' I should at least let you know what I know. I had to tell him, I was afraid he was gonna kill me," Jim said, defensively.

"Thought ya said ya wasn't afraid uh this Riley guy."

"I ain't, it's that gunslinger he's got workin' for him. I already told you, that guy is outta this world. I tell you, ain't nobody gonna out draw him."

"Well shit," Clarence fussed. "I thought we had us uh deal; ya get all the wolves I could trap, uh Long Tom' rifle an' fifty dollars for yer oldest girl when I leave. I was throwin' the horse an' saddle in for nothin'. All ya had ta do was keep yer mouth shut."

"You never said you was gonna kill nobody. Never told me the horse an' saddle belonged to that kid you killed. I suppose that rifle's the one you shot him with. We ain't got no deal no more, you was settin' me up to pin this whole Riley killin' on me!" Jim Johnston was enraged. "You did kill that kid, didn't you?!"

"Alright, alright calm down."

Damn!

Clarence Hobbs' plan had almost worked. He figured the trail would lead the Riley's to Bountiful, and with Jim Johnston's gunfighter past, if he got into it with Riley it would be the death of Riley. That would have left the blond babe alone and his for the taking. He assumed the law would eventually find evidence of the kid's murder at Bountiful and that would be the end of Johnston. Then he would have yet another woman and a couple of girls he could play with.

It could have worked.

Why in hell would Riley, by all accounts, an ordinary albeit very successful rancher, hire a gunslinger for a ranch hand?

You don't rope cows with a gun.

"Calm down!?" Johnston yelped. "You try an' pin a murder on me an' you say, calm down?!"

Clarence was alarmed, he was no match for Johnston if the man went for his gun.

"Take it easy Jim, I ain't even armed, we can talk 'bout this an' work somethin' out."

"Then you better start talkin' while you still can."

And talk Clarence did. He doubled the price for Johnston's daughter; of course the fact that she was only thirteen would make her worth twice that in Tucson, and he agreed to buy back the horse and rifle he had given to Johnston and to pay him for the saddle Jim no longer had. Hobbs knew better than to argue, he would save that for a time when he had the advantage.

After Jim left, Clarence went back to the bar, broke a glass and cursed the damn Riley kid for gettin' in the way.

"Guess I'll just have ta get my monies worth out uh his mother," he fumed quietly.

Clarence was still grumbling when a big man in a western hat with a Colt .45 on his hip and arms that looked like the hind-leg of a beef, ambled into the saloon and found a table near the back.

"Sure make me come ta you!" Clarence groused as he flipped open the trap-door in the bar and sauntered back, sizing the customer up as he went.

He ain't one of my usual Saturday night cowpokes.

"What can I get fer ya mister."

Asshole!

Hobbs grinned at his own frivolity.

"Names Ross Riley," the big man said and Clarence felt his knees buckle slightly. "I'm going to be bringing a small herd of cattle through here in two or three weeks. Taking them to a place called the Kartar Valley about two hundred miles west of here. I need to hire ten, maybe fifteen cowboys to help with the drive. I'll pay two dollars a day to anyone who finishes the drive, a dollar a day to those who don't. If you know anyone who might be looking for work have them be here day after tomorrow at about this time. And I think I'll have a shot of Old Crow."

Returning to the bar Clarence muttered, "So that's blondie's husband. Man's big enough ta hunt bear with uh switch."

Opportunity…

"If he's gonna be here fer uh couple days, she's out at that ranch just wishin' ol' Clarence would come see 'er," he told himself.

Next morning at the crack of dawn, Clarence was on his way to the Running R. He had asked for a couple days off to get a little R and R and smiled at yet another pun. When he arrived at his vantage point above the ranch house, he stepped off his gray cayuse and pulled his eye glass from a saddle bag. There was no movement around the house. For a moment he wondered if the blond could be in town with her husband.

"If she's here, I'll take 'er in er' house or barn."

It was late afternoon and his plan was to settle in for the night, then starting early he'd keep an eye on the place until he could sort out who was where. He was mostly concerned about the location of the hired gunfighter.

By early evening the hired man and the red-haired girl arrived at the ranch.

"Good," Hobbs uttered, "now I know who's there. I just gotta wait an' see who leaves in the mornin'."

After an excellent meal of hamhocks, apple sauce, yams and endless questions about the upcoming wedding, Sam retired to the bunkhouse. Dinner was great, Ruth and Lillian were in good spirits, today's cattle sorting had gone well and life was far better than he could have ever expected, but he was troubled…anxious really, like something terrible was about to happen.

At first Sam assumed it was because of the wedding and concerns about the army, but deep in his gut he knew it was something else. He had worried about the army since the night he ran, this was different.

Clarence awoke to a light rain, a condition that dampened his mood but not his ardor. He built a small fire under a grand fir, warmed a chunk of hard-tack and waited for something to happen at the ranch.

It wasn't long before an odd bronze-colored horse left the ranch with its rider, the hired gun, aboard. Clarence felt his heart beat faster as anticipation rushed through his veins.

Be smart.

He had to think this through; he had the small vile of chloroform, the rags and the hood. He had ropes, he even had a blackjack, anything to immobilize her long enough for him to gain control.

But the girl was still there.

Can I git uh two-fer?…he pondered, the idea was thrilling but stupid.

He mounted his little gray cayuse and worked his way along the familiar route to the wooded area behind the house. From there he made his way on foot to the back of the house.

What now?

He debated his next move. "Ya cain't strike unless yer in strikin' distance?" he told himself.

Hobbs decision was made for him when the front door banged shut and Ruth started down the steps, wearing riding pants and a loose-fitting light-blue top. She was wearing a broad-brimmed hat and carried some type of jacket in her left hand.

Hearing the door shut, Clarence moved to the corner of the house and watched as Ruth made her way toward the barn, then waited until she disappeared inside. He was ready to scurry across the barnyard when the door slammed again.

"Shit," he muttered slipping back around the corner.

Lillian skipped down the steps, red hair dancing in the sun. Clarence was captivated by her round butt as it twitched across the barnyard like she was a puppet. She, too, entered the barn.

Lilly walked past her mother who was currying Cocoa, and led Buttercup from her stall then rummaged around looking for a fresh saddle blanket.

Clarence hurried to the barn door and peaked inside. He caught sight of Ruth. As she bent to her task, Clarence got a glimpse of her shapely bottom encased in the tight tan riding pants. A short distance away, the red-haired girl was brushing down a Palomino.

"This ain't gonna work," he fussed, "unless I take one uhf 'em out."

Ruth and Lillian were excited. They were going to ride over to the Polson ranch to talk about the dresses for the twins to wear for the wedding. The girls were so cute Lillian could hardly wait to see them in emerald- green. She wanted the girl's outfits to match her mother's eyes. It might be silly but that's what she wanted.

"Whoa…"

Sam pulled Bigfoot to a halt. It was that pesky feeling again.

"I need to go back," he said, as if Bigfoot cared.

He knew Ruth and Lillian would probably already be on their way to the Polson place but he was learning to trust his instincts. A strange feeling burrowed its way into Sam's psyche. There was a touch of loneliness along with a kind of anxious nostalgia. He scanned the scattered trees and sage, feeling a kinship, like he was part of the surrounding countryside, not an intruder.

Without thinking his hand moved to the amulet and despite the cool day it felt warm, almost hot, in his hand. Remembering the unbelievable appearance of the wolves at the cabin and at Bountiful, Sam began to move the amulet in a slow circle in front of him. He felt foolish but there was no one around to poke fun or ridicule.

Sam heard the whistling of a high wind but there was no movement among the aspen leaves, no swaying of the pine or fir; just the steady howling of wind as if the mountain peaks were exhaling.

As he continued the circular motion the golden eyes of the wolf began to glow. Even in the light of day they appeared like two tiny lanterns. Sam began to feel lightheaded but was determined to see where this experience might take him.

Without warning the landscape became a blur, the amulet fell from his hand and hung loosely around his neck. His brain was unable to function and he could not fathom what was happening. Unable to focus, he closed his eyes; when he opened them he was flying…not literally, but he had never moved so fast in his life. It was as though Bigfoot's flailing hooves were not touching the ground. Sam wondered if the horse was as stunned as he. Sam had no control over anything but thought he was experiencing some kind of apotheosis.

The Amulet!

He remembered making the circular motion with the amulet. What kind of mystical magic had he unleashed? He wrapped Bigfoot's reins around the saddle horn and took the amulet in both hands then began the circular motion once more.

What have I got to lose?

Sam and Bigfoot skimmed along just above the ground, levitated by some mysterious force, he was looking at the trees, a blur to his tear soaked eyes. He was barely able to breathe as they raced over down logs, along open ridges and down timbered slopes.

It wasn't until they hit the well-worn cattle trail that Sam realized they were on the way back to the Running R. A new fear struck him like an eight-inch dagger to the heart.

Ruth and Lillian!

The amulet is taking me to Ruth and Lillian…They must be in danger!

Clarence took a moment to ponder his predicament.

"Ya should be countin' yer blessings," he whispered. "Mother an' daughter, it's like uh miracle."

Clarence never heard the horse as it burst through the arch gate into the barnyard of the Running R. He was lucky to see the horse and rider at all, so obsessed was he with the situation inside the barn.

He managed to slip around behind the end of the barn just as the rider pulled up in front of the house and a twinge of panic swept over him.

'It's that damn gunslinger! What the hell is he doin' back here?

Now what the hell do I do?' His mind was frantic while he tried to coax himself to stay calm.

"Ruth! Lillian!" Sam called as he went into the kitchen then to the stairway. "Already gone," he whispered, walking out the front door, "might as well check the barn."

He was surprised to find Ruth and Lillian tightening the cinches on their horses.

"So much for an early start," he joked, as he walked up to Lillian.

"Eeiicks!" she squealed. "Sam, what are you doing here? You almost scared the pants off me." Taking a couple of deep breaths she tried to gather her wits, which were scattered around the barn. "Did you forget something?"

Sam looked at Ruth. "I had a bad feeling and needed to make sure you were okay." It was a knowing look only Ruth and Sam understood.

"I think we're alright, aren't we?" Ruth said, glancing Lillian. "Why don't you take a look around, Sam, as long as you're here? You can ride over to the Polson's with us if you're really concerned."

"Now **that** I would worry about," Sam cracked, and chuckled at the thought of hanging around while women discussed bride's maids' dresses. "I will have a look around," he said, puzzled why the amulet would have brought him back here if nothing was wrong.

Clarence couldn't hear what was going on in the barn. With revolver in hand he looked around, searching for options. He could try and sneak away but he had thirty or forty yards of open ground to cover, or he could stay hidden and wait for the hired gun to walk out in the open.

This guy might be fast, he thought...but he ain't faster than a bullet. If I'm gonna get ta enjoy either uh those babes I need ta end this now.

Clarence moved to the corner of the barn.

Come out, come out, where ever ya are, he thought, grinning...an' yer uh dead man!

Sam stepped out through the barn door and danger flashed from his brain to his hand without the benefit of thought.

Not ten feet away, he saw the hole in the barrel end of a Colt .45 pointed directly at him. It looked big enough to walk through.

Gotcha!..Clarence thought, as his finger touched the trigger.

He never heard the shot. The muzzle flash nearly blinded him. It was his final memory. The bullet from Sam's pistol struck Clarence squarely between the eyes.

Buttercup and Cocoa, frightened by the sudden explosion, reared and nearly broke free of their handlers. Ruth and Lillian quickly calmed them then rushed out of the barn, never stopping to consider the danger. They found Sam starring down in disbelief at the prone, faceless body of Clarence Hobbs.

Ruth didn't recognize him immediately; his face was so distorted by the bullet. When she did, she exclaimed, "Oh my God!" and began crying hysterically. "He was here! My God, he was here!" She looked at Sam in amazement and wonder.

Lillian helped her to the house while Ruth explained to Lillian what this meant, how she met Sam and that it was finally over. Her words spilled out in relief like grain pouring from an open sack.

Sam retrieved Hobb's pistol, removed the empty holster from his dead body and placed the .45 in it, then with gun and holster in hand he walked to the house.

"Does this look familiar to you?" he asked Ruth, holding out the gun and holster.

"Oh my God! That's Larry's pistol!" she shrieked. "That horrible little creep killed Larry!"

When Ross returned from Paradise and Horse Plain, Sheriff Baker was with him. Jim Johnston had taken the Long Tom rifle Clarence gave him to the sheriff. He told Sheriff Baker the whole story, the poison traps, the horse and saddle. He claimed he'd sold the horse to a neighbor and when he'd gone to try and buy the horse back it was gone. Ross told Luke to forget the horse. They had the evidence they needed.

They had gone to the saloon to talk to Clarence but the bartender told them he was gone, that he'd taken a couple days off.

Thinking he'd probably felt the noose tightening and made a run for it they were more than a little stunned to find a dead Clarence Hobbs at the Running R.

Larry's gun and holster were more evidence but Luke was relieved this killer would not go to trial.

Shaking Sam's hand, Sheriff Baker said, "You saved me the trouble of chasing this jerk down. I probably would have had to arrest him and go through a trial and you never know what a jury will do. I like this way a helluva lot better."

After a thoughtful moment he added, "I know this won't bring your son back, but if he's watching, maybe it will bring him a little peace."

Sam touched the amulet.

What on God's earth is this thing?

Chapter Thirty-eight
Woman's Perogative

As their wedding date neared, Sam had an epiphany. The only problem was it meant a trip to Kalispell. The herd for Wishbone was gathered and corralled awaiting the drive. Most of the activity around the Running R had something to do with the wedding. When Sam told Ross he wanted a couple of days off Ross had an unpredictable reaction.

"Let's see, you been working here for what, two years or more and I can't remember you ever having a day off. Besides, you and Lilly are going to have your own ranch before long. I'd say it's about time you start acting like you're the boss, so if you want a day or two off, that seems like your business."

"I guess that will take some getting used to," Sam replied. "I never expected anything like this when I came here."

"Well son," Ross said fondly, "life is full of surprises."

Sam smiled at the understatement.

One such surprise was Ruth's sudden change of heart about Wishbone. Just when Ross had finally accepted the idea of moving to the Kartar Valley, Ruth decided she wanted to stay on the Running R.

A woman's prerogative, he mused.

As Sam rode north toward Kalispell his mind was busy. So much had happened since he'd grabbed the leather talisman off that red-haired guy and ran...much of it with no rational explanation. He did not doubt the power of the amulet, he just didn't know where it stopped, and wasn't sure he wanted to.

Resurrection.

The ultimate power, the power to bring the dead back to life, nothing on earth is less understood or more desired than answers to the mysteries of life and death. Sam dared not let his mind go so far, but he knew what he saw in the valley.

Sam shook his head, clearing it of a memory that was rapidly becoming unbelievable. He thought about the amulet and realized he was a little afraid to touch it. Whatever power it possessed it was growing stronger, and he was learning right along with it.

It was clear there was something about using the circular motion with the amulet. The thought ran chills around and around his spine.

The power of the circle, he thought.

He kept the amulet safely tucked away in his shirt the rest of the way to Kalispell, though he was slightly tempted to see if it would whisk him to his destination the way it had taken him back to the Running R.

Sam found exactly what he was looking for in Kalispell. By the time he returned to the ranch he was floating; this time without the help of the amulet. Lillian was excited about the wedding but she was also excited to see her uncle's ranch, it would soon belong to her and Sam. Ruth seemed the most relaxed and happy she'd been since that fateful day when she'd returned from Paradise accompanied by a scruffy-looking young man.

It was hard for Sam to believe when their wedding day finally arrived. He awoke to the sound of cattle bawling in the distance and a blue-jay squawking on the bunkhouse window sill, peeking in like a curious cat.

"A blue-jay on your window has to be a good thing," he muttered, crawling out of bed.

Anxious to see Lillian on a day Sam knew was the happiest of his young life, he quickly dressed and went to the big house. Ruth met him at the door with a plate filled with taters, eggs, side pork and a pot of coffee.

"I'm sorry Sam," she said, with all the sincerity she could muster. "You're going to have to eat in the bunkhouse this morning. It's bad luck to see the bride on your wedding day before she comes down the aisle, or in this case the stairs."

It was not to be a large wedding but it wouldn't be without witnesses.

Tomas and Elizabeth Finley with their two boys and girl arrived around mid-day. The Polson twins and their parents weren't far behind. The Claytons closed up the boarding house in Paradise for a couple of days to attend the wedding and wish the couple well. Even Doc Jenson and John Grimm, and their wives, made the trip from Horse Plain.

The men holed up in the bunkhouse, joking and teasing Sam about his good fortune adding a few off-color comments about the joys of the wedding night. Ross reflected on watching his little girl morph slowly into the stunning young woman she'd become. While sparing himself thoughts of Sam and Lillian's wedding night, he acknowledged inwardly that Samuel DeSoto was about to become a very lucky man. The women, meanwhile, were in the house busily decorating, baking, and dressing. New dresses were the order of the day, some handmade, some store bought and all special for the event. Marge Clayton was putting the final touches on a three-layer cake. As she smoothed the white frosting with blue and green trim while she pondered the placement of the small man and woman carved by the youngest of the Finley boys.

The miniature man and woman were dressed in tiny matching blue jeans, white shirts and leather vests. The man wore a tiny-carved pistol on his hip and the woman held a short rope looped around the man's neck. When Marge carefully placed the diminutive figurines atop the wedding cake, laugher and giggles ensued.

When the wedding march began, played by Doc Jenson on his violin or as he liked to say, 'It's a fiddle if I'm buyin', it's a violin if I'm sellin', and Elizabeth Finley on her flute, making beautiful music no matter what you called the instruments.

As Sam stood nervously awaiting the sight of his bride to be, he briefly thought of Larry and how nice it would have been for everyone if he could have stood next to Sam, best man and beloved brother.

Sam wore the tan-colored suit he found in Kalispell, complete with blue shirt and string tie. Black curls nestled against his collar and splayed onto his shoulders. To anyone who didn't know, he appeared to be of Indian descent, probably a half-breed but devilishly handsome no matter his heritage. He wore new black boots, but the Colt that had become his constant companion was delegated to the bunkhouse.

When Lillian appeared at the top of the staircase, her mannequin-shape perfectly filling her white pearl-enhanced wedding dress, Sam thought his heart would stop. Her red hair, that normally hung straight, tumbled in loose flame-like curls halfway down her back as she clutched her father's arm and slowly descended the staircase.

Sam struggled just to remember to breathe; it was like watching an angel descend from heaven. At that moment he knew he would give his life for this girl…this woman.

He stood transfixed next to John Grimm, a man with the occupational peculiarity of undertaker and reverend. His ties to the Riley's were curiously deep, having presided over the burial of their son and now the imminent marriage of their daughter. Sam let his gaze wander, Ruth cried as she watched her beautiful daughter approach her husband to be and the scene became surreal. He could barely hear the words of John Grimm as his eyes settled on Lillian.

The words 'Do you take this woman?' jerked Sam back to the moment and unimaginable reality.

"I do," he said, barely able to hear his own words.

"And, Lillian, do you take this man?"

Sam held his breath, afraid that to exhale might blow this dream out of his reach.

"I do."

The words were like music from a thousand harps.

"Then with this ring I thee wed!"

Sam's heart leaped into his throat; this was why he had gone to Kalispell. Reaching in his jacket pocket, he pulled out a small white box. Taking Lillian's hand, he slid the 2-carat sapphire ring on her finger.

"To match your eyes," he whispered, and John Grimm said, "You may kiss the bride!"

The women cried, the men cheered and Sam and Lillian embraced in a soft lingering kiss. Of all the impossible things that happened since he ran from that valley - This, he thought…is the most unbelievable of all - and silently wished his mother and father were alive to see this day.

The back-slapping, hand-shaking and well-wishing kisses on the cheek broke his reverie. Holding Lillian's hand, while she slid a long knife through three-layers of cake, convinced him this was not another dream or vision, this was really happening. His feeling of pure joy was challenged only by the enormous pride that threatened to overwhelm him.

Sam and Lillian chose to spend the first night of their honeymoon camping on a small stream north of the Running R where they first kissed. The idea of spending their first night together in a tent appealed to both of them. It was like starting their life together with no frills, just their love for each other and Mother Nature. And both were excited to consummate their love in the place it began with an unexpected kiss. They would spend the next night in Thompson Falls, on their way to Wishbone, to fulfill the 'deal' on the wedding dress.

Daniel Bone and Joe Wright were anxious to head back to Fort Vancouver and Daniel's small fortune. It didn't take much begging from Joe to convince Daniel to take him along to Canada, where his gold mine was located. Joe would rather be a miner than a private in an army with nobody left to fight but Indians.

They had been through a lot together; a couple of hair-raising skirmishes with the Cheyenne and Arapaho on the way from Kansas to Oregon, the loss of Colonel Wolard, along with a thousand soldiers, and the wild story the single survivor told about dead Indians attacking them, was not something easily forgotten. After their night on guard duty and the wild fire and the mysterious appearance of that terrifying Indian, they both knew they had their fill of Indian country.

Both men anxiously awaited the return of the Riley's and their release from what had been a great duty station. Joe still fussed about never having found any 'womens' but now that he was soon to be a civilian, he figured there would be a lot of chances.

Daniel was determined to keep the house in top shape so Missus Riley would be pleased when she returned. He knew he could never have a woman like her but just thinking she could be his friend made him feel warm inside.

"Keep your socks an' skivvies washed, Joe," he harped. "I don't want this house smellin' bad when Missus Riley comes back!"

"You're soundin' uh lot like uh wife, Daniel, 'cept ahm jist gettin' all the naggin' an' none uh the good stuff."

When a large dust cloud drifted down the Columbia, Daniel and Joe danced a little jig across the covered porch of the Wishbone house.

"Hot damn!" Joe yelped. "That's either uh Injun uprisin' or it's the Riley's comin' ta set us free!"

Daniel wasn't sure if he was most excited about leaving Wishbone and getting back to Fort Vancouver and the rest of his life, or the thought of seeing Missus Riley again. He was a little disappointed when, instead of Ruth, her daughter Lillian arrived. Nonetheless, before long both he and Joe were totally captivated by her dazzling beauty, in many ways, a replica of her mother.

With the cattle safely delivered to their new home, Sam took a deep breathe and headed for the house. He was more than a little anxious to see if the two soldiers from Fort Okanogan would recognize him. He introduced himself as Lillian's husband and made a joke about the ranch being hers and that he was only along to do the heavy lifting. The soldiers were so enamored with the lovely Lillian they barely acknowledged his presence.

"Sure would like ta have uh spread like this someday. Might, too, if that Canadian mine uh mine is any good." Daniel laughed at the crazy English language.

With his long curly hair falling around his shoulders and a full horseshoe mustache, Samuel DeSoto bore no resemblance what-so-ever to the frightened wild-eyed corporal who rode into Fort Okanogan, what seemed so very long ago.

After a couple days of preparation, Daniel and Joe were packed with enough supplies to get them to the first downriver trading post. Each received an affectionate hug from Lillian then with each man leading two packhorses, they rode away toward a new life filled with hope and possibilities.

Chapter Thirty-nine
Sitting Bull

THE Ghost Dance movement was so wide spread it was no longer a concern only to Indian Agents on individual reservations. It was a military matter with ramifications all the way to the nation's capitol.

Of course not everyone in the military or the capitol agreed on the best way to handle the situation. Some believed the movement was nothing more than a phenomenon that would run its course and fade away while others saw it as an uprising on the verge of full-scale war.

Senator John Logan grew tired of Indians clinging to the 'old ways' and implored Sitting Bull, "The government feeds you, clothes you and educates your children. Why do you resist becoming civilized, why do you resist becoming white men?"

Most of his anger was aimed at this Hunkpapa Sioux war chief who was revered by most of the Sioux Nation. Logan and fellow Senator, Henry Dawes, believed Sitting Bull to be arrogant and un-cooperative. They preferred speaking with younger, more tolerant Indians like Running Antelope and John Glass.

Because many segments of the great Sioux Nation were fragmented by disagreement, the Indian Bureau was attempting to exclude chiefs like Sitting Bull and Red Cloud from negotiations.

Eventually, a commission was formed to over-see Indian activities on reservation lands…land that once belonged to the Indians but now belonged to the government. Along with their friends in the White House, Newton Edmunds, who referred to himself as a professional negotiator, and the Reverend Sam Hinman, a long-time missionary to the Sioux, began working on a scheme that would effectively take what remaining land the Sioux had and turn it over to the government.

"What the Indians need is less land and more church!" the reverend proclaimed.

He, like so many others, failed to see the similarities between the Ghost Dance movement and Christianity…mainly because they failed to look beyond the dance.

James McLoughlin, known as White Hair to the Indians, was procured to head the effort to make the Sioux 'white' as quickly as possible. McLoughlin, still smarting from a defeat by the Natives in the remote region of the *Okinakane* at a place called Janis, had little tolerance for Indian insubordination. The attack on an advance party of prospectors, led by him and his brother David some thirty years prior, had cost numerous prospectors their lives and the loss of thousands of dollars worth of gold. The gold was never recovered, his family's reputation with the Hudson Bay Company was never regained, and it set back the infusion of miners and the development of the gold fields along the Columbia, Okanogan and Fraser Rivers by two decades. That incident marked the beginning of unexplained, and in some cases unsubstantiated, attacks by a mysterious source believed to be Indian.

McLoughlin described the attack, saying, "We never saw an Indian but arrows and spears darkened the sky. Rocks and trees fell in front and behind us like they were being thrown by the hand of God. There were no war-hoops or mad cries of attack…only the eerie whisper of arrows in flight. Those of us with the best horses were able to escape before the logs and rocks blocked the way. For the rest, those with slower horses or on wagons, it must have been horrible. I beg their forgiveness."

At other times, Agent McLaughlin was much more philosophical, even questioning if the incident ever really happened.

"Sometimes," he said, "it seems like the attack was yesterday, other times, a lifetime ago. In many ways it seems like an apparition, yet there is something about it that stays with me….like a bad dream."

Dr. Valentine McGillycuddy, a former Indian Agent, believed the dance should be allowed to continue.

"If Seventh-Day Adventists can prepare their ascension robes for the second coming and the military has not ordered to stop them," he declared, "why should Indians be any different?"

Agencies on nearly every reservation began setting up a system of courts and tribal police much like those on the Flathead and at Walker Lake. Pine Ridge was no different except emotions were reaching a breaking point. Bureaucrats, running the Indian Bureaus, believed setting up reservation or tribal courts and police would allow Indians more control over their affairs. A lack of understanding, or concern, for the Indian culture resulted in bigger problems than if order continued to be kept by the military.

Indian culture dictated that decisions, control and discipline be administered by tribal chiefs, not by rag-tag policemen appointed by white bureaucrats. Animosity was building among Indians who didn't appreciate being told what to do by other Indians, whom they often regarded as over-zealous and lacking proper authority.

The bureau, the military and Agent McLoughlin were fed up with Sitting Bull and his followers. On a cold December morning, Lieutenant Colonel Bill Drum received orders from General 'Bear Coat' Miles to arrest Sitting Bull and move him to a military prison at Fort Yates.

Lieutenant Bull Head, an Indian policeman appointed by Agent McLoughlin, along with Sergeant Red Tomahawk, found Sitting Bull asleep in his cabin at Standing Rock.

"Wake up, you are under arrest!" Bull Head gruffly announced. "You will come with me to the agency. You are my prisoner!"

Sitting Bull, unaccustomed to being bothered during his sleep muttered, "Go away, come back when I am awake and I will go with you."

"You will go with me now!" Bull Head ordered, pulling the covers off a naked Sitting Bull.

Now angry, Sitting Bull sat up and turned away from his tormenters and declared, "I was told my friend Buffalo Bill Cody is coming to speak with me. I will not leave until I have seen him." He was more used to giving orders than taking them.

"You **will** leave, and now!" Red Tomahawk interjected, puffed up with newfound authority. "When the lieutenant gives you an order you will do it!"

Glaring at the impetuous sergeant, Sitting Bull responded, "I am your chief. You do not tell me what to do."

With no alternative, Sitting Bull got up, put his clothes on and started for the door.

"I will go with you but I am not your prisoner. I have committed no crime and you have no right to arrest me. Bring me my horse and I will **go** with you. You will not **take** me!" the proud chief declared.

When Red Tomahawk opened the cabin door he was stunned to see a huge crowd was gathered. Some were chanting, some were dancing and most were armed. A young warrior named Catch-the-Bear stepped forward.

"You think you will take Sitting Bull but you will not!" he proclaimed.

Bull Head and Red Tomahawk grabbed Sitting Bull by the arms and began dragging him toward his horse.

"Release him!" Catch-the-Bear yelled in anger.

Grabbing a rifle from his brother, Falls-in-Rain, Catch-the-Bear fired a shot, hitting Bull Head. As he fell, Bull Head shot back at Catch-the-Bear but accidently hit Sitting Bull. Enraged and fearing for his life, Red Tomahawk grabbed Sitting Bull as a shield. The chief jerked free and the frightened Indian, Sergeant Red Tomohawk, shot Sitting Bull in the head; ending the life of a living legend, and the great chief many believed to have killed Old Yellow-hair…Brevet General George Armstrong Custer.

As Red Tomahawk ran for his horse, he was struck by a Cheyenne war axe and with its red handle protruding from his back, he fell face down not ten feet from where Sitting Bull's lifeless body lay.

Shots were fired, arrows flung, spears thrown and bodies fell as the battle raged. With the Indian police out-numbered and on the run, only the distant bugle of a detachment of the 7th Cavalry saved them from complete annihilation.

As the cavalry set about restoring order and tending to the wounded, Lieutenant Randle Black and James McLoughlin looked on in astonishment as a white horse reared and turned in a complete circle on hind-legs. It appeared to onlookers that even Sitting Bull's horse, though performing a trick learned in Buffalo Bill's Wild West Show, was doing the Ghost Dance.

It should have been seen as a sign that the Ghost Dance was far bigger than any chief...even Sitting Bull. It was a dance of spirits, animal and human, but of course, neither the white man nor his government or its bureaus belived in signs or spirits.

They didn't need to. They had God on their side!

Chapter Forty

Wounded Knee

Word of Sitting Bull's death spread across the plains and over the shining mountains, carried by drums, 'talking on the wind' and riders from every Indian Nation west of the Great Missouri.

An uprising seemed imminent and ranchers and settlers across the west and southwest were worried. The anger on both sides was deep and far-reaching. Sitting Bull's murder, as it was being called, was committed by 'white Indians': Natives employed to enforce the white man's law on their own people.

Word was that Sitting Bull was gunned down during an illegal arrest, one that Sitting Bull was not even resisting, and that he was killed because a dancing crowd of supporters would not obey the demands of over-zealous Indian police. Enraged Indians, who were already disturbed over the missionary's attempts to convert them and their children to Christianity, danced all the more fervently in hopes of fulfilling the promise of the Ghost Dance to rid the earth of all white men.

Settlers, ranchers, businessmen and even the government disagreed on how the Indian crisis should be handled. The fact that territories like North and South Dakota, Montana, Idaho and Washington were now states only made matters worse. The bureaucracy directing both the Indian Bureaus and the military was far removed from the sight of the problem. Local knowledge no longer trumped political influence and power.

Decisions in matters of Indian affairs were being made at the highest levels of government, including President Benjamin Harrison. Word finally came down in the fall through the Indian Bureau to all reservations in the west: Stop doing the Ghost Dance!

Names were recorded by Indian agents of those Indians who led bands or tribes in defiance of the order and were dubbed 'fomenters' and orders were issued for their arrest. It was these documents, many inaccurate or intentionally misrepresented for the purpose of settling old scores, that ultimately if indirectly, led to the death of Sitting Bull.

People like Ross Riley and Tomas Finley argued on behalf of the Indians.

"They should be able to dance in what ever manner pleases them," Riley expounded. "Yes, Indian children should learn English, but they must also be taught the ways of their people and the language or dialect of their individual tribe or band. Religion should not be taught at all but remain a personal or family choice!"

Trouble along the Columbia and Okanogan Rivers was less obvious than in the Dakotas, Montana and Wyoming, mainly due to the lack of military presence or tribal police, and Indians who wanted to dance could.

For Sam and Lillian, married life on Wishbone was pure bliss. They spent their days exploring the ranch, finding all sorts of little hideaways, hidden ponds and major game trails. Nights were spent discovering all the special nooks and crannies of the amazing house and each other.

On a cold morning in December Sam awoke before daylight with a headache and a feeling something was terribly wrong. He touched the amulet and the sensation intensified, much like when Larry was killed only with out the dream or vision. Several days later, he and Lillian learned of the death of Sitting Bull from a rider, on his way from the agency at Nespelem to the mission near the west end of the Wishbone Ranch. The rider did not know exactly when the killing happened but Sam was sure *he* knew.

The amulet knew.

Towards the end of December, the haunting feeling of impending danger or disaster again stuck in Sam's craw and he told Lillian, "I know the amulet is trying to tell me something. I must learn how to listen and understand. I might have been able to save Larry if I had known how to use its powers."

"Are my mom or dad in trouble? Does it tell you who needs help?" Lillian didn't question the power of the amulet. "It's not the army is it? Do you think Daniel and Joe knew who you were and pretended not to until they got back to Fort Vancouver?"

"No, it is not the army and it is not about me. This thing is far from here and is more like a supplication than a warning. I can feel trouble but I can not see it."

With Sitting Bull dead, the Hunkpapa Sioux were without a leader. Some wanted to retaliate by waging war against the soldiers and even the Indian police. Others believed if they continued the Ghost Dance the white man would disappear with the coming of the water grass. 'Ghost' camps were established where the dance was performed day and night in spite of its ban.

Some sought the guidance from the Sioux Chief, Red Cloud, on the reservation at Pine Ridge but many others fled to Cherry Creek and the camp of the Minniconjou Chief, Big Foot.

As more Hunkpapa Sioux joined Big Foot's camp, he believed they were in danger of attack by soldiers and decided to move his camp and followers to Pine Ridge, where he hoped they would be protected by Red Cloud's good standing with the white man.

As Big Foot led his band of Minneconjou and Sioux toward Pine Ridge he was met by Major Samuel Whitside of the 7th Cavalry. Whitside had been directed to arrest Big Foot whose name appeared on the list of fomenters. The orders came from the War Department in Washington D.C. The plan was to take him to a military camp at Wounded Knee Creek.

"You and your band will follow me," the major told Big Foot, "but first we will collect all of your weapons for safe keeping."

"We will go with you but we will not give up our weapons. We have done nothing wrong," Big Foot declared.

His band consisted of over one hundred warriors and nearly two hundred and fifty women and children. He did not want his warriors to be unarmed in case the soldiers intended to do harm to any of them.

"You will do as you're told or we will do it for you!" Major Whitside demanded.

Big Foot was cold, he was sick, and in no mood to be ordered around.

"Do what you must but our weapons are our pride. You can not take anymore of our pride than you already have without a fight."

"Wait!" John, a half-breed scout shouted. "They **will** fight, Major, and you will have to kill all these women and children. Are you sure you want to do that?"

After a tense hesitation the major replied, "We'll take their weapons when we get to camp." Summoning First Sergeant Mills, Whitside ordered, "Have half the troops fall in behind the prisoners. If any Indian raises a weapon, shoot him."

As the caravan dropped down onto *Chankpe Opi Wakpala,* the Indian name for Wounded Knee Creek, Big Foot's band began to chant.

"Hieyaya, hieya, hieyaya."

This was a sacred place, especially to the Sioux. Somewhere along this stream, while making their way to Canada and a new life, a grieving mother and father buried the heart of their son; the war chief of the Oglala Sioux and hero of the Battle of Little Big Horn…Crazy Horse.

Later that night, the rest of the 7th Cavalry Regiment commanded by Colonel James Forsyth arrived at Wounded Knee. With him, he carried orders to take Big Foot's band to the nearest railroad where they would be loaded and shipped to a military prison in Nebraska.

Colonel Forsyth was drunk when he again demanded that Big Foot and his warriors give up their weapons and that he and his band were to be taken away to a military prison.

Big Foot was enraged. "We have done nothing wrong!" he shouted. "We have stolen nothing. Our guns we paid for with the white man's gold or with fine pelts."

Big Foot's voice, faltered as emotion and illness overtook him. Many warriors gathered around him ready to fight…a larger group of soldiers encircled the warriors.

Big Foot spoke to his warriors, "Do not give the white soldiers your weapons."

Turning to the red-faced colonel, who was trying to sort through his whiskey haze, Big Foot said in painfully clear English, "My people will not raise their weapons against you or your soldiers, but we will not give up what is rightfully ours."

A Minneconjou medicine man, Yellow Bird, stepped forward and threw his rifle at Colonel Forsyth's feet.

"Take my weapon, I do not need it," he declared in a loud voice, then began to dance and yelled to the warriors, "Give them your weapons, it does not matter! They can not harm us if we do the Dance of the Ghosts."

Pulling his colorfully painted shirt over his head he waved it at the soldiers.

"This shirt is sacred! Bullets will fly away from it!" Yellow Bird proclaimed. Pointing to the warriors huddled inside the circle of soldiers he shouted, "Their shirts are sacred! They are Ghost Shirts, bullets can not penetrate them!"

Colonel Forsyth and several of his officers, also inebriated and trying to clear their heads, were caught flat-footed when a wild-eyed Minneconjou, named Black Coyote, broke from the agitated group of Indians shaking his rifle at the soldiers and yelling in his native tongue.

No one saw the shooter; not Colonel Forsyth or Big Foot but as bullets flew, Black Coyote ran wildly through the soldiers firing his rifle. Despite being wounded, he continued shooting and soldiers fell like cordwood onto the frozen ground.

Forsyth and his officers were shocked sober and began shouting orders and directing fire at the Indians who were running helter-skelter, attempting to escape the horrible noise and carnage of the battle they knew had begun.

The screams of women and cries of children mixed indiscriminately amidst the cursing and yelling of soldiers and warriors alike. As Indians ran for tents or teepees, the flash of muzzles and roar of gunfire was like the guts of hell were being heaved onto the battlefield.

At the sound of the first gunshot, Louise Weasel Bear grabbed her two children by the hands and ran for the closest teepee. A grizzled sergeant chased after her, firing as he ran. When a bullet struck her girl child of eight years she stopped then shielded her remaining young son. The sergeant kicked the young boy to the ground and dragged Louise into the teepee. Throwing down his rifle, he struggled to rip the clothes from her body. As he pulled her buckskin skirt up, she pulled her skinning knife from a sheath hanging at her side.

Hidden by the horrible sound of war and the teepee walls, the sergeant freed himself from his trousers and fell between the exposed legs of the Indian woman. As he poised to thrust into her womanhood, she plunged her skinning knife into his heart. Neither his scream nor hers could be distinguished from the others shattering the cold morning air.

Of the thirty-some soldiers found dead after the shooting stopped, only one had a bone-handled skinning knife protruding from the middle of his chest. Three hundred or more Indian warriors, women and children lay dead or dying. Attempts to find the wounded and recover the dead were curtailed when a fierce blizzard blew in from the northeast.

When the troops returned a week later they found frozen bodies embracing one another in a desperate effort to find warmth, others in a crawling position, evidence of a heroic attempt to reach shelter.

Wasumaza, a swift young warrior who some say 'out ran' the white man's bullets, survived the battle along with Yellow Bird, who fought fiercely and was among the few who continued to believe in the Ghost Dance and ghost-shirts after Wounded Knee. As long as anyone would listen, Yellow Bird told of looking down the barrel of the soldier's guns but was never struck by their bullets.

Louise Weasel Bear never understood why a soldier, if he was an honorable man, would attempt to impose himself on a woman he did not even know. From that day forward most of the Sioux Nation no longer believed any of the 7th Cavalry to be honorable.

"The soldiers had no reason to shoot at us, to kill us. We were peaceful Indians. Our Chief Big Foot would have done what the soldiers wanted. He believed the Ghost Dance would soon free us from their oppressive behavior," Yellow Bird declared.

Big Foot's death, falling so closely after the death of Sitting Bull, caused much sadness and disappointment among the tribes at Pine

Ridge and Standing Rock and along the upper Missouri. In the Black Hills and along the Cheyenne River, the Rosebud and the North Platte there was much anger. There was also disillusionment. Why did the Ghost Dance fail to exhume the ancestral warriors and lead the People in a great victory?

Wovoka, a thousand miles away at Walker Lake, heard about the killing at Wounded Knee Creek and mourned. The days of Indian resistance to white man domination were over. The white man had won the war of the plains. The Paiutes still believed in the Ghost Dance but Wovoka yearned for a chance to speak with Standing Wolf or Bent Grass.

If he had led the People astray, Wovoka wanted to know why or how. His knowledge of the Christian belief told him that for believers even a simple mistake could lead to hell and damnation.

For Christians it was all about Jesus, what if the Ghost Dance required belief in Bent Grass, whom he believed was a God or Goddess, or maybe belief in her son Standing Wolf.

The Messiah?

The thought tormented him but he had no way to know for sure without another vision taking him to the valley of the Sematuse, the home of the True People, to heaven.

Wovoka knew he could never mount a horse and ride to that mysterious valley, his only hope was that when he closed his eyes for sleep the Great Spirit would choose, once again, to transport him to the most wonderful place on earth he could imagine.

He smiled at the thought.

Was it really on earth?

Chapter Forty-one
Plains of the Pyramid

Rising above the small village, he looked down at his sleeping body. Peaceful, he thought. His chiseled face was expressionless; were it not for his closed eyes and steady breathing he might be mistaken for dead.

A spattering of wooden buildings spread out below him. The extensive narrow roof of the agency longhouse was the last thing he recognized before soaring above the river like a hungry hawk.

He was soon joined by others, some wearing full headdresses of hawk and eagle feathers, others with headbands adorned with a single feather of the crow or turkey buzzard. Some wore buffalo robes of the plains, others the fur-lined garments of the mountain people.

They moved in silence like bats in the night, down one river and up another to their eventual destination. No one in the ghostly armada knew where they were going, only that the Great Spirit had once again summoned them.

They were armed with war-axes, spears, long bows, arrows and rifles…the white man's rifles. He did not like killing the whites but was convinced they deserved to die. They had killed his people and would kill him if given the chance.

When last called upon by the spirits, he and the other chiefs and warriors of the *Choo-pin-it-pa-loo* had stopped the advancement of prospectors and settlers into the sacred land of the *Okinakane* and Pasayten.

Now the army was sending troops from Fort Simcoe to retaliate against Indians they believed to be responsible for that attack, but they would be punishing and killing Indians who had absolutely nothing to do with that attack or any other. The Great Spirit and the *Choo-pin-it-pa-loo* could not halt such injustice but they, too, could retaliate.

Excitement spread through him as he watched the dark shadow of a river give way to the lighter grasses of the plains. Before the light of day he found himself sitting astride a well-bred Appaloosa. Surrounded by many braves and war chiefs, all mounted on fine horses, they waited impatiently for the break of day.

From the grassy top of a granite pyramid, they watched a long column of bluecoats move noisily north. There were no settlers or prospectors with the soldiers but two giant guns that shoot twice were being pulled by one horse each. These horse soldiers were not on a mission of peace. They were intent on arresting Indians and punishing them for acts they had not committed.

Next to him on a spirited pinto sat a proud war chief, his bronze skin glowing in the morning light. He had much respect for this brave chief born of a Nez Perce mother and a Yakima father. He knew him as Kamiakin.

From this vantage point, he could see as far the eagle soars. If his eyes were those of the eagle, he could have seen all the way to the land of his people, the land where he had fished and hunted as a boy.

They did not speak, each knew why they were here, what had to be done. The bluecoats were between two great rivers, trapped like cayuse in a canyon. That was where they would die.

He watched the soldiers plod slowly north past the great butte, dragging their big guns and hindered by half-a-hundred mules laden with bulging packs.

Army whisky.

A hint of a smile tugged at his tight lips.

"Ah guess ya know we're being watched, Sir," lead packer Tom Beall said, riding alongside the colonel.

"I know," the colonel replied. "I don't expect they're anything more than curious."

From his position in the giant wild rye of the flatland he could see a few Indians atop the high butte to his right.

"Sure thing, colonel, ain't likely them Injuns want to mess with any part of the 5th Cavalry." Beall flashed a toothy grin, his ruddy complexion turning a shade or two darker.

"I hope you're right, colonel," Lieutenant Grier tentatively interjected. "From the top of that butte they've probably been watchin' us since we crossed the Snake."

As the serpentine column faded in the distance, the setting sun warned of the onset of darkness. The chief on the pinto horse gave a series of hand signals and the Indian horde split into five groups.

The bluecoats camped in a narrow canyon that provided shelter from the wind, still chilly in early May and fed by a sizeable stream which provided much needed water for man and animal.

Sunrise found the soldiers surrounded by five bands of Indians, each numbering two hundred or more. There were two bands at the north end of the canyon, one on the east and west canyons rims and one at the south end.

Whatever mission the bluecoats were on, it would end here, in this isolated canyon in the land of the Palouse.

"I, for one, will be damn glad when we reach the Columbia," said Lt. Gaston. "I feel like we been sittin' ducks ever since we crossed the Snake."

"I don't see how crossin' the Columbia is gonna improve things much, replied Captain O.H.P (Oliver Hazard Perry) Taylor. "It's the Indians of the upper Columbia that are causing all the trouble."

"That might be, but these Indians have some way of talkin' to each other. If those mountain Indians are communicatin' to these plains Indians, and if they're pissed," the lieutenant removed his hat and long fingers through his blond hair, "we're hangin' out like a tit in a sand storm."

"I'm sure the colonel knows what he's doin'," O. H. P. retorted. "Besides, Indians are afraid to fight at night and they're sure not goin' to want to attack in the daylight when we can see 'em." He patted his beat up musketoon, a forerunner to the cavalry carbine.

With the swiftness of a striking rattlesnake and the savagery of a wolverine, the strategically placed bands struck. The east and west bands descended on the troops, striking the body of the command while the north and south bands cut off the brigade's head and feet.

Mounted on agile horses, the Indians made slashing attacks on the pinned-down soldiers and lances and arrows found their mark with astonishing accuracy.

Surrounded and cut off from each other, Lieutenants Gaston and Gregg fought to join forces. Captain Winder bravely fought his way across Spring Creek to high ground where he tried to set up the mountain howitzer, but its blasts were no threat to the fast moving warriors.

"Stand up and fight like a man!" Winder yelled at the Indians, as swift horses carried them out of cannon range then charged again while panicky soldiers struggled to reload.

The soldiers fought bravely but were no match for the powerful Indian armada. It may have been a blessing that the expedition's lead packer had replaced many of the boxes of ammunition with whisky, believing the presence of so many armed soldiers would intimidate any Indian force contemplating an attack.

When their ammo ran out, most of the soldiers turned to the whisky to help them face certain, horrible death. Only the lead packer who sabotaged the supplies, the Nez Perce scout who led the soldiers into the trap and the colonel in charge of the command managed to escape. The Great Spirit wanted the commander at Fort Simcoe to think twice before sending troops onto the plains of the pyramid.

When he awoke, he rubbed his eyes and looked around his small one-room cabin. A smile pursed his weathered face.

There was trouble in the Badlands and he wondered how long it would be before the *Choo-pin-it-pa-loo* would ride again?

Chief Joseph could hardly wait…

Chapter Forty-two
Do-over

A COLD wind blew out of the northeast and the winter sky turned gun-barrel blue as Lillian and Sam finished putting out feed for the stock and secured the barn in anticipation of a storm.

"This wind is coming right off the Canadian plains," Lillian said under the cover of the barn.

On the Flathead this kind of wind could turn into a blizzard in a hurry and Sam knew from experience they were something to take serious but there were at least a couple of mountain ranges between the Kartar Valley and the Flathead country to deflect storms.

"I know we need to be prepared but I doubt we'll see anything like you were used to on the Running R," he assured Lilly.

He wasn't quite as confident as he sounded. He remembered one winter at Fort Okanogan when the drifting snow isolated the fort for more than three months.

They were stocked up on supplies and wood, the cattle and horses were fed or had feed available, and the idea of being snowed in with Lillian for a few months didn't seem like anything even resembling punishment.

Still, Sam was anxious for spring. It had nothing to do with cold or wind or snow, it was another of those pesky feelings; nothing he could see or even dream about, it was more like sensing someone else's pain.

He knew it was the amulet. He was no more than a four or five day ride from Pasayten, and he wished he could get rid of the feeling that the amulet wanted him to return there.

Everyday, he left the house feeling like he was being watched and assumed it was the black wolf, although it hadn't shown itself since their search for Larry.

Lillian missed her parents and communication with them was difficult; mail couriers were slow and undependable and based on what word they were able to get, Indian problems seemed to be far worse on the Flathead than around the Okanogan.

Sam had become friendly with a few Indians and bureau agents at the Nespelem Agency. They were especially concerned about growing anger and unrest on reservations in South Dakota and Wyoming and believed the possibility of all-out war was very real.

But not everything was gloom and doom. Sam was in a state of euphoria resulting from a most unexpected surprise. While talking with an agent at Nespelem an Indian entered the building, wearing buckskin leggings with ornamental fringe down the sides and a shirt that looked to be made of silk. On it was an ornate design of an Appalosa horse with colorful feathers decorating its mane and tail, Sam thought he was the best looking Indian he'd ever seen. The man had the blackest, thickest hair and wore it in an unusual style. The forelock was cut about four inches long and stood straight up from his head. Two long braids framed either side of his face while the rest of his hair hung mid-way down his back. He stood straight and proud, his facial features sharp like a hawk or eagle and his eyes were piercing, intelligent, unblinking and focused like a bird of prey. He appeared to be elderly but with a hint of the strong proud physique of a chief.

The young Indian agent, to whom Sam was speaking, stood and took a moment to talk to the Indian then he turned to Sam.

"Sam," he casually said, "I'd like you to meet Joseph, Chief of the Nez Perce."

Sam nearly leaped to his feet. He had heard of Joseph, everyone had heard of Joseph. Extending his hand in anticipation of a handshake he was surprised again when instead, Joseph made a circular movement with his hand. After a few minutes of awkward attempts at small talk, Sam pulled the amulet from inside his shirt.

"Ever seen one of these?" he asked the chief, hoping it might at least serve as a conversation piece.

Joseph's intense, fierce eyes lit up like he was being paid a visit by ancient ancestors.

"That is a most sacred symbol of my people," he said in broken English. "How do you have this?" His voice could not conceal his surprise and wonder.

Sam was beginning to regret his attempt to show off for Joseph.

"It is a long story Chief," he said, sounding weary. "One I will be glad to tell you if you have a lifetime." He was being flippant but he was also dead serious.

He visited with Joseph for over two hours that day. Chief Joseph had much to say about the white soldiers, his run from White Bird, and the amulet.

"Before my birth, it was sacred symbol of Nez Perce people called *Choo-pin-it-pa-loo*. I did not see these great warriors but my grandfather told me they could make themselves invisible."

Joseph looked longingly out the window of the agency building. "If I could have done that for those who fought with me, I would now be in Canada, living free."

It was a thought that rang like a church bell in Sam's head. Was he making the same mistake as Chief Joseph?

Joseph fixed his coal-black eyes on Sam. "You must be a very special human to possess such sacred symbol. Someday when I am old, I shall remember the day I spoke to one who holds the amulet and I will weep with joy."

By the time Sam returned to Wishbone, he had a new understanding and even greater respect for the piece of leather hanging around his neck and for Chief Joseph. There was something about the man that belied his apparent subjucation. A sense of pride and defiance was barely hidden behind those piercing eyes…and he recognized the amulet…

Consider the possibilities.

When the blizzard blew into the Kartar Valley on the last day of December, 1890, Sam and Lillian snuggled under a blanket by a cozy fire and comforted themselves with the belief that any threat of an Indian war would have to wait until spring.

Chinook winds of spring brought the news of Wounded Knee and what was being called a massacre of un-armed women and children. The trading post was selling newspapers from the east and from San Francisco and Seattle with detailed accounts of the killing, including graphic illustrations.

"It is good most Indians can not read," Sam complained to Lillian, "or we would already be at war."

"Do you think the 7th Cavalry would really gun down women and children?" Lillian asked. "The troops that brought mom and dad to Wishbone seemed like good people."

"There is one thing I do know about the army," Sam lamented. "There are good people and bad people, sometimes the bad people are giving the orders."

He thought for a moment before continuing.

"Lillian, it says this massacre at Wounded Knee Creek happened on the 28th day of December, a few days before the blizzard. I think the amulet was trying to tell me Wounded Knee was going to happen." He watched carefully for Lillian's response.

"But why? There's nothing you could have done about it," Lilly questioned.

"I am not so sure," Sam replied. "I know this will sound loco but I am starting to wonder if there is a limit to its powers."

"And what exactly does that mean?"

Lillian looked confused. She knew Sam was obsessed with the little leather circlet and while she had seen some things only it could be responsible for, she was concerned he might be becoming either obsessed or possessed.

He won't even take it off to make love, she thought.

"I do not know what it means. It is like I am suppose to do something but I do not what. The scary part is that I am being drawn back to that valley."

"Are you really sure you could find it?"

"Sí, with the amulet, I could find it alright. I doubt I could miss it if I tried." Sam tried to joke about it but he was convinced it was no laughing matter.

"What are we waiting for?" Lillian chirped. "Let's go see what's bothering you."

"Snow, for one thing, water for another," Sam replied. "The valley is high in the mountains and I am sure there will be a lot of snow until late May, early June and we have to cross the Okanogan River. It can be traicionero, treacherous during high water."

"Fine, on the first of June we go in search of this mysterious valley and the meaning of the amulet." Lillian was being a little theatrical but she was serious as smallpox.

Sam was not sure about Lillian going with him but wasn't ready to have that discussion just yet. When they heard again from Ross and Ruth, things had calmed a little on the Flathead Reservation. The military presence was greatly increased with members of the 7th Cavalry on constant patrol.

Indians were no longer doing the Ghost Dance, at least not in the open, and those who knew about Wounded Knee Creek were discouraged and disillusioned that neither the dance nor the shirts had worked.

"I think I may know why the dance failed at Wounded Knee," Sam told Lillian. "In the valley, the Indian who was dancing wore the amulet and was making the circular motion with it. I do not know how the dance got from that valley to reservations everywhere, but I am pretty sure they missed the most important part…the amulet. And there's one more thing," he added. "I saw the leaves of aspen trees explode into mounted warriors. There are no leaves on the trees in December."

"But if someone from the valley told others about the dance, wouldn't they have told them about the amulet?"

"Maybe they did not know and thought the power came from the dance when it really was the amulet." Sam became very pensive. "I do not know how many of these there are," he said as he pulled the talisman from his shirt, "but what if there are only two, this one and the one that dancer had. I saw what happened there, but maybe when your uncle led us into that valley we interrupted something." He had Lillian's complete attention.

"Like what?" she questioned.

"I took this off a white man. I have never understood what a white man was doing in that valley, but even more why would he have what is obviously something very sacred around his neck?" He rubbed his thumb thoughtfully over the painted wolf. "I do not know who or what that red-haired white man was, but I think he was leaving the valley when we stopped them. Maybe we interfered with some kind of destiny. Not only the fate of Indians but the fate of mankind may have been altered. Maybe I am going loco, Lilly, and I kind of hope so because otherwise this is getting very frightening."

With power comes responsibility.

Sam was having all sorts of crazy thoughts. He knew the amulet had a hold on him from the moment he first shoved it in his pocket. Now that he was back in the land of the *Okinakane* the hold seemed to be getting even stronger. Unless he could somehow talk himself out of it, come June he would find out why.

Among the things that changed between when Sam fled the fort and his return to the area was the influx of civilization, if you could call it that. Small villages, or towns, were popping up along both the Okanogan and the Columbia Rivers. The country was losing its remote and 'godforsaken' feel.

"Indians," Sam lamented, "except for a few lost bands, they are all living on reservations. Children of Salish speaking tribes of the Okanogan are taken at age four or five to the Willamette or Klamath Reservations where Chinook is spoken. Children of the Willamette and Klamath are sent to Colville or Nez Perce Reservations. This is done with a sinister purpose; to rob a generation of their language, heritage and culture. Since the children are unable to communicate in their native tongues they have no choice but to learn a common language…English."

"That's just plain mean and wrong!" Lillian's deep-blue eyes turned virtually black with anger. "But couldn't that be dangerous? I mean if the tribes all speak different languages it's hard for them to organize." Lillian had a quizzical look on her lovely face. "But once they all speak English couldn't that backfire? What if they all band together against the whites?"

"I think the government and the army believe by that time there will be no real Indians left. They will all be at least part white in more ways than one."

The mysterious Indian communication system known as 'talking on the wind' was operating at a frenzied pace. The sound of drums and unspoken words were carried across the wind and water. Something big was happening, something that touched the heart and soul of all Native Peoples.

Ta-keen Eagle and Bent Grass did not see the activity as a danger to the Indians of the valley, but were filled with concern for those Indians not fortunate enough to have been chosen as the True People... Sematuse.

Bent Grass' discussions with Fire-hair Frank and Standing Wolf were enlightening. Their experience in the world outside of the valley of rainbows gave her a new understanding of their unique connection. The lives of many warriors, women and children had been lost, and Bent Grass, Frank and Standing Wolf felt responsible in their own way; Standing Wolf for leaving the valley to spread the belief in the Ghost Dance without a full understanding of its limitations; Frank for failing to protect the amulet which he now understood was vital to the Ghost Dance.

Bent Grass felt responsible for everything. She should have known the dance was powerless without the amulet. She should not have permitted Wovoka to leave the valley armed with only a strong belief. She had allowed an entire Indian Nation to go into battle unarmed and misled.

Until Standing Wolf's father came to the valley with the winter snow so long ago, Bent Grass had no idea there was a world outside the valley. Even then she did not imagine any connection or interaction between the two worlds. It was not until her son brought his friend and follower, Wovoka to the valley that she understood.

She had learned about the desperate conditions Indians on reservations were forced to live under. Most reservations were poor land, of little value to whites and even less to the Indians. There was little or no game and fishing was difficult at best.

The Indian Bureaus and government pledged shipments of food and equipment so the Indians could grow their own but few promises were fulfilled, and when something of value was discovered on a reservation, such as gold or silver or any precious metals, the land was removed from the reservation and opened to settlers or businessmen for purchase.

Bent Grass learned that 'time' had not been kind to the Indian. She had no concept of 'years' but Wovoka had used numbers to keep track of them. It was as if the white man counted years the way Indians counted winters. She had to admit it served some purpose; it gave the white man a way of remembering.

Wovoka told her of a great war when the white man tried to rid the land of his own kind. It seemed the white man's thirst for killing was insatiable. When they finally tired of killing each other they decided to kill all the Native People…Indian and Mexican alike.

Frank and Standing Wolf told her the war between the whites was called 'Civil War', though there was nothing civil about it, and regaled her with stories about how they became friends and why they parted ways and what happened later.

What Bent Grass found most compelling was the way all things in the white man's world happened on the name of a year; start of the Civil War, 1862; end of the Civil War, 1865; white man gives land to Indians in treaty of 1868; white man takes land back from the Indian, 1869; Custer defeated at Little Big Horn, 1876; massacre at Wounded Knee, 1890.

When Wovoka visited the valley the year outside was called 1888. Standing Wolf told her that outside the valley, right now, the year was 1891. The Sematuse had their way of keeping track of events and seasons so none of this 'naming of time' mattered to her at first, and she found it amusing… until it struck her that 'time' in the valley did not change…ever, only people changed…some grew older, some got wiser.

However, the importance of counting time was becoming apparent to Bent Grass. She was having visions she did not understand, other than that she, Fire-hair and Standing Wolf must keep track of time. It was a matter of utmost urgency, though she could not see why or how.

The *mowich*, or mule deer, always came down from the high country and the fish always swam upstream toward the headwaters. There was the time of the first frost, of falling leaves, of snow covered ground, of water grass and dry grass. But time for the Sematuse simply went around in a circle. Bent Grass did not see any reason to count time with numbers. Still, she knew she must. Did time moved forward to some unseen and unknown place? If time began somewhere, it had to end somewhere.

What a silly idea!

Part of the power of the circle, Bent Grass knew, was that you could always return to a place in the circle for a do-over. The past was never gone, only in a different place. In the outside world, with years moving forward, the past was gone forever, there was no going back... or was there?

"Human beings make mistakes," she told Frank. "How can you ever hope to get things right if you can not go back and fix your mistakes?"

After pondering her question, Frank replied, "Perhaps that is why the Indians have lived in harmony with the land for thousands of years, and why the white man has nearly destroyed it in a hundred. The buffalo are gone and iron horses on steel tracks bring more and more white men onto the land like ants to a picnic. When the white man makes mistakes he can't go back and fix them, he can only make new ones. Those mistakes and consequences last forever."

Bent Grass looked toward the great mountain, *Chopaka,* with tears of sadness in her ebony eyes. "But the white man teaches Indians outside this valley to see time their way and the Indians can no longer fix their mistakes. The circle has been broken!" she cried.

"So what does that mean for Indians outside this valley?" Frank asked.

"I am afraid it means hope is lost. There is no longer a way to right the wrongs of the past, no way to bring back the buffalo. Even *Ogle Wa Nagi* has grown tired of the old ways."

Frank looked longingly at his lovely wife, and mother of his longtime friend.

Do-over.

That was something both Frank and Standing Wolf knew something about. Because of this beautiful valley and this mysterious woman, they were both granted the rare gift of a do-over. Only Bent Grass could know the ramifications.

Chapter Forty-three
Resurrection

Not far from the Valley of the Sematuse, Samuel DeSoto would like nothing better than a do-over as he pondered his fate and future. He was only twenty-five with everything a man could want, but he had a past that haunted him and could threaten his otherwise bright future. Most troubling was the amulet; he was afraid of living with it and fearful of being without it.

It was like seeing into the future, knowing when bad things were going to happen but helpless to prevent them from happening. But it also brought good luck…especially for him and he might be learning how to use it to prevent the bad…to alter the future. Maybe even change the past!

He thought of Ruth and her attacker and Larry's murder…were these coincidence or consequence? There was only one way to find out but that meant giving up the amulet, perhaps his life.

Or did it?

What about Lillian? If he returned to the valley, she was insisting upon going with him.

Sitting on the front porch of the Wishbone house, Sam and Lillian watched a spectacular sunset with awe and appreciation. It was late May and the air was soft and warm. They'd made slow, gentle love that the afternoon and both were relaxed and relieved. Sam decided it is the perfect time to talk.

"Lil," he began.

She knew when he called her 'Lil' he had a lot on his mind. "Yes?" she said in measured anticipation.

"Before we go look for that valley and take the amulet back, there are some things I need to ask you."

"Yes?" she said, using the same questioning tone as before.

"What if," he began, "What if I had the power of God? What if I could bring the dead back to life? What if I could take away all bad things that ever happened to the people I care about? Would that be bueno?"

"Do you mean bring Larry back?!" Lillian's eyes were giant sapphires.

Sam was hesitant, afraid to admit what he believed to be true. "Si, bring Larry back. I believe with the amulet I might have the power to bring the dead back to life. I know it sounds loco but I saw Indians come out of thunderclouds and aspen leaves. I do not think there is a limit to the power of the amulet."

Lillian swallowed hard. She knew Sam was dead serious, but the pun did not amuse her. Then she felt a rush of excitement flood over her body and mind.

Bring Larry back?

It was one of those things you wish for, knowing it can never be. She knew the amulet held special powers but wasn't ready to believe it held the power of life and death, especially life after death.

Sam was thinking of a number of things he could do, including erasing anything that creep had done to Ruth.

Why not think big?

Why not go back to before Lillian's uncles and the 5th Cavalry Regiment entered that valley? Why not make that never happen? But if that never happened he would not have met Ruth or Lillian. He would not be a deserter… He would not even have the amulet.

What about Wounded Knee, hundreds had died there. He touched the amulet as a reminder that all of that was real.

For a moment, Lillian was angry at Sam for suggesting that he could do such a thing.

But what if he could?

She fought to get control of her emotions.

"Are you asking if I think you can or if I think you should?" she asked in measured tones.

"I do not know…maybe if you think I should," Sam replied, thinking he might have poked a stick through a hornet's nest.

"What I think, Samuel DeSoto is that you have no right to ask me that. I'm not the one who thinks he's God…you are! Of course I want my brother back; for me, for mom and dad but I don't have the power. If I did I would make my own decisions, not ask a mere mortal what they would do. It's not fair, Sam, it's just not fair!"

There is a lot more to being God than I thought, Sam conceded.

"I did not think you would want me to bring Larry back without warning you." He was on the defensive.

"How would it work, Sam? We've already buried him, people have mourned. People went to trial for his murder, people died because of his murder. Can you bring those people back too?"

"I wanted only to make things right, to fix what I might have caused." Sam was almost pleading.

"What do you mean? Do you think you caused Larry's murder?"

"It is complicated. I have a very bad feeling the magic of this amulet is like a double-edged dagger." Sam was into something he did not want to talk about.

"Explain complicated!" Lillian demanded.

"Bueno…it is like things happen that are good for me but sometimes it is not so good for others. At least it seems that way. It was like when there was no need to keep me on at your ranch then Larry broke his collarbone…that kind of thing. I do not think I had anything to do with his murder." Sam was frazzled.

"Sam," Lillian softened her tone. "I think we need to take the amulet back to the red-haired guy you took it from. Maybe he knows how to use it, maybe he will use it to kill us but at least I will feel like we're doing the right thing." She took his hand and kissed him on the cheek. "I don't want to be married to a God. I want to be married to you."

"But think of the good it could do, has already done," Sam protested.

"Okay, I'll tell you what. Let's take it back to that valley and if the people there want you to keep it, good. If not, we give it back and hope they let us leave or live…or both." To Lilly, it sounded like a perfect compromise.

Sam smiled.

"Deal," he said.

When Sam and Lillian rode around Warrior Lake, named by Daniel Bone and Joe Wright, a band of mounted Indians on the horizon seemed to materialize against an otherwise blue sky. The Indians wore no feathered headdresses and carried no decorated spears, instead these warriors packed rifles with a feather or two tied to the barrel or stock.

The appearance of Indians was commonplace and comforting, Sam and Lillian thought of them as guardians of the Kartar and Wishbone. Sam and Lillian each led a packhorse carrying food for themselves and gifts, which included blankets, knives, whet stones and cloth for the Indians. With no idea what to expect, Sam admitted the whole thing scared him in a way he had not been afraid since his last time in that valley.

Sam watched the mounted warriors on the rocky rim with only a passing interest when suddenly the waters of Warrior Lake began to shimmer as if something huge and shiny was swimming just below the surface. Sam looked at Lillian. Her eyes looked as if they were tiny replicas of the lake itself.

The shimmering turned to boiling white caps as if the lake bottom was on fire. Sam reached for the amulet as a human form began to emerge from the murky water. A black hat broke the surface then shoulder-length curly blond hair tumbled out from under the hat. Amidst the boiling caldron a man with a handle-bar mustache sat atop a raw-boned bay.

Neither Sam nor Lillian even thought of speaking. They were totally transfixed by the unbelievable sight.

"So yer the one!" the apparition said, looking directly at Sam. "Yer the one that made off with the little trinket that's causin' such a ruckus!"

Sam looked quickly at Lilly, her mouth and eyes were both wide open.

The blond man and his horse levitated just above the water's surface. He twisted his moustache and leaned back in the saddle. "That thing hangin' 'round yer neck has got a hold on ya'll, ain't it? Sombitch, ah told that damn Breed it would happen. Ah told him it was alive, it's got a spirit ya know. Ain't got a soul but it's got a spirit."

Sam and Lillian were so mesmerized they hardly heard a word the mirage spoke.

"Ah can see ya got a pure heart. It woulda been quite a tussle if Breed woulda caught up with ya. Ah guess ya'll know it's that piece uh leather makin' ya'll do what yer fixin' ta do."

His flint-blue eyes shifted to the young woman on the Palomino. "Ain't ya just a sight for sore eyes, just as pretty as yer ma, wish ah could give ya'll a big hug but ah ain't quite got that trick figgered out yet."

Lillian looked at Sam, he simply shrugged.

"Ah'm yer Uncle Roy, Missy, ah ain't real fond uh meetin' ya'll this way but ah got somethin' ta tell ya. Ah'm sure ya been told ah'm dead an' ah am. But dead ain't exactly what ya'll think it is. It's more like steppin' sideways through a crack or seam. They call 'em portals, they lead ta a parallel existence, another die-mension."

"Can the amulet bring the dead back to life?" Sam was startled by the sound of his own voice.

"Questions for me have ya? Ah like that." Roy twisted in the saddle as the water beneath the big bay began to swirl. "The only limit to the power uh that thing you call an amulet is when it's used. Ah sure wish ah could show Breed how smart ah got."

The swirling waters of Warrior Lake were beginning to form a whirlpool under the ghostly horse and rider.

"What do you mean, 'when it's used'?" Lillian had found her voice.

"If ya'll git ta where yer fixin' ta go, ya' will find out. Ah wish ah would uh known sooner that ya can find a portal without havin' ta die. Next time we meet ya'll will know what ahm talkin' about."

As abruptly as he appeared, Lilly's Uncle Roy disappeared into the depths of Warrior Lake. For her it was like a dream, for Sam it was a nightmare.

He was sure he never felt so vulnerable in his entire life, not even after the loss of his parents. He had everything to lose and was only doing this because somewhere deep in his conscience he knew it was the right thing. The closer they got to the Okanogan River and the valley, the less sure he felt. Sam silently scolded himself for not leaving well enough alone.

The river crossing was a rather harrowing. The water, while not especially high, was swift and wider than Sam would have preferred but they made it safely to the other side. They camped along the river's west bank and held each other long into the night, both plagued by unanswered questions.

It wasn't words on the wind or distant drums; this time it was a powerful vision, as powerful as the one prior to the arrival of the horse soldiers. Bent Grass asked Frank and Standing Wolf to come to the cave of spirits with her.

"I had a vision of two white people, a man and a woman," she said. "They are coming here. They know where we are and they are coming here!"

"Perhaps it is my friend, Wovoka," Standing Wolf said. "Do you see danger for our people?"

"No," Bent Grass said, "but if it is Wovoka and he is coming here with a woman, he may be in **great** danger." She smiled thinking of Willow.

Becoming serious she said, "I feel the pull of the amulet. I think it is returning to us along with its bearer."

"You said a man and a woman," Standing Wolf stated. "Do you think it is the soldier? Who is the woman?"

"I only know they are coming, not who they are. There is something special about them… very special." Bent Grass touched Frank's arm. "In my vision the woman has fire-hair like yours. Maybe she comes from your tribe."

Frank smiled. Not likely, he thought…unless she comes from a family of wharf rats, his mind flashed by to his boyhood and Monsieur Taureau and Julie… the smile faded.

*

Riding past Janis Crossing, Sam and Lillian took a moment to appreciate the lavender and yellow slopes covered with lupin and sunflowers. The expansive colors were brilliant, almost breathtaking and Lillian muttered, "What a beautiful place, this Mother Earth."

"It is even more beautiful because of you," Sam said, and meant it.

He chose not to mention an eerie feeling that caused him to shiver as his gaze drifted across the river to the strange rock formations.

Standing Wolf was particularly interested in his mother's vision. "If it is the soldier I followed he is clever and cunning. We must not underestimate him again as I did."

"He may be clever but he also has the amulet," Bent Grass interjected. "All of us failed to consider that when you went after him. He has power as long as he has it. If **he** does not have it, then someone else is being drawn to us by the sacred symbol."

Standing Wolf was thinking…Why come back to the valley where he could face an even more terrifying fate than if the army found him?

"Is the amulet telling him what to do, Mother? Why did my amulet not tell me how to find him?"

"One question at a time, my Son," Bent Grass said. "Once the soldier you call Sam, bonded with the amulet it was protecting him but that is not all. Because you were outside our valley, the amulet was also protecting you. That is why it did not tell you how to find Sam."

"So what will happen if he comes here?" Frank was getting anxious. "Shouldn't we be concerned?"

"They pose no danger to us. I do not know when they will be here, only that they will. It is that 'time' thing again. It is different where they are than it is here."

"So how will you know when they are here?" Frank asked, still nervous. "Will the amulet know it was once around my neck?" He thought that was a stupid question but was compelled to ask.

Bent Grass was not much help. She shrugged and said, "I will know when the amulet is here."

*

"That is the river!" Sam said excitedly, "the one that leads to the valley! Roy called it Lost River when the cavalry regiment followed it from the Okanogan into the Pasayten…and oblivion."

The trail ascended away from the river and they rode into a small aspen thicket when the sun was settling into the western sky.

"Let us camp here for the night," Sam said. "I have a feeling tomorrow is going to be a big day."

After a meal of hard-tack and grouse cooked over a campfire they spread out a couple blankets on the ground.

Sam pulled the Lillian close and whispered, "I love you. I will always love you. If something goes bad tomorrow I want you to grab the amulet and do not let go."

He kissed her softly at first, but when she pressed hard against him their kiss was filled with white-hot passion. As his hands moved smoothly over her body, she felt his passion rise to match her need.

Later, lying spent in one another's arms they looked at the star-filled sky. "I have a strange feeling, Lilly." Sam sounded as if he were in a trance, "like a powerful force is calling me." He touched the amulet…

Morning brought a mix of excitement and trepidation. After a valiant attempt to eat breakfast they packed up their gear and headed for the one thing Sam was not sure he could find, the nearly invisible crevice that led into the valley.

Not to worry, the amulet will show the way.

They rode more than an hour before Sam pulled Bigfoot to a halt.

"What is it?" Lillian asked, as she drew back on Buttercup's reins.

"I'm not sure," Sam replied. "I have another odd feeling."

Bent Grass awoke with a start.

"The amulet is very near," she said, as she shook Frank from a sound sleep. "I must go to the cave of *tlchachies*. Find Standing Wolf and wait here, you will know if I need you!"

It was a level of excitement Frank had never seen in his normally serene and composed wife.

*

Sam dismounted and removed Bigfoot's bridle, replaced it with a halter and tied the horse to a stout fir tree, then motioned for Lillian to do the same with Buttercup.

"There's something over there," he said, pointing toward an ominous rock bluff a hundred yards away.

With his Colt .45 on his hip, Sam pulled his carbine from the saddle scabbard. Lillian did not say a word. She didn't know if they were pursuing some kind of animal or if Sam was having another vision.

Following obediently, she stayed close and quiet, anxiously looking for any movement or unusual sight. When Sam stopped unexpectedly, she bumped into him. They both felt it; a blast of cool air coming out of the rock face. If not for that cool air, Sam surmised the opening would not have been found. It was large enough to take a horse through but completely hidden by dense folage. He poked his head into the gap. It was dark but there was an eerie glow, like a candle-lit room on a stormy night. Stepping back, he helped Lillian around the rock outcrop then, peering inside, they waited for their eyes to adjust to the dim light then, holding hands they stepped through the rock fissure. The glow intensified and though they couldn't make out its source, it appeared to be coming from all around them.

"This is more than a cave," Sam whispered to a captivated Lillian. "Much more...," his words trailed off, lost in the moment.

As if ignited by a divine source in what appeared to be some subterranean lair, a flash illuminated the grotto in a flood of light! The sight before them was like nothing either had ever seen. Lillian tightened her grip on Sam's hand and with her other, reached for the amulet hanging around his neck.

Chapter Fourty-four
Holy Ghost

It was nothing like they expected, but what had they expected; a devilish-looking man with greased-back hair in a pin-stripped suit, a wolf-like beast with human arms and legs carrying a pitch fork or maybe an angel with the wings of a dove and playing a harp?

Despite the obvious power of the amulet, Sam and Lillian did not anticipate anything more than a valley filled with Indians, whom they hoped they could convince they meant no harm to, and who would accept the return of the amulet, thank them for their good deed and bid them a safe return to Wishbone.

What they saw was a cave filled with amazing artwork and the captivating sight of a beautiful Indian woman dressed in a white robe waiting to greet them. She had long black-braids and smoldering black eyes that demanded their attention.

Sam's mind was spinning like the spokes of a runaway wagon. She doesn't look dangerous…on the contrary, he thought…She looks more like an angel, not the angel of death, I hope!

"You have found the sacred cave of *tlchachies*," Bent Grass stated. "I am called Bent Grass, seer of the Sematuse."

A cold panic washed over Sam's body. He could not understand a single word the Indian woman said. He looked at Lillian; she stood transfixed, staring at the seraphic looking woman.

"Of course, they have their own language," he muttered.

He was astonished when Lillian spoke, had he not seen her lips moving he would have thought it was the Indian woman. He was also amazed how brave and calm Lilly sounded.

"My name is Lillian. We have something to return. Something we believe is yours," she explained. "We believe it has very powerful medicine."

Bent Grass spoke again, in English. "Forgive me," she said, and repeated her message.

"How do you know our language?" Sam asked, having found his tongue. "My name is Sam," he quickly added.

"Sam," Bent Grass seemed to dwell on his name. "You are the soldier who took the amulet from my husband. You do not look like a soldier."

"Much has changed since that day," Sam replied, feeling more confident but disturbed that she knew who he was. After all, she hadn't turned them into stone yet.

"What is this place?" he asked, looking around in awe.

"It is the way between your world and ours," Bent Grass answered.

Sam and Lillian looked at each other, unable to comprehend what Bent Grass was telling them.

"What do you mean, 'between our worlds'?" Lillian asked.

After what she had seen Sam do with the amulet, she was ready to believe anything.

"Where is the valley I saw?" Sam asked. He was sure there was more here than a cave, phenomenal as it was, and thought…It should be dark as a grave digger's pocket. "How do you make the light?" he asked.

"What is a seer?" Lillian asked. "Are these paintings yours? Did you paint the amulet?"

The question struck Sam and Lillian at the same time. Was this cave a gateway to some kind of heaven and this angelic-looking woman the gatekeeper? Sam's head was spinning like a Texas Tornado.

"I painted the amulet," Bent Grass said. "I have painted two. My son is the bearer of the first…you are the bearer of the second."

The enormity of her statement was not lost on Sam. He had seen and felt the power of the amulet and if this woman was its creator, what did that mean?

"I have found this circulet has great power." Sam knew this was his chance to have all his questions answered. "How does it work? Do you know some kind of magic?"

"I have a gift but the power is in the amulet. I made it so." Bent Grass did not sound boastful, though a touch of pride could be found in her soft voice.

Sam decided this was a good time for a confession.

"When I took the amulet I did so out of fear," he began. "Things were happening I did not believe were possible. I only grabbed at a chance for survival." He waited guardedly for a response, getting none he continued. "The amulet has been good to me. I want to keep it but my wife believes I should return it to the rightful owner." Again, Sam paused a moment before adding, "I did not know it was your husband I took it from." It was a pitiful attempt at an apology but heartfelt.

Bent Grass smiled and Sam and Lillian thought the cave felt a little warmer.

"You, too, have a gift. You have a wise *mahakin*." Bent Grass looked at Lillian with what appeared to be curiosity and amusement. "You have fire-hair like my husband. Perhaps you are from the same tribe."

She made a joke!

Lillian and Sam were astonished that this apparent deity was actually jesting with them.

There is no better time than now, Sam decided.

"Señora Bent Grass, since I have been in possession of this amulet many goods things happened, but also some very bad things," he said, trying not to stumble over his words. "Does the amulet have two sides…good and evil?" He paused, "And if it does, can it be controlled so only good things happen?"

"You were here when the soldiers tried to make us leave the valley. It was bad for them and good for us. Many things have two sides, whether or not something is good depends on which side you are on." Bent Grass seemed pleased with her answer but Sam was frustrated.

"Maybe I do not ask the right question," he said. "If you did not want a bad thing to occur, even if it might be good for you, does the amulet make sure what is best for you will happen, even if it is bad for another person? I do not know any other way to ask it," he concluded.

"The amulet will always protect you," Bent Grass replied. "If a person means you harm it is bad for that person. If something bad happens to a person who did not mean you harm, that is the way of things. Bad things sometimes happen to good people."

Coincidence!

Sam took the first deep breath he could remember since Larry's death. Larry didn't die because of him or the amulet.

"Is there a limit to its powers?" Sam asked, remembering that fateful day when Lillian's uncles and a thousand soldiers died in the worst way imaginable.

"The power of the amulet is limited only by where and when it is used. When inside the valley of the Sematuse it can not change things outside, if outside it can not change things in the valley."

Sam knew this was his only chance for answers and the questions kept coming. "Many Indians were killed while dancing at a place called Wounded Knee Creek. They believed the Ghost Dance would protect them. Could the amulet have saved them?"

Bent Grass studied Sam, trying to decide what and how much to tell him.

"Perhaps it could have," she said, "if the time was right." Bent Grass smiled, she too was learning.

"What is a seer?" Lillian asked again, even though knowing Bent Grass was the maker of the amulet pretty much said it all.

"It is a name given to those who speak with the Great Spirit and who know things," Bent Grass said, gazing at Lillian, "often things that are yet to happen."

Lillian sensed the woman was still being overly modest.

"This is not the way the army came into the valley," Sam declared nervously.

Bent Grass said, "You came in on the sacred trail of the black wolf. That trail closed behind you, the Great Spirit made it so. There is only one opening between the world outside and the valley of the Sematuse."

Sam and Lillian were overwhelmed by everything, the cave, the paintings and this woman who spoke with the Great Spirit. If the Great Spirit was the Indian equivilant of God then who was she, the Holy Ghost?

Sam's hand automatically went to the amulet. This small, round piece of leather had proven its ability to alter reality, could the same be said for the crucifix or the rosary?

"Can we see the valley?" Lillian asked, sounding almost like a child.

With a touch of amusement, Bent Grass looked at the impetuous redhead. She liked this woman-child, and saw goodness in her. Bent Grass was pleased.

"Sam, get your horses and bring them here." She had made a decision.

When he returned with the wild-eyed, snorting and stomping mounts, Bent Grass took Lillian's hand and the cave unexpectedly went black. While waiting for their eyes to adjust, they saw a kaleidoscope of dancing spots; green, red, yellow and white. When the spots cleared, Bent Grass was leading them toward a distant illuminated opening. As they came closer the light intensified, until again they were nearly blinded. As the aperture grew in size Sam felt a sense of trepidation.

"Should Lillian be touching the amulet?" he asked, firmly holding onto the lead ropes of the frightened horses.

"She is safe with me," Bent Grass replied, pleased and amused at his concern. "As bearer of the amulet you and your horses will be safe as well."

Sam gasped as Bent Grass stepped out of the cave and disappeared except for the arm and hand, holding on to Lillian…then she, too, was gone. He sighed with relief when he exited the cave and found Lillian and her mystical guide intact and waiting.

"What happened?" he exclaimed.

"You crossed over," Bent Grass replied. "You have passed through the veil separating your world from our valley."

Sam and Lillian forgot their questions as they gazed out over the glorious scene. An array of meadows, streams, forests and mountains lay before them. A colorful rainbow hung over a serpentine river, several shades darker than the pale-blue sky.

Sam was acutely aware of the difference in the valley from this vantage point than the one he saw on that fateful day.

"What do you mean, 'crossed over', and what veil?" he anxiously inquired.

"Our world is very different from yours," Bent Grass gently replied. "Come with me to our village. I will explain along the way." As the trio set out toward the unseen village, Bent Grass spoke.

"When our ancestors, the old ones, were led into this valley by the spirit of the black wolf they thought they had died and gone to the place of good hunting, fishing and gathering. A kind of happy hunting grounds you might call heaven.

"But then some had babies, some got old and died and some got sick. This is not heaven, but a place where we can be happy living in the old ways. There is no hatred, greed, jealousy or anger but there is one emotion that has remained with us…fear…fear of discovery, fear of being forced to leave this place.

"That fear grew when long ago a few tried to leave the protective veil of the valley and died a horrible death. It was for that reason I had to instruct my son to call upon our ancient ancestors to eradicate the horse soldiers," she looked apologetically at Lillian, "including your uncles…before they drove us from the safety of our home.

"I made this place for the True People, so there would always be Indians on Mother Earth, who would remain true to the old ways." Bent Grass again paused. "Are you with me so far?" she questioned.

"Why would the people die if they tried to leave?" Sam was perplexed. "And what do you mean, you made?" He instantly wished he could take the last question back.

"Everything in the valley travels in a circle. The larger your circle the slower you age. In your world time travels in a straight line with a beginning and an end. That line can be bent into a circle but if the circle is broken, it becomes a straight line and that spirit can not find its way home."

The village came into view and Bent Grass said, "You will meet my husband and my son, perhaps they can explain things I can not. They have lived in both worlds, on both sides of the veil."

As they approached the first teepee with a white buffalo painted on its rawhide cover, two men met them.

"My husband and my son," Bent Grass said, pointing to each.

"I know who you are!" Lillian shouted, struck with a realization she didn't understand. "You're the one my Uncle Roy called Breed. You're him, aren't you? My uncle said he wished he could tell you how smart he's become."

It was Standing Wolf's turn to be stunned. "You talked to Roy?"Lillian answered excitedly, "Yes, on the way here! He was like a mirage or something. He came up out of the lake!"

"Roy is, was, your uncle?" Standing Wolf muttered in disbelief. Looking at Sam he added, "And this is your husband?"

"It is,"Lilly answered proudly.

Bent Grass was all eyes and ears as she watched and listened to the exchange.

"How **is** Roy your uncle?" Standing Wolf asked, confused.

"He **was** my mother's brother," Lillian answered.

Standing Wolf remained silent, trying to process this information.

"We, Sam and I, live on Wishbone, my Uncle Roy's ranch. My mother is his only living relative. The army found us after he disappeared and gave her the deed to his ranch." Lillian was talking nervously to keep from shaking like the leaves of the aspen.

"Neither Roy nor Lance ever mentioned a sister," Standing Wolf said, a little contrite.

"This is a very strange place for a family reunion," Frank interjected with some amusement. Remembering his own reunion he thought, or is it?

"Is my Uncle Roy alive or dead?" Lillian anxiously asked, then added, "And my Uncle Lance?"

"Both…or neither," Bent Grass replied. "Dead is sometimes not what it appears to be."

Lillian's mouth dropped open but no words fell out. Even Sam was momentarily speechless but finally managed to utter, "I don't understand." Yet in a way, he did. "Isn't dead, dead?" He could not help thinking of Larry and the white wolf.

Bent Grass gave Sam a perplexed look. "In your world, perhaps, but in ours I think my Son, or my husband can better explain how death is not always what you expect."

Standing Wolf and Frank, knowing the secret of death in the spirit cave, looked at each other, then at the two wide-eyed visitors.

Standing Wolf spoke first. "When you left the cave of spirits and entered our valley, you died. As you can see, it is not what you expected. At this moment you no longer exist in your world. Of course, the death you experienced was free of the pain associated with dying, but the result is the same. You left one existence and entered another." He glanced at Frank who simply nodded in agreement.

"In your case, because of my mother and your Uncle Roy, you will be able to return to your world; a rare occurance but not impossible as most believe.

"We should have known when you grabbed the amulet and escaped through the spirit trail of the sacred black wolf, more was involved than opportunity or luck.

"Even my mother did not understand that destiny was once again set in motion."

Sam and Lillian moved closer together and he wondered how grabbing the amulet and running for your life could have anything to do with destiny. Sam thought of his family's ranch…Destino. Was the name another coincidence?

Standing Wolf continued, "In the white man's world you believe death means you go to heaven, providing you have accepted the white Jesus as a savior, and hell if you have not. Both places are snake oil sold to the highest bidder. The truth is, there is a place for every believer and non-believer, their own hidden valley within the world around them…a place separated by a secret opening, a vortex in time and space where the only way in is thought to be death."

Frank stepped forward, reached out and tentatively touched the amulet around Sam's neck. It was like saying hello to a friend he wished he had gotten to know better.

Withdrawing his hand, satisfied by the touch, Frank spoke. "Destiny is not determined by choice but by chance. You, like my daughter are innocent players in a cosmic struggle."

Looking at the lovely, red-haired Lillian he smiled, "A kind of spiritual poker-game where all are playing to win and Mother Earth is the prize. There are places and Gods for every belief with saviors, redeemers and trinities as guardians of their believers. By chance, we are part of a game that has been played out over eons. There will be winners and losers, but in the end Mother Earth will decide."

Sam was confused and strangely restless. Looking at Lillian then at Bent Grass he quietly said, "We came here to return the amulet," and pulled the leather circlet over his head.

"Wait!" Bent Grass said. "Do not act in haste. You must keep the amulet. You have become one with it and it with you, but there is more. I received messages in the spirit cave I did not understand. Even the messenger was like none I had ever known."

As she looked at Sam, her eyes seemed to reflect the magnitude of her discovery.

"When you and your *mahakin* entered the cave of spirits the message and the messenger became clear. It is a prophecy really, the revealing of a message left behind by ancient people from another place in another time. You are the message and the messenger. You possess the amulet and the power of the pyramid. It is through you that hope springs eternal."

She took Lillian's hand and said, "Your *mihakin* has a great gift, a special power and now you are one with him, together you hold a power granted not only by the amulet but by the spirits of ancient ancestors.

"Now you must return to your world for it is **you** who will save the People. Watch the night sky for I will give you a sign. A light will emerge from the darkness and the spirit of the amulet will come alive within you. It will tell you what you must do."

With those words, she turned and led the couple to the spirit cave and back into their world.

Chapter Forty-five
Reckoning

Riding down the Lost River and away from the cave of spirits they were silent, lost in thought, each trying to understand what they had seen and heard.

The one called Bent Grass spoke of a new cycle, a galactic circle and the dawn of a new world age, a chance for humans to once again live in harmony with Mother Earth.

She talked of a day when Mother Earth, Sister Sun and all the children of the night would move down a single path. A time to right all errors as the light of truth shined down on all humanity.

Neither he nor Lilly understood what the words of Bent Grass meant but she said they would know what to do. What both agreed upon was that Bent Grass was far more than just a seer of some lost tribe, far more…

Sam abruptly pulled Bigfoot up short. "What in the…!?"

The noise was deafening, like nothing either of them had ever heard before. Bigfoot and Buttercup snorted and stomped as if they'd stepped on a hornets nest.

Covering their ears, Sam and Lillian searched up and down the trail for the source of the awful sound. Then looking up they saw it! Like a giant silver eagle it soared over head, a long white stream of excrement trailing behind it like a diarrheic seagull, painting the otherwise brilliant-blue sky with streaks the color of seagull shit.

"What is it Sam?" Lillian asked, puzzled by the bizarre sight.

"I do not know, but I do not intend to stay here under it," Sam replied, urging his mount away from the hovering mess he expected to hit the ground at any moment.

Their escape was interrupted when they suddenly found themselves on something hard and black. Their horses slipped, skidded and floundered as if on a frozen stream. The huge bird and horrible noise were gone but the mystery was only beginning.

"We have to go back Lilly, something is wrong," Sam said, "terribly wrong."

Badly shaken, Sam and Lillian returned to the spirit cave where they were met by a seemingly expectant Bent Grass. After quietly listening to their story of the giant bird and the ear-splitting noise, Bent Grass smiled.

"You have shared your first vision of the future. There will be more visions. They will not harm you, they will prepare you for things to come. You must understand, your lives will never again be the same."

At the urging of Bent Grass, Sam and Lilly spent one more night in the valley. With her words of support and encouragement, they were convinced the huge silver bird had been a vision.

When they returned to the cave the following morning, Sam's thoughts were profound. He had always looked upon his Spanish heritage with a sense of pride but now he was conflicted. He had never heard of the Mayan and always believed the Spanish were the first inhabitants of the land now called Mexico.

But there was more, so much more. He now understood the power of the amulet as granted by its maker. A power limited only by the wisdom of its bearer.

He thought of Larry, of resurrection and the ramifications of such an act. He had seen Lillian's uncles, Ruth's brothers die an agonizing death in the valley they just left, a valley that now seemed like the most beautiful, serene place on earth.

He was not stupid nor was he a scholar, and much of what Bent Grass told him reeked of voodoo or superstition. He had to admit he always held a fascination for the night sky and the vast array of stars, some even resembling the shapes of objects or animals. It always made him feel humble, perhaps the fascination was more heritage than humility.

He knew the year to be 1891 when he and Lillian entered the aboriginal lair Bent Grass called the spirit cave. So absorbed was he by the wonders of the valley and the teachings of Bent Grass, he had no idea how long he and Lilly had been in the valley. What he was sure of was time no longer mattered. They were now one with the Sematuse. They were part of a mission eons in the making.

Sam and Lillian again shared a secret, much like the black wolf in the trap or the white wolf running with the pack. It was a secret hard to believe but neither held any doubts.

"Sam," Lillian's voice broke his musing like the soft flutter of butterfly wings. "Should we tell Mom and Dad about any of this?"

The sight and sound of his wife only added to the shock and awe of the situation he found himself in.

"No, querida," he answered softly. "I am afraid this is one secret we can not share with anyone."

"But you know how badly I am going to want to tell Mom," Lillian pleaded.

"If you tell your mother it will change nothing. She will humor you, she might even believe that you believe it but in the end, it will be your blessing and your burden."

Sam looked at the world around him in a way he could never have imagined; the mysterious river that led to or from another world, yellow pine standing like proud sentries on the slope above the river. He watched a bald eagle as it soared in search of a meal, its head and tail flashing in the sunlight like beacons of hope.

He looked at his wife, the beautiful Lillian, mounted proudly on her palomino mare. He knew he could never understand how he deserved such a gift but it was not for him to understand, simply to accept, graciously with humility and reverence.

How will it work? He wondered. He knew time would temper his excitement and hone his patience as he watched and waited for the sign he knew would come.

"Lillian," he summoned, feeling an uncommon sense of gratitude.

"No matter how long we share this secret, I am positive there is no one on earth I would rather share it with than you. I love you…"

There was much to consider, but for now they must return to Wishbone, run their ranch, maybe have a family of their own, and be content with their time together. They would tell no one about the valley or their secret, besides…

How do you tell someone you have attained the gift of immortality?

On a bitter cold day in December, while proclaiming, 'peace on earth, goodwill toward men', white soldiers killed the chief of a proud nation and many Indian women and children, stealing the heart and spirit of the People.

While in the spirit cave awaiting the arrival of the amulet, the Great Spirit made it clear to Bent Grass that Samuel DeSoto was the last remaining descendant of the Mayan People and the Spanish Crusaders who overthrew them. The Mayans were a proud people who walked the land long before the Sematuse or the Sioux. Like many other Native Peoples they disappeared, apparently gone from Mother Earth. Or had they?

Bent Grass had seen the light of truth; with Mayan blood flowing through his veins and the amulet around his neck, Sam was joined with a cosmic force more commanding than the god's of the universe. He would wait for the signal in the night sky and when the time was right, he would return the land to all Native People; Mexican and Indian who had lived in harmony with the land before the white man came and took it away.

On another cold December day when Sister Sun stands still in Father Sky, the winter solstice will mark a turning point, a new beginning and the end of the white man's reign over all Native People.

Epilogue

The failure of the Ghost Dance at Wounded Knee Creek and Standing Rock was an unfortunate oversight on the part of the Indians and unnecessary on the part of the 7th Cavalry, because Sitting Bull and Big Foot were prepared to comply with the soldier's orders. Black Coyote, the Minneconjou, widely attributed with firing the first shot at Wounded Knee, was later found to be deaf and confused by actions he could not hear or understand.

Wovoka did not know the essential role of the amulet in the dance, however, the massacre occured in late December, after the aspen leaves had fallen and lay under winter snows, so the spirits of the ancestral warriors could not have heard their call even if the amulet had beckoned them.

The Ghost Shirts, touted by Kicking Bear as being capable of deflecting bullets were nothing more than a superstitious belief driven by audacious hope.

Twenty soldiers received the Medal of Honor for their heroism, including one found with a skinning knife in his chest.

*

Jack Wilson, the Paiute shaman who became known as Wovoka, had actually participated in the original Ghost Dance in 1870 led by the Paiute mystic, Wodziwob, known to the whites as, Gray Hair. When Gray Hair's prophecies did not come true, the dance was eventually abandoned.

Wovoka restarted the movement around 1888 as the result of a vision in which he believed he went on a spiritual journey to heaven and back. He believed God spoke to him and told him to teach the People the Ghost Dance so they might one day return to the old ways. Saddened by the loss of life at Standing Rock and Wounded Knee, he never again spoke of the Ghost Dance. He died in Nevada in 1932 as Jack Wilson; the proud Paiute who still believed God had spoken to him.

The mystery of the Massacre at McLoughlin Canyon near the Janis Rapids on the Okanogan River was never solved. As few as six and as many as one-hundred-sixty settlers and prospectors may have died there. No evidence of any Indians being killed was ever found. The McLoughlin Brothers survived, though the incident would haunt them for a lifetime. Thousands of dollars in gold dust and nuggets were lost, along with claims to several mines along the Fraser River in British Columbia, Canada.

The attack is credited to either a renegade band of Indians called the *Sarsopkins* (Sarsapkins) who lived in what is today the Pasayten Wilderness, or the *Choo-pin-it-pa-loo*, a ghostly band of Nez Perce believed to be angered over the treatment of Chief Joseph. This mysterious band was rumored to have attacked wagon trains and even burned out settlers from White Bird Pass in Idaho to Salmon Arm in southern British Columbia.

In addition to the McLoughlin Canyon attack, another little known but significant battle occurred between Indians and soldiers on the plains between the Snake and Columbia Rivers, known as the Palouse. It was called 'Massacre' at Steptoe Butte…as all Indian victories are referred to in American History. Again the actual number of soldiers killed is sketchy and while the attack was largely attributed to the Spokane and Coeur d' Alene Tribes with some assistance from the Nez Perce, there are some who believe it was carried out by a ghost-like horde of warriors…perhaps Joseph, Kamiakin and the *Choo-pin-it-pa-loo*.

It is uncertain if Lone Frank's gold mine or his treasure of gold coins and currency were ever found. However, in 1904 three men, Herb Curtis, Billy McDaniel and George Louden, part of a crew surveying the border between the U.S and Canada, filed a claim on a mine located on a 7,200 foot mountain crest near Cathedral Peak, deep in the Pasayten Wilderness.

The three men, day laborers at the time and earning two dollars a day, soon made large purchases of land and become among the most prominent ranchers in what is now the Sinlahekin Valley of the upper Okanogan. The Curtis Ranch is now a prosperous family-run apple orchard, and the McDaniel Ranch is a successful cattle ranch. The Louden Ranch is an operating cattle ranch but under different ownership today.

The cattle ranches, one located on Toats Coulee Creek at the gateway to the Pasayten and the other at the base of Chopaka Mountain, are among the largest in the Sinlahekin Valley today. The three men were believed to have sold their claim to an unnamed mining company for $100,000.00 dollars, and although the gold mine was never operational, it apparently made these men very wealthy.

The Wishbone Ranch, located in the Kartar Valley, became part of one of the largest sheep ranches in the northwest in the 1930's. Whether the change in ownership was in some way related to the depression, or if the owners simply sold out and moved back to Montana is unknown. Perhaps they never left at all.

There continue to be reports of strange activities in and around the waters of Warrior Lake, now called Omak Lake. The reports include an agitation or white water stirring under the surface, or unusual wave action across the lake when no wind or other obvious explanation is present. Others claim to have seen a man, perhaps Indian, on a horse the color of the sun, riding along the granite bluffs that overlook the lake. On some occasions, he is reportedly accompanied by a red-haired woman on a Palomino.

Somewhere in the vast expanse of the Pasayten, a Native People live in a valley hidden not only from view but from time; a people who wait for the day when they will again be free to roam the land from mountain peaks to desert sands; a time when the buffalo will again fill the plains and fish will swim up river in search of the headwaters, a day when the True People and Mother Earth will once again live in harmony.

Much has been said and written about the Mayan Calendar and its prophecies regarding the end times. The end of the Mayan Calendar and the end of the current 13 Baktun cycle coincide with a series of rare celestial events believed to be significant, if not apocalyptic, by astronomers, scientists and religious leaders. During the winter solstice, when the sun is at its greatest distance from the celestial equator and is not moving north or south as it enters the sign of Capricorn on December 21, 2012, there will be a perfect alignment of the earth and sun with the galactic equator. It is the day when the Mayan Long Calendar is believed to mark the end of time. Perhaps it is not the end of time as we know it, but rather the end of centuries of injustice to the Native People.